D0495983

DREAMS

The Sarah Midnight Trilogy

Book 1

Daniela Sacerdoti

BLACK & WHITE PUBLISHING

YA

First published 2012
by Black & White Publishing Ltd
29 Ocean Drive, Edinburgh EH6 6JL

3 5 7 9 10 8 6 4 2   12 13 14 15

ISBN: 978 1 84502 370 6

Typeset by RefineCatch Ltd, Suffolk
Printed and bound in Great Britain by the MPG Books Group

This story is for Irene

Acknowledgements

More than I can ever say, thank you Ross, Sorley and Luca.

Thank you to my mum, Ivana Fornera, and my brother, Edoardo Sacerdoti, for encouragement and belief.

Thank you to my mother in law Beth and my father in law Bill, for being just wonderful.

A heartfelt thank you to my lovely editors, Janne Moller, Rachel Reid and Kristen Susienka, without whom Sarah wouldn't be who she is. Thank you for our chats over coffee and for the many times you made me laugh. And for pushing me well out of my comfort zone!

Thank you to my agent, Lindsey Fraser, for believing in me (and for giving the best hugs).

Thank you to Linda Strachan for the very first critique of Sarah and for being such a generous mentor to a new writer.

Many thanks to Ailidh Forlan, Beth Pearson, Heather Arbuckle and Jamie Bell, Sarah's reader panel, for their thoughts and suggestions: you were invaluable!

Finally, thank you to Maire Brennan and Julie Fowlis for Sarah's writing soundtrack.

CONTENTS

Prologue
Night Falling

Loneliness makes me
Love breaks me

You'd never think it could happen to you.

You'd never think that one day you'd stand in a graveyard, rain tapping on a sea of black umbrellas, watching your parents being lowered into the earth, never to come back.

It's happening to me.

They said it was an accident. Only I know the truth.

So here I am, standing on the edge of the deep, black holes dug for them, knowing that they have been murdered; knowing that nobody – nobody – is ever going to believe me.

I can never give up the fight, this fight that has been handed down to me, thrust upon my unwilling shoulders. I'd rather be buried with my parents, my brave mother and father, who lived and died by the Midnight motto: *Don't Let Them Roam.*

My parents were hunters, like their parents and grandparents before them, and scores of ancestors behind me, hundreds of years back, fulfilling the same call.

1

I must follow in their footsteps. I am the only one left to keep the promise. I am the only hunter left.

I am Sarah Midnight.

1
Blackwater

Am I to atone
For my father's mistakes?
Will I fall like he did?

Sarah was kneeling on the cold pavement, before a girl of about her age. The girl was writhing and moaning, trying to free herself from Sarah's grip. Her face glowed feebly in the darkness, white with fear.

And then the girl's expression changed. Fear turned into fury, and a strange sound came from the back of her throat.

There we go, thought Sarah. *It's beginning.*

The girl's eyes started turning black, slowly, slowly, until they were two pools of hatred. Her skin grew a sickly white, her hair stiffened and crumbled, blowing away in the night breeze and leaving a bald, greying skull in its place. Her hands sprouted claws, her clothes ripped to reveal paper-thin skin and long, bony limbs.

The stuff of nightmares. Literally.

Because it had been a dream that told Sarah where to find this girl, and what she had become. Where to find the creature

3

that had possessed the girl's body and soul, destroying every trace of her, and was set to do the same to as many young women as it could. Sarah had dreamt of the demon in the play park, waiting, biding its time for a victim to come along – until Lily appeared. Sarah knew that the dream was telling her to go, in spite of her fear, and hunt the creature like her parents would have done. Except she'd be on her own.

Lily's transformation was now complete, and the creature was about to free itself. Sarah had to act fast. She closed her eyes and started calling her power.

My first time, she thought. *Just like in my dreams.*

For a few terrible seconds Sarah feared it wouldn't happen. She feared that the blackwater, the power she had inherited from her father, would fail her. She feared that her hands would stay cold, and that she would be helpless, turning from hunter to prey in the space of a heartbeat.

You should have been here! You should have been here to teach me!

Grief and anger invaded her, and with them came the release. The blackwater took her like an unstoppable current, and her hands were flooded with heat. Sarah looked down in horror, expecting to see her arms in flames. The creature shrieked under Sarah's touch, a blood-chilling screech. Its skin began to weep and dissolve. After a minute or so, all that was left of the demon was a puddle of dark water, so cold that it was painful to touch.

Sarah sat back on her heels and exhaled slowly, as if an enormous weight had been taken off her shoulders. She looked at her hands dreamily, as if she couldn't quite believe what had just happened, what had come out of her. She'd known about the blackwater for a long time – she'd known that her father had possessed it, and that she was bound to have it too. But to feel it happening . . .

That was different.

Exhilarating and terrible, all at the same time.

Sarah shivered in the chill wind. She was drenched in that strange, dark liquid they called the blackwater, but really was something else, something without a name. She wiped her hands on her jeans, slowly, as if in a daze. She was drained, exhausted.

Her first hunt.

Her parents should have taken her, they should have guided her, but they'd been killed too soon. So she'd had to do it by herself. She had to learn, and learn fast. So many times she had asked her parents to start teaching her . . .

"Back soon, my love." Her mother's hair brushed her cheek softly, as Anne bent over Sarah's bed to kiss her. The gentle light of Sarah's lampshade illuminated Anne's delicate features and made her brown eyes shine. Sarah wanted to throw her arms around her mum and keep her there, keep her home.

"Let me come with you . . ."

"Sarah, darling, we talked about that. It's too dangerous."

"I know!" Sarah's pale face was flushed with the vehemence of her words. "But I want to stay with you. I don't want to be here on my own . . ."

"You're safe. You know that your dad and I saw to that. Nothing can attack you here."

"It's not that. I'm not scared for myself . . ." Sarah hesitated. Words were failing her. *I'm scared you won't come back*, she wanted to say, but the sentence got stuck in her throat. She couldn't put her fear into words. "I need to learn. I'm a Midnight too. I've never used the blackwater. I don't know how to . . ."

"The time will come. I promise. Soon."

"If my gran was alive, she would have taught me!"

Anne took a deep breath. "Yes. Yes, she would have."

"But you won't!"

"We're protecting you, Sarah. Enough now. You're delaying us." James, her father, had walked into Sarah's room, a hard look in his eyes. His big, tall frame was silhouetted against the door. His tone was clear: there would be no more discussion. When her father spoke, Anne listened. Always. Sometimes Sarah wondered if her mother had ever had a will of her own.

"Mum . . ." Sarah called. But Anne had followed James, and she hadn't looked back.

It was another lonely night for Sarah, listening out for her parents' footsteps, wondering when she would be allowed to embrace her rightful inheritance. Wondering what she would do if they didn't come back.

Wondering what the blackwater felt like . . .

"I'm sorry, Lily," Sarah whispered to the girl lying dead on the ground. At least Lily had been the creature's last victim.

Sarah stood up. She picked up the scarf that had fallen in the fight and wrapped it around her neck, a slash of white against her black coat, her hair blowing long and soft in the breeze. She turned away and started walking home. For the last time.

Because tomorrow she'd have to pack, leave her house, the memories of her parents and everything she knew, and move in with her aunt and uncle.

Sarah turned the key in the door and let herself in. She took off her coat and scarf and hung them up, carefully, arranging them on the peg as if everything depended on them hanging straight. She took her shoes off too, and walked onto the wooden floor of her immaculate hallway. She bent down to wipe an invisible stain, and then again, just to make sure.

Once in the kitchen, she started wiping all the surfaces with a cloth, painstakingly, taking great care not to miss a bit. She was so tired that her arms were shaking, but she *had* to do it. She had to.

Her stomach started rumbling. She was hungry, but she knew she wouldn't be able to swallow anything. The knot she'd had in her stomach since her parents' death hadn't allowed her to eat properly for days.

Shadow came to greet her, brushing herself against Sarah's legs with a slow, soft purr. She was completely black but for a little white paw, and her eyes were a deep, golden amber. Sarah had come home from school one day, two years before, to find her sitting on their doorstep. She was just a kitten, but she had a look of defiance, as if to say *I'm meant to live with you, you can't turn me away*. Sarah had opened the door, and the kitten had walked in as if she'd owned the place. She started following Sarah everywhere, and because of that, James suggested calling her 'Sarah's Shadow', which was eventually shortened to Shadow.

"Sarah! Where have you been? I was worried sick!" Aunt Juliet stormed into the kitchen in her dressing gown and slippers.

"Out. I needed air." Sarah refused to look at her.

"Air? It's past midnight!"

Sarah ignored her.

A defiant, impossible teenager, thought Juliet. As if she didn't have enough worry with her own daughters, now she had to look after this difficult, passionate, wonderful girl. Because that's what Juliet thought of Sarah: that she was wonderful. Sarah had no idea, and Juliet would never have said. But Juliet also felt it was her duty to guide Sarah, shape her, mould her — and that's why their relationship didn't stand a chance, because Sarah would *not* be guided, let alone moulded into something she wasn't.

Juliet had a good heart, really, and she meant well. But she could never understand Sarah fully, just like she had never understood her own sister, Anne.

"You can't go wandering around alone at night. There are bad people around, surely you know that!"

Bad people, and plenty of other . . . things, thought Sarah, *wiping the already perfect kitchen table.* Memories of the hunt came flooding back. Lily's terrified face, the terrible heat of the blackwater in her hands . . . *That's how the rest of my life is going to be. Dreaming and hunting, until one day something will get me, like it got my parents.*

A lifetime of dreams. Her own private torture, one that she could never escape.

They had started when she'd turned thirteen, like it usually happened to the Midnight girls. She'd dream of creatures that tormented, hurt, killed innocent people; and in the visions she was *there*, sometimes as a witness, sometimes as the victim. It was Sarah's duty to write it all in her dream diary, down to the last detail, so that her parents would know what and where to hunt. Now that her parents were gone, it was up to her to interpret the dreams.

It had never been difficult. Her dreams had always been detailed, precise, reliable. But since Sarah's parents had died, things had changed. Her dreams had become unpredictable, confused. The information they gave had become muddled, the setting surreal: places she had no idea where to find, places that didn't belong to this world. Sarah was in the dark. Her only guide was her Midnight instinct, albeit weakened by grief and fear.

"Thank goodness you're going back to school soon. A bit of normality. Well, if anything can be normal again," Juliet added with genuine sadness. "When you come and stay with us, no more going out like this without telling me exactly where you're going and when you're coming back."

Sarah threw the cloth across the room in a fit of anger.

"I'm not coming to stay with you! I'm staying here! This is my home!"

Juliet looked at her with tenderness, but Sarah misunderstood. To her it looked like pity, and Sarah couldn't bear to be pitied.

"I know, darling, I know . . ." Juliet put out her hand to touch Sarah's shoulder. Sarah pulled away.

"I'm so sorry that all this had to happen to you. I wish you could stay in your own home, really I do. But your parents decided that you can't live alone until you turn eighteen, and frankly I agree with them. We'll look after you. There's no other way. You can't go against your parents' wishes; you'd lose this house, you'd lose everything. And anyway, you couldn't possibly defy their last wish . . ."

Sarah felt her eyes well up. She thought of her home, her wonderful grey sandstone villa. She thought of her room, painted a light, silvery grey that shimmered in the sunshine and in the moonlight . . . the long, white voile curtains flowing in the breeze every time she opened the window . . . the view from her room, the vast garden, and beyond it, the moors and hills, purple with heather, wild and windy. She thought of her parents' room, their chaotic den with clothes and books all over the floor . . . how upset it always made her, whenever she walked in, to see everything so . . . *out of control*. She thought of her mum's mirrored console, where Anne used to brush her long black hair – the beautiful hair that Sarah had inherited. So many times Sarah had sat at that console, playing with her mum's make-up and perfumes.

Most of all, Sarah thought of the basement, now locked shut. The secret room where Anne and James kept their weapons, and their maps, and the books nobody was supposed to see. Where her mum kept the herbs and stones and candles and all the mysterious items she used for her spells and charms, one of which Sarah was now wearing around her neck, hidden from view: a small red velvet pouch filled with pine needles, a tiny garlic clove, and a pink quartz. A protection charm.

No charm has worked for them though, Sarah thought bitterly.

How on earth could she have explained those things, if somebody found them, if she wasn't there to guard them? How on earth could she get rid of them? Bury them in the garden, or burn them in a big bonfire? Her parents' lives, turning to ash, turning to nothing. Sarah couldn't let this happen.

She *had* to find a way to stay in her home.

"By the way, your cousin called for you today." Juliet's voice interrupted her train of thought.

"My cousin?"

"Harry. He was calling from London. I never met him. Fancy missing your own uncle's funeral."

"They hadn't spoken in years," Sarah answered in a small voice. Her dad and his brother Stewart had fallen out many years before – Sarah had never been told why. A few years after the rift between the brothers, word had come through that both Stewart and his wife had died, leaving Harry to be brought up by distant relatives in New Zealand. He was fifteen. Anne and James got a card once in a while, but neither party had made much effort to keep in touch. Sarah suspected that the argument had been very bitter, to create such distance between the Midnight brothers.

"Well, he said to check your email. Sarah, you're soaking! What happened to you?"

"It rained. At the play park."

"You were at the play park? In the middle of the night?"

Sarah took a deep breath. "I'm tired. I'm going to have a shower and go to bed."

"You've had no dinner. Eat something, at least!" But Sarah had already gone up the stairs and into her room.

She threw herself on the bed, followed by Shadow, who curled up at her feet. Sarah loved feeling Shadow's soft pink nose against her own, and the cat's whiskers brushing her cheek softly.

"It's just us now, baby, just us," Sarah whispered into her fur.

She needed a shower. She dragged herself to the bathroom, while Shadow remained at a safe distance from the water, perched upright on the window sill, her amber eyes glowing in the semi-darkness of the room.

Sarah closed her eyes under the water flow, letting it wash away the blackwater, the adrenaline, the fear. She emerged half an hour later, wrapped in a towel, her long black hair dripping, and sat cross-legged on her bed, trying to keep the duvet as straight as she could. She switched her laptop on.

One new message.

> Hello Sarah, your cousin Harry here. You probably don't remember me, you only saw me once, when you were still a baby. Your parents and mine had their differences and didn't speak for a long time, but Uncle James and I had started writing to each other in the last few months. How cruel that they had to go now, when we had just started getting closer. You must be going through hell. I know what really happened to them. We need to talk. I'm coming back to Scotland. I'd be grateful if you could put me up for a bit.
>
> Take care,
> Harry

Sarah's heart skipped a beat. He knew! She wasn't alone in that terrible knowledge, in knowing why her parents had died so horribly. There was, after all, another Midnight to share the burden. And maybe if Harry came to stay, she wouldn't have to move out.

Feeling that something important might have happened, Shadow jumped on Sarah's bed and sat beside her, looking at the screen.

"Of course, Harry," whispered Sarah under her breath, her fingers moving quickly on the keyboard. "Of course I'll put you up for a bit." She smiled, for the first time since . . . since it all happened.

> Dear Harry,
> They're throwing me out of my house because my parents decided I can't stay here on my own. Come ASAP. Stay at least until I'm 18. ☺
>
> Sarah

Sarah stroked Shadow's fur a couple of times, and a new message popped on the screen.

> I'm at the airport. See you in an hour.

At the airport! He's already here! Sarah's heart began to beat faster. She felt a glimmer of hope, at last. She dried her hair quickly, threw on a pair of leggings and a T-shirt, and went downstairs to the kitchen. She was suddenly hungry, properly hungry, like she could actually *eat*.

Sarah loved cooking; it was her refuge. She was brilliant at baking, and she often made cakes and scones for her parents, to restore them after a night spent hunting. She kept all her cookery books neatly on a shelf in the kitchen, and poured over them, reeling in the domesticity of pasta making and chopping and slow-cooking, when all around her was chaos and fear.

Trying to be as quiet as possible – she didn't particularly care if Juliet was woken up, she just didn't want the hassle – she took flour, oil, salt and yeast out of the cupboard and arranged them on the kitchen table. She mixed and kneaded and moulded, loving the feeling and the smell of the dough in her hands. There, the perfect Sarah-sized little pizza. Now she had to clean everything up, or the mess would have made her too anxious to swallow anything.

When she'd finished, she poured some milk for Shadow, which the kitten barely touched (she was a good hunter, and had had plenty to eat earlier, while Sarah was hunting too) and waited for her pizza to be cooked. Ten minutes later she devoured the whole thing down to the last crumb. She hadn't realized how hungry she really was. That pizza was her first proper meal in weeks.

Sarah was chewing the last morsel when the doorbell rang. She cleaned her fingers and her mouth quickly and sprang to her feet. *Could it be Harry, already?* She stood behind the kitchen door. She wanted the chance to look at him for a minute before he saw her.

She heard Juliet dash down the stairs, probably to check if any unsuitable friends of Sarah's were visiting the house at that time of night.

"Hello. I'm Harry Midnight." A deep, vibrant voice with the hint of a New Zealand accent. "You must be Juliet. Thanks for looking after Sarah. Now you can go. Well, get dressed first."

Sarah stifled a smile.

14

"Chop chop. Don't worry. I'm family. We'll look after each other." The amusement in his voice was palpable.

"There is *no way* I'll leave her alone with . . . with you!" Juliet cried out, as soon as she regained the ability to speak.

"No, I suppose not. Well, we can talk about it tomorrow."

Sarah took a little step forward, still hiding behind the door, to try and catch a glimpse of him. He was tall with blond hair and light-blue eyes, so clear that they almost shone. The whole Midnight family was fair, blond and blue- or green-eyed – Sarah had inherited her black hair from her mother – but in spite of his colouring, Harry looked quite different from James and Stewart. He had stronger features, with a long, straight nose, a soft-lipped mouth, and his most striking trait: those eyes, big, expressive, full of life. And a sharp light in them, a light that said *don't come too close*, like a warning. He was wearing a blue hooded jacket, and jeans that had seen better times – he looked like someone you wouldn't mess with, someone who could look after himself.

Sarah decided she'd seen enough. She ventured into the corridor. Her heart was jumping out of her chest. Her future depended on this man.

"Harry," she whispered. Her voice sounded uncertain, but her gaze told a different story. She was looking straight into Harry's eyes.

She's strong, he thought at once.

"Sarah."

The pale complexion, the small nose and mouth, the way she kept her chin slightly raised in a gesture of pride and defiance; and those eyes, impossibly green. She was a Midnight through and through.

15

Harry's gaze was so intense on her, it suddenly felt too much. "Come on. I'll show you to your room," she said brusquely, to break the spell. "We can talk upstairs," she added, throwing an imperceptible glance at Juliet. Harry understood at once.

They walked upstairs, followed by Shadow, past Juliet, ignoring her as if she'd been a coat hanger. Like a flash, Juliet was on the phone to Trevor. Her voice was drifting from the hallway, and Sarah and Harry could hear bits of what she was saying.

"Like he lived here! As if this was *his* house! I know, I know, he's family. I know there's nothing I can do . . . OK. OK. I'll sleep on it. See you tomorrow."

Was she making the right decision? To let this long-lost cousin into her house, into her life? She had no choice. Her parents had left her no choice. Sarah felt a wave of anger towards them. She didn't like to feel that way, and did her best to shake off the uncomfortable feeling, as if it had never appeared; but a distressing memory kept pushing itself to the forefront of her mind.

The spotlights in Sarah's eyes were blinding as she walked onto the stage of the Royal Concert Hall. She couldn't see the audience; it was just a sea of black, row after row of heads, barely discernible. Sarah had waited for that moment *forever*. It was her first proper performance.

The best music students from secondary schools in the whole country had been selected to accompany some famous artists in a Christmas concert. When her teacher told Sarah that she'd been chosen, she couldn't believe it. She was so excited, and so proud, that even her cleaning and tidying routines had relaxed a little. For a few weeks she was un-characteristically talkative, chatting away about rehearsals, and how friendly the musical director was, and how they were supposed to wear their school uniforms, and how the BBC was going to cover the event . . . On and on she went, telling her parents everything, every week coming home from rehearsals with a spring in her step and a smile on her face.

The Christmas concert was on a Saturday. Aunt Juliet drove her into town, with her cello in its purple case and her ironed uniform arranged carefully on the back seat. Aunt Juliet had insisted on going with her to keep her company and help steady her nerves. Sarah had wanted her mum to go with her, but, her parents explained, it was just *not possible*. They had things to see to, and said so in a way that left no doubt as to the nature of those *things*. Of course they'd be at the concert, though. They wouldn't miss it for the world, Sarah could be sure of that.

When the moment came to go backstage and leave friends and relatives behind, Sarah threw one last anxious glance among the little crowd, hoping to see her parents walk through the glass doors. At that moment, Aunt Juliet's phone started beeping. Sarah's parents were running a little bit late, but they would be there in half an hour.

Plenty of time. There was still nearly an hour to go, before the rest of the audience arrived and everyone was settled. They'd be fine.

Sarah's hands shook with nerves and excitement as she walked on stage, the lights making her hair shine blue-black, and colour rising to her face as she sat with her cello. She couldn't make out anything beyond the stage, but she knew that her parents would have arrived by now, and were sitting watching her. The thought was warming her heart, and filling her with pride. She couldn't wait to show them what she could do.

The singers and fiddlers and harpists and accordionists followed one another, and Sarah felt the happiest she'd ever been. She couldn't know how many people among the audience were admiring that beautiful girl with the long black hair, playing the cello with such passion, such precision. She flew through her parts without making a single mistake, and then it was time to stand up, and drink in the cheering and the clapping, and smile shyly when the artists turned around and gestured at them, the music students, with more clapping rising from the audience to celebrate the new talent, the boys and girls who'd played so well.

There was a flurry of congratulations, and hugs, and bouquets of flowers as everybody's friends and families were allowed backstage. Sarah scoured the little groups, looking for her parents.

Aunt Juliet was there, and she was smiling, but her eyes looked strange.

"Well done, my love! You were amazing!"

Sarah kept looking over Aunt Juliet's shoulder. "Where are Mum and Dad?"

Juliet looked at her for an instant, as if searching for the right words.

But by then, there was no need to say anything. Sarah knew they hadn't come.

* * *

Harry and Sarah sat in the guest bedroom and talked for a while, carefully, uncertainly. Sarah wasn't sure how much she should say, and kept the conversation formal, like a cautious dance. All the while she looked into those impossibly clear eyes, and felt afraid. Soon, exhaustion caught up with her. She wished Harry goodnight and went to bed, too tired to worry, too tired to think, but still finding the nervous energy to arrange the duvet around her the way her own private ritual demanded. She was soon out like a light, drained with grief, with the hunt, and with the relief that maybe she wasn't going to have to leave her home.

But it was the troubled, unquiet sleep that brought her the visions.

Sarah was standing in the dark. She could make out two bodies lying on the ground, motionless, and a semi-circle of dark figures standing around them. She recognized the bodies: they were her parents'. Her stomach lurched. Beside them stood a boy not much older than her, with hair so black that it was nearly blue, and a face as pale as the moon. And someone else: a tall, blond man with something in his hand . . . a dagger, a silver dagger. The man's face kept changing, his features kept blurring.

"Look at him, Sarah."

A woman's voice. A voice dripping with hatred.

Sarah turned round to see where the voice was coming from, and she saw a woman with a face full of sorrow. She had startling, angry blue eyes and high cheekbones, framed by wavy dark-blond hair. She was beautiful – or she would have been, had she not looked so enraged and so full of pain.

"Who are you?" Sarah asked.

"You're alone, Sarah," the woman replied, and smiled a menacing smile that changed her lovely features and made Sarah's skin crawl. With the corner of her eye, she saw that the blond man had raised his dagger, and was walking towards her . . .

Sarah woke up soaked with sweat, and freezing. She reached out for her lamp and switched it on with trembling hands. At once she gasped, and sat up in fear.

There was someone standing beside her bed.

"It's OK, Sarah. Whatever you saw, it was just a dream," whispered the figure, shrouded in semi-darkness. He was tall and blond. Like the man in her dream.

Harry.

Sarah's heart missed a beat. She breathed in deeply, trying to keep herself calm.

"What are you doing in my room?"

"I heard you screaming."

"You weren't sleeping?" Her voice was shaking. She swallowed.

"There won't be much sleeping for a while. I'm watching over you."

"Am I in danger?" Sarah knew the answer already.

Harry leaned over her, and brushed a lock of damp hair away from her face. She realized she was trembling all over, like a leaf in the wind.

"Sarah, I wish I could reassure you and say that everything will be fine, and that there are no monsters under your bed. But you are a Midnight. I know you're brave and strong, and I have to tell you the truth. You're in terrible danger, and you can't trust anyone."

No, I can't trust anyone, thought Sarah, remembering the man in her dream walking towards her with his dagger raised.

I can't trust anyone, including you.

2
Destiny

Finding each other
Among a million possibilities
Always wondering
Was it meant to be

Sean

I knew that sooner or later they'd get to him, and all my efforts to protect him would have been for nothing. His destiny had been decided. I knew it by the way he spoke to me the last day of his life: as if he was dead already.

Harry. My brother.

I've been alone all my life. As my parents died while I was still quite young, I've always resisted making relationships with other people. My grandparents looked after me because they felt it was their duty, but they never made their way into my heart. Friends and acquaintances were just for company. Girlfriends . . . well, girlfriends were a different story, more of a quest, really, a never-satisfied quest for somewhere to be, somewhere to belong.

Then I met Harry Midnight, and he changed my life forever. He changed *me* forever. He showed me how it feels to care for someone more than you care for yourself; he showed me what it means to have a family.

He took me into the secret world behind this one, the terrible, beautiful, dangerous world where the things we see with the corner of our eye, the things we fear are lurking in the shadows, dwell and thrive. Where the imprinted memories of long-ago predators are more than just memories: they come alive.

Thanks to him I became a hunter, I became the person I was always meant to be.

I had just started university in my hometown of Christchurch, New Zealand. Medicine. I had no great passion for it; I just did it because I could, because I didn't know what else to do, and because it seemed like a good way to get myself the life I wanted. Harry was there to follow a family tradition – both his father and his uncle were doctors. I soon got to know a few of his other family traditions, most of them involving danger and death in various degrees.

He was an orphan. His parents were killed when he was a teenager. They had fallen out with their own families in Scotland, and had moved to New Zealand when Harry was a baby. After their death, Harry found himself alone, and ended up being cared for by relatives, just like me.

The first time I saw him was on a freezing winter night. He was standing in a flowerbed not far from the university dormitories, muttering to himself. I was walking back from somebody's room – I can't remember her name; there were a few girls in my life at the time. I thought he must have been drunk, standing in the cold like that, talking to himself. I'm no Samaritan, but I didn't want anyone collapsing outside and ending up getting hypothermia, so I walked up to him.

I'll never forget the first time I saw his face, because I swear, his eyes were the wildest thing I had ever seen. Green, a bright green that was nearly unnatural, with a look in them that would have stopped anyone in his tracks – anyone, or any*thing*. He looked like he was deep in conversation, as if he were discussing something crucial – his face was tight, like a fist. He was waving his hands in the air, tracing invisible symbols with his fingers.

Looking back, I should have known from his eyes how dangerous he was, and how that night I ran the risk of ending up under a bush with a broken neck. The first of many times when Harry and danger would go hand in hand.

When he saw me he stopped talking at once, and his serious expression broke into a smile. He had chosen the 'nothing to see here' approach, as opposed to twisting my neck.

"Lovely night," he said cheerfully.

"Are you OK?"

"Yeah, fine, just having a wander."

I saw at once that he wasn't drunk – no danger of him falling asleep outside then, and no reason for me to be there.

"Right, mate, see you later," I said, walking away.

But fate had other plans.

I often wondered what would have happened had I not seen him that night. What would have happened if I had decided to stay with whatever girl I had at the time, if I'd taken another route to go back to my room, if I had chosen not to speak to him . . .

If I'd legged it when the creature came out of the earth.

"Watch out!" the strange man shouted all of a sudden, when my back was already turned to walk away. I felt something landing on me, something heavy. I fell on the cold, hard ground. I was shocked, enraged – was the man with the crazy eyes looking for a fight? I scrambled to my feet, only to be pushed down again. Someone, or something, was sitting on my back, and wasn't letting me get up again.

It took all my strength to turn around, throw the man on the ground, and sit on top of him. I thought a pair of green eyes would meet mine – but what I saw was something else entirely. A naked, white-faced creature with unseeing eyes. Its skin was like the inside of mushrooms, white and sickly-looking – like something that lived underground, like some monstrous larva. Its features were human, though. As if it had been human once, long ago, and then somehow took another evolutionary route, and became something quite different. Its mouth was open, showing a row of blackened but sharp teeth – and it was trying to snap at me, biting the air, seeking flesh.

I don't panic when I'm afraid; fear makes me sharper, colder, more controlled. My brain geared for survival, and I couldn't see anything else. I pushed my fingers in the creature's eyes and made it howl, a sound that came from beneath the earth, somewhere dark and primeval. Its arms were searching; its mouth was open and snapping. It kept shrieking as I pushed my fingers into its eyes.

I had no time to think that what was happening to me was *impossible*. I had no time to think that such creatures don't exist, that you can only see them at the cinema, or read of them in books. I had no time to consider any of that, because the creature that wasn't supposed to exist was sinking its claws into my arms, into my back, drawing blood, and it was my time to roar in pain and rage.

Just then I realized that the green-eyed man was standing beside us, not moving. He was looking on, as if he'd been watching a football match on TV. Why was he not helping? Was he the creature's master, and was he using it to attack me?

Then I noticed his posture – he had a small dagger in his hand, and he looked ready to strike, if he had to. He was waiting for something. What on earth was he waiting for? For the creature to kill me?

"Help me, you bastard!" I shouted. But he didn't move. An imperceptible smile curled his lips, making me even angrier.

Something came into my mind. The most ancient part of my brain must have registered the information and stored it, and was telling me what to do now, in this life-and-death fight: there was a stone border that ran around the flower bed, the closest thing to a weapon I had at that moment. It was my only chance.

I took my hands off the creature's face – it brought its hands to its eyes, setting me free for long enough to turn my head quickly and locate the stones. One split second, and the demon went for me again. It pushed me down, its mouth snapping – it was so close to my skin that I tensed up, waiting for the bite.

And it came – the creature bit my arm so hard it tore off a chunk of flesh.

I was bleeding, frightened to death, and furious. A strength I didn't know I had surged through me, and I *roared*, a sound I never thought could come out of my throat. That thing would not bite me again. It would pay for what it had done to me.

I shoved my knee in the creature's chest, so hard that its breath was knocked out of its lungs. I got up on my feet, pain tearing through me, blood pouring down my injured arm, and I kicked it in the face, feeling its nose break. I should say I was sickened by it . . . but I wasn't. I was excited, I was triumphant – to hear the bone breaking, to see the creature that had tried to kill me roll on the ground in pain. It made me feel alive, like nothing else before. I threw myself on the demon, and took its bleeding head in my hands. I banged it against the stones, once, twice, until I felt the bone break, and the demon was still.

I was breathing so hard I thought my heart would stop. I looked up at the sky – it was clear, with a million stars. I'll never forget that sky, the night I killed a demon for the first time.

"Impressive."

A voice coming from far away. I shook my head, trying to dispel the fuzzy, unreal feeling that had taken hold of me.

The green-eyed man was smiling. I opened my mouth, but nothing came out. I was shell-shocked.

"Have you done this before?" He sounded interested, polite – as if he'd just asked something like 'ever been scuba diving?'

"Why did you not help me?" I could barely contain my anger. I could have died, and he'd been standing there all along, with a dagger in his hand!

Harry was unfazed. "I wanted to see how far you'd go. You just met a Surari."

"Surari?"

"A demon. Harry Midnight, by the way." He offered me his hand.

I hesitated for a second, then I took it. He pulled me up, and we were face to face. "Sean Hannay."

Our eyes met, and something strange happened: it was as if we'd recognized each other. I saw myself in him. I know he saw himself in me. We belonged to the same place: we belonged to the hunt.

And that was the beginning.

This is what Harry Midnight did for me: he lifted the veil that hides the truth, he showed me the world behind this world. He showed me how the rivers of time flow parallel and should never be allowed to touch, how the creatures from the beginning of time must be stopped from seeping into this world, and if they make it here, they must be destroyed without mercy. He taught me that we all live in danger, a great and immediate danger. When we sleep in our beds, we are not safe; when we go to work, we're not safe; when we walk down the streets of our cities, we're not safe. Our own children are not safe; nobody is safe, at any time, day or night, wherever we are.

Most people are not aware of it, yet – the Secret Families do all they can to keep it from us. Most people choose not to see anyway; they choose to believe what they want to, and nothing else. They want to pretend that none of this is happening, that it's not real. It's all just a nightmare that will dissolve as dawn breaks. Soon this is a choice they won't be allowed to make. Soon many more people will know what we know, and the whole world will be forced to see.

I joined the fight because I loved the thrill of it. Yes, I *loved* hunting – that's all there was to it. But as I saw what we're really facing, as I discovered what's really threatening us, it wasn't a thrill any more. It became a survival mission for the whole human race. I made Harry's mission mine, and now I live for it. I'm not part of a Secret Family – they're not made, they're born. I'm one of those around them, one of their Gamekeepers. Just like traditional gamekeepers hunt and cull the wild animals on the estates they look after, so *we* hunt and cull . . . but it's not wild animals for us, of course; not deer, or pheasant, or hare. For us, the *game* is the demons. The Secret Council, formed by the heads of the most prominent Secret Families – or Sabha, in the ancient language – gave us the name of Gamekeepers. I think it must be their idea of a joke.

Anyway, to become a Gamekeeper takes years of training and steady nerves. They test us over and over again to make sure they have our absolute loyalty. We are then allowed to go back to our old lives, keeping them up like veneers. Each one of us is assigned to a particular family by the Council, but we can be called away at any time to perform missions for different families, and be sent wherever the Sabha need us. We have to be ready at a moment's notice to be sent anywhere in the world, to do anything they ask of us. We come from all walks of life, young and old, men and women, stumbling into a world we could never have imagined existed. Only one thing we have in common: to serve the Secret Families, with all that it entails.

Mary Anne, my then-girlfriend, and I weren't assigned to a family as such, but to an individual: Harry Midnight, who had found us and trained us both. The Midnight family had no Gamekeepers, Harry had told me. They wanted nothing to do with the Sabha. But that didn't apply to Harry. His parents had chosen to be part of the Secret Families and remained loyal to the Sabha.

These days, being a Gamekeeper carries with it a good chance of getting killed. So many of us are dead already; so many friends of mine are gone. A shiver is shaking the whole world, the breeze that comes before a gale has started blowing. The cracks into this world have started showing, and it won't be long before the war begins. The rivers of time are being pushed together, the passages are being opened – things that should never see the light are coming in, either taking advantage of the openings of their own accord, or because they're being summoned. We're fighting to keep this world ours; but those who stake a claim to it – a deeper, more ancient claim than ours – are getting stronger by the day. The balance of power is shifting, more swiftly than we could have ever predicted. There's an Enemy at the gates – a faceless Enemy who's a mystery to us, who uses the demons as its servants. A demon himself? Nobody knows. It's all been so quick; the threat has been so sudden, sweeping over us like a tsunami. We weren't ready. The Sabha weren't ready. The Gamekeepers weren't ready. There had been no time to prepare, no time to find a way to defend themselves before the destruction began.

The Secret Families – people like Harry, people who fight and die every day to keep this world ours – are being targeted, one by one, family after family. The ancient network of protection all over Europe, all over the world, is being ripped apart.

If it disappears, there will be nothing else for us to do but hide, and pray that when they find us, they'll decide to kill us quickly – and by us, I mean you and me, and each and every member of the human race. If the Secret Families are destroyed, there's nowhere for humanity to go – it would mean that the tide had turned, for the first time in millions of years. It would mean that this world is no longer ours. It would mean that it's the Time of Demons again.

Before it all started, it was just hunting. And hunting was fun. I loved being a Gamekeeper. I soon realized that things were changing; I could see the creatures' numbers multiplying, I could feel them becoming stronger, more vicious – but for a while it was just *incredible*. I woke up every evening (that's the way we worked, sleeping through the day, hunting through the night) raring to go, full of adrenaline, ready for the fight, ready to smell their blood.

It was Harry, Elodie, Mary Anne and me.

Elodie is the heir to the Brun family, the Secret Family from Lyon – or should I say she *was* . . . God, not knowing if she's dead or alive is killing me. Harry adored her. To see the bond between them made me long to find something like that too . . . but I don't hold much hope. Love seems to be one of those things that happen to other people.

I was with Mary Anne, and she was a wonderful Gamekeeper – strong and brave, with a total and absolute disdain for fear. She ignored danger – she just went ahead with anything she had to do. No wonder Harry had seen the potential in her, and trained her as he'd done with me.

She was also beautiful, funny and warm. But I didn't love her. Harry and Elodie had something so deep and all-encompassing. They lived for each other – I'm not sure I could ever feel that way for anyone, and I certainly don't think that anyone could feel that way for me.

We were an amazing team, the four of us. We thought nothing could beat us. Until we were called to Japan to contain the Taizu threat – and that's when everything started going wrong.

It was the Ayanami family who'd called us. They are one of the greatest Secret Families in the world. Again, maybe I should say *were*. They were facing an invasion of Taizu spirits – silent, deadly creatures that can kill dozens with a single touch, leaving no trace. They make it look like the victims have had a heart attack, but the truth is that their breath has been taken away. You know what they say about cats stealing babies' breath, and because of that they should be kept away from cribs and cots? Those are not cats; they're the Taizu taking on an animal form.

We started hunting in earnest – but it didn't take long to realize that the threat was greater than it looked. The Ayanami, the Shinji and the Tokuda – the three Japanese Secret Families, the clans of the Plains, the Mountains and the Sea – were alarmed, and many Gamekeepers were sent by the Sabha to help them, from all over the world.

Six months later, most of the Gamekeepers sent to Japan were dead, and the three Families had been destroyed – drowned, suffocated in their beds, gassed in their own cars, clawed to death, devoured. It was carnage.

Only little Aiko, the three-year-old daughter of the Ayanami chief, was saved, and flown to Italy in great secrecy to be looked after by some local Gamekeepers in a little mountain village in the Alps.

With fear and destruction all around us, Harry changed. He became more and more despondent, more and more afraid.

He told me he had to go to London as soon as possible, to meet with the Sabha. He was convinced that only by fighting together, guided by the Sabha, could the Secret Families face a threat as big as this. I wanted to go with him, but the plight of the Japanese people was too strong for me to ignore. I had to try and help. Harry and Elodie flew to London, while Mary Anne and I kept fighting in Japan.

It was a terrible time. We did all we could, and then the time for a decision came: we knew that if we stayed in Japan any longer, we would be killed, like so many other Gamekeepers. Mary Anne decided to fly back to New Zealand and continue the fight there. I chose to reach Harry and Elodie in London. We parted ways, with a hint of sadness on my part, and heartbreak on hers. There was nothing I could have done to help her pain. I'd tried to love her – I really tried – but I couldn't.

When I saw Harry again, in London, I was shocked. He looked like a haunted man, his eyes opaque, his cheeks hollow. I hated myself for having left him. I should have stayed with him; I should have kept protecting him. What had possessed me to stay in Japan, to fight a hopeless cause?

Harry had been meeting with the Sabha many times. The heads of the Secret Families of Europe were flocking into London to try and find a way to face the crisis. His faith in the Sabha was complete, absolute.

The day I arrived he found an excuse for Elodie to go out – she left without arguing, with a sense of resignation, because she knew she couldn't have said no. She looked so frightened, so lost – her brown eyes big with apprehension, her long willowy hair down on her shoulders as if to protect her, her thin frame looking even frailer than usual. I barely had time to give her a quick hug, to whisper 'it'll be OK' in her ears, and she was gone.

I dreaded what was coming. I felt in my bones that Harry wanted to tell me what to do in the event of his death – because I could see he had no doubt that it would come soon.

He sat me down in the living room of their Mayfair townhouse. From the window I could see the beautiful, square symmetry of the houses all around, and the grey English sky weighing over London, heavy with imminent rain.

He took a deep breath – it sounded strange, rasping – then he began.

"I've recently been in touch with my Uncle James in Scotland. You know we hadn't spoken for years . . ."

"Yes."

"He's a fool. He's trying to keep going as if everything is normal. He *knows*! But he's refusing to acknowledge the magnitude of what's happening. It's as if he's denying the existence of a wider world . . ."

"That can't be. Nobody can keep going like nothing is happening." I thought of the innocent people in Japan, unaware of the battle, caught in the middle of it. Even their lives had been changed, and they were just bystanders – how could a Secret Family remain untouched?

"He's refusing to make provisions for his daughter, my cousin," Harry continued. "Her name is Sarah. She's nearly seventeen. She's the Dreamer of her family." I knew what that meant – each Secret Family has one Dreamer in its midst, someone who through their dreams tells the family about any demons in their surroundings, and where to find them. If the Dreamer gets killed, the power will pass on to another member of the family. "When they strike, she'll either die, or be left to face it all alone, without allies. And they'll strike soon. I know for sure that these are my uncle's last days. Sean, there's something I need you to do for me."

"Of course, Harry. Of course." To see such fear in the eyes of a man who was like a brother to me – no less than if we'd shared the same blood – I felt like my heart was breaking.

"You must look after Sarah. When something happens to me – and it'll be soon – you must go to Scotland and protect her. I can only trust you. I don't have long to live."

All of a sudden the pain I felt turned to anger. Harry was a hunter, and yet he was letting himself be killed without putting up a fight. How could he do this to Elodie, to me, to himself?

"I don't want to hear you talking like this, Harry. It's like you're dead already!"

"You don't understand, Sean. I *am* dead already. Look. Look at me."

I looked. And I saw. The gauntness, the mortal pallor, the rasping breath. The opaque eyes, covered by a milky film. I had seen it happening in Japan, I knew the signs – but with Harry, I had willed myself not to see.

"Poison," I whispered, horrified.

"One touch was enough. Or maybe it was in my food. It's just a matter of time now."

"Oh, Harry. Who did it? Who was it?" I would strangle them with my own two hands, no matter how long it took me to find them.

35

"It's difficult to believe, I know. But, Sean . . . it was the Sabha who did this to me." He shook his head, as if he couldn't believe his own words.

My heart skipped a beat. How could that be? How could a member of a Secret Family betray us all?

"The Sabha? Oh, God . . ."

"I used to think they were just in denial, that they hadn't had enough time to act. But now I know. They've been infiltrated – or even turned. That's why I can only ask *you* to look after Sarah," Harry continued. "I can't trust anyone else. I can't be sure of anyone . . . We have to take matters into our own hands."

"Who will listen to us, Harry? Who will believe that the Sabha are now an enemy?"

"Not many. We managed to get to Aiko through the Ayanamis' Gamekeepers; we're old friends, they believed me. And then there's the Flynns. Our families go way back, so I know I can trust them, and they know they can trust me. I've sent Mike to get Niall Flynn and take him to Louisiana, somewhere out of the way."

"Mike Prudhomme? He's the best Gamekeeper I know."

"Yes. He and I go back a long way too. Niall is lucky, very lucky. And so is Sarah, with you."

I nodded. I was at a loss for words. I hoped with all my heart I would not let Harry down.

"Nobody else can know what we're doing. If the Sabha find out, you're all dead . . ." Harry's breath failed him, and he held his chest. I wished I could have breathed for him. "I want you and Mike to keep in constant touch. You need his help. Only you will know how to contact them."

"Yes. Yes."

The room was spinning around me. Nowhere to go, nobody to trust.

"What about Elodie? She must come with me to Scotland."

"She can't." Despair flooded Harry's face. "She's being driven to the Thames now. There's a boat waiting for her. She's going to Italy, where Aiko Ayanami is. She needs to help the Gamekeepers protect her. You're safer apart than together . . . You and Sarah, Elodie and Aiko, Mike and Niall. If you're all together and they find you . . ."

I nodded. He was right. "I just can't believe it. I thought we were fighting the Valaya. The Enemy. Now we have to worry about the Sabha too."

"I believe that the Enemy and the Sabha are now one."

We looked at each other, Harry's words weighing between us like stones in our hearts.

"Sean. Elodie is now my wife." The shadow of a smile appeared on Harry's lips.

"Your . . . wife?"

"We got married yesterday. We knew there wasn't much time left."

Harry and Elodie had got married, and the day after their wedding they'd already been separated. I felt a deep sorrow take hold. It's still with me, and I'm sure that it'll never let me go, for the rest of my life. I felt the walls closing in on me and I thought I'd suffocate, just like it was slowly happening to Harry. I walked to the window and looked at the sky.

"The heirs of the Secret Families must be kept alive, no matter what. Do you understand? Sarah must be kept alive. She might be the one who saves us all, in the end. Each and every heir needs to survive, and so many have died already."

"I'll do anything I can, Harry. I promise you. Maybe I should take her into hiding too, like Aiko and Niall. Somewhere secret . . ."

"Sarah would never go with you, believe me. She doesn't even know about the existence of other Secret Families, about the Sabha, or the true nature of the Surari. My uncle kept all that from her. If she were to know the truth now she might go to the Sabha, and we'd lose her. You have to keep up the pretence; you have to win her trust slowly . . ." Harry coughed again, a painful, burning cough that made me flinch. I nodded, overwhelmed by all these revelations. "Which is why I want you to have all this. This house, my belongings, everything. I want you to *become* me. Here's everything you need . . ." He handed me a leather briefcase. "Leave here as soon as you can. They won't be long."

I struggled to take in what Harry had just said. "You want me to *become* you?"

"It's the only way. Sarah will never let you in otherwise. She'll never trust you. You don't know the Midnights. They're proud, and diffident. They won't accept help from outsiders. The only time I saw her she was just a baby. She doesn't know my face at all, and any pictures they have of me – if they have any – will be from when I last saw them, when I was eight years old. We're both blond, and your eyes could pass as Midnight eyes. She'll believe you."

"I want to stay with you until . . . until the end."

"It's too dangerous. Listen to me now. You're the closest thing to a family I'll ever have. You and Elodie. You must survive this. You must help Sarah survive. You have to go. Now."

The green of his eyes was burning into mine. I nodded. I couldn't speak.

"They're coming to finish me off in style." He smiled bitterly. "I know what they want to do to me. I won't let them."

And that was it. I looked into his face one last time, into his brave, wild Midnight eyes.

That was the last I saw of him.

I rented a room somewhere in the East End, out of the way. I went through Harry's briefcase. He'd been very thorough: all the documents I needed, pages and pages of information about the Midnights, people I could call if I needed help, the deeds of his Mayfair house with a note attached to it: *If you need somewhere to stay, when it'll be safe again.*

Among the documents and papers was a photograph. It was a picture of a girl with long black hair, and Harry's green eyes: Sarah Midnight. The quality of the photograph was terrible, dark and grainy, so I couldn't make out her face very well. I stared at it for a long time.

That night I watched the news on my laptop. I heard what I was expecting to hear: that a man known as Sean Hannay had been found floating in the Thames. I prayed and prayed that Elodie was safe in Italy, somewhere hidden and secure, somewhere she and Aiko, and whoever else found their way there, could find refuge. It had been too late for Harry.

The last thing I could do for him was to follow his instructions. To become Harry Midnight.

I accessed Harry's email account. And there it was, the email he'd been dreading, from the Midnights' solicitors.

> This is to let you know that your aunt and uncle, James
> and Anne Midnight, were killed last night in a traffic
> accident . . .

I deleted it at once. There was no way I'd bring attention on Harry – on *me*.

Time to go. I walked out into the dark night, looking for a taxi that would take me to Heathrow Airport, and from there to Scotland, the green, windswept place where I would find Sarah Midnight.

3
A New World

Alone what seemed forever –
Then your beacon shone

"You *have* to go to school, Sarah. I know you're upset, but we need to keep the routine going. You can't sit around the house all day, it'll make you worse . . ." Juliet was going on and on, busying herself around the toaster, spreading crumbs everywhere. Sarah felt her skin crawl at the sight of the mess her aunt was making. She had to get up and pick the crumbs up with a wet sponge, then dry the surface with a kitchen cloth, carefully. To see her cleaning seemed to upset Juliet, which irritated Sarah even more. Only when she was happy that every single crumb had been picked up, and only once she'd gone over the surface a couple of times for good measure, could Sarah sit back at the kitchen table, in front of the frothy cappuccino she had made herself. She looked mutinous.

"I can't go, it's as simple as that. I've got stuff to do."

"Like what?"

"Just . . . things."

Juliet rolled her eyes. Her niece must be the most stubborn, strong-headed girl in the whole of Scotland. In a fit of frustration, she threw her hands in the air.

"All right, then. Just for today. You're going back to school on Monday though . . ."

"She's going today."

Sarah looked up in surprise. Harry had walked into the room, barefoot, wearing jeans and a white T-shirt, his blond hair wet from the shower.

"She needs to go *today*. You're right, Juliet. We need to keep some sort of normality here. I'll see to that."

Juliet looked at him, incredulously. Was he really on her side?

"Yes. Good. I'm glad we see eye to eye." Juliet took the last sip of her cappuccino and went upstairs to get dressed, a satisfied smile on her face for having won the battle, albeit with a bit of help.

Sarah was outraged. How dare he interfere in her life like that?

"What did you do that for?" she whispered, as soon as Juliet was out of earshot. "I need to sort out my parents' things. You know that. I told you last night."

"I know. But to do that, you need Juliet out of your hair. And to get her out of your hair, you need to show her you're sorted. That we can manage by ourselves, and that I can look after you."

"Oh! Of course. Then I can stay home for a few days."

"Who said that?" said Harry, his blue eyes twinkling.

"*You* said . . ."

"I said we need to show her we're sorted. And letting you miss school is not part of the plan. You're going. Double maths and all."

He's enjoying this!

Sarah stopped in her tracks. *What did he just say?*

"How do you know I've got double maths?"

"Do you actually have it? I took a wild guess."

Sarah eyed him suspiciously.

"I guessed. Seriously!" He put his hands up in a declaration of innocence.

"I don't believe you for a second. How on earth would you know what I've got on today?" She was shaking. *He creeps into my room at night, and he knows my timetable?*

"Ok, then. I went through your stuff." He said this in an even tone, as if it was a perfectly normal thing to do.

"You *what?*"

"I had to. I was looking for something."

"Oh. Right. And did you find it?" Sarcasm was her only option. The alternative would have been to slap him.

"Not yet. Now go, or you'll be late. Actually, wait . . ."

Sarah turned to face him. She was pale with anger.

"What?" she hissed.

"Do you have a minute to make me a cappuccino? Yours looks amazing."

Sarah gasped in outrage. She looked for a suitable answer, but all she could muster was a feeble, "Make your own!" She was so angry that she was nearly in tears. She ran up the stairs, and slammed the door to her room.

He's right, a little voice inside her said. *If we show them that we're fine, that we're in control, they'll let Harry stay and I won't have to leave my home. Right now, it's the best thing to do.*

OK, so he got that right. But what about going through my stuff?

43

Sarah looked around her. Her room was her sanctuary. The idea of someone touching her things . . . And what on earth could he be looking for? She took a deep breath. She'd have to wait until after school for an explanation.

She took a quick shower, dried her hair, and got dressed in her uniform: a short black skirt, black tights, a white shirt, and a grey jumper, with a grey and blue tie. Everything she wore had to be spotlessly clean, perfectly ironed and sitting straight. She just couldn't have it any other way. She examined herself mercilessly, adjusting her skirt, smoothing down her shirt, undoing its buttons and doing them up again. She tied her silky hair back in a high ponytail, making sure not even a single hair escaped from it, grabbed her bag and was ready to go . . . But hesitated.

She went back to stand in front of the mirror, and did it all over again. She adjusted her skirt, smoothed her shirt, undid her hair and did it up again, and she knotted and unknotted her tie until it was perfectly straight.

Now she was ready.

To think that many girls in school were envious of her beauty, of her obstinate perfection. If they knew how exhausting, how heartbreaking it was for her, to keep doing those rituals of perfection – how much she would have loved to throw on her uniform and run out of the door without feeling that, if she'd done that, the world would collapse around her. How she would have loved to be able to stop tidying, to stop cleaning, to stop straightening things. How she would have loved to lie on her bed and read a book without worrying about upsetting the duvet, to have a shower without having to throw herself on all fours on the floor with a facecloth and dry every single drop, to get out of the house without worrying to the point of tears if she had left everything the way it was supposed to be.

Her obsessions drove her parents crazy. Her parents – her mum especially – would have been happy to live in chaos. They couldn't understand – or maybe they didn't want to see – that Sarah's constant cleaning and tidying wasn't simply a character trait, but came from her terrible anxiety, a chronic state of terror that had consumed her since she was a child.

Night after night Sarah had lain in an empty house, waiting to hear the key in the door, and her parents' footsteps on the stairs. Only then, when she knew that her parents were back from the hunt, that they were alive, could she breathe again. Every evening, just after her parents went out, Sarah would clean every surface in her kitchen, she'd practise her cello, she'd tidy her room until everything was sitting perfectly straight; and then she'd slip into bed, arranging the duvet and pillows around her in a way that only she knew, in the way they had to be. If she did all that every night, in the right order, her parents would come home safe. It was her secret pact with God, with destiny, with the universe – she didn't know with whom or what, but it seemed to work.

As it was working so well, Sarah decided to extend it to every part of her life – her hair had to be perfectly braided, her school uniform impeccable, her books arranged by colour, her shoes neatly aligned against the wall, following an invisible line of perfection. If anything was out of place she'd be beside herself with anxiety, because something terrible was going to happen to her parents, and it'd be all her fault. Before she knew it, her life had been taken over by the tidying and cleaning and arranging and straightening, and not a moment of her day was spent without some sort of ritual.

James and Anne understood nothing of this. They fooled themselves that Sarah was simply a very tidy, precise little girl. It had been Aunt Juliet who noticed that something was not right, and she had mentioned it to Anne.

But Anne had said that Juliet was worrying over nothing.

Sarah understood. They were Midnights. They had to hunt. They had to live that dangerous, impossible life. If their daughter was terrified, exhausted with all the tasks she set herself, they'd rather not see. It would have been too much to bear. So the secret pact went on, swallowing Sarah's life bit by bit.

When her dreams started she got even worse. Nearly every night – especially around the full moon – Sarah dreamt. And nearly every night she woke up to an empty house, screaming. She'd get up and start tidying, until every single object in her room was perfectly aligned to the invisible grid she had in her head. This calmed her a bit, but not completely.

In the end, her pact hadn't worked. The force she'd made it with – God, the universe, whatever it was – didn't keep their part of the deal, and one night she waited in vain for the sound of the key in the door, the footsteps and soft voices. Instead, it was the police, to tell her that her parents were dead.

Harry came out of the kitchen as Sarah was in the hall, putting her jacket on and wrapping her long, cream scarf around her neck – twice, that was the way she *needed* to do it.

"Be good," he teased. Sarah looked at him, her eyes green, narrowed, like a cat's.

"Goodness. You're scaring me." And he meant it. The Midnight gaze could be very intense, and occasionally it could have a strange effect on people. And on other things as well. He'd seen the real Harry using it a few times.

"Look, Sarah. You need to trust me. Right now, you have no choice." He was suddenly serious.

"I know. Otherwise you'd be out the door by now." Sarah used the iciest tone she could find, and turned away.

Then she spun round.

"When exactly did you go through my stuff?"

"While you were sleeping."

Sarah was aghast.

"How? I'm a very light sleeper. I would have heard you." Her voice was shaking, and she hated herself for it.

"Let's just say I've got my methods." Harry held her gaze. They faced each other for a few seconds.

It was Harry who looked away.

"I'll see you this afternoon. Come straight home, there's a lot of work to be done."

Sarah didn't answer, and walked down the gravelly path, towards the wrought-iron gate that marked the entrance to her home.

"Sarah! Sarah, wait, I'll give you a lift!" Juliet's shrill voice reached her just as she was stepping onto the road, but she ignored it.

Juliet stood on the doorstep beside Harry, and sighed.

"Well, I think I'll go home now. I'll be back this afternoon."

"Why hurry, Juliet? Do stay," said Harry, and his eyes were steely. He laid a hand on Juliet's arm, and led her back into the house.

Sarah stood frozen on the school's stone steps. Keira McCarthy had just passed her, blue shadows under her eyes, her pale face set in sorrow.

Keira's older sister had disappeared two weeks before, at the same time that Sarah's parents died. She had vanished into thin air. Sarah knew that they were never going to see her again. Because it was she, Lily McCarthy, that Sarah had turned into blackwater. There had been no way to just kill the demon and save Lily. But at least she had been the creature's last victim. The third and last. Two other girls had disappeared, not far from there. Sarah thought of the creature's sickly yellow skin, the long, thin claws, the full horror of the hunt rushing back . . .

"Sarah. It's good to see you back."

Sarah jumped out of her skin. A tall man with a handful of papers in his hands had appeared at her side. The head teacher, Mr McIntyre.

"Sorry, I didn't mean to startle you." He took her elbow in a familiar, gentle gesture.

"Hello, Mr McIntyre." Sarah waited for her heart to slow down.

"Sarah, I want you to know . . . Well, if you need to talk, you know where I am."

She felt choked for a second. She looked into Mr McIntyre's kind face. He and her mum were not only colleagues, but good friends. Anne had taught music at the Trinity Academy for many years. As much as it could be difficult to go to the same school her mum taught at, Sarah enjoyed seeing Anne around, exchanging a few quick words, a look. At least that way she got to see her mother, which didn't happen often, given that she and her father were out hunting nearly every night.

Sarah couldn't believe that she would never see her mother again. She blinked a few times. She wouldn't let the tears fall onto her cheeks; she'd keep them all in, even if they'd suffocate her.

"Thank you," she said hurriedly, and walked away. In her haste, she bumped into someone.

"Oh, I'm sorry . . ."

"Sarah!" She felt a pair of arms squeezing her affectionately. A distinct scent of bluebells enveloped her.

"Bryony." Sarah returned the hug, hiding her face in her friend's sweet-smelling hair. It was wonderful to see her again.

"You're back! This place was a desert without you. Oh, Sarah, I'm so sorry. I wanted to come to the funeral, half the school wanted to, but we weren't allowed. They said family only. But to me you *are* family . . ."

Bryony had been Sarah's best friend since they were three years old. She was a petite girl, with bright, curly red hair that she wore loose on her shoulders like a little beacon. While Sarah was quiet and kept herself to herself, Bryony was chatty, lively, and popular with everyone. She was forever trying to drag Sarah to parties and clubs and after-school classes, without much success. Sarah spent most of her time practising her cello.

"Are you coming tonight?"

"Coming . . . where?"

"To my house. I'm having Leigh and Alice up; we'll get chips and watch a film or something . . . I know it's kind of . . . well, it's so soon after . . . but a bit of company will do you good. My dad can come and collect you. You know, with those girls disappearing . . ."

Nobody else is going to disappear now. At least, not at that creature's hands.

"Bryony, sorry, I just can't. You have no idea how much I've got to sort out . . ."

No, you really have no idea.

"Of course, sorry." Bryony's face fell. "What's going to happen now? I saw Siobhan a couple of days ago. She said you'd be moving in with them . . ."

"No. That's not going to happen." Sarah's eyes were blazing.

"You can always come and stay with us. You know the way my mum is, she'd have you any day, just fit an extra bed somewhere . . ."

Sarah smiled, in spite of her sadness. Bryony was the eldest of five children, and they always seemed to have a crowd staying at their large, messy, cheery house. Sarah was sure that Bryony meant it — that had she asked, her mum and dad would have taken her in. But that was impossible.

"Thank you, but I'm sorted, for now. My cousin arrived yesterday. From London." The thought of Harry made her tense up. *The man with the dagger, the one I saw in my dream, looked just like him. He was standing at the end of my bed when I woke up. He went through my stuff in the middle of the night.*

The girls walked down the corridor to their Maths class, and sat together. Mr Combs, a young man with an incredibly boring, monotone voice, was standing at the desk already, waiting for the bell.

"I didn't even know you had anyone on the Midnight side of the family," whispered Bryony.

"I only saw him once."

"How long is he staying for?"

"I don't know. Hopefully long enough so that I don't have to move."

Mr Combs called for attention, and the double Maths period started crawling slowly to the eleven o'clock mark.

Juliet lay slumped across the living-room floor, her face white as marble, her eyes closed, her hair spread on the carpet. Shadow was sitting upright beside her, her tail tapping menacingly, keeping guard in case *he* came back.

What is a small cat to do, when a six-foot-tall man decides he wants her out of the picture? Shadow knew she didn't stand a chance, but she was brave, and fearless. She didn't run away. She kept watch.

If he came back, Shadow wasn't going to give in without a fight.

Sean was calmly sipping a cup of coffee, sitting at the computer in the basement. James Midnight's inbox was on the screen, and Sean was scrolling down through his emails, looking for . . . There. There it was. The solicitor's note.

> I am sorry to inform you that your nephew, Harry Midnight, has disappeared. He has been reported missing by his housekeeper, Mrs Elizabeth Boyle. Please contact me if . . .

Delete.

Delete, delete, *delete*.

His body was overflowing with anger, white-hot anger, and his heart was pounding.

Harry is dead. Harry is never coming back.

Then he took a hold of himself. He focused on his breathing, in and out, in and out . . . Slowly . . .

After a few minutes he felt calm again. He switched the computer off and stood up.

Harry Midnight, I'll keep my promise to you. If it's the last thing I do, I won't let you down.

Sarah was sitting in the canteen. In front of her, on a tray, was a ham sandwich. She was looking at it with disgust. Plastic bread, plastic ham, probably made two weeks before. She had no intention of eating it.

"Come on, Miss Fussy, it's just a sandwich!" laughed Bryony.

"No way," said Sarah, and started peeling an orange.

"Why no lunch with you anyway?" asked Alice, snatching the sandwich from her tray.

"No time this morning . . ."

"What? Super-organized Sarah, no time to—Ouch!" Bryony had kicked Alice under the table.

"Sorry, I didn't mean . . . I didn't think . . . Things must be up in the air for you right now . . ." Alice scrambled.

"It's OK, Alice, really. I know what you mean." No time to do anything, that morning. Too busy fending off Harry and Aunt Juliet . . .

All of a sudden something clicked in her mind. Harry had wanted her to go to school. He'd *insisted* she get out of the house.

Harry had wanted her out.

So that he could be there alone.

How could she have been so *stupid*?

Sarah sprang to her feet and started gathering her stuff quickly.

"Bryony, please tell Mr McIntyre I've gone home. Tell him I'll be OK, my aunt is there. I'll text you later ..."

"Sarah, are you OK?"

"I'm OK, don't worry," she said breathlessly, and she was out of the lunch hall and down the steps already, running like her life depended on it, up towards the main street and down Cross Street, then up the hill to Gateside Road. Her side was pulsing in agony, and she thought her lungs would explode, but she kept running, among the flaming colours of the Scottish autumn, through the iron gate and up the gravelly path.

4
Illusion

If life wants to devour my soul
I'll fight to the last breath

"Aunt Juliet!" Sarah called, bursting into the hall. "Aunt Juliet!"

She checked the downstairs rooms, feeling her panic rising, until Juliet appeared at the top of the stairs, her hair in a mess, looking vague, as if she'd just woken up.

"Sarah, what are you doing here? Why are you not in school?"

"Aunt Juliet . . . you're fine . . . "

"Of course I am. What are you doing home already?"

"I . . . I skipped gym. I wasn't feeling well."

Shadow had jumped down from the sofa and was brushing herself against Sarah's legs. She looked electric.

"Did you run all the way? You're so out of breath! You should have called, I would have come to get you . . . "

"It's OK. I'm OK. Just need a drink." Sarah picked Shadow up and looked into her eyes. They were enormous. She was trying to tell her something.

"Go and sit down, I'll get you a drink and some lunch, maybe? What about a ham sandwich?"

Just the thing.

"No thanks. Water will do. Where's Harry?"

"Well, we had a nice chat this morning, about your mum and dad. He asked me so many questions . . . He made me a cup of tea, then . . ." Juliet looked confused for a second. "Then he went downstairs, I think. Yes, he went downstairs. He's still in the basement."

The basement? How did he get in? The door is always locked! She felt frantically under her jumper and around her neck. Her key was still there, hanging on a silver chain. So where did he find another key?

"And what did you do? After your chat, I mean?" she asked Juliet, trying to sound casual.

"I . . . I . . ." That look of confusion again. "I sat here, watching TV, I think . . ." She shook her head. "Funny that, I can't remember! I must have fallen asleep . . . "

Sarah felt a knot in her stomach. "Well, never mind, Aunt Juliet, don't worry. I'll cook you lunch. I'll just go and say hello to Harry."

Say hello, indeed.

"Hi Sarah. You're back already. No gym?" Harry seemed to materialize between them, silently. They hadn't heard him coming.

Sarah felt her heart pounding in her chest.

"No gym," she replied in a clipped tone.

"Exercise is good for you, Sarah. It makes you strong, and resilient." His tone was mocking. For the second time that day, Sarah felt like slapping him.

"She got her exercise anyway, she ran all the way here!" laughed Juliet.

"Ran? Why? Was something on fire?" Harry's eyes were wide with innocence.

"I just wanted home, that's all."

"Well, *I* need to get home for a bit," Juliet intervened, putting her hand on Sarah's arm. "Trevor must be drowning, with the girls and the house. I'll be back tonight."

"You don't need to, Aunt Juliet," said Sarah quickly.

"Better if I do."

"We're OK, Juliet. I've got it in hand," said Harry.

Juliet looked uncertain for a second. Sarah looked at Harry. His handsome face, his clear blue eyes. The picture of reliability.

"OK then. OK. As you're here . . . "

Sarah saw her aunt to the door, and gave her a big, tight hug. Juliet was surprised, but pleased.

"Take care, baby, see you tomorrow." She looked into Sarah's face. She was struck by how young, how vulnerable she looked. A child of seventeen. A young woman of seventeen. Alone in the world, but for her and Trevor.

And Harry.

The moment passed, and Sarah looked away.

"What did you do to her?" Sarah growled as soon as Juliet was out of the door.

"I don't know what you mean."

"You know very well what I mean. She was *confused*. She couldn't remember what happened this morning. I thought you'd sent me to school because you wanted to be here alone, but you wanted to be alone *with her.* You asked her questions about my mum and dad. What did you do to her?" she repeated, in a staccato voice, her green eyes blazing. Shadow was beside her, her tail moving rhythmically, menacingly.

She looks just like Harry.

"I just needed to speak to her. I convinced her to stay for a while longer, and we had a cup of tea."

"And then?"

"Then I sent her to sleep."

What? "How?"

"Like I did to you last night. Like this." He turned quickly and placed his hand on Shadow's head. Shadow didn't even have time to protest, or jump away, before she fell in a little heap at their feet.

"Shadow!" Sarah threw herself beside the cat, horrified. She put a hand on Shadow's soft, furry back . . . she was still breathing. She seemed fine. She was just asleep.

"See? It's nothing bad. Something I picked up in Japan. I can send people – well, any living creature – to sleep, a deep sleep. They don't wake up until I say. That's all, no damage done."

"Wake her up *now!*" Sarah was shaking. If Harry had hurt Shadow . . . She felt her hands warming up, the blackwater starting to flow . . .

Harry leaned down and touched Shadow between her ears, gently. The cat opened her eyes and got up slowly, drunkenly, looking at Sarah as if to ask *what just happened to me?* Sarah scooped her up and hid her face in the cat's soft fur, breathing her in with relief.

"Come with me." Harry strode out of the living room, into the kitchen, and down the spiral staircase that led to the basement. The door was locked. He took a little key from his pocket, and unlocked it.

Sarah was speechless.

"Where did you find that key?"

"A tool of the trade. Everybody should have one." He smiled.

"You're basically a burglar," she said dryly.

His smile widened into a mischievous grin. "If it's needed."

The basement was in semi-darkness. It was chilly, and a musty smell saturated the air. Harry switched the lamps on, their warm golden light cutting the shadows and pervading the room. Sarah walked over to switch on the electric heaters, and she was enveloped by a cloud of sudden heat. With the light, and the heat, and the golden glow reflected on the wall, Sarah had the overwhelming feeling that her parents were there . . .

She turned towards James's desk, and had to blink, once, twice.

Dad?

But it wasn't him. It was just Harry. She felt breathless. That breathlessness, that sense of not being able to inhale, of being about to suffocate, was happening more and more.

"Come and look." The computer screen came to life. Harry took out a memory stick from his pocket. "This is what I was looking for last night."

"What is it?"

"You'll see . . . There. This is what your mum and dad had been facing in the last few months."

A series of pictures flashed on the screen. People. Normal people. Men, women, young and old. Snapped in the car, hanging up the washing, in the supermarket, at a restaurant.

"I don't understand. These are just . . . people. It was *demons* that killed my mum and dad. We hunt demons, not people!"

"Look closer." Harry clicked on the photo of a blond woman, snapped as she was calling a taxi. She was turning away, so her profile was barely visible. He zoomed in, and again, and again, until the screen was filled with the detail of her neck. There was a tiny black mark just behind her ear. Harry zoomed in once more.

"See that?"

Sarah squinted a little. "It looks like a tattoo. Like a . . . a circle. A ring."

"Exactly. That ring is the symbol of the Valaya. They're people, yes, but they're worse than the demons we hunt."

Sarah felt her knees give way. She sat down beside Harry.

"These are the people who . . . "

"Killed your parents. And many others. Yes."

"Va . . . Valaya?"

"Yes."

Sarah shook her head. "Why should I believe you? I don't even know you. Why should I listen to you?"

"Sarah, you don't have a choice."

"Oh yes I do!" she shouted. "I could throw you out. Move in with my aunt and uncle, forget about all this . . . "

"That is not possible."

"I don't trust you. I want you out of here now!"

"Sarah, be quiet."

"Don't you dare tell me what to do! You come here with a bunch of stories that make no sense—"

"Sarah."

"Pack your bags now!"

Before she knew it, Harry had clasped a hand over her mouth, and was holding her tight. She couldn't move or speak; she could hardly breathe.

How could she have been so *stupid*, she asked herself for the second time that day. She closed her eyes and felt her hands beginning to warm up. Soon she'd be able to strike. Her heart was racing and she felt dizzy, but she was strong enough to do it, to use the blackwater. Harry would see, if he thought she was a helpless little girl, he could think again.

"Listen to me," Harry whispered urgently. "They're here. They're here *now*. They've come for you. I'll let go of you. But not a sound. If we don't get rid of them, we'll be dead in about . . . let's see . . . three minutes. OK?"

What?

"OK?"

She nodded frantically.

Harry let go of her slowly, turning her face towards him, so he could look her in the eye. Her green eyes met his blue ones. She saw that Harry's expression was steely, tense, ready for the fight.

He's not lying.

"Where?" she mouthed.

"Listen."

Scratching. She could hear scratching behind the steel door, and growling, a deep, throaty growling that chilled her blood.

"Is there another way out?" he whispered.

She shook her head.

They looked at each other, and in wordless agreement, they knew what to do. They got up slowly, making no noise. Sarah pointed at the big wooden wardrobe in the corner, a piece of furniture that was six feet high and nearly as wide. Sarah unhooked the silver chain around her neck, and took another key off it, a smaller one. She opened the wardrobe, as quietly as she could. Inside it there was a collection of weapons: James's arsenal.

Sarah hated that wardrobe, and she hated the weapons in it. She shrugged her shoulders and gestured at them, as if to say *your choice*.

On both sides of the doors there were some hooks, and two little *sgian-dubh* in leather pouches were hanging from them. *Sgian-dubh*, the Scottish name for a ceremonial knife – although for the Midnight men, they were a lot more than just ceremonial. Sarah had often seen her parents putting them back carefully after a hunt. Harry took them off their hooks, handed her one, and kept one for himself.

"Our best bet," he whispered. "Go open the door, and hide behind it."

Sarah nodded. *Yes, I'll open the door. No, I won't hide behind it.*

"Can you use your hands?" she whispered.

"I don't have the blackwater," he replied quietly. The real Harry didn't either, so he didn't have to make up a story. James had inherited it, but Stewart hadn't, and neither had Harry.

Sarah tip-toed to the door. There was no more scratching, no more growling. Everything seemed quiet. She began to turn the handle, slowly, slowly. The growling started again.

Sarah took a deep breath. Her hands were burning up. She was ready. In one fluid movement, she opened the door and jumped back, just as a black, smooth, liquid creature pounced into the room, aiming straight for her. For a split second, they were face to face. The creature had human features, with watery blue eyes, pale skin and broken veins all over its nose. A middle-aged man's face.

Then it opened its mouth. It was full of teeth as sharp as a dog's.

Sarah screamed in horror and let go of her dagger, putting out her hands to use the blackwater. In an endless instant, she realized she had made a bad decision. A very, *very* bad decision. She should have stepped aside, like Harry had said. She wasn't ready; it was going to bite her face off . . .

It's all lost. Mum, Dad, I'm sorry.

She closed her eyes and waited.

It didn't come. She heard a thud, and then silence.

She opened her eyes, cautiously. *I'm still alive. I'm whole.*

The creature was on the floor, Harry's dagger sticking out of its side.

"Now, Sarah!" he called, shaking her out of her shock.

Sarah closed her eyes, focusing on her hands burning, burning . . . She crouched beside the demon, and put her hands on its head. Now she could see it properly. It had the body of a dog, with hard, black hair and a long tail, and its human face looked sickeningly out of place. Sarah shivered with disgust as its fur started weeping. After a minute all that was left was blackwater, dripping from Sarah's hands.

She couldn't move. She was petrified, as if she had turned to stone.

Had Juliet not gone home, she would have died. Had Harry not arrived, they both would have died. A million terrible possibilities swept through her mind. She didn't move for a while, crouching on the floor, trembling. Harry kneeled beside her.

"Are you OK?"

Sarah looked at her wet, blackened hands. She nodded.

"This is just the beginning," Harry whispered gently.

Sarah looked at him. "Are they coming for me?"

"Yes."

"Why?"

Harry hesitated. He couldn't tell her the whole story – he couldn't tell her how the heirs of the Secret Families were being killed one by one, all over the world, because this would have led to her asking questions. Not only would his deception be revealed, but she'd put herself in harm's way. Someone in the Sabha had betrayed Harry and killed him – they'd do the same with her. The time would come for her to know the truth; but for now, all he could do was keep her alive. The less attention they drew to themselves, the better were their chances of survival. Italy was sheltering Elodie and Aiko, Scotland would shelter Sarah.

"Because they want to destroy the Midnights." He resolved to answer. "With your family gone, there would be nobody left to fight them. And we can only imagine what they'd do if they could take over, roam undisturbed . . ."

Sarah stood up, raised her chin the way James used to do, and looked at Harry with an even, steady gaze. She was terrified, but she had no choice. Her Midnight blood dictated her fate.

"Let them come."

It took a long time for Sarah to fall asleep that night. The day had been so strange, so full of shocks that she was still reeling with it all. She lay in her bed with the lights off, looking out of the window to the black moors and the sky above them. She had only been a hunter for two days, and already she had turned into prey, just like she had feared. Everything she had learnt that day was swirling in her mind like a crazy carousel, and she couldn't stop it.

Harry was frightening, with those clear, sometimes cold eyes – and still, something in her responded to him in a way that she couldn't understand. He'd saved her life, he'd opened her eyes to an even greater danger than she'd imagined. He was arrogant, he made fun of her – but he looked at her as if she were infinitely precious, something to keep, and protect. He was so full of contradictions, so difficult to decipher – she just couldn't decide who he was.

The dream from the night before kept going round and round in her head. Another one of those strange visions she'd had since her parents had died. Usually it was straightforward: she saw terrible creatures doing terrible things, and she had to remember as many details as possible to figure out where this was happening, so that her parents could go and stop it. That was it. But everything had changed now. The dreams had become mysterious, cryptic.

She had seen the people who killed her parents – the Valaya – but who was that pale, black-haired boy? She thought she'd seen him somewhere before, but she couldn't remember where, or when. And that woman, the beautiful, blond woman who seemed to hate her with all her might . . .

You're alone, she'd said.

Sarah shivered at the memory. Who was she? What had Sarah done to her, to be hated so? It was like a poem in a foreign language: she couldn't understand a word, but if she found the key, she would be able to translate it.

At last, Sarah's eyes closed without her being aware of it, and she drifted away, exhausted, into a mercifully dreamless sleep.

5
Mistress

Frozen in the moment
Nothing moved as I died
Nobody knows that I died
Nobody
But he who killed me

Cathy

It took a long, long time to turn myself into the Mistress. The rage and emptiness I felt sped up the process, the hopelessness I lived with was my fuel. Another ten years to find them, my Valaya, the ones who'd help me, and we were ready.

That day of twenty years ago, when my heart broke – that day I knew that light was lost to me forever. I was caught in the glare of the Midnight light, and burnt to a cinder. All that was left was darkness, and I learnt to live in it, while James and Anne went shining on as if nothing had happened, as if I were nothing but a memory, a painful memory to be erased as quickly as possible.

Time to move on, he'd said.

I had been a Midnight for a short while – I had been the one chosen to carry the inheritance, to be the daughter they'd lost. Me, the motherless, fatherless child whom they took in as their own. James and I grew up together; we were each other's world, each other's best friend and companion. We fell in love, under Morag's approving gaze. It was perfect. We got married.

I adored him.

And then it all fell apart.

"It's a girl," Morag said without the shadow of a doubt. "I can see it now."

She was sitting beside me, as if to watch over me, a hand on my stomach, her eyes closed. She hadn't let me out of her sight since she found out I was pregnant. She knew first, before me, before James, before any medical test could pick it up. She said she saw the spark start in me. I was so happy at that moment, I didn't even have words to describe the feeling. Her approval was all I wanted.

And James's love. I'd made him proud. I was eighteen, and I had everything. Out of our window, the sea was breaking against the Islay shore time and time again, a sound that was sweet to me, the sound of home.

I was home.

"You'll train her. And she'll be a Dreamer." James was beaming, looking at his mother.

"Yes. We'll look after her." Morag's face was pained for a moment. I knew she was thinking of Mairead, her lost daughter. Another reason why I could help her, why I could help them all. To soften the pain for the loss of Mairead.

That night I went to sleep with Morag's words dancing in my memory: it's a *girl*. My daughter. Faith Midnight.

The next morning I woke up in a soaking bed. Four months too soon, my daughter was ready to come into the world.

Her body wasn't, of course.

I held her like a doll, very white, very still. I was too shocked to cry. James was crying by my bed; Morag was standing beside the window, looking on like the thirteenth fairy, the one who curses Sleeping Beauty at her christening. I know now that she could see what was ahead, what the doctor was going to find out.

The next day I was taken to hospital because of complications, and there we were told. They said it'd been a miracle that I carried Faith as long as I did. It was a miracle she'd stayed five months inside me, because I wasn't meant to have any children at all, ever.

"There are ways. It's very soon to think of all that now, but you can look into adoption . . ." As the doctor said that, his hand kindly holding mine, Morag laughed.

She *laughed*.

Of course, adoption doesn't bestow the Midnight talents. Witchcraft can be learnt, but not the Dreaming, nor the blackwater, or the deadly Midnight gaze. They can only be carried with the blood. Morag laughed her bitter laugh, and I cried and cried, because I had lost my daughter and because I knew what was coming. I knew what Morag would say next.

I knew what Morag would say, but I never, ever thought that James would take her side. *James loves me*, I said to myself over and over again.

After a week I was home. We watched from the window the little white coffin being carried away — I was too ill to go with her; I could barely stand. That's the time they chose to tell me.

"Cathy, darling. Do take your time. Take as long as you need. We'll find you somewhere to stay, wherever you like."

Morag's words didn't sink in for a few minutes. Blood was ringing in my ears and the room was spinning. Already. Already, she was sending me away!

"James . . ." I pleaded.

He was distraught, I could see it. He sat on the bed and held me close, stroking my hair, letting me cry on his shoulder. His own tears wetted my nightgown.

"My love . . ."

Surely he wouldn't let me go? Surely he'd say no to Morag; he'd say that he wanted me no matter what?

"Cathy . . ." He held me so tight, I was *sure* he wouldn't let me go. He loved me truly, he loved me too much to do that.

And then he took me by the shoulders, and looked into my eyes. His face was so handsome, as ever, with those incredible green eyes, eyes like a wood in spring.

"Take all the time that you need," he said.

My heart broke at that moment, and was never whole again. James, my one and only love, my husband, was sending me away too.

I tried to leave quietly. I tried to hold my head high as I stepped into the car. I hated myself when, instead, I ran into James's arms and begged him not to let me go.

"I'm sorry. I'm so sorry," he said. "I can't go against my family . . ."

68

It was the final humiliation as Morag took my arm and led me back into the car. I looked into her face, searching for the love she used to feel for me, searching for some compassion. I found none.

I was broken, alone. Useless. Mourning my daughter, mourning my lost love, mourning the family that had been mine.

Mourning the mother I would never be.

Anne slithered in among the Midnights, in my place. Maybe she had been waiting, hoping, I don't know. I remember where I was when I found out. Cruelly enough, I read it in a *magazine*. You see, Anne and I had been studying music together. She was brilliant, absolutely brilliant, heading for a great career. She was already making a name for herself, even though she was so young. I had followed her success with joy, and a sense of pride, because she was my *friend*. We'd always been in competition, but once I had become James's wife, my career was of no importance to me any more, so I didn't begrudge Anne at all.

James and Anne had met through me, in passing. Barely exchanged a word. She was so different from me, with her black hair, small, shy, always trying to hide away. I really didn't think that James would give her a second glance.

And now they had got married. The magazine had printed page after page of their wedding on Islay, Anne standing in white against the backdrop of the sea, James with smiling eyes, so handsome in his kilt. And Morag. Tall, proud, unsmiling, photographed as she's looking over at her son and his wife, looking at them like she owned them.

I remember feeling ill with jealousy, and stumbling towards the river, thinking there was only one way left for me to take. I sat on a stone bench and watched the swirling waters, trying to find the courage to dive. I wanted the water to close over my head. I wanted not to see any more, or hear any more, or *be* any more. I wanted the pain to stop.

I couldn't. My limbs would not respond. I couldn't switch off the instinct to exist. I couldn't wish myself dead hard enough.

So I went on and I lived. I did what Anne used to do before she was married, and it was now me in the magazines, me on TV and in concert halls over the world. I was barren but I had a talent that I didn't even know I possessed, until then. My fingers flew on the piano as quick as fluttering birds. I put all my sorrow into my music, and people responded.

But it was a cold, joyless path I'd taken.

Nothing was left of me. From the outside it looked as if I'd built a wonderful life for myself: Cathy, the young musical talent, the concert pianist, the composer that swept up all prizes. But like it often happens, things are not what they seem. Anne was fulfilling the only dream that mattered to her – James and his mission, the mission that had been mine, and that she had now made hers. I knew how happy she was, because I knew how happy I would have been, in her place. I would have given it all away, my music, my work, my life, to be a Midnight again, to be with James.

While Anne lived with James, while she learnt all her magical skills from Morag Midnight, I was running and running on a treadmill, getting nowhere, or at least nowhere that mattered. People standing up to clap and cheer; the prizes, the all-important gigs I got; it was all a whirl of nothing to me.

Contrary to what many people thought, it wasn't Anne who'd lost our lifelong competition, it was me. It was *me*, the famous, rich one, who'd lost everything. Any chance of happiness I ever had was gone. My life was empty, and set to stay that way.

Word came through they'd had a daughter. I was playing in Hong Kong when I found out. I felt so ill I thought I'd pass out. Their life paraded in front of me like a trophy, torment-ing me every day, every night, while I played my soulless music all around the world. I knew James pitied me for the choice he'd made, the one that left me out in the cold. Anne didn't pity me; she didn't hate me, she wasn't scared of me – she simply didn't think of me at all. I didn't even deserve a thought; I was so far removed from their lives. I didn't matter. I never existed.

I was in a haze for what seemed like years, sleepwalking through my life, wishing I was dead. When I came back to myself, I could see clearly: I had to be like the Midnights, I had to *become* them, in order to destroy them.

The Midnights had set fire to my life, burnt it down, and walked away – but they had left something behind, like a precious stone, intact under the ash and dust of my existence. It was a little nugget of knowledge, a black seed that I could plant, and watch while it grew, its pale roots feeding on my dreams. Secret knowledge the Midnights wouldn't touch, waiting to be cracked, waiting to come to life. And I did it, I brought it to life.

Like Anne, I don't come from a magical family. The blood that runs in my veins is as common and plain as hers. But she had mentors – James and Morag, who took her by the hand into the amazing, exciting, dangerous world they lived in. I was only taught briefly, so briefly. I did the rest myself.

It took ten years to learn how to open the rivers of time – ten years to learn how to slip them into our reality, the creatures that walked the earth before we came. *Demons* is one of the many names they were given through time; in fact they are *Surari*, in the ancient language of the first human tribes. Legends and myths talk about them; the folklore of every country in the world has stories about them. *Supernatural creatures*, they're called sometimes – but there's nothing supernatural about them; they're creatures of nature like us, just a lot more ancient. They seem unnatural because they don't belong to this time, because they should not be here, among us.

But they are, and they keep coming.

The Midnight motto is: *Don't Let Them Roam*. My motto is: *Let Them Come.*

The Midnights and the other Secret Families around the world were entrusted with the duty to send the demons back where they came from, to the primeval waters that covered the Earth at the beginning of time – while it's me, and those like me, who force the flow of time in order to get them here.

The Surari we're allowed to call are only as powerful as the magic that summons them. Some of us, like the members of my Valaya, can only call Ferals, the animal-like demons with great strength but very limited understanding. Ferals are brutal, senseless beasts. They can also fall into our world by chance, through a fold in time and space, unknowing, unwilling, and find themselves lost and raging in a strange land. They end up living in the sewage system, in condemned buildings, in the few corners of wilderness we have left, and scavenge and kill to survive.

Some of us – like me, of course – have enough knowledge, enough power to call the Sentient ones, the strongest ones, the ones that do more, so much more than just kill without a reason. The Sentient demons *want* to be called, they long to come back and rule the earth again, and we can use this desire of theirs for our own gain. They have Slaves themselves, minions they use as we would use guard dogs.

It's not easy to keep the Sentients in check – it takes all our skills and infinite vigilance to keep them under control and to stop them from taking over, bending the Ferals to their will. I can feel the Sentient ones planning to turn the Valaya from a coven of humans each with a demon servant, into a coven of demons each with a human servant. I can feel them conniving, waiting, biding their time. They'll never succeed – it's my bidding, or the dark waters of the world before time. I won't show any mercy, for anyone. What mercy was ever shown to me?

My Valaya is not the only one. Just as there are many Secret Families around the world, there are also many more of us. Many Valaya, many Masters and Mistresses, each with their own demon, each with their own territory. And above all of us . . .

I can't say. I can't say who leads us all, the One whose orders I follow. All I know is that the Time of Demons is coming again, and it'll be us, the Masters and Mistresses all over the world, who will rise up and rule. The Secret Families will be gone forever, and nothing, nobody will be there to stop us. It has started already. The heirs of the Secret Families have started falling all over the world, a harvest of blood.

But Sarah – Sarah is mine. It'll be me who puts an end to her life.

James and Anne stayed in the light, the golden couple and their perfect world. I longed for the dark – what else did I have left? I wanted to be like them – I wanted to *be* them – all I could do was to become their reversed image, their negative.

You might say I *live* in a nightmare – truth is, my life turned into a nightmare the day I met the Midnights. I've been tied to this wheel, and I can never be free until they are all dead, every last one of them.

It was the Midnights that taught me how to lie, and I learnt well. I'm Cathy Duggan, when everyone is looking; in my heart, I am Catherine Hollow, the Mistress.

6
Dawn

I call on my nightmares
Again and again
I am
My own destruction

Sarah was at the window with Shadow asleep in her lap, watching the first light spreading on the moors. Strange how even when our life has been broken and put back together in a way we can't recognize, even when we want everything to look different, because *we* are different – even then, the stars don't change their place, the wind blows like it always has done, and dawn still breaks. The world looks the same, and still nothing is the same. Like an imperceptible shift of the earth's axis has happened: it's invisible to the eye, but it has enormous consequences.

Sarah was dressed already: black leggings, a blouse and short black skirt, and her ever-present boots. Her hair was tied back in her usual perfect ponytail. She had only slept for four hours, but her sleep had been heavy. She felt rested, in a strange, charged kind of way. Like a coil ready to spring.

She thought of what happened the night before, of the demon-dog that had attacked her in her own home. Never, never before had a creature dared to attack the Midnight home. But with her parents gone . . .

One thing is for sure: I'm not going to sit here and wait to be killed.

The Valaya. Human beings, not demons. People like her, like her friends, her teachers, her neighbours, her classmates. People who looked into the abyss and decided they liked it, that that's where they belonged; who formed an alliance with the ancient forces of the land, to claim it back for themselves. She never thought that anyone would ever willingly ally themselves with demons. Not after all she'd seen.

For the thousandth time, she went through the list of names she had copied from her parents' files the night before.

> *Michael Sheridan*
> *Sheila Douglas*
> *John Burton*
> *Katy McHarg*
> *Simon Knowles*
> *Mary Brennan*
> *Catherine Hollow*

Sarah took her head in her hands. *I've never hurt a human being before. I don't want to, I can't . . .*

A knock on the door.

"Sarah, are you awake?" It was Harry.

"Yes, come in."

He looked terrible, with purple shadows under his eyes, a faded T-shirt and the same jeans as the day before.

"Did you sleep OK?" he asked.

"Not much, but OK. How did you . . . not sleep?"

Harry smiled. "Exactly. Would you like some coffee?"

"I'll make it." Even in the most dramatic of circumstances, Sarah wasn't going to relinquish her perfect cappuccino.

On her way downstairs, she stood at the mirror and looked at herself. She couldn't help a warm feeling spreading through her veins, somehow, even in the midst of all that fear, all that grief. Because Harry was there, and she wasn't alone.

Sitting at the breakfast table, Harry and Sarah were sipping their cappuccinos in silence. Suddenly the phone rang. They both jumped, as if they'd received an electric shock.

"It's just the phone," laughed Harry. "Talk about nerves!"

No wonder.

Sarah went to answer it, and in a few minutes, she was back.

"It was Aunt Juliet. They wanted me to spend the day with them. I managed to convince her I'm too busy."

"You are. Today we begin."

Sarah felt a knot of fear in her stomach. *What do we begin?*

"What's the first name on the list?" Harry's clear eyes were shining. Sarah could see how excited he was. *He loves hunting, just like my parents did.*

The realization came at once: *I'm not like them. I hate all this. It's my duty, but I'd never choose it.*

"Michael Sheridan," Sarah read. "Harry . . . "

"Great. Let's go get the daggers."

"How do you know where to find him?"

Harry lifted his iPhone. "I've got . . . people. Friends who find out things for me."

"Right." *Dodgy*. "Harry, I can't . . . "

"You can't what? You don't want to just sit here waiting for the next attack, do you?"

"No. But I can't hunt human beings."

"We won't be hunting *them*, the people on the list. We're after the Surari they called to their service. It took the Valaya years to gain enough knowledge to summon them. They'd need years to summon others. In the meantime, they'll be helpless, or as good as."

Sarah closed her eyes. So many things to learn, so much knowledge to make hers. A whole new world, a new life. A terrifying one, worse than the one she had before. And that one was bad enough.

How much I hate all this, she thought, and immediately she felt breathless, anxiety weighing on her lungs and stopping them from filling up with air.

"Harry, if we go around looking for demons in the middle of the day, someone will see us and there'll be panic!"

"Let's say that today we go for a lookaround. Just to see how the land lies. Let's go get the daggers. By the way, do you mind if I use your father's? I have a dagger of my own, but his feels great in the hand. So light. A real treat."

"The *sgian-dubh*? Of course. You can have it. But if it's just a *lookaround*, why the daggers?"

"You can't go wrong with a dagger. I learnt that in Japan . . . The hard way." Harry raised his left arm. There was a deep, white scar from his elbow to his wrist. He smiled, that arrogant smile again. With a dimple on his left cheek, she

78

noticed. "Also, there's quite a few things I can do with a blade."

"What do you mean?"

"You'll see."

"You take the dagger, then. I've got the blackwater," said Sarah stubbornly.

"Take the dagger. Trust me."

"I don't." Her expression was so mutinous, so childish, that he couldn't help smiling. "OK then. Let's say you do this as a favour. For your long-lost cousin."

Sarah gave in. She rolled her eyes, and walked towards the spiral staircase to get to the basement.

"Your dagger is not in the basement. It's under your pillow."

"Under my pillow? How did it get there?"

Harry smiled, and didn't answer. Sarah felt her stomach tighten. *He'd done it again. He sent me to sleep. How creepy is this? He can put me to sleep, and I won't remember a thing.*

She walked upstairs to her room, and took out the dagger from under her pillow. Upsetting her perfect bed made her skin crawl. She made her bed again, carefully. Then she tore the duvet away and made it once more, from scratch. She took a deep breath. *Better.*

She went back downstairs, holding the dagger with two fingers, as if it was something vaguely revolting.

"Are you wearing socks?" asked Harry.

"What?"

Harry lifted up his jeans around his right ankle, to reveal the *sgian-dubh* tied to it with a leather strap.

Oh. "No."

"Right then. Turn around."

"Why?"

"Just turn around. And lift up your top."

"What?"

"I want to show you where to carry a dagger. Mary Anne showed me."

Mary Anne? Right.

Sarah blushed deeply, but she obeyed. She turned around, and lifted her top. Harry slipped the dagger into her bra, right over her spine, touching her skin with warm, light fingers. Sarah pulled down her top quickly, and stepped away.

"Try and move."

"I can't feel anything."

"Exactly. Now try and get the *sgian-dubh*."

Sarah raised her arm, lifted it behind her back, and her hand curled around the dagger. She took it out smoothly.

"Perfect."

"I don't like being armed."

"You don't have a choice."

No. I wasn't given a choice when I was born a Midnight.

7
A Place Between
the Water and the Sky

Tomorrow it will be time
To unravel all your secrets

Grand Isle, Louisiana

The road was a white ribbon among the mangroves, between patches of wetland and ponds of still water. The air was heavy and full of moisture, without a hint of a breeze. Just on the horizon, shimmering at the edge of their vision, was the sea.

"So . . . do you play the Cajun accordion?" Niall's face was untroubled, open. The face of someone who didn't think too hard about things.

Or didn't think at all, Mike had suspected a few times since they'd met, a few days before.

"Do I what?"

"Play the Cajun accordion. The official Louisiana instrument."

"Of course. And I eat jambalaya while performing voodoo rituals."

"Do you?" Niall's eyes were huge with enthusiasm.

"No."

"Oh. Oh well." A pause. Then, "Jesus, is that an alligator?"

"It's a fallen tree, Niall." Mike sighed. This Irish boy was testing his patience beyond belief.

"Was it? Anyway, apparently the music is great in these parts. Can we look for some?"

"This is not a holiday."

"I know, but if we can kill two birds with one stone . . . "

"Will you take this seriously?" Mike was exasperated. Since he'd picked Niall up in that castaway village he came from, Skerry or whatever the name was, he had behaved as if he was going on some fun trip. Had it not been for Niall's mother looking straight into his eyes and saying, with that sing-song accent of theirs – *look after him, please* . . . Had it not been for what Mary Flynn had said, Mike would have thought that the Flynn family were completely unconcerned. Or unaware. But no, they knew and they were afraid.

It was just Niall, being . . . being Niall.

"I *am* taking it seriously. Look. I've got a Swiss knife."

"You what?"

"A Swiss knife. In my pocket."

"Great. Just great. That will save our lives for sure." Mike switched the radio on and set the volume as high as he could.

Niall Flynn, Secret heir of the Flynn family. And certifiably mad. I'm supposed to keep him alive. Good luck to me. And as if the Enemy wasn't enough, I also have the Sabha to watch out for.

82

His phone made a buzzing sound.

"It's a message. Can you get it?"

"Sure thing. It's from Sean. He asks if we're nearly there."
Y–E–S, he typed. "There. Sent. I'm amazed there's reception down here."

"Not for most people, there isn't. For us, yes."

"It really is in the middle of nowhere."

"Says the man from Donegal."

Niall laughed. "Good point, I suppose."

Mike had chosen their hiding place. Somewhere that would keep Niall safe, and from where they could help Sean with his mission. Sean Hannay was the only other Gamekeeper who knew where they were headed: Mike's home of Grand Isle, Louisiana – a part of it that was well, well away from the beaten track. Somewhere on a beach, surrounded by marsh-lands where people rarely ventured.

Grand Isle. The most beautiful place on earth, thought Mike. *At least I get to see home before they kill me.*

The shack was just that. A shack.

"Aw, this is lovely," commented Niall, not a trace of irony in his voice.

You've got to give him that: he's easy to please, thought Mike, looking around the dusty, damp, spider-infested little cabin that they were to call home for . . . well, who knew how long?

They put themselves to work, and in a few hours the cabin was clean, the generator was going, buzzing away, and the computers were up.

"There. To you the privilege to speak to Sean for the first time, from our Grand Isle hideaway." Mike handed Niall the iPhone, on speaker. After just one beep, Sean's voice filled the room.

"Mike?"

"It's Niall."

"All OK? Are you clear?"

"I think so. And what a beautiful place. The sea is just incredible, and the beach . . . "

"Er . . . yes. OK. Is Mike there?"

"I'm here, Sean."

"Is the boy for real?"

"Oh yes he is. A ray of sunshine for us all." Mike rolled his eyes. Niall laughed, and his eyes shone in a mischievous way that made Mike smile. A genuine smile.

"I need your help with something, Mike."

"Fire away."

Mike

That's what I'm supposed to do. Help Sean from somewhere safe. Send him the info he needs.

Looking after a Secret heir, that wasn't in the plan. I knew nothing of all this sorry mess until I nearly got eaten by that . . . thing, whatever it was. That thing that came out of my filing cabinet. Seriously: my filing cabinet.

Hey, becoming a Gamekeeper wasn't the plan in the first place! I was just a photographer, and in my spare time, a hacker. That's all. Until my filing cabinet became some sort of a nest to a Feral – that's what they call them. And because of that, I met Harry Midnight.

I wonder how many people in the world end up saying that: I was just a . . . whatever – accountant, mailman, housewife or something – until I met Harry Midnight. He's changed quite a few people's lives. Including mine. The Gamekeeper training was the hardest thing I've ever done, but I did it, and I became one of their best. I have no Secret talents, no magical powers; but man, they need me. Especially now that the Sabha is dirty as hell, and there's only us left to fight, the small group Harry knew to be loyal. As far as we know. It's not looking good, but, what can I say, I've always loved a challenge.

"Thank you, Mike."

"And how's the heron?" Heron, the code name for Sarah. So that if they were intercepted, no connection would be made between them and the Midnights.

"The heron's fine. Frightened. But in one piece."

"Let's keep it that way."

"Hey Sean, what's the craic out there in Scotland? Did you get to anything?" Niall intervened.

"Anything . . . like what?"

"Any gigs?"

"Aaaand, we're out. Goodnight, Sean." Mike brought his hands to his temples, massaging them in little circular movements.

"'Night. And Niall . . . "

"Yes?"

"Get a grip."

"Will do," Niall replied cheerfully, without resentment. He was impossible to upset.

"Are you all like this where you come from?" Mike was busying himself with the provisions: tinned food, dry biscuits and, of course, a few bottles of Bourbon to steady frayed nerves.

"Nah. Just me. Now why don't you pour us something while I go get dinner?"

"There's no shops for miles around. Tonight it's beans and canned peaches." Mike waved a can in the air.

"No need for shops. See you later."

"Give me a minute, I'll come with you."

"I don't think you can. Back in an hour." Niall grabbed a couple of plastic bags they had used to pack Mike's equipment, and he was out of the door.

"Better not leave you alone . . ."

"I'll be fine!" he called, disappearing in the humid, mosquito-infested Louisiana night.

After an hour, as promised, Niall was back. The bags were full of freshly caught fish, alive and still writhing.

Mike was speechless.

"How did you do that?"

Niall shrugged. "Bonfire on the beach?"

"With a big neon sign saying 'Secret heir here, please attack'?"

"Aw, come on, nobody knows we're here. You said it yourself. We're clear. And we can't cook all this on a camping stove. Come on."

A driftwood fire was crackling green and blue, casting strange shadows on Niall's face. Once again Mike wondered what made this boy so special for *them* to hunt him. To hunt them all, so savagely.

"So, what's your talent?"

"I play everything I can get my hands on. Fiddle, *uilleann* pipes, flute, you name it, I can play it."

"Right. Great. That's a talent indeed. But I meant, what's your Secret talent? You know, those crazy things that you heirs can do."

"Oh, yes. I sing."

OK.

"I got that. You play everything, and you sing. A one-man band. But what can you do, you know . . . as a family. As a Secret Family."

"Told you, we sing. We can sing to hypnotize, to stun, to kill. To heal as well."

"That's amazing." Mike was genuinely impressed.

"I suppose so. Oh, and I'm the Dreamer of my family. I get dreams about demons, then we go and sing them down." Niall's face seemed suddenly different. Older.

"Oh." *He's a Dreamer. I don't envy you, man.*

They didn't speak for a while. They watched the fire flickering and crackling and hissing. The noise of the bonfire and the lapping of the waves were the only sounds.

Niall broke the silence. "Anyway, you don't play the Cajun accordion, then? 'Cause you never really answered . . . Hey, where are you going?"

"To pour myself another Bourbon. I've earned it."

87

8
Spirits of the Air

I see the shadows behind the smiles
Longer than my days last my nights

They took James's Land Rover. Harry drove like a madman. Sarah was clinging to her seat, praying to survive the ride.

"Where did you learn to drive?" she asked, her teeth clenched. She was even paler than usual.

Harry smiled and said nothing.

"If we get there alive, I'll drive us back."

"You don't have a driving licence."

"It'd still be safer."

Half an hour later they had crossed the city. Harry stopped in front of a dark, imposing Victorian building. A green plaque announced that the building hosted the Crocketford Community Library.

"Come on."

"Wait, Harry . . . "

"Wait for what?"

Sarah opened her mouth to reply. Nothing came out. *Yes, wait for what?*

"OK, then. Let's go," she said grudgingly. She brought her hands to her forehead. She could feel a headache coming on.

They walked into the neon-lit entrance. It looked more like a church than a library, with vaulted ceilings and grey stone walls. There was a musty smell all around, and a subtle dampness pervaded the air, like in most ancient places. The cold neon light was completely unsuited to the place, and gave it a sterile look, like a surgical theatre.

Sarah lifted her eyes to the dark, impossibly high ceiling, and her head spun.

It all happened in an instant. She had just enough time to set her eyes on the stone arcs above her, then the church-turned-library faded away.

Sarah found herself in semi-darkness. The smell of moss and wet earth hit her. She threw her hands forward, trying to feel her way out, and they met icy, hard stone. She blinked, over and over again, trying to get used to the muted light, and she noticed a wedge of sunlight coming from somewhere behind her. She turned around, and threw herself on her knees, trying to reach it. She crawled on, and squeezed herself through the passage, hitting her shoulders on the hard stone in her haste to get out. The first things she saw when she emerged were the huge grey stones standing in a circle all around her. She realized that she had come out from somewhere under those stones.

She was on a grassy hill, under a purple sky, in a place that seemed suspended in time. The clouds were galloping on over her head, and the wind was roaring in her ears. Every colour seemed heightened, and the light was strange, sharp and yet muted, feeble, like an eternal dusk. She looked around, to see if anyone else was there. She realized she was alone, and she waited.

Something was brought to her by the wind, something tiny and black, like a little seed. It flew towards her face and hid in her neck. Sarah brought her hands up, and felt a sharp pain just above her breast.

There was something there. She took off her T-shirt as quickly as she could, and the wind gave her goose bumps. She could see it now, the little black thing attached to her skin, like a leech. It was feeding on her blood, and it had started growing, growing, becoming more and more swollen the more it drank from her. Sarah tried to call the blackwater, but her hands would not heat up. She couldn't make her hands burn; she was so cold, and suddenly so weak . . .

Sarah whimpered and tried to prize the demon off her skin, but it wouldn't move. She started to feel faint. It was now as big as a football, and full of her blood. She was shivering, as the demon fed on her.

She closed her eyes, and waited for death. It had happened so many times before in her dreams, she had died so many times, and every time was as painful and terrifying as the first. She curled up, feeling a single tear roll down her cheek.

Sarah blinked, and in that split second, someone appeared in front of her.

It was the pale, black-haired boy she had dreamt of before. He was looking at her with wide eyes, as if he'd been hit by a thunderbolt. His eyes shone like obsidian; his skin was white; his hair was so dark it was nearly blue. A little poem she had read once in a book of fairy tales came back to her:

> Red as blood
> White as snow
> Black as black
> Is the wing of the crow

"It's *you*," he said simply, like he'd known her forever. Like he'd recognized her.

Sarah looked into his eyes. She thought she'd seen a flickering fire in them, like burning coal. But as she blinked, the little fire was gone already. The pale boy was holding something, clutching it to his heart with both his hands, but Sarah couldn't see what it was. A strange feeling came over her, as if all her thoughts had disappeared, as if she couldn't think any more. She felt as if the sky and the earth had swapped places – disorientated, dizzy.

I should be in pain, I should be afraid. But I can't feel anything.

He kneeled beside her and touched her hair gently, slowly. With his touch, Sarah felt as if all thoughts had escaped from her head, and only one was left: that *he* was there, there with her. His black eyes were like a spell, leading her beyond the fear and the pain, as if the whole world had disappeared and lay forgotten. She couldn't look away; she was lost in his gaze, as if she'd dived into a dark pool and was drowning slowly.

The boy lifted one hand, and placed a finger onto the swollen creature attached to Sarah's chest. Just one finger, just one touch, and the demon burst into blue flames, burning until it turned into a little pile of ash, blowing away in the wind.

Why I am not burnt? I should be burnt, I should be cold, but I can't feel anything. I should be terrified, and I'm not. I can't think.

The black-eyed boy took off his jacket and covered her with it. She was so weak she couldn't move. All she wanted was to keep looking into his eyes.

"It's you," he repeated, as if he couldn't quite believe what he saw.

What does he mean?

"Yes. It's me, I'm Sarah Midnight."

"I'll stay with you until the dream finishes," he whispered. He had a deep, warm voice. It sounded as if it came from somewhere far away, somewhere a bit echoey. Like a cave.

Sarah sighed, and closed her eyes again. He held her hand until the vision disappeared.

Sarah opened her eyes to realize she was leaning against Harry, her head on his shoulder and his arms around her waist, sustaining her so that she wouldn't fall. He was propping her up against a cold stone wall. She tried to free herself, but she found that her legs were still shaky and had to hold on for a little while longer.

The second she realized it actually felt quite good to be leaning on Harry, that his body felt strong – so much stronger than hers, so safe – she took a wobbly step back, blushing.

"Are you OK?"

Sarah nodded.

"A vision?" he whispered.

She nodded again.

"Does it happen when you're awake as well?"

"Sometimes. Not often. Did anyone see?"

"No. I held you as you fell. I pretended we were locked in a passionate embrace." He smiled, a smile that wanted to be cocky, but was somehow shy. Sarah looked away.

"What did you see?"

"A demon, but I don't know where. Some weird place. Unreal. I'll tell you later, in the car. Let's go." *Another strange one. No hint as to where that leech thing is . . . And that pale, black-eyed boy again . . .*

They walked on into the main hall. Tucked against the back wall was the counter, covered in books and leaflets, and dotted at regular intervals with computers. Three bored-looking employees sat in front of them, two women and a man.

"It's him."

Sarah followed Harry's gaze. A middle-aged man, nearly bald, with a shirt that strained on his considerable stomach. A man like many others, the kind of man that could be your teacher, or someone who checks your ticket on a train, or a neighbour you'd say hello to on a sunny morning, as he mows his lawn. Nobody, looking at him, could begin to imagine the secrets he hid, the terrible things he'd done.

Michael Sheridan, the first name on her parents' list.

That sorry excuse for a human being killed my parents. Sarah felt sick.

"What shall we do?"

"We'll ask him to send his demon back where it came from."

"Here? In front of everyone?" Sarah whispered urgently, gesturing towards the pensioners in the computers' bay, the group of schoolchildren listening to a story, the middle-aged woman scouring the DVD shelves.

Harry walked towards the counter, resolutely.

"Good—" Michael raised his head from the form he was filling in, and saw Sarah. "—Morning," he finished. Slowly, he opened his mouth in a smile. Like a crocodile baring its teeth. Sarah felt a chill down her spine. *This place is full of evil*, she thought. She felt it all around her, as thick as cobwebs.

"I'm looking for a horror book. A new release," Harry said coolly. *Very apt excuse*, thought Sarah.

"Of course. The horror section is in the back. Follow me." Michael sounded jovial, happy to help. *Creep.*

They walked on. The library was bigger than Sarah would have thought, with rooms and rooms one after the other, and bookshelves at strange angles, like a labyrinth. Sarah's heart was beating too fast, and her instinct had kicked in: she could feel her hands tickling, getting ready.

"Here we are." Michael stopped and turned around. "The horror section. Sarah Midnight, I'm honoured to meet you in person." He smiled his toothy smile. There was a little blob of saliva at the corners of his mouth.

"And I'm disgusted to meet you."

Michael's smile didn't waver, only his eyes got colder.

"I wasn't expecting you'd still be alive," he said, as if he were discussing the weather. Sarah felt afraid. And then she felt a deep, consuming rage burning her from head to toe.

"You're nothing, Michael Sheridan. Without your demon, you're nothing," she whispered, hitting him with her green gaze. Michael stepped back, imperceptibly.

"We've come to ask you to leave us alone," intervened Harry, an icy, white light in his eyes. "To send the demons back where they belong, and to dissolve the Valaya. If you do all this, we'll let you go."

"You'll let us go?" laughed Michael, a fat, hearty laugh, as if he'd never heard anything so funny before.

"It's what I said." Harry ignored Michael's laughter, and looked at him evenly. Sarah admired Harry's courage. He seemed never to lose his nerve.

"This is the last day of your lives," murmured Michael, taking a step towards Sarah. Harry slipped between them at once.

Right at that moment, someone entered the room and started browsing the shelves.

"What about this one? It's supposed to be very good," said Michael quickly, picking a book at random from a shelf. There was nothing left to say.

Harry took Sarah by the arm and led her out of the book-labyrinth, into the fresh, chilly October air. Sarah breathed deeply, trying to forget Michael's sweaty body odour and the musty smell of the library.

"It worked a treat," she muttered.

"It was worth a try. At least we saw one of them in the flesh. I don't know how I didn't kill him there and then . . . "

Sarah winced. She hated thinking about killing; she hated talking about killing; she hated anything to do with killing and violence and inflicting pain. She had enough of it in her dreams. She was still struggling with the idea of hunting down Surari – demons, creatures, whatever you want to call them – but *human beings*?

Harry didn't seem to have such qualms. He was different from her mum and dad, in so many ways.

"Oh . . ." Harry jumped.

"You OK?"

"Yes. Yes, fine."

"What shall we do now?"

"We'll go home." Harry was scratching his neck furiously.

"Are you sure you're OK?"

"Yes, yes. Just a bit itchy here, on my neck."

"Let me see." Sarah slid her hands inside his collar, gently. Her face pressed against his chest. He smelled good, she thought. He smelled . . . familiar. He smelled of soap, and of the sea.

"I can't feel anything." Her voice came out small.

"It's OK, let's go." They got back into the car, and started driving towards the motorway. Sarah was looking out of the window, lost in thought.

And then it hit her. *It's like in my dream!*

"Stop the car!"

"What? Why? Ouch," said Harry suddenly, putting a hand to his chest.

"Harry, stop the car. It's like in my dream! The demon from my dream!"

Harry had suddenly paled, and looked in great pain. As soon as he could he stopped the car, and they jumped out. They'd been driving along Charlotte Gardens, and they ran in, as fast as they could. Without a word, frantically, Harry ripped his jacket and his shirt off. To their horror, they saw a flash of red on his clothes and on his chest.

"Harry. In your shirt," Sarah murmured, her voice even, vibrant with controlled panic. Something abominable, something black and shiny had fallen off him and was writhing on the grass. They jumped back with a gasp. Harry was holding his chest: he had a small, round wound on his collarbone, and it was bleeding.

"I think it's . . ."

"Michael's demon. That's what I saw in my vision," Sarah finished for him. *Of course. That's what Michael had meant when he'd said that this was the last day of their lives.* She took a step towards it, hands raised and ready . . .

"Watch out!" shouted Harry suddenly, and grabbed her by the arm.

Sarah barely had the time to see that the little creature had a round mouth full of minuscule little suckers, before it jumped towards her face. It all happened very fast. Harry pushed Sarah away, just as the demon was about to attach itself onto her face. With a horrible sound the demon bit Harry instead – and this time deeply, mercilessly. He fell on the ground, clutching his chest. Sarah screamed and tried to grab the creature, to prise it off Harry's skin, but it wouldn't move. She could see its black body inflating, as it kept drinking Harry's blood at incredible speed.

Sarah closed her eyes and started concentrating on her hands, desperately trying to warm them up, desperately trying to call the blackwater. *Hurry up!*

Harry whimpered and closed his eyes, and his head fell back. He had fainted. The demon was now as big as a cat, swollen with blood.

Oh my God . . .

Sarah lost her concentration again. She closed her eyes, felt her hands warming up once more. *It's not working. It's not working.* Panic overtook her.

In despair, Sarah asked for help, a silent prayer.

Mum, Dad, help us!

And someone listened. She felt a gust of wind on her back, but it wasn't wind, it was a flapping of wings – and at the same time, the deafening cawing of a flight of ravens exploded in her ears. Instinctively Sarah covered her head with her hands, ducking, but the ravens ignored her, and flew straight over Harry, covering him in a sea of black feathers, pecking and cawing and flapping their wings. Sarah gasped in fear; she could see that some of the ravens were already stained with red – Harry's blood. But before she could move, the ravens pulled away, as if of one will. As suddenly as they had come, they flew away in a flurry of wings and more cawing, disappearing into the sky.

The demon-leech was on the grass beside Harry, in a pool of black and red blood. It was pulsing in silent agony, biting the air, opening and closing its round mouth like a fish out of water. Sarah knew she had to make sure that the demon-leech was finished before she ran to Harry. She raised her hands – finally, they were burning – and placed them on the hot, slimy black skin of the creature. With one sudden, single gush the demon dissolved into blackwater, mixed with all the blood it had drunk, soaking the ground with red-black liquid.

Sarah threw herself on Harry, who was lying bare-chested and bloodied on the grass. His face was white; his chest was covered in bruises – the round wound caused by the demon, and dozens of little wounds all around it, where the ravens had pecked to prize it away.

"Wake up . . . please wake up," she whispered breathlessly. She took his hand into her own, trying to find his pulse. Faint, but there. He was still alive. She covered him with his bloodied shirt and jacket, then she took her own jacket off and laid it on him as well.

"Harry . . ."

I can't lose him.

I can't lose him like I've lost my parents. I'd be alone.

I'd be completely alone.

Sarah brushed Harry's hair away from his forehead, tenderly, in a gesture that mirrored what he'd done to her the night he'd arrived. Her touch left a trace of blood on Harry's skin. She looked at her hands. They were wet with the blackwater, and with the blood that had leaked out of the creature when she had dissolved it. She'd been so worried about Harry that she hadn't even noticed. She dried her hands on her skirt and on the dead leaves, and placed them on Harry's chest, trying to give him her energy, her warmth. His skin felt so cold.

Sarah tried to inhale. She was breathless with fear again, her chest weighed down like she'd been buried alive.

Wake up, wake up.

A distant cawing came from the sky. The flight of ravens was still visible, like a black stain against the clouds. Sarah looked up, blinking at the white sky, dizzy from trying to follow the birds in their ascent.

"Sarah." Harry had opened his eyes.

"Harry!" Sarah squeezed his hands and inhaled deeply, air filling her lungs at last. She could breathe again.

"The demon . . ."

"It's gone, don't worry . . . how do you feel?"

"Like I've been hit by a train." He pulled himself up, slowly, holding on to Sarah's hands.

"You lost a lot of blood. That disgusting thing was *full* of your blood! Had it not been for the ravens . . ."

"The ravens?"

"They saved your life! They pulled that thing off you and pecked it. There, look." She pointed at the sky, but above them there were only clouds. The flight was gone.

"Look, I know it's hard to believe it, but really, it was ravens that saved us. But how can it be? A demon, pecked to death by . . . by birds!"

"Unless . . ." Harry whispered.

"Unless?"

"Unless they weren't real ravens." Harry's voice faded, and he dropped his head in his hands.

Sarah wanted to ask what he meant, but he looked so pale, and his lips had a hint of blue. She remembered how quickly she had weakened in her dream, how soon she had started to lose consciousness, when the leech was attached to her. Sarah stroked his face again, and Harry put his hand on hers.

You're still with me . . .

"I'm going to take you home. We can take a taxi, come and get the car tomorrow."

"I can drive."

"Are you sure?"

"Perfectly sure. One dead, six to go." He attempted a smile.

"Harry . . ."

"Yes?"

"I thought I'd lost you."

Harry looked at her with his clear eyes, and Sarah felt like she was diving in a loch of icy waters, falling endlessly, helplessly.

They were barely in the door when Juliet phoned to invite them for dinner. Sarah looked across the hall and into the living room, where Harry was lying on a sofa, deathly pale, a glass of whisky beside him. The journey home had been ghastly, with Harry concentrating furiously on the driving, trying not to lose consciousness again.

"I'm sorry, Juliet, we can't. It's just that . . ." She thought quickly. "Bryony is coming for dinner; we'll watch a DVD, she'll stay over . . ."

Shadow purred against her legs. She loved Bryony. Once more, Sarah wondered how much Shadow really understood of the human world. She seemed to always know what was going on.

"Yes, I'm here. Yes. Of course. Speak to you soon."

Sarah put the phone down.

"Sorry, Shadow, Bryony is not coming, it was just an excuse to get Juliet out of our hair."

Shadow stopped purring, and walked away on silent paws, in a huff.

"You did the right thing. We can't risk it. If they attack us at Juliet's we'd put them all in danger." Harry's voice was still feeble.

In a moment of clarity, one of those moments where things are grasped and understood all of a sudden with unquestionable insight, Sarah saw how much Harry *loved* that strange arrangement, just the two of them. He was right; they couldn't put their family and friends in danger – it was their duty to stay away from them for a while – but he didn't seem to mind much, being alone with her so often.

I like it too, thought Sarah suddenly, unexpectedly. She had been alone so often as a child, and this was the first time she'd lived with someone who actually spent their nights at home. It was like a suspended time, an in-between time where Harry was with her, always. Even when she was sleeping.

She took in Harry's pale, handsome face. *My cousin. He could be my brother. He could be my best friend. He could be . . .*

"I know it's dangerous for you, going to school," Harry interrupted her thoughts. *Thankfully.* "But it's a risk we have to take. If you stopped going to school we'd get into trouble."

"I couldn't anyway. The audition with the RCS is in a few weeks. I *must* get a place."

"What is that?"

"The Royal Conservatoire of Scotland."

"Wow. Is that what you want to do? Teach music like your mum?"

"No, I don't want to teach music. I want to *make* music. I want to compose, and play all over the world. I'll try and get into the Royal Scottish Orchestra, for a start."

Harry smiled. "You'll be amazing. I know that."

Sarah smiled back, and looked away. "Well, it all depends . . . you know. This crazy life I have. I don't know how much time I'll have to do what I want to do. What about you? What did you do in New Zealand?"

"I studied medicine, like my dad. And your dad."

"What will you do next?"

"You mean apart from making sure you stay alive? That's a full-time job in itself." He laughed.

"I mean, when we'll be free."

Once a Gamekeeper, always a Gamekeeper.

"I'm not sure. Qualify as a doctor, maybe. I don't really *need* to work. My clients in Japan were very generous. I can live on it for the rest of my life."

"I don't really need to work either – neither did my parents. They did it because they loved their jobs, though sometimes they were so tired in the morning, they couldn't even speak."

Harry nodded.

"So when is this audition?"

"The thirtieth of November."

"You must work hard, then. I'll help you. We've got to try and keep things normal."

"Just as well, or I'd be stuck here alone with you!" she teased him.

He looked at her with those piercing eyes. "Would that be so bad?" he said, and it was a bit like a whisper, like something said while lying on the same pillow. Sarah felt her blood rising to her cheeks.

"I'm going to cook dinner," she said quickly. Too raw, too intimate. She wasn't ready. She was scared.

She ran into the kitchen and busied herself. She was trying to stop her heart from running away like a wild horse, but it was no use. The thought came anyway: *to be alone with Harry in this house. No, it wouldn't be bad at all.* She rejected that thought, pushed it away with all her strength, because that was not the way she was supposed to feel, not right now. Not in the middle of all this. Not for her cousin!

"Smells good." Harry had followed her into the kitchen, in that silent way that unnerved her. She jumped. *Something else he learnt in Japan?*

"Quiche with a side of peas and potatoes."

"Nice."

She desperately tried to think of something to say, something to break the silence. Maybe that was the right time to try and learn more about what was happening to her. And a way to change the subject.

"Harry, who are these people?" she asked, putting the dish she had prepared into the oven and closing the door carefully. "The Valaya, I mean. Why are they doing this?"

Harry took a deep breath. How much could he tell her, without giving away his deceit, without leading her into the hands of the Sabha? He'd have to tell her about the other Secret Families sooner or later, about the Valaya all over Europe, and the shadowy puppeteer behind them all. She'd have to know that once they'd eliminated the Scottish Valaya, there would be more of them, more enemies, more danger. That it was going to take a long, long time for the war to be over – if ever. But not now, not yet. Once they were safe from the present threat, he'd reveal his true identity, and explain what was really going on.

Not yet.

"They want to rule Scotland, and from here, they want to spread. They want to call more demons, and use them for their own means . . . They're fools."

"Because the demons won't let them, will they? People like Michael . . . they think that the demons are at their service, that they've got them under control, but they haven't."

"Exactly. The Surari used *them* to come into this world, not the other way round. It's not easy for the creatures to seep into our reality without dissolving. The Valaya helped them, so they played the game. But once they're here, they won't be doing the Valaya's bidding. These forces are a lot older, a lot more powerful than we can imagine. They used to rule the earth. We snatched it from them, and they want it back."

Sarah nodded. Her parents had told her about that, and how the Midnights were the only beacon for humanity, in a wilderness of danger.

But how can it be? Only the Midnights, for the whole world? A million questions were swirling in her head, her outlook on the world changing by the minute.

"You said you hunted in Japan. So . . . we're not the only ones? There are demons all over the world? And demon-hunters like us?"

"Sarah, don't worry about all this now. Let's focus on staying alive."

He's hiding things from me. Just like my parents did. But he's right. All that matters now is to survive.

"How did the Valaya summon the demons? I had no idea you could actually *call* them."

"They learnt the dark arts. Spells written in cursed books that I never want to set my eyes on, and I hope you won't either. Even just looking at one of those books can sicken you, infect you. It must have taken years of study, to do what they did, to summon demons like these ones. That leech thing – a little bit longer, a little bit more feeding, and it would have multiplied into dozens, hundreds of them . . . can you imagine?"

Sarah shivered. "I don't want to know about those books. I never want to learn those kinds of spells. Actually, I don't want to know about any of this."

"Like I said, let's just focus on staying alive. It's the best way, believe me."

Sarah nodded. But she had one more question.

"Today, when you said they weren't *real* ravens, what did you mean?"

Harry took a deep breath, and shook his head. "It's hard to believe . . . But I think they might have been spirits of the air."

"Spirits of the air?"

"Some call them Elementals, or in the ancient language, Dhatu. They're spirits of the elements – air, earth, fire and water. They take the shape of animals somehow related to their elements. I've seen some spirits of the water taking the shape of seals, for example. They're very, very rare. I have no idea why they decided to help us."

"Could someone be controlling them?"

"They're difficult, nearly impossible to tame. I'll see what I can find out." Harry gestured at his phone.

"It's amazing. They looked like normal ravens, and then . . . they just did what they did. I couldn't believe my eyes."

"Things are not always what they seem."

"That's your favourite saying, isn't it?" smiled Sarah. "A bit like your motto."

Harry smiled, an anxious smile. *It applies to me too.*

The oven beeped, and shook them out of their thoughts. Sarah took out the quiche and set the table carefully, beautifully. It was lovely to be sharing dinner with someone. Her parents were always on the go, always heading somewhere. She lit two silver candles, and placed them in the middle of the table, as the final touch.

She felt peaceful, in spite of the storm raging in her life. Harry was eating heartily, and she took it as a compliment.

"You need to build yourself up, after you lost all that blood."

"Don't mind if I do." Harry took a second helping of the quiche. "You've got to eat up too; you're so pale and thin, Sarah."

"I'm starving. I hadn't eaten for ages after . . . you know. When you arrived, I got my appetite back."

"I'm glad to hear that. You love cooking, don't you?"

Sarah nodded. Her mouth was full. "I always cooked for my parents," she answered as soon as she could.

"I love cooking too."

"Seriously?"

"Yes, believe it or not. And I'm not bad at it. I'll bake your birthday cake. It's the twenty-second of October, isn't it? Your birthday?" *It was in Harry's files.*

"Yes. Are you not worried about your street cred? Baking a cake, I mean?" she laughed.

"Not at all. Cooking is cool. I'll make you one shaped like the moon."

"Why the moon?"

"Because you remind me of the moon," he said, and looked into his bowl. Sarah blushed.

"When is your birthday?" she asked quickly, moving the conversation on.

"Not long to go either. It's the sixteenth of November."

"You're a Scorpio."

"Yes. Do you know anything about star signs?"

"Not really. There's a few books about these kind of things in my grandmother's library in Islay, but I never really looked at them. Bryony knows about these things. I'm a Libra. I'm supposed to be balanced, but I'm as moody as anything."

"That's true, yes."

"Hey, you're supposed to say no, of course you aren't!"

"But you *are*."

Sarah laughed. He was looking a bit better. His skin had that very un-Scottish golden glow again, the light from the silver candles dancing on his handsome face.

"OK, then, I'm moody!"

"A nice moody, though," he conceded.

Sarah smiled, and wished that the evening would never end.

9
He Came in a Dream

Suddenly it seems
That nothing matters but you

Sarah lay in her bed, thinking what a strange day it had been. Half of it horrific, half of it peaceful and lovely. She couldn't believe she'd been so suspicious of Harry, when he first arrived. It felt like he'd been there forever. She closed her eyes, listening to the soft sound of the radio coming from his room, and drifted away . . .

Time to slip into that strange, trance-like kind of sleep, and the vision took her. It often happened like that. Sometimes it was so quick that she'd close her eyes in her bed, and open them in a different world.

That night she didn't find herself in that surreal, strangely-lit world her dreams had taken her to lately – those grassy plains under a purple sky. Instead she was standing in her garden, under one of the oak trees. Golden-red leaves were falling and swirling all around her, floating on little whirlpools. The sky was bright blue, clear, cloudless.

She brushed a leaf out of her hair, and turned around, checking to see if she was alone. She looked towards the oak, and back. Someone had appeared right in front of her.

"Sarah."

She knew that voice. It was the pale, black-eyed boy again. Sarah felt a deep, sudden joy invade her, and with it came a sense of disorientation, as if a strange fog had risen in her mind, to cloud her thoughts. *There he is! He's back!* That was all she could think, as if every other consideration had been dissolved.

"Who are you? Are you a demon?" Her voice sounded strange to her own ears, muffled, like sounds on snowy days.

"I'm not a demon," he said, and he sounded . . . pleading. Yes, that was it. Pleading. There was sadness in his voice. *Why?*

"Who are you, then?"

"I was sent to you."

"Who sent you?"

He didn't answer; he just stroked her face, tracing her lips gently with his finger. "I never thought you'd be so beautiful." He said it simply, as if he'd been making small talk.

Sarah blushed, and didn't know what to say. *Of course, I have to be as hopeless in my dreams as I am in reality.*

"The spirits of the air," he whispered. "The ravens today. It was me who sent them."

"You?"

"I won't let anything happen to you, my Sarah." He took her face in his hands. For a second, she thought he was going to kiss her. Instead, he spoke again.

"Sarah . . ." His voice was like velvet, like warm water. Like a spell.

"Yes."

"I'll be back soon."

Don't go. "When?"

"Soon." His eyes were burning into hers. Her mind clouded over. There was nothing left to say, nothing left to do but let herself float away . . .

"Soon," she echoed.

Sarah opened her eyes, and she was in her room. Her head was fuzzy, as if she'd just woken up from an anaesthetic. *Oh no, I'm awake. Please, let me fall asleep again. Let me see him again.*

She sighed, a sigh of regret, a sigh of joy, and closed her eyes again, savouring the moment. She wanted more of him, and then some more. A deep, deep happiness invaded her, in spite of all that was happening. As if the new world she was entering could hide some beautiful surprises, and not only misery and fear. As if she were standing at the edge of a warm sea, and all she had to do was dive.

I don't even know his name.

She thought of the golden leaves swirling around him. She thought of how all her thoughts had left her mind, as if carried away by an invisible force.

She didn't write that dream down. It was a secret, something only for her to know.

Sarah drifted back to sleep, a dreamless sleep, and resurfaced at dawn. The grey, cold light of the early morning was sweeping the room as she pushed the blankets off. A shower of leaves fell off the bed, red, yellow, golden, swirling around for a few seconds before landing on the floor, one by one.

It could only be *his* doing. Sarah looked at the leaves in wonder. They were so beautiful. They were dead, or dying, their bright colours one last breath before the end – but their agony was amazing to see. Sarah untangled a red one from her hair.

Leaf. In my heart, I'll call him Leaf.

10
Chosen

Salvation comes like fire

Leaf

It's her, then. The one my father chose for me.

I was expecting . . . Oh, I don't know what I was expecting. I only know that I was dreading it, I was dreading to find out who was to share all this with me, if she'd drag me deeper, if she'd make it all even worse.

But she won't. She's my salvation. I burn, she's water; I suffocate, she's air – I can just imagine, when I am one with her, how light will flood my eyes, how the night will part and let me out into the day. When I break her, the light she has inside will come out, like a seal breaks to reveal the hidden message – and she'll have to share that light with me. I'll be saved, and she'll be the one who falls. I'll burn her down; I'll kill her and give her life again. I'll be true to her. I'll never leave her, never.

113

She smells of light and life, she smells of wind. I can see her, sitting in the darkness with a crown of fire, surrounded by spirits, her skin as white as my mother's.

I wish I could just take her, but that's not how it works. She has to come willingly. She has to need me as much as I need her, and there's a long way to go, before I win her trust. To make her want me was a good start. I could feel her fear dissolving into desire – it makes it all so much easier, that the one he chose for me is not only ready for the taking, she's also longing to be taken. She's *asking* to be taken away from all this. My influence works a lot better this way; it sinks deeper.

Before anything else, though, I have to keep her alive. I could stop her enemies right now. I could destroy them all. But I won't. They'll attack, and I'll be there to save her. I'll be her protector, her guardian angel. She'll fall for me, and when the time comes, she'll follow me.

I used to dread my new life, now I long for it. My father made the right choice. There can be nobody else but her.

11
Constellation

Why did you let me love you
If you had to go?

Castelmonte, Italy

Elodie

Harry and I were like a two-star constellation. Eternal,
unmoveable.

Meant to be.

Now that his star has been taken from me, I'm wandering
through this black, infinitely lonely universe, half of something, half of nothing.

I was sixteen when I met Harry. He had come to Lyon to
speak to my father, Arnaut Brun, the chief of the Brun family,
the most powerful Secret Family in France. My father now lies
in the cemetery of Saint Michel, our family chapel, having
died in the terrible knowledge that his wife and daughter
were to follow the same fate, at the hands of the same faceless
enemy.

He was right about my mother, although not the way he thought. They didn't come for her. She just lost the will to live when my father died, and withered day after day until one night sleep turned into death. As for me, I was far away already. I had followed Harry Midnight, the mesmerising heir of the Midnight family, to Japan, and then to London.

My life turned out so different from what my parents had planned for me. I was supposed to marry some heir from a Secret Family, maybe Vincent Didier, the eldest of the Didier sons. That would have been a perfect match, a perfect alliance, and our children would have carried incredible powers in their blood.

But Harry came along, and as soon as I looked into his eyes, I knew I could never marry Vincent. I knew there could be nobody else but Harry. I also knew that my parents would never, ever accept him as their son-in-law. The Midnight legacy was strong but tainted by its divide, and because of that Harry would never sit in the Sabha, among the chiefs of the most prestigious Secret Families. He was not one a Brun heir could ever marry. He was not *one of our kind*, my father cruelly said.

I'll never forget the day my mother turned her back to me, as if I wasn't her daughter any more. I'll never forget the day my father took my ring away, the ancient heirloom of the Brun family, given to the firstborn of each generation.

I never regretted it. I could lose my family, my inheritance, the world I'd known as a child – it was all worth it, to be with Harry Midnight.

But the day Sean arrived in London, I knew it was the last time I'd ever see Harry.

To leave him was like having my heart torn out.

When I was a child my parents and I used to spend every summer in Lac Blanc, in our country house – that was before the woods became too dangerous, before too many things started to seep through. We used to take long walks along the lakeshore, watching the water dance and shimmer.

One day, during one of our walks, my father stopped suddenly. He turned around, arms outstretched to block our way.

"Better to go back, Marcelle," he said, and gestured at something lying on the road. My mother led me away in a hurry, and we double-backed towards our house, away from whatever had stopped my father in his tracks.

But it'd been too late. I had seen already. It was a swan, lying open and bloodied on the pebbles, its feathers stained with red, its head thrown back at a strange angle, its chest half-eaten.

At the time I thought it was an omen. I thought that one day that would be me.

To leave Harry that day made me feel as if I were that swan, slaughtered, lying opened and naked for everyone to see. My heart eaten away by something sharp-toothed, something strong and merciless.

I accepted I had to go because I have a duty. We all have to fight, regardless of whether we want to keep on living or not.

And I don't. Because there's no life for me without Harry.

I'll do all I can to protect Aiko, the only heir left in the whole of Japan, and to help our brave, selfless Gamekeepers, the Frison family. This little corner of Italy is the only safe haven left, as far as we know. The Sabha have been infiltrated, and there's nobody we can trust. What's happening beyond this village in the mountains, what's happening beyond the Alps, is a mystery to us. Nobody will contact us in any way, because anything could give us away.

We're safe, for now. Until they find us. And when they do, I must be here to protect Aiko at all costs.

"It's not the first time there's been an enemy at the door," Leandro Frison had said, remembering the War. "I was a young boy, but we all had to fight. There was no hiding away; you had to choose a side. And that's what we're doing now."

I know what Harry had to ask Sean. He asked him to protect his cousin, Sarah Midnight, the last heir of the secluded, mysterious Midnight family. The only family in Europe – or the only one we know of – who refused to be part of the Sabha, and adhere to its rulings. The only family – a clan, they call themselves – who remained a mystery even to my father and the greatest, most prestigious Secret Families. I can only imagine how precious, how unique their powers must be. I caught a glimpse of them as Harry told me about his uncle, his fearsome grandmother, Morag Midnight, and their mansion on a Scottish island. I imagine it to be some-where windy and wild; I imagine salt-encrusted rocks and grey waves, and the cry of seagulls above.

There's only Sarah left. I wish I could have gone to protect her, but I don't get to choose what to do with my life any more, not now that our world is crumbling. My place is here with Aiko.

Who's doing all this? Who has created the Valaya, and who controls them all? Nobody knows, not for sure.

But Harry had his suspicions, and he left me a trail to follow. Unwillingly, of course – he didn't want to put this burden on my shoulders. I had to go behind his back, ignoring his desire to keep me safe, and find out all he had discovered about the traitors in the Sabha, and how they could lead to our real enemy, the one who started it all.

I'm trying to keep faith, I'm trying to believe that there's still hope, and that this fight won't start spilling into the world beyond the Secret Families. I hope that the world will still be shielded from what comes out of the woods, the soil, the water. I'm praying that we can still keep all this hidden from view, that the only ones who'll notice are a few eccentrics spinning their conspiracy theories on the web, so that the truth about the Time of Demons gets mixed up with alien landings and Loch Ness monsters, and because of that, nobody will believe it's coming for real.

The only way is to protect the heirs one by one – to crush the Valaya one by one – until we can raise our heads out of this hiding place, and follow the trail I stole from Harry's files. To go and find the root of all evil, and destroy it once and for all.

Two letters. And a book of stories. That's all I have.

It'll have to do.

I'm supposed to have visions where I see the future. This is the strongest of my powers. They come to me in water, in mirrors, in glass, or they come like dreams, when I'm asleep.

Except it doesn't work any more.

The power I've had since I was thirteen disappeared the day I left London. The Frisons say that it must be shock, that it'll come back. Every day I walk to the little stream at the edge of the village, with its white-grey waters coming straight from the glaciers – so cold that I can barely touch it. I lean over it, and all I see is my reflection, my hair falling like willow branches, and a pair of melancholic brown eyes. Eyes that must belong to someone else – they're too sad, too old to be mine.

I'm only twenty, and I've lived a lifetime. I'm a twenty-year-old widow, a Secret heir with no powers.

If they come, I'll fight them with my bare hands. After all, when I die it'll be the time I see Harry again. I promised him.

"I'll never leave you." Harry's hand ran over Elodie's shoulder, down her arm and coming to rest on her hip. She lay in a lazy heap on their bed.

"And I'll never leave *you*."

London was silent, peaceful, that night of long ago, before it all went wrong. It was just them awake in the night; it was just them alive in the whole of the world, in the whole of the universe. Lost in love.

"Don't fall asleep. Stay with me," Elodie whispered in his ear. Her breath smelled faintly of the ice-cream they had eaten strolling in Hyde Park, a few hours before. Pistachio ice cream, her favourite.

"Why waste time sleeping?" She enveloped him in her arms. She wanted to be as close to him as possible. She wanted to be one with him, so that he could never leave.

"You see, when I'm happy, I sleep," he said hazily.

Elodie laughed. "And when you're not happy, you're hyper."

"Exactly."

"Sleep, then." She held him as he drifted away, keeping him safe, her face snuggled against his back and her hands resting on his chest.

"If you leave, I'll follow," she whispered.

"I know."

It's a promise.

Every day I hope it's the day I get to keep my promise.

12
Remember Me

Strong in my blood
Discovering all
The past and the future
And all in between

"Chicken with almonds and raisins . . . Sarah is back to her old self!" Bryony was looking at Sarah's lunch with appreciation. They were sitting in the school canteen, at their usual table, the one beside the window. A cold, grey light was seeping from it – it was a dull day, and the glass was covered in a million little drops of moisture.

Sarah couldn't help but smile. Her life was in complete chaos, and still Bryony could make her smile. *What would I do without her?*

"Yes, well, I took a bit of time to cook yesterday."

"What did you do at the weekend?"

What did I do at the weekend? Good question. I went looking for a lunatic who's part of a secret society of freaks. Oh, and a demon nearly killed my cousin.

"Nothing much, really. I watched TV, cooked, tidied a bit."
She was used to lying to Bryony. She'd done it for years.

Bryony was her best friend, and still she knew so little about
Sarah's life – her real life, not the one that she and her parents
presented to the world, like the window of a department
store, all done up to look perfect, but completely unreal.

*James Midnight, GP. Anne Midnight, music teacher. One daughter,
Sarah Midnight, a really good girl, doing great in school. A normal
family.*

Until dusk. When darkness falls, and everything changes.

"I saw your cousin drop you off this morning," said Bryony.

"Did you?"

"You never told me he was so gorgeous. He looks like an
actor!"

Sarah blushed and looked away. "I didn't notice."

"Maybe I'll invite him for a coffee, what do you think?"

"Bryony!" *That's all I need right now.*

"Just joking! Don't worry. How long had you not seen him
for?"

"Since I was a wee girl. His dad and my dad . . ." Sarah felt
breathless for a moment, as always when she mentioned her
parents. "They fell out, years ago. I don't know why. My uncle
and his family moved to New Zealand, and they never met
again."

"What a shame." Bryony had a crowd of aunts, uncles and
cousins, and they were very close. Sarah often wondered what
her life would have been like, had she had brothers and sisters,
and a big family. She envied Bryony a little. Especially now,
when she felt so alone.

"Hello . . ."

A tall, lanky boy had appeared beside their table. He was wearing the school uniform, a white shirt worn out of his trousers, a black cardigan, and the blue and grey tie. His straight brown hair came to his neck, framing an open, friendly face.

Jack McAllister. A sweet, kind boy, one of Bryony's best and oldest friends, who'd had a crush on Sarah since they were five years old. Bryony had been trying to convince her to go out with him for the last few years. It was her pet project.

"Can I join you?"

"Of course!" said Bryony with a smile, and glanced at Sarah.

Sarah pretended not to notice.

"I'm going to get a Coke." Bryony stood up. *Very strategic. I'll get you back, Bryony.*

"Sarah . . . I haven't seen you since . . . since . . ." He stumbled.

"Yes. Well . . . I've been at home for a while."

"I just wanted to say that I'm sorry. I'm really sorry, Sarah."

"Thank you." Jack was a lovely person, and a good friend. *And that's it.*

He fidgeted with his tie. His cheeks were scarlet.

"Would you like to go out, later on? A coffee, maybe?"

Er . . . no?

"I'm sorry, I really can't. I have so much to do today." *That's true, anyway.*

Jack's face fell, and Sarah felt terrible. "Of course . . . maybe another time."

He looked desolate. Sarah couldn't bear it.

"Things are not easy at home right now." She struggled to continue. It felt strange to be confiding in anyone. She hardly ever did that, and words came out with great effort. "But when it all settles down again, I'll go for coffee with you."

Why did I say that?

Jack's face lit up. "Great! Great! I'll buy you a hazelnut latte if you like!"

Sarah smiled. He had remembered that hazelnut latte was her favourite.

Out of the corner of her eye she saw Bryony standing at the vending machine, drinking her Coke and looking at them in a way that spoke louder than words . . . and the spell was broken. Why was everybody trying to make decisions for her? Why did everybody seem to have plans for her life?

"Anyway. Bye Jack." She started gathering her jacket, her bag, her books as quickly as she could.

"Sarah, wait . . ."

"Sorry, Jack, I really have to go."

"This fell out of your books." He handed her a leaf, a bright-red autumn leaf.

Sarah's heart skipped a beat.

"It fell out of my books?"

"It must have. I saw it falling when you grabbed your stuff. It's just a leaf!" He shrugged, wondering why she looked so spooked.

Sarah took the leaf, and placed it carefully in one of her books, turning away.

"Bye then, I'll give you a call . . ."

But Sarah had gone already.

"How was school?"

"Fine."

"Who was that boy you sat with in the canteen?"

What?

For a moment, Sarah was speechless.

"How did you know who I was talking to?"

"I don't. That's why I'm asking you." Harry's impossibly clear eyes weren't giving anything away.

"Do you follow me around? Were you in school with me?" whispered Sarah. She was too bewildered to be angry.

"Of course! Do you think I would have allowed you to go to school alone, not knowing when the Valaya might attack?"

Allowed me?

"They wouldn't attack me in a busy school, in the light of day."

"They'd find a way to make it look like an accident. I promised to protect you, Sarah, and I will."

Sarah nodded, uncertain.

He follows me in school, hiding somewhere. He's watching me.

She didn't know whether to feel horrified or strangely comforted. Harry must have seen her consternation. He took her hand.

"I won't leave you alone," he said.

His hand was strong, and so much bigger than hers. Sarah squeezed it. She heard a voice saying something. Her voice.

"No. Don't leave me alone."

What am I saying? She was startled. Those words had come out from the bottom of her soul, as unstoppable as a sigh.

They looked at each other, and a current of recognition passed between them. Two people adrift, holding on to each other.

That night, Harry and Sarah went down to the basement. They had decided to wait for the Valaya's next move, and in the meanwhile prepare themselves the best they could. Harry started examining James's weaponry, some of which he had inherited from his Midnight ancestors, and some accumulated in his brief life. Sarah stood at the oak table, going through her mother's magical equipment. Harry was beside himself with excitement. Having been a hunter for a long time, he had a profound knowledge of the weapons needed for each hunt, for each creature – and he had never come across an arsenal as rich as James's.

"Have you seen this, Sarah? A knife to cut ghost matter!" His eyes were shining.

But Sarah didn't answer. She was barely listening, lost in melancholic thoughts, as she looked at Anne's things. The way they reminded her of her mother was painful enough – but the way she had no idea how to use any of them made it even worse. Her mother had chosen not to give Sarah her rightful inheritance of knowledge – she'd chosen to leave her in the dark.

There were jars and jars of herbs, meticulously labelled. Some came from the garden, and they were plain, everyday herbs; some were different kinds of seaweed, collected by her mother when they went to their home in Islay; and some were a mystery. The labels said the weirdest things, like 'Kelpie's Mane', 'Selkie Skin', 'Tree Blood', 'Sea Spirit'. Sarah knew that those names weren't flights of fancy, poetic names that her mother had made up – she knew that they meant what they said, somehow. Sarah examined the jar labelled 'Sea Spirit'. It was a grey powder, nothing much to look at. She opened it and slid her finger in. It felt wet, like water. She took a closer look – no mistake, it was dust – but it definitely felt like water. She put her whole hand in it, splashing gently inside the jar. When she took her hand out it was perfectly dry.

Sarah opened a little box. It was full to the brim with brightly coloured stones, rubies, emeralds, pieces of obsidian and amber, and a few diamonds, as big as her fingernails. She also had some lumps of gold, silver and copper, and a few plain-looking stones that, Sarah was sure, must have had some special qualities invisible to the eye. There were several other boxes. Some were made of cardboard, with flowery patterns in pastel colours, in her mother's delicate taste; some were wooden. There was an oak one with the Midnight coat of arms, an intricate M woven around a dagger, burnt into its lid. She opened them all, one by one. Some looked like harmless sewing baskets, full of different coloured threads, pieces of string, little velvet pouches and fabric. A few had candles in them, of all colours, shapes and sizes. One was more like a chest, and it wouldn't have looked out of place in a pirate film. It was made of heavy, dark wood, and had a brass lock. Sarah tried to open it, but to no avail.

"Harry, look. This one is locked."

"Mmmm . . . do you want me to try with this?"

Sarah turned around. Harry had a huge butcher's knife in his hand, and looked very pleased with himself. Sarah felt quite ill, wondering what it might have been used for.

"Er . . . no thanks."

"Wait." Harry took out a key from his pocket, the one he'd used to unlock the basement door when he'd just arrived. "My universal key."

He fussed with the lock for a few minutes, then he shrugged.

"No."

"Oh . . ."

"What is it?"

"I think I know where the key is."

Sarah ran upstairs, followed by Harry, to her parents' room. Her mother kept some antique dolls on the windowsill: Morag's dolls from when she was a little girl. Sarah had never been allowed to play with them, but she had often looked at them in wonder – they were a little girl's ultimate dream. She had often asked herself why one of them – the fair-haired one with the blue velvet dress – had a key around her neck, like a necklace.

Sarah touched the doll gently, stroked her hair, smoothed her dress – then she lifted the key from around her neck, and put her carefully back in her place. Harry looked at the doll again and again. He thought he'd seen her before, somewhere, but couldn't quite remember where.

"Maybe . . . or maybe not," said Sarah, wrapping the chain around her fingers.

"Worth a try." Harry threw one last look at the doll as they left the room, and a chill went down his spine. *Where did I see her before?*

Sarah slipped the key in the lock of the wooden chest. It worked. It turned smoothly, easily, and the chest opened.

She lifted the lid slowly, with Harry looking over her shoulder.

"What is it?"

"They look like . . . scrolls."

Sarah took out one of them, and smoothed it down on the table. It was very old, but not antique, and it showed the traces of where it had been folded time and time again, like a grid. It looked like a map.

"Oh my God, Sarah."

"What? What is it?"

"This is one of the Secret Maps!" Harry leaned on it with his palms, reverentially. "These maps are pure gold, Sarah. They're virtually impossible to find . . ."

The map they had lifted out was a map of the British Isles – but it was full of weird symbols and writings. The legend was very strange. Sarah couldn't make sense of it.

"This one is for landmarks. Look. Hollow hills . . . under-ground streams . . . Oh, I knew it! I always knew there was a city there! Look, it's all underwater now . . ."

Sarah took out another one, and unrolled it.

"This one is a map of Scotland, look . . ."

"Of course . . . Callanish . . . Loch Glass . . . Rosslyn Chapel . . . and Edinburgh, look! Quite a lot going on here. Amazing."

They examined a few others. One had strange shapes and signs all over it, and different coloured lines, bending and circling, forming spirals, waves, curls, some continuing into the sea, some stopping abruptly. They reminded Harry of the Maori tattoos he'd seen in New Zealand.

"What is this?" asked Sarah.

"Ley lines and electromagnetic fields. Useful for things like unusual bird migrations, crop circles, blackouts . . . Had I had one in Japan . . ." He shook his head.

"This one is huge." Sarah unfolded a map that took up a good quarter of the table. "It's London."

"The Secret Map of London . . ." Harry was in awe.

"Is there one of Edinburgh, I wonder?"

"There it is. It's the twin of the London one. Sarah, these maps are worth millions. My clients in Japan would kill for these. Literally."

If the Sabha knew what treasures the Midnights hold, all the knowledge they have . . .

Sarah sighed. "Pretty useful then?"

"You can say that again. With these, and James's arsenal . . ."

"Harry."

"Yes?"

"It's all yours. My dad's stuff, I mean," said Sarah, folding the maps carefully back into their chest.

"What?"

"You're my dad's only nephew. His things belong to you. I wouldn't even know how to use all these . . . weapons." She said the word with just a touch of revulsion.

"You can learn."

Sarah shook her head, frowning. "I'm not my father. I have the blackwater, and my dreams. I'll learn my mum's spells," she gestured at Anne's equipment carefully arranged on the oak table, "but I won't fight the way you and my parents did." Harry nodded, in wordless understanding. "I want you to say yes. It's the Midnight inheritance, it's yours too."

Harry looked away.

The Midnight inheritance . . .

"Very well."

Sarah smiled, a rare smile that lit up her green eyes for a second, like the secluded heart of a forest, so remote that nobody can step into it.

"At least you know what to do with them. With my mum's things, I don't know where to start . . ."

"She never taught you her spells?"

"No. She thought there'd be time . . ." The usual wave of sadness that drenched her every time she thought of Anne.

"I don't know, Sarah. She knew her life was in danger. She'd known it for months. What was she thinking, to leave you so . . . unarmed? James didn't teach you to hunt either, you had to do the first one yourself . . ." His voice trailed away. He'd seen her eyes welling up.

"I'm sorry. I didn't mean to upset you."

"It's OK. I know you're right. I don't know why they didn't teach me. They were never here, they were so busy . . ."

Too busy to save their daughter's life?

"Now that I think about it, my mum did say something about it, once . . ."

It was a warm, balmy July night. Anne and Sarah were in the garden, in the small patch that Anne had planted with healing and magical herbs.

"For protection, and purification," said Sarah, touching the rosemary bush.

"Well done."

"There's so much more to learn . . . When will you teach me?"

Anne looked away, holding her black hair back with her hand as she leaned to collect some thyme.

"I taught you a few spells already."

"Little girls' spells! Not the real ones, to use for proper hunting. I'm sixteen, Mum, it's time!"

"I know, darling, I know . . . But those spells are not harmless. They can be very dangerous. Your grandmother only allowed me to learn them after I got married."

"But I'm ready!"

Anne looked into her eyes. *My wonderful child*, she thought. *My woman-child* . . .

"I'll think about it."

Sarah smiled. "Is it a yes?"

"It's an 'I'll think about it'!"

"When? Soon?"

"Soon," conceded Anne. "If something happens to me . . ."

Sarah's smile vanished. "Don't say that."

"We have to be ready. If something happens to me, you must know that I haven't left you unprepared. If I won't be here to teach you my spells, you have to know that I found a way for you to know them."

Sarah shivered, in spite of the summer warmth. Anne's words sounded like a premonition.

"She said she found a way for you to know them?"

Sarah nodded. She couldn't speak. *Don't cry don't cry don't cry.*

"Oh, Sarah. Don't worry. We'll find out what she meant. I'll help you, promise. Listen, it's been a long day, why don't you go and get some rest?"

"Ok. But I'll practise for an hour, first. Harry . . ."

"Yes?"

"If a dream comes . . ."

"I'll be awake."

"Thank you." They looked at each other, connected for a moment.

Sarah took out her cello, and stood at the window.

When she played, Sarah felt serene, peaceful, as if reality had been suspended. Her music mirrored her passionate nature, the dark, vibrant tones of the cello singing her own sorrow, her own loneliness. James had often said that she *was* a cello, in a way.

She closed her eyes, and lost herself in music. She knew her audition piece inside out, she'd been practising it for so long – and she mastered it perfectly. Her music teacher, Mr Sands, had helped so much. He took a lot of pride in that dedicated, talented, obsessive young woman.

"To be a great musician, you have to be obsessed with it. Eat it, drink it, breathe it," Mr Sands had said to her once. And she certainly did.

Mr Sands had often looked at her hands, and wondered why they were so dry, red and raw looking. She caught him looking a few times, and she decided to lie once more.

"I have psoriasis."

"Oh. It must be agony, to play."

"It is, yes," she said, and didn't offer any details. *The pain distracts me from what really hurts*, she could have said, but didn't. It was none of his business. To think that she did so much with her hands. That's where her soul lay. That's where her power lay. And still, she destroyed them, she made them bleed.

The last few notes lingered in the air. Sarah put away her cello in its purple case, and started getting ready to go to bed. She got changed into her shorts and T-shirt, wrapped herself in her white woollen cardigan, and sat on the windowsill. She leaned against the cold glass. She saw Shadow, out for her nightly hunt, a black, silent silhouette against the white gravel.

Sarah watched the sky getting darker, the purple clouds closing on the moors as if to imprison them, and the first star lighting up in the west. Venus was scintillatingly white, like one of her mother's gems. Sarah's ruling planet, the planet of beauty and love . . .

She could see her profile reflected in the window. She was always a bit surprised, when she saw her reflection – as if she didn't recognize who she saw. She thought she'd see a child, the child she used to be – and instead she saw a young woman. When did she grow up? She must have missed it. Because inside, she still felt like a little girl. A little girl who hadn't been much loved, who had been left alone a lot.

A wounded one.

Sarah shivered. She was cold and tired. She couldn't keep her eyes open, but she was afraid of what she was going to see in her sleep.

Maybe Leaf is going to visit me . . .

That hope convinced her to slip into bed. She did her usual ritual with the duvet and the pillows, adjusting them, and then again, just to make sure. She closed her eyes, and sleep took her away almost at once.

The visions started, but it wasn't a nightmare. Her mother was standing in front of her bed, and she was smiling.

"Mum!"

Anne had her black hair loose on her shoulders, and she was wearing her favourite nightdress, white and flowing. In one hand she had a book with a blue cover, her other was curled up in a fist. She was holding something, but Sarah couldn't see what it was.

Silently, Anne sat on Sarah's bed. She opened the book, and showed her the first page.

Anne's Diary, for Sarah.

"It's for me . . . You wrote it for me!"

Anne nodded, and then she spoke, for the first and last time in the dream. Her voice seemed to come from far away, like the echo of a voice that had disappeared long ago.

"It's my spells. Be strong. I love you, my darling Sarah . . ."

"I love you too, Mum. Where is the diary? Is it here, in this house?"

Anne opened her hand, palm up. She was holding a little blue velvet pouch . . .

Sarah woke up with a sigh, her face drenched with tears.

Mum!

She got up and ran downstairs. She was cold, but it didn't matter. She went into the kitchen, and down the wrought-iron stairs, icy under her bare feet. She took the little key from the chain and unlocked the door.

It was pitch dark. Sarah felt the wall with her hands, looking for the switch. She put the light on, and immediately she saw a shadow on the floor, mixed with hers, so that she couldn't have said where her shadow ended and the stranger's began. She gasped, and turned around.

It was Harry.

"Is everything OK?"

"Oh, it's you! You frightened me. You're always so silent."

"I heard a noise. I wasn't sleeping. I promised you I'd stay awake."

"I had a dream . . . I saw my mum. She gave me a message."

Harry's eyes widened, his heart racing. *It can't be . . . she can't be back from the dead to tell her . . .*

"What did she say?" His chest was going up and down, fast.

"She wrote a diary for me in the last months of her life," Sarah whispered in the semi-darkness. Harry breathed a sigh of relief. For a second, he had felt the room spinning around him.

"To teach me her spells. In case something happened to her. That's what she meant when she'd said she found a way for me to know them."

"Did she say where it is?"

"Not exactly. She showed me . . . wait . . ." Sarah surveyed her mother's belongings on the oak table, looking for the blue pouch. "This. Maybe there's a message in it. Maybe it says where the diary is . . ." Sarah started undoing the little strings, impatiently. She poured the contents of the pouch on the table.

Nothing. Nothing, except some dry, sweet-smelling dust.

"What is it?"

"I think it's . . . dry leaves." Instinctively, Sarah took a bit of it between her fingertips, and smelled it.

"Thyme. Of course – I know where the diary is!" she said, running up the winding stairs, followed by Harry. She ran down the corridor and opened the heavy wooden door. The cold night enveloped her and chilled her to the bones, but she didn't care. She ran down the stony steps and on to the gravel. Her bare feet were hurting her, but she couldn't go back and get a pair of shoes, she couldn't wait. She had to find the diary.

She ran to the back of the house, across the garden, and towards Anne's patch. She kneeled on the damp soil, and started digging under the thyme bush, careful not to hurt its roots.

She felt something warm and soft around her shoulders. Harry had brought her the white woollen cardigan, and had kneeled beside her.

The new moon was watching them, a baby moon in the sky beyond the garden, shining on the moors and on the whole of Scotland. Harry took everything in, the beauty of that clear night, and Sarah's face, determined, impatient, anxious, with her black hair like a silky waterfall on her shoulders. The light of the moon was reflected in her skin – he had often thought that Sarah was like the moon, white, luminous, distant.

Untouchable.

"There it is!" Sarah took out a parcel wrapped in oilcloth, tied with string. She opened it carefully. Inside, there was a blue book.

Sarah cleaned her hands on her bare legs, took the diary out, and opened it with reverence. Page after page of her mother's writing. Pictures, drawings, samples of dried herbs in little transparent bags . . . spells, stories, recipes, all in Anne's graceful script. She felt tears of joy pouring down her cheeks. Harry held her in his arms, and she let him. She closed her eyes, lost in silent joy, her face against Harry's chest, his arms around her waist, and her mother's diary cradled between them.

13
The Sapphire's Song

Watch over me as I go
Watch over me though you can't be there

Sarah woke slowly, peacefully, after a deep sleep. She came back to the surface, blinking, feeling she'd been sleeping for days, when it had only been three hours. She caught a glimpse of the clock on her bedside table.

Half eight!

She jumped out of bed, disturbing Shadow, who leapt up with an outraged miaow.

Sarah had only half an hour to wash, get dressed and run to school. Impossible.

"Oh, no," she moaned, rubbing her face with her hands. She'd spent most of the night reading her mother's diary, and had fallen asleep well after dawn.

She couldn't wait to be out of Trinity. At least at the RCS she was going to have a bit more freedom on how to organize her work . . . if she managed to get in. And considering what the Midnight way of life was – well, she was going to need a lot of freedom.

She had a quick shower, dried her hair and put her uniform on, very, very carefully. She looked at herself in the mirror, and immediately she felt breathless. No, that wasn't *right*. She sighed in frustration, undid the buttons of her shirt and did them up again – a hurried version of her morning rituals. There was no more time. That would have to do. She noticed deep blue shadows under her eyes. Like a vampire.

I look like the living dead.

Sarah sighed. She didn't like the feeling of make-up on her skin, but this was an emergency. She grabbed some concealer and spread a bit of it under her eyes. She looked at herself critically. Not much better. *Oh well, I hope I look alluring, as opposed to just exhausted.*

"Sarah, it's late! I'll give you a lift!"

Harry. Hearing his voice gave her an involuntary, sudden bout of joy.

"Coming!" she called. With one last smoothing of her tights, she ran downstairs.

"I made you some toast and jam."

Immediately Sarah looked at the toaster, anxiety forming a knot in her stomach already, but Harry had picked up every single crumb. She breathed deeply. *Thank you.*

"I'm not very hungry, and it's late."

"Sarah, you've got to eat. I'm going to sit here until you finish at least one slice."

Sarah rolled her eyes. "You're worse than Aunt Juliet!"

He laughed. A dimply laugh, Sarah noticed.

"You learnt to use the coffee machine? Well done!" she said mischievously.

"Not sleeping has its advantages."

"Do you often not sleep?"

"Pretty much. I'm an insomniac; I have been since I was a child."

He was wearing a checkered shirt with its sleeves rolled up – he always did that, rolled his sleeves up, Sarah thought fondly. She caught a glimpse of his scar, whiter than the rest of his arm. The sun streaming from the window made his blond hair shine.

He looks . . . strong. Yes, that's the word. Strong and luminous, like a warrior of the sun.

And there it was again. Another little bout of joy. How long had it been, since she'd woken up happy? Long, long before her parents' death.

"Will you be at school with me?"

"Yes. You won't see me, but I'll be there."

Sarah nodded. She was safe, then. She put the last bit of toast in her mouth, and cleaned her hands.

"Ready," she said. They ran out, with Sarah barely stopping to straighten the coats in the entrance.

"Oh, and Sarah?" he said casually, as they were walking down the gravelly path.

"That boy you were talking to, yesterday . . ."

"Jack."

"Well, whatever his name, he's not for you." Harry's tone was deliberately casual.

Sarah's cheeks grew scarlet. "That is up to me, Harry."

Harry smiled arrogantly. "I know. And I know you've already decided."

"How would you know that?"

"I saw how you looked at him."

"And how did I look at him?" She crossed her arms.

"Like you look at Aunt Juliet." Harry opened the car.

He's right. Still, how dare he!

They got into Harry's car, a newly bought black Fiat Bravo. He'd said he wanted to keep the Land Rover for Sarah, that it wasn't fair for him to use it. Sarah loved the Bravo. Its design was exquisite, both inside and outside, so much nicer than her parents' Land Rover, big and intimidating like an army tank. Sure, it wasn't very roomy, but her cello sat comfortably in the back, and that was enough. Harry noticed her looking around with satisfaction, and it pleased him, in a childish way.

"What do you have on today?"

Sarah was still sulking after his comment about Jack.

"Have you not checked my timetable?" she retorted.

Harry smiled placidly. "Not for today, no."

"I'm going to spend most of the day practising with Mr Sands."

"A good day, then."

"Yes. What will you do? I mean, apart from following me around like a creepy stalker?"

"Ha ha. I need to speak to some friends."

"Those mysterious friends who seem to know every-thing?"

"Those ones, yes."

"And who would they be?"

"They prefer it if people don't know about them."

"Men or women?" asked Sarah. Harry stifled a smile.

"Men."

"Right. Did you hunt with them?"

"Maybe."

Sarah rolled her eyes. She didn't like hearing about those friends of his. They reminded her of his life before her, a life she didn't want him to go back to.

"Harry?"

"Mmmm."

"When all this is finished, you *will* work as a doctor, won't you?"

Harry looked at her quickly, before bringing his eyes back on the road. *It'll be a long time before it's finished. A lot longer than you imagine. If it ever finishes, and if we're alive to see its end.*

"What brought this on?"

Sarah shrugged her shoulders.

"I don't know. Maybe I'll keep hunting, just because I love it." *I have no choice. It'll be a long time before we're free. If ever.*

"No," she whispered.

"No?"

"I mean, don't do it. Don't do what my parents did."

"It's what I've always done."

"I don't want . . . I don't want you to . . ." she stumbled.

"You don't need to worry about me. I can look after myself!" laughed Harry.

Sarah was upset, and she didn't say a word for the rest of the journey. They arrived at the school in silence.

"Are you OK? You're quiet."

Sarah nodded, and she got out of the Bravo. She took her cello from the back seat.

"Harry . . ."

"Yes." She looked like a child, her face full of worry, her cheeks flushed.

"Don't go hunting at night. Stay with me," she said, and walked away quickly, without giving Harry time to answer, and without looking back.

Harry was still for a while, holding onto the wheel, following the splash of her purple cello case through the car park and up the steps, until it disappeared.

"Your hands are better," said Mr Sands.

"Yes."

"Are they less sore?"

"Yes." *Everything is a little bit less sore, these days.*

She wondered where Harry was, if he was watching her right now, if he was listening.

At the end of the school day Sarah hurried out, nearly running. She stood at the top of the stairs with Bryony, Alice and Leigh, looking around the car park, until she spotted Harry's car.

"Bye girls!"

"Sarah, wait! Are you coming to my house tonight?" asked Bryony.

"I can't, sorry, Mr Sands gave me lots to do. I've got to go, there's Harry."

"*That's* your cousin?" exclaimed Alice, looking at the tall blond man leaning on his car with his arms crossed. Sarah rolled her eyes. *Here we go again.*

"Does he have a girlfriend?" Alice added, and then, as Sarah was trying to pretend she didn't hear, "You've *got* to introduce us, Sarah."

Sarah frowned, and stormed off. Alice could be such a pain in the neck. *I'll leave them to gossip in peace.*

"See you tomorrow, Sarah!" she heard Leigh calling.

"See you, Leigh!" Sarah called back, feeling a bit guilty for having walked away so abruptly. Leigh was a sweetheart.

"Hello. So, the red-haired one is Bryony, then?"

"Yes, why?" answered Sarah irritably.

"Nothing, just that I've heard so much about her. The blond one is very pretty. Who would that be?" he added. Sarah knew he was winding her up, but she couldn't help rising to the bait.

"Alice," she said crossly. "She's too young for you!"

"I'm only twenty-two," he retorted, putting Sarah's cello in the back, carefully.

"Harry!"

"I'm just teasing you. I'm not looking for a girlfriend." He laughed, and got into the car.

"Did you not have one in New Zealand?" asked Sarah, trying to keep her tone casual.

"I did. Mary Anne. She wasn't the one."

Mary Anne. The one who carried a knife in her bra. Ugh.

"Did you tell her that?"

"She sort of knew. Especially when she read my note. That made it pretty clear."

"Your note? You left her with a *note*?" Sarah was horrified.

"The plane to London was about to leave. I didn't have time to call her."

"Right." *What a gentleman. Poor Mary Anne,* thought Sarah, but she didn't say anything.

"It was one of those things."

"A girlfriend is not just 'one of those things', Harry!"

"Yes, well, I'm still to find the right one." His words echoed between them like ripples of sound.

The right one.

Sarah looked away.

"Anyway, four days, and still nothing. I think they'll attack soon." Harry quickly changed the subject.

I think so too, I think they'll be on us again very, very soon. And I know that tonight I'll dream. I feel it in my bones.

Just thinking of another vision made Sarah shiver. But there was no way to avoid it. There was nowhere to hide, her dreams always found her. If they had something to tell her, they would, mercilessly.

"I read of a spell, yesterday, in my mother's diary. I want to try it as soon as we get home."

"What is it?"

"My mum calls it the sapphire's song. It should tell us if someone is trying to get into the house."

Harry nodded. "It sounds good."

"Yes, hopefully I can make it work. Harry, I was wondering . . . why did my grandmother not teach my dad and Uncle Stewart her spells, but she taught my mum?"

"Traditionally, in the Midnight family it's the women taking care of the witchcraft sort of thing, if you want to call it that."

Or so Harry told me.

"But she didn't have any daughters, so had my dad or Uncle Stewart not married the knowledge would have been lost."

"She did have a daughter. Your father's sister. Our aunt," he corrected himself quickly. Sarah looked blank. "Did you not know?"

"What? I have an aunt?" Sarah couldn't believe what she was hearing. *There's aunts and cousins sprouting all around me*, she thought, flabbergasted.

"Her name was Mairead. She was killed when she was thirteen. She had barely started having her dreams. I can't believe you didn't know!"

Sarah felt her eyes well up. "I can't believe nobody ever told me. Are there any pictures of her?"

"I don't have any pictures of her, I'm sorry." *The picture that Harry showed me is still in his house in London.*

"I never knew."

"The Midnights seem to be very good at keeping secrets," said Harry, and he meant it.

"How did it happen? How did she die?"

"I don't know. I was very young. They never told me the details. I only know that it wasn't an accident. She was killed."

"It's terrible. She was just a child . . . They must have been distraught."

"Yes." *Harry talked about it with great sadness.* "I'm surprised that James never told you."

"And my mum didn't either. There were three of them, then? Are there other aunts and uncles I should know about?"

"Just them."

"Mairead . . . That's why my name is Sarah Mairead."

"She was called Mairead Elizabeth Midnight."

"What did she look like?"

"She was blond, but her face was so much like yours, the same eyes, the same expression."

Mairead Elizabeth Midnight. And she looked like me. Another lost girl.

They were silent for a while.

"Can I help you with your spell, or do you want to be alone?"

Sarah thought about it for a minute. "Stay," she said finally.

"Very well. Let's go. I'll get us a cup of tea."

"You're like an old woman, with your cups of tea!" said Sarah, and Harry laughed, trying to lighten the mood.

He couldn't believe they had never told her. Why did they keep Mairead's existence from Sarah? Were they trying to spare her the sadness of Mairead's death? Sarah's parents didn't have a good track record in trying to spare her suffering, or protect her from painful things.

It was a mystery. *Another one.*

They made some tea, and went upstairs to Sarah's room to get Anne's diary. The room was freezing, as the window had been open since that morning. The curtains were flowing in the breeze, and the silvery-grey walls were glimmering subtly. The wooden floor looked as if on fire, strewn with the light from the setting sun.

Sarah took her mum's diary from the little drawer in her bedside table, and sat on the bed. Shadow had jumped on her lap, deliberately ignoring Harry. Since he had sent her to sleep, Shadow didn't trust him.

"Let me see . . . There it is, the sapphire's song.

My Sarah, if you fear an attack in your own home, do this: take my sapphires, there's two of them in the wooden

148

box. Pulverize some rosemary, some garlic and some dulse in the little mortar. Coat the sapphire in the pulverized plants. Then say:

Sing if the seal is broken.

Lick your finger and touch the sapphires. After you've recited the invocation, don't speak any more, don't say a word, for all the time you'll want the sapphire to keep guard. If you speak, the sapphires will be silenced. Put a gem in the attic, right in the middle of it, and keep one for yourself. If someone tries to get in, the sapphire will tell you. Remember, don't say a word, or the sapphires won't sing.

"That's it."

"It seems pretty clear," said Harry. They went back down into the basement, and Sarah started putting some dried leaves into her mother's stone mortar.

And then: "Sarah." A tense, sudden whisper that made her look up in alarm. "Did you hear anything?"

"No, nothing." Her heart had started racing. She tried to take a breath that didn't come.

"I think I heard a noise. Stay here."

Harry took out the *sgian-dubh.*

"I'm coming with you."

"No, stay here and lock the door."

"You might need me."

"Don't contradict me, Sarah."

'Don't contradict me'? Did he really just say that?

Sarah looked him in the eye, defiantly, and walked to the spiral staircase. Harry threw his hands in the air. *Of course she'd do that.*

"At least get your dagger!"

Sarah turned her back to him and lifted her shirt quickly, to show him the *sgian-dubh*.

Harry nodded. "Good call."

Slowly, carefully, they went through the whole house, the kitchen, the living rooms, the dining room, the library, the bedrooms, the bathrooms, James's study. *This house is endless!* thought Harry.

Nothing. Nobody there, human or otherwise.

"It was your imagination."

"Maybe." Harry wasn't convinced.

They went back into the basement, and Sarah started again from where she had stopped. She took out the sapphires, and arranged them carefully in front of her. She had already put some dried rosemary and some garlic into the mortar; she added the dried dulse, and pulverized the whole lot. She coated the sapphires in the mixture.

"I'm saying goodbye now. I won't be allowed to speak any more."

Harry nodded.

"*Sing if the seal is broken,*" Sarah invoked. She licked her index finger, and touched the sapphires, one by one.

And now it's silence.

She didn't mind. She found the idea of not talking for a while strangely attractive. Holding the sapphires with great care, she went up the spiral staircase and up to the second floor, followed by Harry. They walked down the corridor, past their rooms, and to the landing in between the guest bedrooms. Sarah opened a door on her left, and took out a long stick with a hook at the top. She used it to open a trapdoor just above their heads, and as she did that, a steel ladder came down too. They climbed up the ladder, and into the attic.

Sarah placed a sapphire right in the middle of the floor, and kept one close to her heart. They exchanged a glance.

My first real spell.

14
Music

No more words between us
Just a song

Grand Isle, Louisiana

"He doesn't have a clue, Sean. But he's a great fisherman." Mike was surfing the Net while talking to Sean. Niall was on the beach, as usual.

"What?"

"He goes out fishing every night. Takes the boat out himself. Without a rod, a net, nothing. Comes back with more fish than we can eat."

"Right. Have you heard him singing?"

Mike rolled his eyes. "All the bloody time. I'm now familiar with every single Irish song ever written, past, present and a few future ones, too. But no, he hasn't been singing the way you mean. Thankfully he didn't need to."

"Yeah. It means you're still in the clear."

"Hopefully it'll stay that way. How are things with you?"

"Not much weirder than usual. The heron . . . she's fine."

Mike's eyes widened. The way he'd said Sarah's code name, *heron* – the tenderness in his voice. It all sounded very, very personal.

Has he fallen for her? That'd make things pretty complicated.

"Anyway, I'll turn in. Will send you the Signal." The Signal was the text they sent each other every morning and night, to make sure they were OK. To make sure they were still alive.

"Yeah. Here comes Niall. God spare me."

Mike could hear Sean laughing as he pressed the 'end call' button.

"There. Our dinner." Niall threw a wet bag on the shack's uneven wooden floor. His brown hair was dripping.

"Crayfish." Mike's face fell.

"And clams," Niall added cheerfully.

"Great. I mean, I love shellfish but we're eating nothing else. I'm turning into a seal."

The shadow of a smile flickered over Niall's lips, so quick that you might have thought it never really happened. A moth was dancing around the gaslight, projecting strange shadows on the walls and on their faces.

A pause, with Niall inspecting the peeling paint on the window frame, lost in thought.

"I wonder when we can go home," he said. He looked very young, very pale. *He's only seventeen*, Mike pondered. *And his life was pretty complicated already, before all this started.*

"Soon. We'll find a way."

"We don't even know who's after us. Who's behind all this."

"Not yet. But we will. And we'll sort it. Now, why don't you sing something for me? That will cheer you up."

"Seriously?"

"No."

"Thought so. Going to light the fire." Niall shrugged his shoulders good-naturedly. He was impossible to irritate. He was so mellow.

"You do that."

"By the way, I'm going out tonight."

"You are what?"

"Going out. Looking for a party."

"You're not."

"I am."

"Niall, you can't go out. It's dangerous. We can't bring attention to ourselves, you know that."

"Try and stop me."

"I will!"

"You can't."

"Jesus, Niall . . ."

"Come with me."

"No way. I'm not going, and neither are you."

"We are going out. You don't want me to stun you with my magical voice and stuff, do you?"

"Go away, Niall."

"Just one night. One night. You'll come, won't you?"

Mike sighed. "Fine, fine. I'll show you a Louisiana night out. Brace yourself."

An hour later they were standing right in the centre of a blaze of accordions and fiddles, dancing clumsily with a glass in their hand. When the tune came to an end, Niall's grey eyes were shining with the drinking and the happiness of that stolen night.

"That was amazing!"

"That was Cajun, my friend!" exclaimed Mike, his arm around a pretty French-speaking girl. "That was *our* music!"

Niall gave Mike his glass to hold. He stepped just under the little wooden stage, and whispered something to one of the fiddlers. The fiddler nodded and handed his instrument to Niall. A crowd of expectant eyes turned onto him.

"This is for the heron." Niall's voice was clear and foreign-sounding in the awaiting silence.

He began to play. It was a haunting, melancholic tune that spoke of misty hills, of wind and of the grey Atlantic. It spoke of his home far away, of regret, and fear of the future. The room had fallen silent; they were mesmerized.

When Niall came off the stage the audience was speechless, and so was Mike. All he could do was hand Niall back his glass.

A small, sweet-faced girl was beside them like a shot. "That was incredible. I loved it," she said, with eyes that left no doubt as to what she really meant.

Niall was smug. "Thank you . . ."

"Caroline."

"Caroline. Fancy a walk?"

"Sure!"

The music had started flowing again. Niall whispered in Mike's ear, "Fiddlers always get the girls, my friend."

"Do they? Well, not *this* fiddler. It's bed for you, young man."

"What are you, his father?" Caroline had her hands on her hips, her eyes narrowed, petulant.

"Do I *look* like his father?" laughed Mike, gesturing at his black skin beside Niall's milky complexion.

"He's my bodyguard. He's FBI." Niall's face was perfectly straight.

"Come on!" Mike dragged him away, out into the warm, balmy night.

"Mike!"

"She could be one of them. She could be anyone! You couldn't possibly be alone with her," he whispered once they were out of earshot.

"You're just jealous."

Mike's hearty laughter filled the darkness around them. "I feel your pain, man."

A riveting tune like a flowing river was spilling out of the bar, its notes tumbling out of the open door, lingering, following them home. A memory already, a little light in the dark times that were to come.

"By the way, that was amazing. The tune you played. I'm impressed."

"Thanks. Do you want to hear another song?"

"No. Come on, we need to send the Signal and then we can call it a day."

"I'm going for a swim."

"Seriously?"

"Oh, yes."

He lives in the water, thought Mike. But he was sleepy, and a bit drunk, and decided he'd ponder the matter tomorrow.

15
Apnoea

Broken glass in my throat
The words I can't speak
The things you should know

Tonight I'll dream, I can feel it, Sarah wrote in her notebook.

"I'll be awake, don't worry," Harry reassured her. He whispered goodnight, and closed the door behind him.

Sarah put the sapphire beside the diary, she arranged the duvet and the pillow, and then again, and then once more. It was past one o'clock, and she was drained, but she didn't want to fall asleep. She was too scared of what she might dream. She felt electric, from her toes to the top of her head. When it came to her power, Sarah was like a cat; she could feel a storm coming.

She switched the light back on, and got up. For an exhausting hour and a half she straightened, sorted, arranged, lined up and organized anything she could get her hands on. When she'd finished, she was so tired she felt faint. She thought she'd lie down for a minute, and then maybe clean her bathroom again, but her eyelids were so heavy, she couldn't help it.

Suddenly and heavy like a stone, sleep took her. She tried to resist, but it was no use. She whimpered in her sleep.

Sarah opened her eyes in the semi-darkness, and a smell of damp, mossy soil filled her nostrils. She could make out a wall of cold, grey stone. At once, she knew where she was: in the little cave under the standing stones. It was the same place she'd seen in the vision she'd had in the library.

Maybe I'll see Leaf again . . .

The thought spurred her on. Sarah remembered how to get out of that dark place. She threw herself on the floor and started crawling towards the little wedge of light. She squeezed herself through the hole, and walked out into the muted light and the wind. She looked around frantically.

Leaf, where are you?

There was nobody there. Nobody but her and the stones.

Suddenly, Sarah felt breathless. She just could not inhale; it was like one of those grey stones was weighing on her chest. Panic took hold. She fell on her knees on the wet grass, holding her throat . . .

She woke up with a jolt. She opened her eyes, and instead of the purple sky she saw a white, chalky face, a few inches from her own. A demon was sitting on her chest, its hands around her throat. Sarah tried to call the blackwater, but quickly realized it was no use. She was slowly suffocating: there was no way she could have focused on her power. Black spots started dancing before her eyes . . .

Right at that moment, Harry burst into the room. *He's awake, like he promised*, Sarah thought confusedly.

"Sarah!" Harry's voice seemed to come from afar. She felt as if she were floating away, leaving her body behind. The black spots were multiplying – she couldn't see any more. A thought flashed into her mind, sudden and painful: *Is this the last night of my life? Are these my last moments?*

Just when Sarah thought it was all over, the grip around her neck began to lose strength. She managed to take a quick, raspy breath, and because of that, right at the last minute, she didn't lose consciousness. The white hands let go completely, and she started inhaling greedily, as deeply as she could, coughing and holding her chest. She got herself on her knees, and stood up shakily. Her lungs hurt with the effort.

Finally, Sarah could see what had attacked her: a hairless, naked and impossibly tall creature, with a flat face, two holes for nostrils, and a cut for a mouth. She blinked, over and over again, trying to make sense of what was before her.

Harry stood with his hands raised, holding the *sgian-dubh*. He was making small, quick movements with the blade, as if writing on air.

There are quite a few things I can do with a blade, he had said. Now Sarah knew what he meant. At that moment Harry roared, and his movements got stronger, sharper. Stab wounds started appearing all over the demon's body, and from the wounds black blood was spraying everywhere, on the walls, on the floor, on the mirror. Sweat was pouring from Harry's forehead as he kept weaving his spell.

Wounded over and over again, the demon howled in anger and blindly threw itself towards the window. It hit Harry with its flailing arms, and he fell on the wooden floor, banging his head with a thud that made Sarah feel sick.

"Harry!"

The bleeding creature continued his blind run and jumped through the window, shattering the glass.

"Harry . . ."

"I'm fine, I'm fine."

"You're bleeding . . ." Sarah kneeled down and took his head in her lap. The demon's black blood and Harry's red were mixing on her hands, on her legs, even in her hair.

Harry closed his eyes. "Ouch . . ."

Sarah brushed his bloody hair away from his face. "Maybe we should go to the hospital."

"Absolutely not."

"We can say you fell . . ."

"I'm a doctor, remember? My professional opinion is that we stay at home."

He dragged himself up, helped by Sarah, and faltered to the window.

"Has it gone?"

"I don't know."

"Why did the spell not work?" whispered Sarah.

"Because the demon was in the house already, I think. Hiding somewhere."

"Hiding? How could . . . Oh God, Harry. I left the window open! That's how he came in!"

"I think the spell only works if someone is trying to get into the house *after* the spell has been cast." Harry leaned on Sarah's desk, heavily, holding his head.

"Harry, are you OK?" Sarah slipped an arm around his waist.

"Just a bit dizzy."

"Lie down."

"I need some coffee."

"You think that caffeine fixes everything!"

"It pretty much does."

"Right, OK. Lie down and I'll make you some coffee."

"You can't go downstairs by yourself; I need to come with you."

"No, you lie down."

"Sarah! That *thing* could be downstairs! It could be in the garden! We need to check the whole house, and then cast the spell again!"

"You're so . . . argumentative!"

"*Me?* You are!"

Sarah looked at him, her eyes flashing. She was looking for a stinging answer, when she saw how pale he was.

"Let me at least clean you up a bit," she said softly.

Sarah washed Harry's hair as much as she could. She disinfected the wound and wanted to bandage it, but Harry was having none of it.

"I'll look like a mummy!"

"Now is not the time to think of your looks."

"Do you have any painkillers?"

"I've got codeine. My mum and dad used it a lot."

Harry swallowed a couple of caplets, and dragged Sarah out of the bathroom. "Come on."

"Thank you, by the way," she muttered.

"For what?"

"Saving my life. Again."

"Oh yes, that. You're welcome . . . *by the way*."

Had she not been so freaked out, she would have smiled.

"That thing you did with the dagger . . . it was incredible."

"It's a skill. It can be taught." *Harry taught me.*

"Can you teach me?"

"Of course. I'll teach you all I know."

"To send people to sleep as well?"

"No."

"Why?"

"In case you use it on me, of course."

This time, she *had* to smile.

They did their caffeine stop. Harry downed a double espresso in one gulp.

"All better. Let's go."

Coffee as a cure for a concussion. And he has a degree in Medicine!

They checked the whole house all over again, Harry with the *sgian-dubh* ready, Sarah with her hands burning. There was some black blood on the gravel, and it led to the gate. It looked like the creature had gone.

"I wonder whose demon it was," said Sarah, thinking of the list of names.

"We'll find out soon enough. It was another Feral. Do you know what they are?"

"No."

Have they not taught her anything?

"Slaves, Ferals and Sentients. The Slaves are ferocious, but mainly stupid. The Ferals are somewhere in between beasts and thinking creatures. The Sentients . . . Those are the ones we need to fear the most."

"Have you ever met one?"

"Many times. Hopefully you never will," he whispered. But he knew it was a vain hope.

Sarah washed the sapphires in water and salt, as her mother's diary said to do when using something for more than one spell, then she went through the motions again.

Now she couldn't speak any more. She was back in her silent little bubble.

Her room was a disaster. There was blood everywhere, both Harry's and the creature's. It was freezing, because the glass had been shattered and the cold night air had filled the room.

"I'll help you clean up," Harry offered and Sarah nodded thankfully.

Harry boarded up the window with some wood he found in the garage, and Sarah scrubbed and cleaned in silence until all the blood was washed away. She looked at the window, sadly. *It looks as if we are under siege. It's awful.*

She grabbed her notebook, and scribbled in it.

When we were attacked I was dreaming.

"What did you see?"

Nothing yet. It was just starting.

"Call if you need me. And don't dare clean or tidy any more, OK? You need some rest. I'm going to have a shower."

Sarah nodded again.

But she couldn't stop herself. She'd been so scared, she felt so violated by the attack in her room, that she had to keep scrubbing and disinfecting until her hands bled. Because of her boarded-up window, she couldn't even see that dawn had broken. She fell asleep on the floor.

She woke up with a jolt, three hours later. Her whole body was sore, and her head was exploding. She tried to get up and get ready, but she felt so dizzy that she had to lie back down. Her hands were agony: she looked at them and winced. They were raw and bleeding. Sarah was horrified, but felt too ill to do something about it. She checked her forehead; it was boiling.

Shadow had come back from the hunt while Sarah was still cleaning. The smell of bleach hurt her little pink nose, but she had stayed, out of loyalty, and had slept on the floor beside Sarah. She now jumped on the bed, and stretched herself.

Sarah moaned. She dragged herself to the bathroom, and managed to find some paracetamol. She took two, trying to drink a bit, but her throat was swollen and painful. She climbed into bed, praying a vision wouldn't come, and fell into a light, fretful sleep.

After about an hour, Harry knocked at the door.

"Sarah, are you OK? It's nearly half seven."

Sarah woke up at once. She couldn't speak because of the spell, and her throat was so sore it would have been agony anyway. She got up slowly, painfully, and opened the door. One look at her, and Harry realized there was something wrong. Her green eyes were unnaturally bright, she was white as a sheet, and her cheeks and lips were ruby red.

"Oh, Sarah . . . Come on, lie down." He checked her forehead. His hand was so cool against her hot skin. "You're burning up. Have you taken anything?"

Sarah nodded. It hurt terribly to move her neck. She raised a hand towards Harry's forehead, and touched his hair lightly, asking a question with her eyes.

"I'm fine, it was just a bruise . . ." He gasped, noticing her hands. "Sarah! What have you done?"

Sarah looked away.

"My God, Sarah. What are you doing to yourself?"

Harry disappeared into the bathroom, pottered about, and emerged with the first pot of cream he could find. He sat beside her on the bed and opened it. He scooped some sweet-smelling cream out, covered her hands in it, and rubbed it in. The relief was incredible. Sarah closed her eyes, letting Harry massage her hands softly. It was such relief, such comfort, she wished he'd never stop.

"Sarah, your poor hands . . . I'm going to phone the school to say you're not coming in today. I'll be right back." A few minutes later, Harry returned with a cup of coffee.

Of course. That'll fix me. Harry's panacea for all ailments, she thought with tenderness.

"Nothing?" he asked, gesturing to the sapphire on Sarah's bedside table.

Sarah shook her head, slowly. She closed her eyes. There wasn't a bit of her that didn't hurt.

"Where's your mobile?"

Sarah pointed at her bag, resting on the armchair by the window.

Harry dug it out and put it on the bedside table, beside the sapphire and the dream diary.

"If you need me just send me a text or call me. I'll be in the basement."

Sarah didn't have the energy to nod again, and she just looked at him with shiny, sickened eyes.

As soon as Harry left the room, Sarah fell asleep again. Again she prayed not to dream, but it didn't work that way. The visions had no mercy; they didn't care if she was sick or healthy.

The dream that the Feral had interrupted started again. Sarah tried to wake up, she tried to resist, but she couldn't. She was standing among the stones again, and she felt as ill as she did in the real world. The wind against her cheeks and the wet grass under her feet were blissfully cold against her burning skin. Something was moving in the distance – a hooded figure, running towards her. Her heart started racing. She fell on her knees, trying in vain to get up again. The figure kept coming closer and closer . . . Until it was there, right in front of her. A lone raven landed beside her, and cawed.

Could it be . . . ?

The hooded figure crouched in front of her, and took the hood off his face. It was Leaf. Sarah felt so relieved she threw her arms around his neck. He had a pungent smell, something that it took her a few seconds to recognize. Soil and moss and wood, and . . . smoke. Wood smoke.

"Darling Sarah," he whispered, stroking her hair. "I came to warn you."

She held on to him, as if to stop him from disappearing again. All her thoughts left her fevered mind, and she let herself go against his chest.

"Sarah, watch out!" shouted Leaf suddenly. Sarah jerked her head up, and felt dizzy for it. She saw a white creature in the distance, galloping towards them in huge strides.

The sapphire was singing, a wordless, impossibly high-pitched song.

Sarah opened her eyes, and whimpered. She was sore all over. With trembling hands, she looked for her mobile on the bedside table, grabbed it, and rang Harry.

As the phone was ringing, she dragged herself up. Shadow was pacing up and down, her tail dancing behind her in the hunting rhythm. As soon as Sarah opened the door, Shadow ran out, quick as lightning. Sarah followed her down the stairs, her legs shaking.

Harry . . . please let him be OK . . .

"Harry!" she tried to call. She didn't have to worry about breaking the spell now, but she had lost her voice. A rough, weak sound came out, too feeble to be heard from the basement.

"Sarah?" Harry appeared in the hall, his phone in hand. Sarah could have fainted from sheer relief.

"The sapphire sang!" she managed to whisper.

"Get the dagger," he said calmly, taking out the *sgian-dubh.*

Sarah was about to turn around to get the dagger – she hadn't thought of keeping it with her; the fever had made her confused, she couldn't think straight – when she saw something white from the corner of her eye.

The demon that had attacked them earlier had come out of the kitchen, its white skin broken and encrusted with blood from the wounds that Harry had inflicted on it earlier.

How did it get in? Sarah asked herself, confused. And then: *That's it. This time it will kill me.* She felt her legs giving way, and she let herself slide to the floor. She looked at her hands, praying her power would work, even if she was so ill. She felt them warming up slowly, too slowly.

Harry stood in front of the Feral, tracing his symbols with the dagger and whispering secret words to himself. Sarah saw the demon shudder as Harry's magic was starting to work, but Harry groaned softly and brought his hands to his head in pain. The spell was broken.

"Sarah, get the gun! On my bed," he managed to cry out before the creature was on him, lifting him up as if he'd been a rag doll, and throwing him against the wall. The *sgian-dubh* had fallen out of his hand.

Sarah heard his words, but it took her a few seconds to process them. Her head was swimming, she felt disconnected from her body and the world around her – she could see stars already, she knew she wasn't going to be standing for much longer . . . the sickness, together with the shock and exhaustion, was making her body shut down.

The gun. Get Harry's gun.

She got up slowly and disappeared into the landing. For a second it looked like the Feral couldn't decide whether to finish Harry off, or to follow Sarah. In that instant of indecision, Harry dragged himself to where his *sgian-dubh* was lying, and raised his hands again, trying to summon the strength to cast the spell. As it saw what was happening, the demon threw itself at Harry, with all its might. Harry used the dagger to shield himself. He knew it wasn't going to be enough to stop it, but at least it'd slow the Feral down for a while. Harry tried to get its knee, but he missed, and stabbed its thigh instead. The demon screeched again, and black blood spurted from the wound. Harry tried to stab it again, but the demon grabbed his arms and lifted him up, holding him close so that they were face to face.

Harry looked into the Surari's eyes – red, ancient, full of an anger that went beyond human comprehension. He readied himself to die.

"Sarah, run!" was the only thought that was left in his head, and the only thing he could say.

The Feral was about to break Harry's neck, when a sudden noise, like a cork being popped, made it stop. It looked over its shoulder. Sarah was standing on top of the stairs with the gun pointed towards them. She had fired, and grazed the demon's side. Her arms were shaking so badly that she could barely keep the gun up. The demon let Harry go, and Harry fell to the floor with a thud, feeling something crack.

My ankle. Shit, my ankle.

The Feral put its head up, and howled – a terrible, other-worldly howl that made Sarah's and Harry's skin crawl. Sarah raised the gun once more. She fired, and missed again.

"Sarah," whispered Harry in despair. The dagger had fallen and disappeared out of sight. Harry knew that the demon's next move would be to attack Sarah, and tried to drag himself up. His ankle gave way, and he fell again. He realized that all hope was gone. There was nothing he could do.

The demon jumped, one mighty, incredible jump that took it to the top of the stairs, and in front of Sarah.

I don't want to die like this, like a lamb to the slaughter. I'm a Midnight.

She threw the gun away and raised her hands, like in a spell, or a curse. The demon hesitated, then threw itself at her. Sarah screamed in terror, forcing herself to keep her eyes open as the demon's hands crowded over her face.

One split second later, it was all over.

Blackwater was dripping down the stairs.

Harry was standing in the hall, frozen.

Sarah was drenched, and unconscious.

Shadow ran to Sarah and started licking her face. Harry shook himself and limped up the stairs.

"Sarah . . . Sarah." He took her wrist. Her heart was still beating.

She's alive.

He cradled her for a few minutes, wondering had Sarah died, what would he have done? How could he have kept on fighting, in a world without her?

"You're all I have," he whispered, even if she couldn't hear. It had become his mantra, something to pull him through all the deceit, something to help him go on.

Harry carried Sarah to her room, limping painfully, with Shadow circling them round and round, and put her on the bed, gently. She was burning, and she was drenched in that horrible blackwater, like the stuff you'd find at the bottom of some mossy, rotten well.

He went into the bathroom and wetted two towels. With one he washed her face, her arms, her legs, trying to erase every trace of the blackwater. Then he folded the other one four times, and placed it on her forehead to cool her down.

Sarah whimpered and curled up on her side.

She's sleeping. Thank you . . . God? Whatever it is that kept her with me.

He sat beside her bed, to watch her while she was sleeping, to listen to her breathing like you would listen to a song.

"Mary Brennan's demon is dead, but you haven't won."

A woman's voice filled the room, and Harry jumped up, looking around. He saw that something was shining on Sarah's bedside table. The sapphire was singing again.

Mary Brennan. The second-last name on the list.

Harry took the sapphire. How could it be? How could something speak through that stone? He considered washing it in salty water, like Sarah had done, to break the spell. But he stopped himself. He had to hear what it said, if the sapphire chose to speak again. He sat in Sarah's armchair, holding the gem in his hands, waiting for Sarah to wake up. Shadow was on the windowsill, erect, alert. She didn't like Harry being in Sarah's room.

A low sound broke the silence, just a few guitar notes. Harry realized it was Sarah's mobile, its screen shining blue on her bedside table.

A message. Harry didn't hesitate to read it.

For that hazelnut latte, call me. Jack.

In your dreams, mate. He erased it, and felt ashamed at once.

He took her hand, and Sarah clung to it in her sleep, whispering something: his name. Harry leaned his head on the bed, and after a few minutes, he was asleep too.

16
Voices

I should have listened to the voice of danger
But I listened to the one of desire

Cathy

Tonight my mind is burning. Tonight I feel like there's a fire in my head, and it hurts like hell. How did they survive again? And why, why the order to send the demons one by one? I was given no reason for this, and it makes no sense to me. I have no choice but to do what He says, or He'll just crush us all, and my revenge on the Midnights will never be complete.

We're dancing a senseless dance with Sarah and her pretend-cousin. Sarah and I are playing a piece together, her cello and my piano fusing and melting in a melody of hate. A melody of love, a twisted love with no place to be.

I'm in so much pain. If I try to sleep, the visions from hell come at once. The price to pay for using the Dark Arts. I never thought it would be like this.

The instructions to my Valaya are clear: kill Sean, bring me Sarah. They keep failing. The Surari get slaughtered, and the humans die. Heart failure, strokes, whatever name you want to give to what happens to them after their demon dies: the fire in the brain. The fire that tortures me tonight.

Michael has started feeling strange already. His ears are ringing, little black lights are dancing in front of his eyes. He's putting it down to stress. He's planning to summon another Feral – it'll take a long time, but it'll be worth it, he thinks. He doesn't know that the flames have started and that they'll consume him soon, very, very soon. As for Mary, nothing yet. The little spark is there, right between her eyes, but she's still to feel any symptoms.

Next out on this deadly dance is Sheila. Her Surari is stronger than Mary's and Michael's, I know I can count on it. I don't know how Sarah and Sean managed to survive up to now – luck, or skill or even destiny, this blind cruel design that inflicts itself on us – but this time, it will be over for them.

Oh, how it burns. Every thought I think tonight is like being branded over and over again with a white-hot blade. Like some monstrous blacksmith working in my head.

Please let it be over soon, because there's only hatred and pain left of me.

Morag hadn't taught me for long, but I was good at witch-craft. Very, very good. It came naturally to me, like I was destined to do this. Morag had wondered many times if there was Secret blood in me, somewhere in my family history, because I took to magic like a seagull takes to the air.

Witchcraft is not about good and bad. The Dark Arts, White Magic, really the distinction is just a matter of naming something the way you want it to be. White Magic can kill; the Dark Arts can free you, so which is good and which is bad?

And anyway, good and bad didn't really exist for me any more. I had been innocent and now I didn't know what was right and what was wrong, and I didn't care.

The night before I was set to leave the Islay mansion, I had slipped some books into my suitcase. I'd done it in despair, taking them from Morag's desk at random, trying to keep something of them with me. I'd taken the books, and Morag's knife, the one engraved with her name.

When I could bring myself to look at the books, a long, long time later, I realized that one of them was different from the others. I suppose I should say it was a big, black book with red letters burnt into its cover like wounds, but it wasn't. The book that changed my life was anonymous looking, with a red fabric cover worn out by use, its pages thumbed over and over again – yes, the Midnight family had used the forbidden book a lot, it seemed.

The title was simply 'Valaya', the *ring*.

At the beginning, I wasn't thinking about revenge. I could not think of James in those terms. I had contained my hatred and anger because I couldn't bear the thought of hurting James, though he had hurt me so much.

But then, as I used the book the way it should be used – no half-hearted stuff for me – *He* heard me. He started talking to me, and His voice gave me a reason to be. His struggle was mine, His war coincided with mine. We could help each other. He whispered in my ear over and over again that it would be right to feel that way, to feel that I wanted to destroy them.

He told me that I *did* feel that way already, that I had always wanted to hurt them since James had left me. He said revenge was the only way I could set myself free. I allowed myself to believe that I could be free of pain, by inflicting pain on them.

The discovery exalted me: I hardly slept, I hardly ate for months, learning all I needed to learn, moulding my heart and my soul around the new rules, the new life that was opening in front of me. A year it took to master the arts enough to call my demon. When Nocturne appeared, hurt and bleeding and dazed from the passage, I couldn't believe my eyes, I couldn't believe how powerful I had become. He was proud of me, like Morag used to be.

And then, ten long years to find the others. Ten years I lived on hatred and barely much else. I played like I was possessed, and I got even better, going from strength to strength as my body grew weaker. When the Valaya was ready, it was time to do what I had dreamt of for so long. The Midnights knew I was coming, but they hadn't known it for long enough to get ready, properly ready. By then Morag was dead, and that had been a disappointment. I would have enjoyed finishing her myself, but sure, you can't have everything.

The day after I'd killed James and Anne I felt like I was going to die. Ill, pained in all my bones. Like I'd been poisoned. I could barely move. Nocturne kept vigil hidden in the trees, and my pupils from the Valaya looked after me, fed me, cared for me, as I lay trying to stop myself from moaning in agony.

I knew then what price I was really paying for using the Dark Arts. I knew that the sickness would get better, but not go away. I thought it was a price I *could* pay; I thought it was a fair bargain.

I listened to Him as He sang to me through the pain-filled nights that followed, and His voice made me feel even more determined to finish the job. To claim Sarah for my own at last, to take her life and kill her. Faith hadn't been allowed to live, and soon Sarah would be dead too. Only fair, don't you think?

And if death was in the cards for me too, that would be a relief. That would be the answers to my prayers. Because the instant I had pushed Morag's knife into James's heart, in that moment I remembered that before I had opened that cursed book, killing would have been as alien to me as eating human flesh.

Since He had started talking to me the Cathy I used to be was gone, and there I was, cutting Anne's throat from ear to ear, because that was slower and more painful than stopping her heart with a single stab. Looking into her eyes as she bled to death, I watched my people clean up, so that the butchering would take the name of *accident*.

And so it was done. Another Cathy had been born when I had opened the book, slowly as I worked through its pages, like a long, painful labour.

The moment I realized what had happened to me was the moment I knew there would be no real freedom from pain, nor from memories. Then the moment passed, and the woman I was lay forgotten, and Anne's blood on my body adorned me like a scarlet cloak.

17
Beneath It All

Some might call it love
This thing that holds us hostage

Leaf

Too close, this time. I punished Cathy for it, of course. Once the door was open in her consciousness, once she had started encroaching on our territory, she was fair game for us. They're all the same, really. They look at the Dark Arts as something they can use; they have a near-complete certainty that they can control the forces they summon. They are wrong. It's easy for my father and me to slip into their minds, look at them day and night with eyes that never sleep. This time, Catherine went too far with Sarah. She's playing our game, I know that, and she's doing me a great service – what better way to win somebody's heart, than to be their saviour? But she has to suffer for the pain she's inflicting on Sarah, even if she's doing it to my advantage. That is my decision.

Let the punishment come, until Catherine's time to serve us is over. As for Sarah, pain and fear are great teachers. They will purify her, they will mould her, they will get her ready for me.

18
Cascade

Silver pages
Under the moon
Memories
Of you and me

"She's still pretty unwell. No, I don't think she'll be back before Monday. Thanks, I will. Bye."

Harry put the phone down. That instant, it rang again.

"Yes?"

"Harry, it's Juliet. Sarah wasn't answering her mobile last night, and I'm worried."

"Hi Juliet, she's got the flu, she didn't go to school today."

"The flu? Does she have a temperature?"

"Yes."

"I'm coming up."

"You don't need to. It really is just flu, and a very sore throat." *And a Feral trying to kill her.*

"I need to see how she is. I'm coming up right now, I'll cook you lunch."

Harry sighed. Better to let her see with her own eyes that everything was fine.

"Ok then. I never say no to a nice lunch." Juliet giggled. Harry could be very charming, when he wanted to.

"Trevor and the girls will come too. Trevor is here for a couple of days; he's going back to Newcastle tomorrow."

"Great, then we can finally meet." *Finally*, he thought, sarcastically. *I can't wait.*

"Who was it?" Sarah had appeared at the top of the stairs. She'd had a shower, and had put on a fresh pair of jeans and a T-shirt. She felt a bit better, after having slept a dreamless sleep for a few hours.

"Juliet. They're coming to see you."

"They?"

"Trevor, and the girls too. Don't look *too* happy!" smiled Harry. "Back to bed now, you've got to rest. I'll make you a cup of coffee."

"Sure, caffeine man. How's your ankle?" She smiled.

"Yep, that's me. My ankle is OK, it was just a sprain. I'm walking, anyway. Oh, I phoned the glass repair guy, he'll come later to fix your window, so you don't have to feel like you live in an abandoned warehouse."

"Thank you. Are you coming up to share a coffee with me?"

"I'll be straight up."

Sarah was still weak. She was leaning on her pillow, her face the same colour as the sheets, the blackness of her hair a startling contrast, like a raven on the snow.

"Here's your coffee. I need to speak to you. Yesterday, while you were unconscious, the sapphire spoke. It was a woman's voice. She said that the demon we killed belonged to Mary Brennan, and that we haven't won."

Sarah frowned. "I thought the spell only worked to tell us if there was an intruder?"

Harry shrugged. "I thought so too. Here's the sapphire. I took it in case it spoke while you were sleeping." Harry took the gem from his pocket, and put it in Sarah's hands.

"Strange. Maybe that's what my mum meant, when she said that spells hardly ever work like you expect. She said they can be dangerous, too."

Sarah closed her eyes and took a deep sigh. She curled up, and her hair fell to cover her face like a silky curtain. Harry felt this irresistible desire to run his hands through her hair . . . He raised a hand . . . and stopped himself.

He was supposed to be her cousin. Had he shown any signs of how he felt, she would have been completely freaked out, and rightly so.

It was his turn to sigh, in frustration.

"Something else. This arrived for you this morning." It was a white envelope. "It doesn't have a stamp, so it must have been delivered by hand. Somebody put it through the letterbox."

Sarah took it. It had her name on it, written in an elaborate, old-fashioned handwriting, like an illuminated manuscript of long ago.

Sarah opened it. Inside, a red leaf. Her heart started pounding.

"What is it?"

"It's . . ." she hesitated.

Harry winced. "Jack?"

"No, of course not." Sarah felt guilty. She didn't want Harry to worry after all they'd been through. She took a deep breath. She had promised not to tell anyone.

"I—I see someone, in my visions. I don't know who he is. He gives me leaves."

"In your dreams?"

"Yes. And he left a couple of leaves around. In real life, I mean."

Harry frowned. "You have no idea who he is?"

Sarah shook her head. "I call him Leaf. I don't know his real name."

She didn't say that she had felt his eyes look straight into her soul. She didn't say that whenever he was around, her mind seemed to freeze.

"Sarah, listen to me. If he makes contact again you need to tell me. We don't know who he is; he could be one of the Valaya, or a demon . . ." Harry's clear eyes were full of worry.

"He's the one who sent the ravens."

"What?"

"The spirits of the air. The ones that saved us from the demon-leech. He sent them."

Harry was taken aback. "How do you know?"

"He told me. In a dream."

"He can control Elementals?" *A Secret heir? A Gamekeeper? A demon? Or just a human being with incredible powers?*

"Looks like it."

"We can't take risks, Sarah. You must tell me if he visits you again. In dreams, or in real life."

"I know," answered Sarah, and she let her arm fall, so that her hand dangled from the bed. The leaf fell on the floor, silently.

They heard a key in the door, followed by a cheery, shrill voice from the hall. "Anybody home?"

Harry and Sarah looked at each other. Sarah rolled her eyes.

"We're upstairs! Come on up!"

Juliet walked in to the room, followed by Trevor and two blond girls, one of about Sarah's age, and one who looked a bit younger. Sarah's room filled with a mix of perfumes, the women's flowery ones, and Trevor's aftershave. Shadow sneezed.

"Oh my goodness, what happened to the window?"

"I'm afraid that was me. I was trying to get some nails off the wall for Sarah, my hand slipped and . . . Well, it was just a tiny crack, but it would have been dangerous. Someone is coming to fix it later."

A tiny crack. There had been nothing left of the window, nothing, thought Sarah, and she shivered at the memory.

"Anyway, I'm Harry. Sarah's cousin." Harry extended his hand to Trevor, who took it absently.

"Pleasure." Trevor had salt and pepper hair, expensive golf clothes and a condescending smile.

I hate golf clothes, Harry thought to himself.

He looks like he's climbed out of a skip, thought Trevor.

Sarah and Trevor were never close. The sisters, Anne and Juliet, couldn't have chosen more different husbands. James had led Anne into the crazy Midnight world, while Trevor had given Juliet a comfortable, prosperous, middle-class life. Trevor was so different from Sarah's family, so completely unaware of anything beyond his golf club, his DIY passion, and his beloved silver four-by-four, that Sarah never warmed to him. Trevor found Sarah difficult, mainly because he couldn't understand her.

Juliet and Anne had never been close either. There was no animosity between them, they were just as different as night and day, ever since they were children.

When Anne had met James, she was consumed by him. She didn't see anyone else, she didn't want anyone else. The chasm between the sisters grew wider. Juliet often thought that James and Anne were a unit in themselves, that even their own daughter wasn't as close to them as they were to each other.

She suspected that James's hold over Anne was the reason why they were so isolated, as a family. There was something about him that Juliet couldn't quite decipher, but it scared her. A sense of natural dominance, a charisma that made him different. And that mother of his, Morag . . . Now that was one frightening woman. Anne adored her, but Juliet thought she was a witch.

They had turned Anne into a Midnight, taken her for themselves, and she didn't seem to need or want anything else. The Midnight family was a mystery to Juliet. She'd visited their mansion on Islay, once, and she had been intimidated, even scared. Room after room of dusty books and antiques, rows of ancestors looking at her from the walls . . . Juliet couldn't help thinking of the Addams family. She thought that if only Anne had married someone else, someone *normal*, their lives would have been so different.

But in spite of all that, the sisters loved each other, and Juliet had been devastated when Anne had died. She had always had a soft spot for Sarah – so thoughtful, so bright, compared to her giggly, flirtatious daughters. But Sarah thought that Juliet wasn't a patch on her wonderful mum.

If only she'd known how many times Juliet had begged Anne to pay more attention to Sarah, to spend more time with her, seeing how anxious, how frightened Sarah always seemed to be. Little did she know that what she saw of Sarah's life was just the tip of the iceberg.

Juliet knew nothing of the Midnight mission, of course, and she was very much frozen out of the unit that James and Anne had formed, so close, so self-sufficient. She could never have suspected what really went on in Sarah's life – how her parents were out nearly every night, how sometimes they even went away for days . . . If Juliet wasn't available to look after her, they'd leave her by herself, with instruction that if someone called at the door, she was to say that her mum and dad were at the shops. Sarah was never going to know how much Juliet had been trying to look out for her, and how her parents had dismissed Juliet over and over again, thinking that Sarah was going to be fine, that she *had* to be fine. That was the life given to them by destiny, and they had no choice. They had been blind to their daughter's suffering, while Juliet *saw*.

And still, Sarah idolized them, and saw Juliet as some sort of pale, lifeless imitation of her brilliant mother.

Juliet would never have said. She would never have told Sarah how she thought that James and Anne didn't look after her properly, that their lives should have revolved around their precious daughter, as much as hers and Trevor's revolved around theirs. She would never have told Sarah how she deserved more time, and more attention, and that no daughter of hers would have been allowed to get so anxious without receiving some sort of help, some comfort. Juliet could never have gone behind her sister's back when she was alive, and she certainly couldn't badmouth her and James now that they were dead. Sarah wouldn't have listened anyway.

But in her heart, Juliet was *furious* – she was furious that that lovely, sensitive, beautiful little girl would make her hands bleed with her obsessive cleaning, thinking that nobody would have noticed – and indeed nobody had, nobody but Juliet. Sarah's father was a doctor, for God's sake – had he not seen her hands? They didn't even seem to notice that Sarah would take two hours to get ready in the morning, because she had to put her uniform on and take it off at least twice, do her hair in a certain way, and straighten her skirt twenty times, breaking out in a sweat if something looked even slightly wrong. On her way out, she had to wipe the whole kitchen, line up her shoes so that they were sitting perfectly, adjust the coats on the coat hanger – that was a job, they were never quite straight enough – and finally, as her last task, she had to polish the bloody telephone in the hall because one single fingerprint on it would have made her start everything all over again. And all that was before she got to school. By the time she'd finished, she was exhausted already – and indeed, Juliet was exhausted just looking at her.

Every time Anne and James asked her to look after Sarah, Juliet would go home in a state, reeling over her little niece's state of mind. But she didn't know how to put it into words. Trevor just didn't understand the extent of it, and Juliet couldn't explain.

Nobody knew. Nobody had ever known. Anne never mentioned any of Sarah's teachers noticing – but even if they had, Anne and James would have brushed them off, like they'd done with her.

Maybe she could speak to Harry, one day. Maybe he could help Sarah.

"And these are Siobhan and Sally, our daughters." The two blond girls were wearing the school uniform, but they had transformed it into something entirely different. A black miniskirt, a lot shorter than Sarah's, bare legs, an insane amount of lip gloss, and shocking pink nail polish.

Shocking being the key word.

Harry shook their hands. The eldest, Siobhan, blushed.

"Nice to meet you."

"Nice to meet you too," said Sally. Siobhan didn't say anything; she just stared at him, with shiny eyes and a smile that managed to be coy and very, very clear in its message, all at the same time.

How do women do it? thought Harry, amused.

Sarah's stomach did a flip. Her cousins irritated her no end. Trust Siobhan to go and flirt with Harry!

"How are you, sweetheart?" Juliet put her hand on Sarah's forehead. Sarah didn't like being touched. *Why do they not leave me alone?* she thought, and immediately felt ungrateful.

"I brought you some chocolates, and a little present."

Sally sat on her bed, upsetting her covers. Sarah's chest tightened.

"Why are you not in school?" she asked them.

"We went to the dentist. We thought we'd come and see you with Mum and Dad before going back."

Lucky me.

"Open my present," Juliet intervened.

Sarah started ripping the wrapping paper, and Juliet saw her hands, broken and raw from the night before. She swallowed. How she longed to take Sarah home with her.

"Thank you, it's beautiful." Sarah was genuinely touched. She couldn't believe her eyes. It was the perfect present. A set of a diary and a photo album, both with a silky, silvery cover. The diary had a purple ribbon as a bookmark, and it was so white, so smooth, so different from her thick, black dream diary. It smelled of new, untouched paper.

"I thought you'd like something that would help you let off some steam, you know . . . You could write your thoughts in it, or if you have any worries. Things always feel easier to tackle if you get them off your chest."

"And the album is for Aunt Anne's and Uncle James's pictures," Sally added.

"Thank you. Really," Sarah said, and her eyes welled up. Juliet's eyes were suspiciously shiny too.

"I'll go prepare lunch. I bought some groceries for you." Juliet blinked, turning away quickly.

"Thank you," she whispered.

"Sally and Siobhan can keep you company for a bit."

Great.

The second the door closed, Siobhan sat on Sarah's bed excitedly.

"Sarah! *That's* your cousin?"

Sally rolled her eyes. Bryony, Alice, and now Siobhan. *Who knows why Harry seems to impress my friends so much. Ok, he's gorgeous, let's face it. But this is too much!*

"*Your* cousin too, as it happens, though not by blood." Her head was hurting again.

"How old is he?"

"Twenty-two." Sarah's staccato tone gave away her irritation.

"Does he have a girlfriend?"

Sarah felt her heart sinking.

"Yes," she lied. *Stay away from him.*

"In New Zealand? He'll forget her soon, it's too far."

"*The Mistress is watching.*"

"What was that?" said Sally.

Sarah jumped up. The sapphire! The sapphire was singing again! She grabbed the stone and hid her hand behind her back.

"What was it, Sarah?" repeated Siobhan.

"My MP3 player. I forgot to switch it off," she said, with a dry mouth.

"OK, whatever, do you know if Harry would be available for some driving lessons?" Siobhan brushed her blond hair away with an affected gesture.

That was the last straw. Sarah was exasperated.

"Sorry, girls, I'm not feeling so good again, I'd like to sleep for a bit."

"Of course, Sarah, sorry. Siobhan, let's go."

"Maybe you could ask him . . ."

"Let's go!" Sally dragged Siobhan out, unceremoniously. The girls left behind them a cloud of perfume that made Shadow sneeze all evening.

Sarah breathed in deeply, and looked at the sapphire. It was still shining. She sent Harry a text to tell him, hoping that he'd read it right away.

The sapphire sang again.

After a few minutes, the phone lit up.

We need to get rid of Juliet and co, just in case.

Sarah got up with great effort, and went down to the kitchen. The walls were spinning all around her, and her head felt like it was going to explode. She was clutching the sapphire, in case it spoke again. Hopefully not while the McKettricks were around.

"Sarah, darling, lunch is nearly ready. Will I bring it up to you? Have you taken anything, this morning? I brought you some paracetamol and some vitamins, just to build you up a bit."

"Thank you. Actually, I'll take two paracetamol and just go to sleep."

"Of course, I'll leave something for you in the oven. We'll eat in the dining room. Don't worry, we won't disturb you."

"I have a terrible headache."

"Mum, Sarah is trying to say that she wants some peace and quiet. She doesn't want four people for lunch. Leave her the roast in the oven, and let's go." Sarah looked at Sally. Not half as silly as she remembered her. She was only fourteen, and still she seemed to be the only member of the McKettrick family who actually could grasp what was going on around her.

"Sally's right," Trevor intervened. "Let's leave them in peace. Come on, girls."

"Of course, sorry, I should have thought. Promise me you'll eat something. And the medicines are just there, in the Boots bag."

"Don't worry; I'll make sure she eats," said Harry, and actually, he meant it. Juliet and Harry looked at each other, and for a second, they understood each other. Harry nodded imperceptibly, as if to say *don't worry, I'll look after her.*

"Right. I want you to rest all afternoon and all evening, OK? No getting up and cleaning." She took Sarah's hands into hers, and squeezed them.

Sure, I'll get a lot of rest, with an attack coming. As for the cleaning, had you not made a mess in the kitchen . . .

"Call me, Sarah has my number!" Siobhan managed to whisper in Harry's ear, with an innocent look.

"Sure . . . Not," whispered Harry, as soon as they were out of earshot.

"He's your cousin, you freak!" shouted Sarah at the closed door.

"Am I really related to her?"

"Not by blood. I suppose that's a consolation."

"Anyway. What did the sapphire say, exactly?"

"*The Mistress is watching.* What Mistress?"

"The leader of the Valaya. The one who started it."

"Is she human?"

"I think so."

"Who is she?"

"I don't *know!*"

Sarah rolled her eyes.

"I can't know everything!" protested Harry. And then he looked at her more closely. "Sarah, you look terrible."

"Thanks."

"No, seriously. Come here, sit down. Have this." Harry took the paracetamol box out of the bag, and took two caplets out of the blister. Then he poured her a glass of water. "Take them."

Sarah swallowed them.

Harry put his hand on her forehead. "You're burning again. Come on, let's take you to lie down."

"If they attack . . ."

"If they attack, I'll see to them. As soon as you're better we'll go looking for them. Enough waiting here."

Sarah nodded. She was scared, but she wanted to take charge of things. *I want to be the hunter, not the hunted.*

Sarah leaned against Harry. He smelled of coffee, and of the sea, a sort of salty scent that made her think of Islay. He helped her to one of the sofas, and covered her with a throw. Sarah watched the flames in the fireplace dancing their hypnotic dance.

"You need some rest. Close your eyes."

"I can't sleep. I'll dream again . . ."

"Come to the kitchen then, there's Aunt Juliet's roast waiting for you," he teased.

Sarah smiled, in spite of herself.

"I'll put the TV on. Let's see if there's some soap repeat."

He really is like an old woman. Soaps and endless cups of tea. She felt herself relaxing, as if the world had pressed "pause".

Reassured by Harry's presence and the soft background noise of the TV, Sarah's eyes got heavier and heavier, until she found herself suspended somewhere between wakefulness and sleep.

"Lie beside me," she whispered groggily.

Harry smiled. "No, silly."

She curled up under the throw, and fell asleep. As soon as he was sure that she was in deep sleep, Harry carried her upstairs.

Lie beside me, she'd said, and the words echoed in his mind with unbearable intensity.

Yes, yes, he wanted to say.

Harry switched the TV off and sat on the window seat, watching the afternoon turning into dusk. He kept thinking of what the sapphire had said. *The Mistress*. The Valaya had managed to keep her identity secret somehow. Who was she? One of the list, or someone else? Five Surari to go. And the Mistress. And after that . . . the bigger battle, the war.

Once more, Harry wondered if they were going to survive. In front of Sarah, his faith never wavered. He was brave, even arrogant. But truth was, he was afraid. To be besieged, to be tracked down and hunted like some sort of helpless creature . . . he hated it. It enraged him. And it frightened him.

He'd never been frightened before, maybe because dying had never seemed such a terrible option. It's not that he wanted to, he very much preferred to stay alive, but if it had to happen, oh well, the hunt was worth the risk. But now, he felt responsible for Sarah. And he desperately, desperately wanted her to survive this. He wanted her to be happy. He wanted to see her smiling, and he wanted her to sleep peacefully, without waking up crying in fear. And he wanted to stay alive too, so that he could be with her.

When had he started to feel like that? He'd only been with her for a few weeks, so how could she have seeped into his thoughts, into his heart, so quickly?

The first time he'd seen her, the night he arrived, he'd thought she was beautiful. But it was the same night, when he heard her screaming and he'd gone to try and comfort her, when he'd seen her black hair on the pillow, and he had breathed in her scent as she had just woken up . . . It was then that he'd felt that sudden, incredible wave, that Sarah wave, drench him and take him away from the shore, and out to sea.

And those hands of hers. It broke his heart to see them dry and cracked, bleeding with that obsessive thing she had about cleaning. How could they have put her through all that? *The Midnight mission*, he thought in spite. A little girl made to dream of horrific things every night, left alone to scrub and line up her stupid shoes until dawn.

He wanted to hold her hands against his chest, make her still, so that she could rest. He wanted to heal her, and with her, to heal himself.

Something else bothered him. Those leaves. The guy who sent the ravens, and visited Sarah in her dreams. If he could control the spirits of the elements, it meant that he was incredibly powerful. Someone you wouldn't want as an enemy. Why did he help them? Who was he? Had he been a Secret heir, Harry would have known about him.

Leaf.

Sarah had seemed strange, when she was talking about him. She'd looked away, and she'd been uncharacteristically sub-missive – Sarah submissive, that wasn't something you saw every day. She'd agreed too readily to let him know if he contacted her. He feared that the vision must have told her more; he feared that more had happened.

His gut told him to watch out for the leaves: to keep Sarah safe from a possible danger – and because he'd seen something in her face when she spoke about that boy, something that he couldn't put into words. He didn't *want* to put into words. He wasn't jealous. He couldn't allow himself to be jealous.

Harry rubbed his face with his hands, exasperated by his own thoughts. He hadn't planned to fall for Sarah. He *couldn't* have planned for it. She had entered his blood, she had become part of him. Maybe it was a Midnight thing. Harry had been his only true friend, and Sarah his only . . .

Harry stopped his thoughts at once. He couldn't think it. He couldn't think the word. No point in torturing himself, if all he could ever do in her eyes, and in the eyes of the world, was be her family. He knocked down the whisky he had poured for himself.

"Harry!" Sarah's voice resonated through the house, distressed.

He ran upstairs, praying that it was a dream, that it wasn't another attack.

Sarah had felt the tide turning, her sleep changing into the trance-like state that brought her the visions. She tried to get up and go back downstairs, in the safety of the living room, with the TV and the lights on, but it was too late. The dream had taken her away already, and there was nothing she could do, nothing but get through it.

She was in that strange place again, the grassy meadows. It was the middle of the night, a clear, moonlit night. She was crouching on the grass, and she was cold, a cold too deep to be natural. She could feel a presence, something invisible, threatening.

A little white cloud materialized in front of Sarah, swirling onto itself like a sphere of milky mist, as if it had been alive.

The sphere moved down to her hands, and started covering her left hand with mist, moving up her arm, and onto her chest.

Sarah started feeling breathless again. She often did when she was scared, or upset – but this time it was different. It was as if the little cloud was stealing her air, making her lose consciousness slowly. She was falling asleep, a deadly sleep . . .

Suddenly, Sarah realized there was someone else there. She was on her knees, paralyzed in the mist's grip, so she couldn't see who it was; but she was hoping . . .

"Not Sarah!" a man's voice shouted out.

Leaf?

The mist left her, and started twirling in front of her eyes. Sarah fell to the ground. The mist floated before her for a few seconds, and then it seemed to condense into a sort of creature whose features kept changing and changing. It hovered over Sarah, waiting for the right time to strike again. Sarah tried to cover her face with her hands, but she couldn't move. A whisper caressed her ear: *Sheila*, it said.

"No!" shouted the voice again.

Sarah was slipping away. With one last, enormous effort, she managed to look up, ever so slightly . . . and she saw Leaf's pained face. He was kneeling beside her, whispering. At first she couldn't hear what he was saying, but then she made out some words.

"I'm too late. I'm too late . . . Sarah, no . . ." Sarah saw that his cheeks were wet with tears.

At that moment the misty creature engulfed her again, and she felt her life leaving her, trickling away like a little stream she couldn't stop . . . She died, and she felt every second of it, every terrifying moment, until she was no more.

She opened her eyes in the darkness, and sat up, panting. She put her hands on her heart, making sure it was still beating. She was drenched in sweat. The rain was tapping on the windows, incessant, pouring over the hills and moors around it. The wind had risen suddenly, and it was howling among the oaks in her garden, shrieking like a banshee around Sarah's window, and lifting dead leaves in little whirlpools.

I can't take it. I can't take it any more.

She realized that Harry was sitting on her bed.

"It's OK. You know it was just a dream," he was saying. She must have called him in her sleep. She looked into his clear eyes, as if clinging to them.

"I died," she whispered.

"Oh, Sarah . . ." Harry dried her tears with soft fingers.

How did she manage, all that time, waking up alone in an empty house? How did she manage before I arrived?

"It was like some sort of mist. It took my breath away. It sent me to sleep, and then it killed me."

She didn't tell him about Leaf. She wanted to, she desperately wanted to, but she couldn't. *Why? Why can I not say his name?*

"Don't worry. I'll protect you, you know that." He took her hands in his. They were still shaking from the vision.

"I know," she whispered. Harry took her hands to his chest, in a gesture so loving that it broke her heart.

"I'll make sure nothing happens to you. You're all I have." His secret mantra. He'd said it aloud.

Sarah's heart skipped a beat. Nobody had ever said anything like that to her. Even for her parents, she wasn't *all*. Their mission came first.

"You're all I have." *So this is how it feels to be somebody's world.*

With Harry sitting on the bed, her hands in his, she felt herself unknotting. She was tired, so tired. Maybe she wasn't going to get up and tidy her room, like she normally did after a frightening dream. Maybe she was just going to stay in bed . . .

She leaned back on the pillow.

"Try and get some sleep now." Harry tucked her in, like you would a child. Sarah thought that he hadn't done it the right way, that her duvet wasn't lying the way it was supposed to, but she didn't rearrange it. She wanted to leave it the way Harry had done it. Also, her very bones refused to get up.

"Is this the way my life is going to be? Forever?" she whispered, looking into Harry's face, clinging to his blue eyes like a lifeline.

"I don't know." *I wish I could make it stop.*

"Sometimes I feel like I can't take it any more. How did my grandmother manage? Years of this . . ."

"She was very strong. She lived for her mission. She was hard, ruthless even. She didn't want anything else, but to hunt."

"But I do. I want my music. I want to fall in love."

With whom? Who will you fall for, my Sarah?

"Don't think about this now. Try and get some sleep."

Sleep. Her own private torture.

She was too tired to stop it.

If I dream again, I swear, it'll kill me. For real.

19
Strange Flowers

The strange flowers of darkness
For a little while, forever

Leaf
I'll be there. I'll keep you safe. This dream will not come true.
I'll burn them all before they can touch you.

20
A Dream of Ravens

Signs and omens
The many names of fear

"I'll do my best. Yes. Speak later." Mike was just ending a conversation with Sean when Niall walked into the shack, his hair dripping. He'd been swimming. Again.

"Hey Niall, listen here. Sean just asked me to find out something about this guy who came on the scene. He appeared in Sarah's dreams. It looks like he saved their lives. Coffee?"

"Aye, thanks."

"Sure. So, yes. This guy. He sent some ravens to help Sean and Sarah dispatch a Feral or two. Not *real* ravens. Spirits of the air, you know, Elementals. You don't happen to know anything about this kind of thing?"

Niall didn't reply. Mike looked up, and saw that he had grown pale. Lines of worry were suddenly etched on his young face. To see Niall worried was like seeing the tide standing still. It looked strange at best. Chilling at worst.

"Niall?"

He shook his head.

"Sorry. It's just that . . . I used to dream of ravens. When I was a wee boy. And they weren't nice dreams, if you know what I mean."

"There. Have this." Mike handed him the coffee and also poured some Bourbon for both of them. "Sean is on guard anyway. Doesn't trust the guy. He made it quite clear to Sarah."

"What's his name?"

"They don't know. They call him Leaf, because he gives her leaves. As gifts. Weird, I know. Ever dreamt anything about leaves?"

Niall shook his head. "No. But those ravens . . ."

"Yes?"

"Nothing. Nothing. Just memories."

Just things that I'd rather forget.

21
Rejection

Easier to give in
Than to fight for happiness
This is what happens
Unless someone fights for you

Cathy

I was Cathy Midnight. For two years, that was my name.

Morag had chosen me because I'm strong, so much stronger than Anne could ever be. Had Sarah been our daughter – mine and James's – she would have been strong too, not helpless and frightened like she is now. I see her; I see her shaking and crying – what a shame for the Midnights, to have their fate resting on her useless shoulders. How horrified Morag would be, if she could see her granddaughter tossing and turning into her destiny, instead of accepting it, instead of being proud of it. They were fools to send me away, and look at them now. The Midnights are finished – with that strange man pretending to be one of them, and Sarah believing him.

Yes, they've dissolved another one of my Surari – maybe the Midnight blood is having the best of her, and giving her the will to fight, for a change – but it'll all end soon. This is the way I want it: when we finally meet I want us to be *alone*.

When I killed James and Anne, I made it quick for James and slow for Anne. I was going to kill Sarah too. And then I changed my mind. It wasn't an act of mercy – far from it. I called it off because I wanted Sarah to know who her parents were, before she died. I wanted her to understand how cruel, how selfish they really were, under that golden exterior. She idolized them, I know – I know a lot about her, a lot more than she can imagine. I left her alive because it was time for her to hate her parents, for leaving her alone and helpless. And I enjoyed it, in a bitter way that was more pain than joy.

Beautiful, sweet Sarah Midnight, the one who should have been my daughter. She plays so well, the world should stop to listen. I fall asleep to her music. Not only do I watch her, I listen to her too . . .

If I didn't hate Sarah so much, I'd love her with an intensity that only a mother could experience.

Closer, closer. Every step brings me closer to her.

And when Sean is unmasked and Sarah is alone, then she'll know how I've felt all these years.

It'll be her time to die, and my time to be free.

22
Mist

Save me from my secrets

Sarah walked straight to the coffee machine without uttering a word, her face like thunder. A grey, rainy dawn was breaking in the sky.

"Sit down. I'll get you a coffee." Harry looked up from his iPhone, and did a double take. He could never get used to how she looked, to how much he loved her face, her hair, her body. She was wearing jeans and a long purple top, her hair tied back in a long braid, giving her an old-fashioned sort of look, like a character out of a Victorian novel.

"You look lovely," Harry blurted out, and immediately busied himself with coffee-making. Sarah blushed and didn't reply.

"Anyway, let's lie low. I say you're not going back to school until Monday."

"Good." Four days at home. Bliss. Sarah loved school, especially the music lessons, but she was finding going to school, and her dreams, and all that was happening around her, just too much. She was constantly afraid that she'd be attacked there, and that someone would get hurt.

Sarah downed her coffee. "See you later."

"Where are you going?" Harry was alarmed. He didn't like her going out alone.

"Just into the garden," shouted Sarah, already out of the door. Harry grabbed his jacket and followed her. He was about to step out when the phone rang, and he walked back in to answer.

Sarah walked down the sandstone steps . . . and there it was. A leaf. A golden one, a million different shades of yellow-gold. An oak leaf, perfectly beautiful, with its map of symmetrical veins running through it. Sarah felt the world spinning around her, and her legs gave way for a second. She was so happy, so happy, in a strange, dazed sort of way. It was as if mist had come over her eyes, and all she could see, all she could think about, was that perfect, beautiful leaf. As if nothing else mattered.

He'd found the way to say 'I'm here', though for some reason he couldn't stop, he couldn't talk.

As Harry appeared in the doorway, Sarah hid the leaf behind her back, and blanked her expression quickly. Part of her knew that she was breaking Harry's trust; part of her wanted desperately to tell him. But she just couldn't. Something was stopping her, and she couldn't figure out what it was.

"Who was it on the phone?" she asked Harry coolly.

"Marketing."

Sarah let Harry walk on into the garden, and as soon as he turned his back, she hid the leaf in the pocket of one of the jackets hanging in the hall. She stroked it one last time, before running out again.

When? When will I see him again?

She ran across the garden and into her mother's corner. She kneeled on the damp, black soil, under a steely sky, and looked up. The clouds were galloping, galloping, like wild horses. With delicate fingers, Sarah touched the rosemary, the sage, the thyme, the mint . . . Who'd guess that these humble herbs hide such power?

"Can I help?"

"It's OK, don't worry. I just don't want my mum's herb garden to be neglected. It's up to me to look after it now."

"Do you want some peace? Do you want me to go?"

"No, stay." Sarah smiled unexpectedly, one of those rare smiles that lit up her face.

Harry sat on the little stone wall that framed the herb garden, and breathed in the fresh morning air. He looked around him: the green lawns strewn with leaves, the oak trees at the back, the duck pond in the distance, covered with water lilies. A miniature park, just for the Midnights.

"This house is amazing."

"Yes. I hope I never have to leave."

"You won't. Don't worry. I'll see to that."

Sarah looked up, frowning. She couldn't bear the idea of being made empty, flippant promises. She looked at him with dark, serious eyes – and Harry met her gaze. She saw that his face was solemn too.

He means it.

A quick, near-imperceptible smile lingered on her lips – it was all she would allow herself, for now. She couldn't let herself believe he'd really stay, yet.

They sat in peaceful silence, Sarah weeding, Harry lost in thought. After a short while, Sarah got up to stretch her legs.

"Cup of tea?" asked Harry.

"I knew you'd say that!" she laughed, but stopped abruptly.

She'd heard a noise, a faint noise, like a sigh. They'd both heard it, and they both looked around, alarmed.

"Did you hear something?" Sarah whispered.

Harry nodded. He was tense, alert, looking around like an animal that just smelled a predator's scent. He freed his *sgian-dubh*, readying himself for a fight, or a spell.

A raven landed beside them in a flurry of wings and feathers.

"Harry . . ."

Harry shook his head, and brought a finger to his lips.

Sarah felt something at the base of her neck, a gentle, imperceptible touch that gave her goose bumps. A tiny sigh resounded in her ears, so low she barely heard it. Suddenly her arms felt cold.

"Harry," she whispered again, looking down. A white, icy mist was enveloping her arms slowly, threading itself from thin air, as if an invisible silkworm were spinning it. *Like in my dream.*

"Oh my God . . ."

Harry started tracing his runes and whispering his secret words. The mist was climbing up Sarah's arms, towards her chest. It felt cold and numb, like an anaesthetic, slowly running through her system, sending her to sleep. It got to her neck, and was swirling around her like a caress, soft and deadly. Sarah's head started lolling. She tried to keep her eyes open, but she couldn't. The mist covered her face, and she fell on the cold, hard ground.

Harry threw himself on the ground beside her, and kept weaving his spell, but it was no use. There was no stopping the mist. The raven cawed three times, as if calling for help. But how could help ever arrive in time, when Sarah was already barely breathing? Harry kept whispering his secret words, even if it was no use; he kept murmuring, like a prayer or an invocation.

"Sarah!" A voice filled the air, coming from the edge of the garden. A boy, standing on the garden wall. His hair was so black it was nearly blue, and he was dressed in black from top to toe – he looked like a moving piece of night, like he'd been made of darkness. Harry stopped his spell abruptly and jumped up, his *sgian-dubh* raised in defence.

"No need for that. I'm here to help Sarah."

Harry nodded. As much as he hated himself for it, he had no choice but to put the dagger down, slowly, reluctantly. There was no time to lose. Sarah's sleep was slowly turning into unconsciousness – the next step would be death. Her breathing was shallow, barely-there sighs that couldn't keep her alive for long.

"Sarah . . ."

At the sound of Leaf's voice, she opened her eyes a little.

"Leaf," she whispered.

Harry felt a bitter taste in his mouth, like bile rising. He had to accept Leaf's help. He looked at the boy with hostility, and for a second it seemed to Harry that his eyes were burning, like those coals that look cold, but if you turn them they glow red under the ash. A dark, deep glow. It was just a moment, then Leaf's eyes turned black again.

Is he human?

Leaf kneeled beside Sarah, sank his hands into the mist, and started weaving it around his fingers, like a cobweb, or spun silk. As soon as it touched Leaf's hands the mist dissolved in a million little droplets that evaporated quickly.

Fire against water, thought Harry. A strange thought took shape in his head, passing quickly and fading away, like a falling star: *he is fire.*

Leaf worked for a few minutes in complete silence, Sarah's breathing becoming slowly deeper and more regular as he dissolved the mist, until she regained consciousness. She sat up, rubbing her face. She was deadly pale, and her lips were blue. Harry went to hold her, and he was startled at how cold she felt.

"Sarah, let me warm you," He started rubbing her arms and holding her close, but Sarah's eyes never left Leaf's face.

Now it's me who's burning, Harry thought. He wanted to throw the black-eyed boy over the wall; he wanted to drag Sarah in the house and lock the door.

She's mine.

"Harry! Leaf is hurt," whispered Sarah, her face full of worry. She freed herself from Harry's arms and went to the black-eyed boy. Leaf seemed to have paled more and more as he was weaving the mist, and his skin, pale already, had taken on a blue tinge. He tried to speak, but all of a sudden, he fell on his knees. He curled up on the ground, his eyes closed, trembling. Sarah put her hands on him – he was freezing cold.

"We need to warm him up!"

Harry didn't move.

"Leaf . . ." She put her arm around his shoulder. "Harry, please, a blanket."

Still, Harry didn't move.

"I'm fine. I'm fine," Leaf whispered, still curled up. "Don't worry. I'll be OK in a minute. It needs to work its way out of me . . ."

Sarah watched him anxiously for a couple of minutes, until he finally sat up, slowly. He wasn't shaking any more. The mist had gone through his system, and left him. Both Sarah and Harry were watching him intensely: Sarah with apprehension; Harry pondering how desperately he wanted that strange boy to disappear.

Suddenly, Harry spotted something out of the corner of his eye, something white and stringy, like a wavy ribbon of steam taking shape in the air.

"Sarah. It's back."

The thread of mist had already started circling slowly around the three of them, and the air was turning colder, colder. Sarah froze. She could already feel her breath becoming shallower.

"Don't move." Leaf stood up, raised a hand and traced a run in the air while making a deep, weird howling sound, like an animal call.

And there she was, strong, proud, with eyes of pure amber and whiskers vibrating with rage. It was a wildcat – or looked like one. Sparks were springing from her paws and from her whiskers, as she started circling slowly, in the opposite direction from the mist.

"A spirit of fire!" whispered Harry.

The wildcat jumped into the air, and trapped a thread of mist into her claws. She jumped again and again, shredding the mist with her paws, as sparks flew all around her. She jumped so close to Sarah and Harry that they thought she'd cut them with her claws – but she always avoided them at the last second.

Thread after thread, the mist was gone. The wildcat stood with her claws sunk into the earth, rolled her head back and gave a deep, growly miaow. She shuddered, and a little blue lightning came from the sky, through her fur and down to her claws. Her fur stood up, electrified. Then she seemed to relax. She stretched slowly, with a deep, languid yawn.

The wildcat looked at them one last time – her amber eyes were the same colour as Shadow's, but a bit darker – and jumped away, disappearing among the oak trees, followed by the ravens flying away into the darkening sky.

Sarah was speechless. It was one of the most amazing things she'd ever seen in her life. *A spirit of fire.*

"That was *incredible!*" she said, and her eyes were shining.

"The demon won't be back again," whispered Leaf. "I have to go."

Sarah felt a stabbing through the heart. "Don't go. Stay," she pleaded, and it was such a raw, vulnerable thing to say that Harry felt sick to his stomach.

"I'm sorry, I have to." Leaf stood close to Sarah, so close that she could feel his warm breath on her neck. "Think of me," he whispered in her ear, making her knees go soft. Her mind emptied, as it always seemed to do when Leaf was around.

Sarah watched him walk away, a tide of loneliness filling her, rising slowly with every step he took. He jumped over the wall and disappeared – and Sarah's heart overflowed with invisible tears. *He never stops. He never gives me time to speak to him.* She felt her eyes welling up, and hated herself for it.

"What did he say to you?" asked Harry.

"Nothing. Just to take care."

For a second Harry imagined how it would be to put his hands around Leaf's neck and feel it snap.

"Four to go," he whispered darkly, and walked away without looking back, wishing that Leaf had stayed where he belonged, in Sarah's dreams.

Sarah followed him into the house and went straight upstairs – she wanted to be alone. She wasn't surprised when she found a golden leaf on her pillow, waiting for her.

23
Asleep

To be innocent again
To know right from wrong, the way I used to
Before you came along

Sarah was lying on her bed listening to her iPod, with the golden leaf resting on her chest. The door opened slightly. Her heart skipped a beat, and she jumped up in alarm, ripping the headphones out of her ears. She was still shaken. It was terrifying to be attacked in her own home, never to feel truly safe. How long was that fear going to last?

Forever, said a voice inside her head.

"Sarah?"

Thank God, it was Harry. She hurried to open the door.

"Sorry, I didn't hear you." She gestured to her iPod, and went to sit on the windowsill, hugging her knees. Harry sat on her bed.

He looks so kind. He looks so . . . Harry. Sarah had to fight the impulse to walk up to him and hold him, and hide her face in his chest. She took a deep breath.

"I wanted to speak to you about that boy, Leaf," he began.

I knew it.

"Yes." She could see he was upset, but she didn't want to give anything away. She didn't know what to say, anyway. It was all such a mystery. And her own feelings were the biggest mystery of all. The strange bond she felt with Leaf was inexplicable. Like a spell.

"Is he human, do you think?"

"I don't know. I think so. He's clearly not one of the Valaya. He saved my life. And yours."

I should have saved your life. "You must tell me if you see him again."

Sarah didn't reply. She was suddenly angry, with Harry, with Leaf, with her enemies, with her parents, with the whole world. She didn't even know why. Her sense of disappointment, of betrayal, was all-consuming, like a grey hole in the middle of her life.

"Sarah?"

"I'll tell you." *I won't. I can't. I want to, but I can't.*

Harry sighed. *She won't. She's used to keeping secrets; she'll keep this one and she'll keep it well.*

They were silent for a minute, a black cloud on Harry's forehead, his eyes lowered to the floor, in quiet anger. Sarah felt a rising tide of anxiety take hold of her, until she started shaking with fear. She curled up into herself, bringing her knees closer to her chest, her hair falling on her face to hide her, to protect her.

Am I making a mistake? Is Leaf someone to fear? Why does he not stop and talk to me, at least tell me his real name?

"I know who the demon-mist belonged to," she murmured. "I heard it in my dreams. Sheila Douglas."

Harry's face set into something hard, something that made him look like a stranger and made Sarah feel terribly, infinitely alone.

"I'm going to find her. She's got to pay," he said coldly, calmly.

Sarah brought a hand to her chest. She was breathless again.

"Harry, there's no point, her demon is dead. You said it yourself: once the demons are destroyed, the humans die. Don't go."

"I don't care. She's got to pay," he repeated.

"Harry!"

Harry took Sarah by the shoulders, and looked her in the eye. They faced each other for a long moment. *How easy it would be to kiss her now, to claim her for my own, to squash whatever there is between her and Leaf . . .*

"I have to keep you alive, Sarah."

"Not by killing other people," she whispered, her voice breaking.

"Whatever it takes."

"No, that's not the way . . ."

But Harry had gone already. Sarah ran after him.

"You won't hurt her, will you?"

Harry was speechless. He turned around abruptly, and Sarah nearly bumped into him.

"Sarah. These are your parents' killers. And they want to kill you too. Do you realize that?"

"Of course I do! But I don't want human blood on my hands! Or yours! That's not the way it's meant to be!"

"I won't kill her, if that's what you're afraid of."

"What will you do?"

"Teach her a lesson."

They had got to the garage. He started the car. His eyes were very cold, very clear, and Sarah felt afraid.

"Jump in. I can't leave you here alone," he called, looking straight ahead.

I can't leave you alone either, thought Sarah, and slipped into the car.

They were quiet throughout the journey, and Sarah looked out of the window. The city streets, the blond sandstone tenements under a heavy sky, the grey castle, rising from the volcano, watching over the city like a sentinel.

Princes Street was busy and full of life: people walking fast in the chilly afternoon air, huddled up in coats and scarves, tourists taking pictures of the sights, and a very, very noisy piper playing over the traffic noise.

"There we are. New You, third floor. Fancy a new nose?"

Sarah sighed, and looked down. She felt nervous, on edge. She slipped a hand under her top, to check that the dagger was there, and flexed her hands nervously in an unconscious gesture, as if to get them ready.

"I'll go myself, if you want." Harry's eyes were hard.

"No. I'm coming." *Better keep an eye on you.*

Harry's pocket beeped, and he took out his iPhone.

"Again? Who do you speak to all the time?"

"My friends, you know that."

"*Those* friends?"

"Yes."

"Who *are* they?" Sarah was exasperated. Harry's friends seemed to be in her life a lot, and to know so much, while she didn't even know their names.

"They're good people to know. People I can trust."

"Have you known them long?"

Harry didn't reply. Sarah knew he wouldn't say any more.

"Right. Let's go. Oh, Sarah?"

"Yes?"

"Have you taken your vitamins? The ones Juliet brought?"

Sarah was flabbergasted. She was taken by surprise, and she couldn't help laughing.

"What?"

"You were pretty ill yesterday, and with all that's happening . . ."

"Yes, Mum. I took them this morning."

"Ha ha."

She was touched. The way Harry could be focused, and cold, and ruthless one second, and then warm and caring the next – it made her heart beat faster; it made her want to solve his mystery, to own the whole of him, not just some parts, the ones he allowed her to know.

"You're still a bit pale."

"I'm always pale. It's the famous Midnight ghostly complexion. You don't have it, though," she noticed, looking at his golden skin.

"That's the southern hemisphere for you."

They walked in. Everything looked polished, luxurious. A place for people who wanted to buy new bodies.

"How can I help?" asked the receptionist.

"My wife and I . . ."

Wife?

". . . are looking for a consultation. We'd like some advice on . . . procedures."

"Sure. Your names?"

"Harry and Sarah Midnight. We'd like to see Ms Douglas. She's been recommended to us."

"Right, let me see . . . nothing until next week, I'm afraid."

"We're family friends. I'm sure if you tell her we're here she'll see us straight away."

"Very well, I'll try." She picked up the phone. "Ms Douglas? There's a Harry Midnight and a Sarah Midnight here to see you for a consultation. They said you might want to see them straight away. Sure. I'll show them in."

Sarah's chest was tight. Here we go . . .

"Follow me, please," the receptionist said suavely. She led them down a softly lit corridor, and knocked at a door.

"Come on in!" A clipped, hard voice called. The receptionist disappeared, discreetly, leaving behind a cloud of perfume. Sheila Douglas was standing at her desk, her face a mask of hatred and disbelief.

"How can you still be alive?" she whispered, a whisper that was like a scream.

"Sorry to disappoint." Harry shrugged.

"Is my demon . . . is it . . . ?"

"Dead and buried, yes. Well, dissolved. Sorry."

"How did you . . . ? How? It was strong . . . it killed so many . . . it can't be. You're bluffing."

"It was hard to kill, I'll give you that. We needed some help. But here we are."

Sheila made a sound between a sob and a grunt, so incongruous with her polished persona that Sarah felt her chest tighten some more. *What's going to happen now? Is she going to try to kill us? Or is Harry going to try to kill her?* She didn't know what was worse.

"You don't think you're safe now, do you? Because the Valaya is not finished. We won't rest until you're dead."

"We know. There's a few more Surari, and that Mistress woman, isn't there?" Harry's tone was flippant, but Sarah knew him well enough to detect the steel in his voice.

"How do you know of her?"

"The sapphires told us," answered Harry cryptically.

"The Mistress awaits you, yes. Even if you managed to kill us all, there'd be her at the end of it. Oh . . ." Sheila brought a hand to her head, as if in sudden pain.

Sarah gasped. Was that Harry? Doing that to her?

"Who is she? Who is the Mistress?" pressed Harry.

"I've said enough. Now go!" Sheila took her head in her hands, her face contorted in pain. Sarah tried to breathe in again, but found that she couldn't. Her chest was so tight, she thought she'd suffocate.

"Are you scared, Sarah? Because you should be!" Sheila looked up, her eyes shining with a frantic light. "You, little Sarah, you'll be in a grave with your parents soon. What do you think you're doing?" she screeched, looking somewhere over Sarah's shoulder.

Sarah followed her gaze and turned around. Harry had his dagger in his hand, and his eyes were icy. Sarah swallowed. He looked ready to kill; he looked like he *wanted* to kill.

"Are you going to stab me?" Sheila laughed again, then she brought her hand to her forehead, in pain again.

"Harry, no!" *He can't. That's not the Midnight mission. We don't kill human beings!*

Harry ignored Sarah. He raised the hand carrying the dagger and started tracing his runes with the tip of the s*gian-dubh*, cutting the air. Sheila had her eyes fixed on the blade, as if she'd been hypnotized. Sarah was expecting her to start shuddering, and was bracing herself for wounds to appear all over Sheila's body like it had happened to the white Feral, but nothing happened.

Nothing.

With one last, sharp movement, Harry put down the *sgian-dubh* and slipped it back in his sock. His cold, clear eyes betrayed no emotion.

"What have you done to me?" screeched Sheila, jumping up. Her chair fell backwards.

"Is everything OK, Ms Douglas?" The receptionist opened the door ever so slightly, enough to put her head in.

"Yes, yes, of course. I just need to finish this consultation." Sheila's voice sounded hoarse. Frightened. The receptionist looked at them suspiciously, but closed the door, muttering an apology.

"Do you want to know what I did, Ms Douglas?" said Harry, his tone even, his face hard as stone. "Let's just say that whenever I choose, you'll fall asleep. It might happen when you're in the car . . . or you might be turning the gas on, or stepping down the stairs . . . Well, you get the drift."

Sheila looked at him, wide-eyed. "I don't believe you." Her expression and her voice said the opposite.

Harry raised a hand, as if he was blessing her, and traced something in the air. Sheila fell on the floor, out cold. Sarah clasped her hands on her mouth.

Harry raised his hand again, and traced the same symbol, in reverse. Sheila opened her eyes suddenly, gasping, struggling for breath.

"You'll pay for this," she hissed, looking at him like you'd look at a raging dog: with anger, and fear.

"If the Valaya bothers us again, I'll make you fall asleep. If I don't wake you up, it'll take you hours to wake up by yourself. In the meanwhile, anything could happen. And I hope it does."

"I wouldn't be able to stop them, not even if I wanted to! You'll gain nothing from killing me!" Sheila spat.

"At least I will have had some satisfaction. I hope you die a painful death, Sheila Douglas, for wishing Sarah in her grave."

Sarah was horrified to hear him speaking like that. *As if he were just like them. As if he were one of the Valaya, and no better.*

The last thing Sarah saw as they walked out was Sheila sitting at her desk with her head in her hands, her eyes semi-closed, as if she were in the grip of a terrible pain.

The noise of traffic in Princes Street hit them like a wall. The heavens had opened. They ran to the car under the pouring rain.

"What are we going to do now?" Sarah dried her face with her hands, her long hair soaking.

"We wait. They won't be long."

No, they won't be long. Maybe now, maybe this afternoon, this evening, tonight. There'll be no rest, no rest until the Valaya has been defeated. And after that, there'd be something else. No rest forever.

No rest, until sooner or later something manages to kill us.

24
The Life That Could Have Been Mine

Wait for me, I'm coming home
Light the fire and close the curtains
After love was gone
Love arrived

The phone rang while Sarah was practising her cello. She stopped, reluctantly, and dragged herself out of the state of grace she always fell into when she was playing – that suspended state of perfect concentration that had her mind, her body, her heart and her soul aligned with each other, like a constellation. For all the years she wasn't allowed to tell anyone what really went on in her life, Sarah could speak through her music. Music was everything to her, her respite from constant fear, from loneliness and loss. Her refuge and her way to ask the world to be seen, to be loved.

"Hello? Hi Bryony. Yes, she's here. Sarah!" she heard Harry say as he answered the phone.

"Coming," she called, sighing. She was always happy to speak to Bryony, but she *needed* to practise. The audition was only seven weeks away, and with all that was going on . . .

"Hi . . . Better. I'm not sure . . . maybe another time . . . Yes, I know I haven't been out in ages . . . Bryony, I have to practise, seriously. No, I'm not putting it off a year, of course I can do it. I know, I know. OK. Just for an hour, then. See you in a bit. Bye."

She looked at Harry and shrugged her shoulders, as if to say *what could I do?*

"Sarah . . ." Harry's voice was full of reproach.

"Oh, don't give me a hard time now. I've got to go. We're just going to the Royal Mall. I'll be back in an hour or two."

"You know it's dangerous. If they attack you they could hurt Bryony too . . ."

"I haven't been out in weeks, I haven't seen anyone in weeks . . . Bryony sounded strange. I can't lose her. I don't want to lose her."

"Does she not understand all that you went through?"

"Of course she does. But she doesn't see why I'm not leaning on her. We always leaned on each other, all these years."

"It doesn't change the fact that you'd put her in danger."

"I know," Sarah sighed. "Oh, you're right. I'll phone her and say I can't go. Once this nightmare is finished, maybe I'll be able to have a life again . . ."

I'm like a curse. The thought weighed like a stone in her heart. Sarah looked so desolate that Harry felt for her. He thought for a minute.

"Listen, what if I follow you? Like I follow you in school? I'll keep an eye on you all. If something happens, I'll be there."

"Oh, Harry, if you could do that . . ."

"It won't take the danger away, but it'll help."

"You can follow me in that super-creepy way of yours. We won't see you but you'll be there, like a spy!" She smiled.

"I'm not super-creepy!" protested Harry.

"Well, you follow me everywhere, and if that's not creepy I don't know what is," Sarah teased him.

"It's *not* creepy!" Harry insisted. Sarah raised her eyebrows.

"Well, maybe a bit. But it saved your life at least once."

"Did it?"

Harry nodded.

"Seriously?"

"Yes."

"Well, that means it works, then. You can drive me and then hang around. In the bushes, or something."

"There are no bushes in the shopping centre."

"There are, a few sorry-looking ones. I think they're plastic. Or you can steal a uniform from a security guard . . ."

Harry smiled. "That's not how it's done."

"How do you do it? Is it a bit like when you walk around all silent, and I can't hear you coming and you scare the life out of me?"

"The same principle, yes."

"A useful skill."

"Very."

Harry really was frightened for Sarah's friends, in case of an attack. That was the truth. But there was another reason why he didn't want her to go, something he couldn't even admit to himself. He knew it was wrong to feel that way, but he couldn't help it.

He'd never been so possessive with anyone. After having lost his parents when he was thirteen, he had sworn he was never, ever going to have a family. He couldn't bear the thought of getting close to someone, and then losing them again. Girlfriends and friends had come and gone, leaving no trace, until the real Harry had come along. Harry Midnight had been the first person to seep into his heart, his first true friend.

And he had died too.

Then Sarah appeared out of the blue, like someone from a dream. All the terror and grief he'd felt at the loss of his parents, and of Harry, transferred onto her. The desire to protect her, to *save* her, had overwhelmed him. It was so strong that he didn't know what to do with it. He wanted to growl, to circle around her like a wild dog. He knew that his feelings for Sarah went beyond affection; he was under no illusion about the way he loved her. He couldn't bear the idea of something happening to her. He couldn't bear the idea of someone taking her away.

Another man.

There, he'd said it, even if just in his head.

He also knew that he had no right to her, that he could never, ever let his feelings come to the surface – he was supposed to be her cousin, so she believed, so the world believed. Being near her, being her family, had to be enough for him.

And if she said once more *lie beside me*, the way she did the other day? Would he be able to laugh it off again? Or would he lie beside Sarah and let his heart, not his head, decide what was right and what was wrong?

He wanted to be her whole world. Danger kept them close; she needed him, and he wanted to keep it that way.

"Hey, what are you thinking?"

"Nothing. Come on, let's go."

"OK. I'm just going to get dressed."

After forty minutes (*What on earth is she doing?*) Sarah was back. Her long hair was loose, and it came down past her shoulders, black and shiny. She had chosen black leggings and black pumps, and a jumper in a blue-grey shade that showed her white, soft shoulders. She had a silvery eye-shadow that made her eyes shine, and a light lip-gloss. Her cheeks were pink with happiness.

Harry was speechless.

Sarah saw how he was looking at her, that he was unable to look away. She realized she didn't want him to, and it scared her.

"I'll get my jacket," she muttered.

"I'll warm the car," he muttered back.

While he got into the Bravo, Harry realized that there was nothing more he wanted than to run his hands through her hair.

"Yes! We managed to get you out!" Bryony hugged Sarah tight. Sarah breathed in the sweet bluebell scent of hers and felt happy, perfectly happy, like when they were children and they were allowed a sleepover in each other's house. Bryony had a purple fabric flower pinned in her hair, on one side of her face. Her taste in clothes had always been eccentric, bright and colourful. She suffered, having to wear a grey and blue uniform all week, and came alive at the weekend, when she could express her creativity and play with colours the way she loved. Sarah thought she looked amazing, so vibrant and cheerful and full of life.

"Hey Sarah!"

Alice and Leigh had arrived, and Sarah hugged them both. They looked great too. Alice with her blond asymmetric bob, and big blue eyes. She was very tall, and very pretty – she and Sarah's cousin Siobhan were the main contenders for the title of prettiest girl in Trinity Academy. Leigh had long, straight brown hair and freckles. She was the less flamboyant of the three, but just as pretty.

The four girls were so different that they gelled perfectly, compensating for each other, giving each other what the others lacked. Bryony was arty, eccentric, full of life; Alice was sultry and confident, older than her years; Leigh was sweet and generous, with a life that had no clouds. And Sarah was shy, a bit melancholic, the darkest of the four – with those strange parents that her friends couldn't decipher.

They made a beeline for Accessorize, their favourite shop. It had everything, from jewellery to bags, hats and scarves, pretty stationery and even underwear and slippers. Everything was arranged by shade and colour, and shone under the bright lights – girls and women flocked like magpies. They raided the shop, and Sarah loved every minute. It was the first time she'd gone shopping in a long time. The Halloween stock was out, a whole range of jewellery shaped like pumpkins, bats and little witches on brooms. Right up Sarah's street.

"What did you buy?" Alice asked her.

"These . . ." She brushed her hair away, and showed her the earrings she'd just bought. Two tiny silver moons. "And this . . ."

She took her new necklace in her fingers: it was a little black cat.

"It looks like your Shadow!"

"Exactly. What did you get?"

"Over-the-knee stockings. To show your cousin!" laughed Alice.

Sarah looked furtively around, wondering if he'd heard. After all, he was there, but she didn't know *where*.

"Look at my loot." Bryony had bought some bat-shaped earrings and a bat pendant. "For Halloween!"

"Cute!" The girls approved.

Leigh had bought a knitted pink across-the-shoulder bag, a matching little purse, and a few pieces of jewellery. Her dad was a famous sports commentator, and she always had a lot in the way of pocket money – unlike Bryony, who had four brothers and sisters to share with, and was always broke.

"Hey girls." A tall boy wearing jeans and an orange T-shirt had approached them. Jack. Sarah tensed up.

"Hi Jack, look at you, very trendy," smiled Bryony.

"You too, I could see you from a mile away with those tights" he replied, good-naturedly. "So what are you doing? Who are you with?"

"Not Michael, if that's what you were fishing for." Bryony blushed, and Alice and Leigh laughed. Bryony had had a crush on Michael for a long time – three months, which was ages, by her standards. Sarah didn't join in the laughter – she was busy trying to look around without being noticed, to see if Harry was near. She was hoping that he wouldn't see Jack. She knew it would upset him.

"Sarah, that hazelnut latte . . ." Jack said hopefully.

Sarah opened her mouth, but nothing came out. She didn't know what to say. She really wanted to be with her girlfriends. The last thing she wanted was to leave them, and go for coffee with Jack.

And if Harry saw us . . .

So what if Harry saw us? It's none of his business! He's my cousin, not my—my . . .

She refused to finish the thought.

Bryony noticed Sarah's unease, and came to her rescue.

"Thanks, why not?" she said brightly. "Let's go to Starbucks, what do you think?" Jack looked at Bryony, puzzled. She flashed him a smile. *She has finally taken the hint*, thought Sarah, relieved, and started breathing again. She was saved.

They sat on the brown sofas upstairs, looking down at the shoppers through the transparent barriers. The evening was closing in, and the blue lights on the glass walls, made to look like water trickling down the sides of the building, came on. Sarah took it all in. It was brilliant to be out with her friends. To be normal, or at least pretend to be. She sipped her hazelnut latte, listening to Jack and the girls chatting, without saying much. She felt Jack's eyes on her whenever he thought she wasn't looking.

"It's your birthday soon. Less than two weeks away. What are we going to do?" Bryony asked Sarah.

"I don't feel like celebrating this year. It's just . . . it's too soon."

"I know," replied Bryony, and Leigh nodded in agreement. "But maybe we could take you out for lunch? Just girls. Sorry, Jack, no offence!"

"None taken. Maybe I can treat Sarah to a day in town instead."
Oh God.

"We'll see. I don't know . . . I have the audition soon," she stumbled.

"Right, sorted. It's lunch with the girls for your birthday." Bryony came to her rescue again.

"OK then," Sarah conceded with a smile.

"And Cousin Harry too," added Alice, with a straight face, and they all laughed.

"I'll text you for our day in town," added Jack. *He's pushing his luck.*

"OK." *Not.*

"It's nearly six o'clock. Why don't we go to my house and do a horror-film marathon? My brother brought a pile of them home the other day."

"Why not?" said Alice.

"I'll get fish and chips for everyone. Who's going to be there?" offered Leigh.

"Aw, thanks Leigh! It'd be just my mum and my sisters. The boys are at football on a Friday night."

"OK. Let's go to Alpino's then." The girls started gathering their things.

"Sorry, Bryony, I can't," whispered Sarah. Bryony's face fell.

"Oh, Sarah, we have to practically beg you to be with us. Shutting yourself off like this can't be good for you . . ." Leigh's blue eyes were full of concern.

Sarah was mortified. She hated the idea of her friends thinking she was avoiding them, as if she didn't want, or need, their company any more. It wasn't true. She needed them more than ever.

"Don't leave us out of your life, even if things must be so hard for you," Leigh went on. Bryony didn't say anything. She was just looking at Sarah with those warm, velvety brown eyes that said more than a million words.

"It's just that—that since my parents died . . . I find it difficult to go out, to see people."

And there's some sort of secret society hunting me. That, too, doesn't help.

Sarah tried to breathe in, but her chest was heavy again.

What I wouldn't give to be able to explain, to tell the truth. What I wouldn't give for them to know me for who I really am. But I can't.

"OK, I'll come. But just for a wee while."

Let's hope for the best . . .

"I couldn't say no. I know, I know . . . Yes, I've got the dagger with me. Oh, and Harry . . ." Sarah breathed in. "Keep an eye on us. Please."

She felt her chest tightening. If something happened to her friends . . .

Maybe it'll be OK. Maybe, for once, it'll be OK.

They took the bus back. It was full of students like them, chatting and laughing. Sarah was looking around nervously, watching for anything uncanny. The people around her looked so carefree. Young. As she should have been.

The life that should have been mine.

They went to Alpino's to get fish and chips, and walked up to Gateside Road. It was dark already, a cold, misty autumn night. Jack walked beside her, and with a subtle, quick gesture, he took her hand.

Oh, no. No, no, no, no. He doesn't seem to get the message!

Sarah blushed, and slipped her hand out of his. She hurried beside Bryony, pretending it had never happened.

In spite of her apprehension, it was a lovely night. Sarah felt a million miles away from her crazy life, away from her dreams, the Surari, the Valaya. She felt like a girl having fun, a *normal* girl.

They were all on Bryony's sofas – Alice, Leigh, Jack, and Kate and Olivia, Bryony's sisters. Sarah had managed to slip between Alice and Leigh, so that she wouldn't have to sit beside Jack. Even Bryony's mum, a sweet, maternal woman, joined them for a while. Mrs McPherson always had a thought and a word for Sarah.

"How are you, pet? You know you're always welcome here," she said, stroking her face.

"Thank you, Mrs McPherson," said Sarah gratefully. *Imagine having a mum like this, a family like this . . .*

Mrs McPherson had prepared a huge amount of popcorn, and the creamiest, most decadent chocolate cake Sarah had ever tasted. They watched three horror DVDs, one after the other. Zombies followed vampires, and then it was the turn of a serial killer with a scary mask. The girls were *oohing* and *aahing* in fear, Sarah was joining in, pretending to be scared too. Her own life was a lot more frightening.

"I really have to go now," she said after the serial killer in the scary mask had finally been slain.

"I'll ask my dad to drive you." Bryony got up.

"No need, I'll phone Harry." She had had a wonderful time, but she was looking forward to getting into Harry's Bravo, and then home, the two of them in the living room, chatting in peace. She'd missed him. And she had to finish her daily cello practice, anyway.

Ten minutes after Sarah's call, Harry knocked at the McPherson door.

"That was quick!"

He was here already, that's why.

"Thank you, Bryony!" Sarah hugged her friends, while Harry was chatting with Mrs McPherson. Sarah slipped behind him and out into the night, before Jack could try and hug her too.

Just like she'd imagined, getting into the Bravo was lovely. It was warm, comfortable and it smelled good.

"Thanks for watching over me," she said with a smile.

"Did you have fun?" *With Jack?* Harry wanted to add, but restrained himself.

"It was great."

"They seem a nice bunch of people."

"Yes. We've all known each other since we were children."

"Jack, too?" He paused. "Is he special?" Harry tried to sound casual, but he was dying to hear the answer.

Sarah shook her head. Bryony, Alice, Leigh and all her friends fell in love once a month, and changed boyfriends like they changed outfits. Especially Bryony, who had such a cheery, sunny attitude to love and dating – she saw it all as a big game. Sarah, on the other hand, had never fallen for anyone; she'd never had a boyfriend, a serious one. And she had never been kissed.

She didn't like talking about those things. She thought that if she'd said she was waiting for the right person they'd laugh at her, like she had fancied herself some damsel from old times. Like she didn't belong here, now.

"I'm waiting for the right person. Like my mum waited for my dad." She immediately regretted her answer. He was going to laugh. He was going to make a joke of it.

"It's a good plan," said Harry. Sarah's heart flew away, like a butterfly in a blue sky. *He understands.*

"Is there anyone that you think might be the right one?" He kept his eyes on the road, as if what he had just asked didn't matter much, just small talk.

Leaf? I never felt that way before. I was never even remotely interested in anyone before. He makes me feel . . . like I'm floating. He makes me feel like there's nobody else in the world but us. When he's around, I could forget my own name . . .

And still . . .

Harry. Her cousin. *Stop it!*

"No."

Harry felt immensely relieved, and then immensely sad. The person she was waiting for could never be him. Unless he told her the truth.

They spent the rest of their evening like Sarah had hoped, in the living room, with a dancing fire and the delicate light of a table lamp. Harry sipped a whisky, lost in thought, and Sarah watched the flames.

"I need to finish my daily practice."

"Is it OK if I listen?"

"Of course."

Harry loved hearing Sarah playing. The dark, melancholic sound of her cello was like an echo of his own thoughts, as if he were hearing the music of his soul. As if he were looking in a mirror. Also, Sarah was beautiful when she played. Focused, her eyes closed, graceful movements, her hair flowing like waves. It worked on Harry like a spell.

When she'd finished, she sighed. She would have rather stayed where she was, in her own little music bubble, immune to the reality of her life.

"What shall I do now? I'm trying not to go to sleep."

"I know. I'll be awake anyway, don't worry."

"You need to sleep, once in a while."

"I never sleep."

"You're not a vampire, are you?" laughed Sarah.

"I know it's *the* thing to be at the moment, but no, sorry to disappoint!"

"Werewolf?

"No."

"Fallen angel?"

"Nope."

"A boring, old human being then."

"That's me." They laughed.

They were silent for a bit, Sarah looking out of the window, leaning her head on her cello, and Harry looking at her.

"John Burton, the next name on the list," he whispered after a while.

"Tomorrow?"

"Tomorrow."

Sarah opened her eyes. Like she had predicted, the dream had come. She was standing in a sea of heather, and an icy wind howled in her ears. She looked up – a milky, white sky was above her, not the purple surreal one of the place she had been seeing in her dreams recently. She realized she was standing on a little round hill. The heathery moors seemed to go on forever, creasing up in more of those little mounds. She was cold, wearing only shorts and a T-shirt, her feet bare. She shivered.

Sarah waited. Someone would turn up, something would happen. *Let it be Leaf. Let it be Leaf and not a demon,* she prayed silently.

A figure took shape in the distance, running towards her. Sarah waited for it to come closer, so that she could make out who it was . . . a girl. A red-haired girl. Bryony? No, the girl's hair was long and straight.

"Sarah! Help!" Sarah steeled herself to stay still, waiting to see if she was friend or foe.

"Sarah!" The girl was getting closer and closer, and Sarah could make out her features. She'd seen her somewhere before.

"Help!"

Of course, Angela! Angela Cunningham! She'd gone to Sarah's primary school for a year, then her family had moved away. Sarah hadn't seen her for years.

Angela was now standing right in front of her. She was breathless with the run, and tears were streaming down her face. She looked terrified. "They're coming to get me!" she whispered.

"Who? Who's coming to get you?"

"The soil people. Only you can save me, Sarah . . ."

"Soil people? Where are they? Where are *we*, Angela?" she thought to ask, so she'd know where to find her.

"Roslin. Hillside. Sarah!" A white hand had come out of the grass, and had curled around Angela's ankle – a hand that had sprouted from the earth, like in one of the horror movies she'd seen at Bryony's. Angela screamed in terror.

Sarah threw herself on the ground and grabbed the ghostly hand, trying to dissolve it with blackwater – but it didn't work. Another hand grabbed Angela's leg, and started pulling her down, underground.

Angela kept screaming and calling, out of her mind with terror, and Sarah took hold of her, trying to keep her on the surface – but it was no use; the white hands were too strong, they pulled and pulled until Angela was underground from the waist down.

"Angela! Angela!" Sarah was crying too now. She knew there was nothing she could do. She watched Angela being dragged down, still screaming and crying for help, until her mouth was full of soil and she couldn't call any more. Her red hair lingered on the surface for a few seconds, one of her hands desperately feeling for something to hold on to – Sarah held it for an instant, until it disappeared under the ground.

"Angela," she called again, though she knew it was no use. The only sound left now was Sarah's heavy, frightened breathing. She knew what would happen next.

Then something brushed Sarah's right foot, and she knew they had come back for her. She jumped up as fast as she could, and scanned the ground around her feet, waiting to spot a white hand coming out of the ground. She hugged herself in the cold wind, shaking uncontrollably. It was her turn; she'd be dragged down now, her mouth would fill with soil like Angela's . . .

They're coming. They're coming for me.

Finally, the white hand appeared and curled around her ankle. Sarah screamed and tried to free herself, but the creature's grip was too strong. She felt a hand grabbing her other ankle too, and she lost her balance, falling in to the heather.

A face emerged from the soil, a human face, but mortally pale. The creature leaned on its arms to climb out completely, and jumped on Sarah, holding her down. Its face was so close that she could smell its rotten breath. It opened its mouth and sank its teeth into Sarah's shoulder with all its strength. Sarah yelled with pain and fear, and felt blood pouring down her arm . . .

Sarah opened her eyes in the darkness. The pain was unbearable.

"Sarah!" Harry burst through the door and switched on the light. He never knew if Sarah was screaming because of a dream, or because a demon was attacking. He was living on a knife's edge, his nerves frayed, his insomnia worse than ever.

"Harry!" She felt her shoulder. It was wet. She looked at her hand, expecting it to be full of blood, but it was just sweat. Still, it ached as if she'd been bitten for real.

Harry sat on her bed and took both her hands in his. "It's OK. It's over. There's nobody here, just you and me . . ." He looked her in the eye and whispered to her, to lead her out of her terror. Sarah was trembling all over, and she was desperately trying to take a breath. Harry thought once more how heavy a burden the Dreamers had to carry.

"What did you see?" he asked, when she had calmed a little.

"This girl I knew, Angela. We went to school together . . ." Sarah put her hand on her chest, trying to slow down her racing heart. "She was asking for help. There was a sort of . . . a sort of zombie coming out of the earth, like *Night of the*

Living Dead or something. It dragged her underground right in front of my eyes. I tried to pull her back up, but I couldn't. It dragged her down . . . Then it came back, it came out of the earth and bit my shoulder."

"Do you know where you were?"

"Somewhere near Roslin, a few miles from here. She was so scared. She asked for my help, and I couldn't help her." Sarah's eyes were huge. Harry squeezed her hand tight. "I need to look for her. She needs me. Maybe I can save her."

"Sarah, not now. You can't do this now. We've got the Valaya after us. We can't be distracted."

"Distracted?" Sarah was so upset, she could hardly turn her thoughts into words. "The demon dragged her underground. She couldn't breathe! She kept calling me . . ."

"You're just putting yourself in danger. As if we needed more of that!"

"I need to take the risk. I have to."

Harry sighed. "Let's think about it tomorrow morning. Get some sleep now . . ."

Sarah shook her head. "I can't."

"Do you want me to stay with you?"

She nodded.

"OK." Harry went out of the room, and reappeared a minute later with his duvet and a pillow. He switched the light off, and arranged the duvet on the floor, wrapping himself in it.

"I'm so comfortable . . . not."

Had she not been so terrified, Sarah would have laughed.

25
Soil

Deep in my soul, where it's dark
I'll meet you in secret
Away from their eyes
Away from the light
Where our kisses
Cannot be counted

"Are you ready?" asked Harry.

"I'm not going to look for John Burton, Harry. I'm going to Roslin." Sarah was wearing jeans, trainers and her black waterproof jacket, with the cream scarf wrapped twice around her neck. She had a black, leather-bound volume in her hands.

"Sarah, please . . ."

"Harry, I've got to go. Do you understand? I've got to go."

"We're going to Craigmillar to find John Burton. End of."

"I'm going to Roslin to find Angela."

"Sarah. We have enough on our hands . . ."

"I can't hold myself responsible for Angela's death. I've got to see for myself."

"Jesus, Sarah!"

"I'm going."

"Fine. Fine." He ran his hands through his hair, exasperated. "We need to find out where she stays. I'll ask my friends. What's her second name?"

"We don't need your friends this time. I know where she is. Recently my dreams have been strange, but this one was textbook. It was a real place. Look." Sarah handed Harry the black leather-bound book she was holding. It was her dream diary, the one that her parents had given her when she turned thirteen.

I've never seen anything more un-Sarah-like. It's . . . sinister, thought Harry, taking it from her.

"Angela told me they were in Roslin, somewhere called *Hillside.*" She pointed at the word on the page, written in bold black letters. "Also, I noticed something out the corner of my eye when I was up there. A farm, a whitewashed building. I think that's where Angela lives now."

Harry looked at her. *She has taken charge.*

"Right. Let's go." He wasn't convinced. He had a bad feeling about it all. The Valaya had to be involved, one way or another.

"There's something I need to do first," Sarah called, disappearing up the stairs. Alone with Sarah's dream diary, Harry started looking through it. Page after page of horrifying visions, Sarah's childish handwriting distorted with fear and shaking hands. *She's written most of this in the middle of the night, waking up in terror.*

He could just imagine her, feverishly writing down everything she could remember, alone in that big house. Most children worry about a monster under the bed – Sarah saw monsters every night, and they were real. Like a dark fairy tale she found herself thrown into, one where no prince would come and save her. Harry skimmed through the entries . . . 12 October 2008. A few days before her fourteenth birthday.

> *I know we were in the Botanic Gardens; I've been there before, with my school. There were two of them. They took us to the hole and covered us with soil, and we couldn't breathe. The other girl died first, then I did . . .*

It went on and on, four years of fear. An entry marked 14 August 2010. She'd been fifteen years old.

> *She was swimming in the pond, and I couldn't see her properly, just her hair floating on the water. It was green. She took the man down with her and then she came out of the water. Her teeth were black. She tried to get me, but I was too far from the water, so she hid again among the reeds and waited for someone else. The man she drowned came back up, and his eyes were gone . . .*

Harry swallowed. Not even *he* had seen such horrors, hunting on the other side of the world. He could only imagine what it must have been like for Sarah, so young, seeing all that. And then getting up to straighten anything she could get her hands on, to scrub and polish until she was exhausted. Did her parents not know? Was anyone there to help her? Did anyone *care*?

Sarah went down to the basement and stood in front of the oak table. Her mother's diary was there. She had been through it all three times, looking for a protection spell. She couldn't find anything but the basic one, the one she'd known since she was a child. She was so frustrated she could have screamed. *A protection spell that works, is it too much to ask? Morag most certainly taught my mum one, a proper one. She must have forgotten to include it. How do you forget something like that?* With a sigh, she started preparing a basic little pouch. She didn't have that much faith in it working, but it was all she had. She crushed some pine needles in a mortar, some garlic and some salt. She put it all into a red leather pouch, and held it tight in her hands, her eyes closed. Then she had a thought. She took the pink quartz out of her own protection pouch, and slipped it into the one she'd made for Harry. *To keep you safe.*

"I'll tie it around your neck. There, three knots. The way it should be."

Harry felt her cool fingers on his skin, and closed his eyes for a split second. "Thank you."

They got into the car and drove out of the city, towards Roslin. Sarah was looking out of the window in silence, taking in the beauty of the landscape. It was an ocean of grass and heather, open and swept by sea winds. They were leaving clear skies behind, and driving towards a gathering of grey clouds. Everything looked expectant, tense, waiting for the storm to hit.

"We shouldn't be far. I think it's past that hill . . . Let's stop here."

"Did we remember to bring a picnic?" joked Harry.

They parked in the middle of nowhere. They couldn't see the village from there, or any buildings for that matter. They were less than an hour from Edinburgh, and still it looked wild, like a Hebridean island.

"This way." Sarah led them.

They walked on for about twenty minutes, until they got to a big whitewashed building, with a brown roof and a big sign: *Hillside*.

Sarah pointed at the sign. "That's what Angela said."

"OK. So here we are. What do we do?" Harry asked.

It's not me asking that question. It's him. Harry is asking me what to do. It was exciting, and a bit scary.

"Let's have a look around first, then we'll knock at the door."

"I could go for an ice cream, could you?" asked Harry, pointing at a sign reading '*Homemade ice cream – organic eggs*'.

"It's only open in the summer, Harry." She rolled her eyes.

"Oh well."

They walked away from the farm. Sarah's instinct led them up a tiny, rounded hill. She turned around. It was like a snapshot from her dream.

"It happened here." Her heart was racing. She could still see Angela's terrified face, her screams as she was dragged underground . . . She took a deep breath. Harry was standing beside her, alert, ready to get his *sgian-dubh*.

"I'm here!" shouted Sarah unexpectedly, at the top of her voice. "I'm Sarah Midnight, come and get me! Come out!"

She's getting stronger, thought Harry. *About time, too.*

243

Sarah's voice echoed through the moors. Nothing happened. And then, another voice, calling from the bottom of the hill.

"Sarah? Is that you?"

They both turned around at the same time. A girl of Sarah's age was walking up the little mound. Her red hair was blowing over her face.

"Sarah Midnight?"

"Angela! You're alive!"

Angela looked at her, puzzled. "Alive? Yes, of course. Are *you* OK?"

"I'm good, yes, I'm good. Your family owns that farm, then?" Sarah pointed at the whitewashed building.

"Yes, we do. It's ours. It's still ours, yes."

Still?

"What are you doing up here anyway?" Angela continued.

"We are . . . hill walking. Yes. This is my cousin, Harry. He's just arrived from London."

"Come in for a cup of coffee. My mum and my sister are home. Remember Lorna?"

"Yes, yes, of course." Lorna was Angela's sister, two years older than them. She was blind since birth. "And you're all fine, yes?"

"Yes, of course we're fine, why shouldn't we be?" Angela laughed.

Sarah and Harry exchanged a look. Harry shrugged his shoulders. They walked together down the hill, towards Hillside.

"Come in."

"Angela, I need to talk to you. There's something important I need to tell you," Sarah began, wondering how on earth she was going to explain the whole thing.

"Mum, she's arrived!" Angela interrupted her.

She's arrived?

Something registered in Sarah's mind. Something not right. Angela's mum walked out into the hall. "Hello, Sarah. Remember me? Can I get you anything? A cup of tea? Ice cream?" She seemed nervous.

"Sarah," whispered Harry.

"I know," Sarah replied. *Something is very, very wrong.*

"Come in, come into the living room."

"Actually, we have to go."

"So soon? You *can't*." Angela was just behind them, blocking the way.

"Sarah, is that you?" Lorna had appeared on top of the stairs. Her unseeing eyes were looking straight ahead. She was holding on to the banister.

"Lorna? Yes, it's me, Sarah Midnight."

"Sarah, you need to go . . . you need to run."

"Lorna!" Angela scolded her. "Ignore her. Come and sit down."

"Sarah, run! Listen to me, run!"

"Lorna!" Angela ran up the stairs and pushed her sister away. They disappeared from view. Sarah could hear their urgent voices, whispering.

"We really need to go now," intervened Harry, taking Sarah by her arm.

"I'm so sorry, but you really can't." Angela's mum was nearly pleading. "We were going to lose everything. With my husband gone, and Lorna like this, we needed the money desperately."

"She's here," they heard Angela saying from upstairs, and caught a glimpse of her on the landing, talking on a mobile phone.

"Who was that, Angela?" asked Harry calmly.

"Someone called Katy. They said that sooner or later Sarah would turn up here. All we had to do was get her in the house." Angela's eyes were wide. "They paid all our debts . . . I'm so sorry . . ."

"They're going to kill her! How could you!" shrieked Lorna, appearing behind her.

"Katy? Katy McHarg?" pressed Harry.

Sarah swallowed.

"Yes. Katy McHarg. Of course they're not going to kill Sarah! They just need to get the stuff back, the stuff her parents stole! And then they'll let you go," she added, looking at Sarah pleadingly. She was desperately trying to hold on to the lies she'd been told, but it was beginning to dawn on her that there was more.

"My parents didn't steal anything, Angela. Katy lied to you. Lorna is right. They want to kill me."

Angela's mum started shaking her head. "Oh my God, what have we done? It can't be!"

"I *saw* the thing that came with Katy . . . the way I see things before they happen. That horrible *thing,* it's up on the hill! I *knew* they were lying. I knew they were dangerous, I told you!" Lorna was distraught.

"I've heard enough." Harry ran to the top of the stairs, and before she could slip away, he touched Angela between her eyes. She fell down the stairs, and lay in a heap at the bottom. Lorna screamed.

"What have you done to her?" shouted Angela's mum, crouching beside her daughter.

"She's just asleep. And so are you," he said, running down

the stairs and touching the woman between her eyes. Angela and her mum lay one on top of the other on the stone floor.

"And be thankful I have no time to teach you a lesson," Harry added, and Sarah shivered. She knew he meant it.

"What's going on? What are you doing?" Lorna had come down the stairs, slowly, her eyes wide with fear.

"It's OK, Lorna. I sent them to sleep. They'll wake up in a few hours. Now lock yourself in, do you hear me? Don't let anyone in. Especially Katy McHarg. We need to go."

"It's on the hill, Sarah, don't go there!" they heard Lorna shouting as they were running out, her desperate voice trailing away in the distance.

"Those cows!" whispered Sarah.

"I knew it was the Valaya!"

"I had to help Angela."

"You have to toughen up, that's what you need to do. No more stunts like this. No more helping people who come in dreams, do you understand?"

"Let's go." Sarah walked on, her cheeks scarlet. *I'd do it again.*

They barely had time to take a step towards the hill before the demon answered Katy's call. A hand came out of the heather right in front of them, then another one. Then a head.

Sarah started shaking. She flexed her hands.

"Harry . . ."

"I'm here. I'm here." Harry's *sgian-dubh* was ready.

I'll never get used to all this. How did my parents do it for so long? How did they not lose their minds?

247

Sarah saw that the demon had no irises; its eyes were completely white. It was blind, like Lorna. The demon lifted itself out, faltering, then it found its balance.

"Who are you?" asked Sarah.

"What are you *doing*?" Harry was shocked. She was *talking* to that creature!

The demon was shocked too. It wasn't expecting to be spoken to.

"Katy . . . Soil," it said with a rasping voice. *It can speak!* thought Harry. *It must be something between a Feral and a Sentient . . . some sort of missing link.*

"You're Katy's demon, and you come from the soil," repeated Sarah.

The demon raised his head and sniffed the air. "Yes."

"She asked you to kill me."

"Bring Midnight."

"Not kill?"

That was too much elaborating for the soil demon. It jumped towards her, and she thought she could easily avoid it, as it was blind, but it predicted her move somehow, and jumped on her. They fell on the heather, and Sarah's breath was knocked out of her in the fall.

"Back soil," the creature rasped. Harry was already on it, the *sgian-dubh* in his hand, ready to start tracing the runes that would stop the demon in its tracks.

"Wait! Harry, wait!" Sarah screamed. "*Back soil.* You need to go back to the soil. You don't need to do this." Sarah was trying desperately to avoid killing, this time.

"Sarah, for God's sake!" shouted Harry, and the spell he was weaving was broken. The demon froze. For a second.

And then it was too late. It had its teeth into Sarah, and she wailed in pain. Harry threw himself on the demon, stabbing it time and time again, all over its back. But that didn't seem to stop it. It freed itself, shaking Harry away.

Harry fell on his back, and Sarah lay on the ground, holding her mangled arm. The demon had taken a whole chunk off her shoulder, and her jacket was drenched in blood.

With a huge effort Harry gathered the threads of his concentration, and started tracing his secret symbols again, whispering to himself. The soil demon faltered, but didn't fall; it charged Sarah again. She whimpered and put up her bloodied hands, feeling them warming up. The demon went to bite her again.

"No!" she screamed, and grabbed its face. The demon sank its fangs into her hand, but at the contact with Sarah's hand its skin started weeping. Just one more instant with its mouth against Sarah's hand, and the demon would turn into water. Sarah tried to stay still, with the creature's teeth tearing into her flesh . . . a second more, just a second more . . . but the pain was more than she could bear. She bit her lip not to cry out, arching her body in agony.

Harry couldn't take it any more; he couldn't stand to see her suffer. He closed his eyes and his movements became sharper, angrier. The soil demon howled and let go of Sarah, who curled herself up, holding her hand and trembling in pain.

Harry's *sgian-dubh* had a life of its own, and his whispers had become words, secret words that Sarah had never heard before. The demon shuddered and a red stain appeared on his chest – a bleeding wound. But it stayed on its feet, and in a monstrous effort, it threw itself on Harry, grabbing him by the shoulders. The *sgian-dubh* fell on the grass. Harry and the soil demon were locked together, and the demon started sinking into the earth, trying to drag Harry underground.

But Sarah had got up, and she was upon them. Seeing Harry sinking underground filled her with blind terror. She screamed with all her might. Harry's legs were now completely out of sight, and he was trying to hold on to the grass. His face was nearly as white as the creature's. Sarah grabbed the soil demon by its hair. She felt the blackwater invade her, move from her head to her chest and her arms, and down into her hands. The demon's skin started weeping again.

The demon howled in pain, and let go of Harry. Summoning all its strength, the demon propelled itself underground, disappearing from view.

"Harry!" Sarah took him by the arm with her one good hand, desperately pulling him out.

"It's gone. The bloody thing has gone!" Harry was panting and covered in mud.

"It's somewhere beneath us. It'll be back . . ."

"We need to *call* it back. We need to destroy it."

"But how?"

At that moment a thud resounded from the farm. The door opened violently, so violently that it was taken from its hinges. It all happened in an instant: the soil demon appeared, framed in the doorstep. It was dragging something behind it – a body. A red-haired girl.

Angela, still unconscious.

"No," whispered Sarah.

As soon as the demon stood on soil it started sinking into the earth, carrying Angela with it. It had all been so quick, so quiet, that Harry and Sarah couldn't move, couldn't scream.

Angela's hands lingered on the surface for a few seconds. Sarah shook herself and ran to her, desperately reaching towards Angela's hands. She managed to hold on to Angela's fingers for an instant, before they disappeared too. Sarah started digging the ground with her bare hands, sobbing and calling Angela's name. Harry pulled her back, and held her tight.

"Sarah. Sarah. Look at me."

"Angela! Angela!"

"Sarah! Listen!" Harry took her by the shoulders and shook her roughly. "It's coming back. Do you understand? It's coming back for us. We need to be ready."

"Yes. Yes."

"Stand up. Come on."

They stood up, holding on to each other. Sarah's wounded shoulder and hand were bleeding profusely. She was shaking in shock and pain.

"It's coming. Can you feel it?" whispered Harry. The ground beneath their feet had started to vibrate.

"Yes. I'm ready." Sarah raised her hands.

And then it was on them. The demon's hands sprouted from the soil, clawing, trying to grab their ankles.

"Take his hands, I'll hold you!" Harry wrapped his arms around Sarah's waist, so that if the demon tried it would have both of them to contend with. Sarah held on to those cold, white fingers. A low growl resounded from under the earth, dimmed by the soil. The demon's skin started weeping.

A mop of black hair appeared, and two blind, staring eyes. The demon tried to pull itself out, but Sarah was clutching its hands, hurting it, burning it. Another growl, and Sarah answered with a yell that was rage itself, crouching over the demon's hands like a lioness devouring her prey. In a few seconds, all that was left of the creature was a patch of black and red grass.

Sarah didn't utter a word throughout the journey back. She was still and silent. Harry cleaned her wounds and dressed them. He helped her wash and change, and gave her some sugary tea for the shock. He held her, he spoke to her, he stroked her hair. Nothing. She wouldn't move, she wouldn't speak.

Then, suddenly, she got up from the sofa where Harry had settled her, and walked upstairs to her parents' room.

Without warning, without a word, she started wrecking the place with a fury Harry had never seen in anyone but himself. Shadow was looking on, terrified, but too loyal to leave. Harry felt that it would have been wrong, very wrong, to stop her. He stood by, making sure she wouldn't hurt herself.

Sarah threw everything on the floor, all the perfume bottles on her mother's dressing table, all their photographs. She broke everything she could break; she opened the wardrobes and pulled everything out; she took the pictures from the walls and threw them out of the window. She grabbed a chair and threw it against her mother's mirror, smashing it into a thousand little pieces.

Next, Sarah ran down into the kitchen. Her dream diary, her book of fear, was still on the table. Black, huge, thick with nightmares.

I hate it.

She grabbed it and took it to the living room. She lit the fire, quickly, efficiently, and kneeled in front of the flames. She started ripping the pages of the diary and thrust them into the fire one by one, with Harry looking on, distraught, but still and silent. He could see fresh, red blood seeping from the bandage on Sarah's hand.

Soon all that was left of the diary was the leather cover with her name in silver letters. The dream diary her parents had given her, that they used like some sort of sick manual, the recording of four years of terror, was gone.

Her parents knew they were in danger – they'd always been in danger, but those last few months, especially so. Still, they hadn't taught her anything that would help her survive. They'd been too busy hunting to tell her what was going on, to prepare her for what was coming. Did they not think that they had to teach her, to show her, to make her strong? Did they not care?

Burying a magical diary in the garden. Too little, too late. Anne could have given Sarah the only thing she needed instead – her time. They never had any time for her. Except when she'd had a dream, and they needed to know what she'd seen. They never saw her, they never *looked*. Anne had said that the spells were too dangerous, that she wasn't ready to learn – and put her in even more danger by not teaching her.

Sarah sighed, suddenly exhausted. The flames had consumed the diary. All that was left was a mound of ash in the fireplace; the leather cover had become an empty shell.

She stood up, pale as the moon.

She was free.

She grabbed the empty cover, and walked out of the house.

"Sarah." Harry followed her. She seemed calm, but he didn't think it was the time to leave her alone. They walked down the hill to Cross Street and past the railway bridge.

"Where are we going?" whispered Harry. Sarah didn't reply, but walked on under the iron arch and into the small park. Suddenly Harry realized what she was going to do. He followed her along the path, onto the grass, and down the slope that led to the river. He watched her throwing the leather cover into the water, with all her strength, so that it wouldn't get stuck among the reeds. It made an arc across the air, and fell in the river with hardly a splash, hardly a ripple.

Sarah stood very close to Harry, and took his hand, without looking at him, without speaking. He held her hand tight, and they watched what was left of the diary float away in the dark waters.

Much later on, Sarah decided that Harry's chest was the only place to be, and let him hold her through the night, until dawn broke. He lay still, afraid of even breathing, in case it all got too much for him. He followed her profile with his eyes, wishing that eyes could touch – her lovely face, the curve of her breasts, her hips, the gentle landscape of her body. He held her wounded hand against his chest.

I'm not your cousin. I'm not a Midnight. I'm not one of your cursed family.

"I'm a man who's barely older than you. And I'm in love with you," he whispered when he was sure she was asleep.

Only Shadow, the keeper of their secrets, heard him.

Sarah woke up exhausted, but feeling like a weight had been taken off her chest. She opened her eyes, and the first thing she saw was Harry's shoulder. She was wrapped around him, curled up against him – their limbs entwined as if belonging to one body, her hair all over him like seaweed on a rock.

She had to get up, she knew that, but one moment, just one more moment against him.

"Three to go," she said quietly, quietly in his ear. He woke up with her warm breath on his neck, and trembled, rigid with the effort to lie still and not turn around and hold her in his arms. A few seconds of torture, a few seconds of inhaling her just-awake scent and feeling her soft hair on his arm, and she was gone.

26
In My Blood

If I could turn to fire
I know what would burn first

Sarah freed herself from Harry's arms, gently, believing that he was still asleep, and tiptoed to the window.

She opened it quietly and let the air in. She stood there, inhaling deeply, her eyes closed. Her chest wasn't tight any more; she couldn't feel that terrible weight over her lungs that stopped them from filling with air. She didn't have to try desperately to breathe, so that she'd end up hyperventilating, her heart racing, sure that this time she'd suffocate.

She felt awful about having destroyed her parents' room, and even worse about having burned her dream diary – but now she could finally breathe. The anger that had weighed on her since her parents had died – no, the anger that had weighed on her for years; that burning, bitter, secret anger that she'd felt every single time they'd left her alone – had gone.

Harry followed her with his gaze as she got up – the grace and beauty of her body like a stab through the heart.

"Morning," he whispered.

Sarah was suddenly aware of how raw, how intimate a moment that was, and crossed her arms. She wanted to get dressed. She wanted him out of her bed. She wasn't ready.

"I'll make you a cup of coffee." She grabbed her jumper and wrapped it around her.

"Thank you. How's your shoulder? And your hand?"

"Bloody sore."

"I'm sorry."

"That's how it goes, Harry. I won't be a minute." She went for the door, then turned around. "I have something to do this morning."

"Please, don't start cleaning, Sarah. I can't stand to see you like that."

"No, I won't. I mean, I'm going to have to clean up the mess in my parents' room, sooner or later. But it's not what I need to do now."

"I'll sort your parents' room for you."

Sarah thought about it for a minute.

"Thank you."

Sarah made some coffee, went down to the basement, and closed the door behind her. She stood in front of her mothers' things and surveyed them, a determined expression on her face. She was going to study Anne's diary, and work out for herself everything her mother hadn't told her, or written down.

She took a deep, free breath, and sat at the table, the diary in front of her. She started going through all the spells Anne had written, one by one, locating the right equipment for each one, learning invocations, rehearsing them. After the strange results they'd had with the sapphire's song, she knew that those spells would work in weird, unexpected ways. Some were very scary, they even needed human blood to work – and they made her think of what her ancestors might have done, in ancient times. *Or not so ancient*, she thought with a shiver. The formidable Midnight women. She wished she'd known more about them. She wished she'd had time to get to know her grandmother better. Morag had died when Sarah was just seven; drowned after stumbling into the sea on a misty night, at their house on Islay. Her things were still there.

I need to go to Islay. When all this is finished, that's where I'll go.

They used to go to Islay as often as they could, to the stately home that had belonged to the Midnights for countless generations. Sarah loved going there; she loved the smell of the sea and the salty wind in her hair. When she was a child she used to dream of living on Islay, to be able to sit on the beach and listen to the sea every day, for hours. They hadn't gone there for over two years. Her parents had said that it was because the house was in need of repairs, but now she suspected it was because of the Valaya being after them.

Sarah thought of her grandparents' enormous library, shelf after shelf of books, floor to ceiling. Maybe she'd find some help there. Maybe she could find the magical knowledge she needed, learn more about the demon world – learn more about Mairead, the aunt she didn't know she'd had.

Sarah worked intensely for hours. After a while, Harry put his head round the door.

"I need to go out for a bit, but I can't leave you here alone, just in case. Can you come with me? We won't be long, and then you can go back to your spells."

"Sure." She really didn't want to stop, but she knew that it must be something important, or he wouldn't have asked.

"Sorry, it's just that I have this craving for Indian food. I must have a lamb biryani right now; we'll only be a minute."

"*What?* You interrupt my work because you want a lamb biryani?"

"Just winding you up."

"I hope so," she growled.

"It's a Starbucks I need."

"Harry, I'm warning you . . ."

"OK, OK sorry. We're going to British Home Stores, I'll tell you later what it's for. We might go to Starbucks anyway, you know? For a hazelnut latte?"

"How do you know . . . Oh, no point in asking."

Harry smiled, one of his dimply smiles.

They got into the car. "Can't wait to have my driving licence."

"You can take your mum and dad's Land Rover; it's a brilliant car, very powerful."

Sarah frowned. "No, I hate it," she said passionately. Harry didn't ask for details. He sensed that she must have some bad memories tied to that car, and didn't want to upset her.

"You can use this one, if you want."

"Thanks. By the way, Siobhan wanted driving lessons."

Harry laughed. "I'm not surprised! I saw the way she was looking at me. That girl is priceless . . ."

"A lot of guys would pay to be in your shoes, you know. She's very popular."

"No wonder, she's very pretty," Harry conceded.

Sarah felt cold. "Do you think so?" She was resolutely looking out of the window.

"No," he laughed. "I mean yes, but she's too . . . pink and shiny for me. And blond."

"Right. And . . . what was Mary Anne like?"

"She was cool."

"That's all?"

"Well, she was tough. A good laugh. I cared for her, we were good friends. Anyway, tell Siobhan that my driving lessons are just for you," he added with a wink, changing the subject.

"I'll be eighteen. You won't need to live with me any more."

Harry's smile vanished. Sarah realized what she'd just said.

"Of course," said Harry, trying to sound flippant.

Stay, she would have liked to say. But why would he have wanted to?

She looked at Harry from under her lashes. His expression was unreadable, his clear eyes fixed on the road.

They were quiet for the rest of the journey.

"Can you wait for me outside?" Harry asked as they were about to go into the shop.

"Sure." Sarah strolled up and down, window shopping, and after twenty minutes Harry came out, holding a British Home Stores bag that clanked as he walked.

"What is that?"

"Never you mind. So do you want that latte?"

"OK then." She knew she had to get back to her work, but she loved the idea of sitting with Harry in peace, for a while.

They sat on the brown sofas. Harry closed his eyes.

"God, I haven't slept a wink. In case you freaked out again."
I couldn't relax, lying beside you — I didn't trust myself.

"Sorry."

"That's OK. It was horrible." He touched her injured shoulder softly.

"Yes. It's the first time I've been really hurt. My mum and dad didn't get hurt often, but when they did they had a job of hiding it. My dad told me that our grandfather had both his legs broken, once."

"Yes, I'd heard that," he lied.

"It was a shock. When it bit me."

"I noticed."

Sarah half-smiled. Incredible, that he could make jokes about something that hurt her so deeply, and still make her smile.

"At least I'm still alive," she said, shivering at the thought of what had happened to Angela.

Harry guessed her thoughts. "She was on their side," he said coolly. Sarah expected him to be like that.

"She was deceived."

"They won't mess with you again, that's for sure. Shall we go?"

Sarah looked at him and his cold eyes, wondering how someone could be so dangerous, and so kind, all at the same time.

"Come and see . . ."

Sarah walked into her parents' room. The clothes had been picked up, the million pieces from the broken mirror had been hoovered up, and the whole place had been restored to order.

Sarah's eyes fell on the dressing table. The photograph display was back in its place. Harry had replaced all the broken frames.

That's what he'd gone to British Home Stores for.

She looked at the photographs, one by one. Anne and James on their wedding day; a little Sarah on the beach; Morag and Hamish Midnight standing gravely in front of their Islay mansion, and another one of Sarah with her cello, after the concert for schools in the Queen's Hall.

"Thank you," she murmured, and she couldn't say any more.

This is the time. This is the time I kiss her.

I can't.

She slipped her hand in his, and no more words were needed.

Harry was in his room, standing in front of the open window. The night was dark and quiet, a restful place to be. He was readying himself to keep a promise.

He raised his hand, and made a quick gesture with his fingers.

Somewhere, Sheila Douglas fell asleep. She happened to be on her way home from the clinic.

Unbeknown to Harry, that was the merciful way – because the fire had already started burning in her head.

27
The White Swan

You taught me the meaning of sacrifice
Bitter consolation
For the loss of you

Castelmonte

Elodie

I have to remind myself every day why I'm doing this, why I accepted to be sent here. Why, the day I saw a vision of Castelmonte's red roofs and white-topped mountains appear in my bathroom mirror, as Harry was trying to convince me we'd meet again soon, I went away without protesting.

I know that Harry is dead. He was dead already when I left, still walking and speaking and still breathing, but he was dead.

I must protect Aiko. Other heirs might be sent here as well, and they'll need my help too. But to be holed up here, away from the battle, waiting for *them* to come for us . . . it's like slow torture; it's like being tied down to a chair while everyone around you is fighting and dying, while you're somehow, miraculously, saved.

Harry died, and I was saved.

I wish it had been the other way round.

Castelmonte is beautiful in the autumn light, the sun still shining even if summer is long gone. People live slowly here, alternating between their homes, the little grocery shop, the bar where men go to play cards and drink red wine, and their orchards and vineyards. It's an idyllic life that Harry would have loved.

We used to talk about settling down, having children. One day. I look at the olive-skinned boys and girls running in the village square, and I imagine a little blond boy with the Midnight eyes, running around with them.

But that will never happen, because Harry will not come back.

Widows should be old, shouldn't they? They should be old ladies dressed in cardigans and tweed skirts, getting together for tea and biscuits. They should have knitting bags and reading glasses.

And look at me. The mirror in my room – the attic room with the window that frames a snapshot of the Alps – shows a young girl in jeans, a camisole and trainers, long blond hair around a tired face, and eyes full of sorrow. I might feel like a widow, but I don't *look* like one.

That's because I shouldn't be; it's all been a mistake, a terrible mistake. A trick of fate.

Marina Frison is my age, and she's about to get married. That's the way it should be. She has a kind smile and an infectious laugh, and the sunny demeanour of someone who never suffered greatly. She'll make a great wife, and a great mother.

Marina's company fills my days. Her chat and laughter make everything look a little less dark, a little less hopeless. Aiko adores her, and I adore them both.

Aiko is small for her age. She's three, but you might think she's barely two – tiny, with a silky black bob and almond eyes, and chubby little hands. She's too young to fully realize what happened, that her whole family has been exterminated and that she'll never see her parents again. Still, there's something solemn about her, something wise, even. Something deep and knowing in her eyes, a memory of sadness, of loss.

Marina and Aiko have created a bond so loving, so intense that it is heartbreaking to witness, surrounded by all this death and danger. Aiko thinks of the Frisons as her family, and she and Marina behave as a mother and daughter. I watch them cuddling on the rocking chair, and I feel afraid, so afraid for them.

Marina looks at me anxiously, as if seeing the sorrow in my eyes pains her greatly. One day, it just came out. I told her that my husband is dead, that the love of my life is dead. That I can never love again.

"You don't know that," she said in her Italian sing-song accent, cradling Aiko on her lap. "Only the sky knows that," she added, paraphrasing an expression they have in these mountains, one that I've often heard: Our lives are in the hands of the heavens.

The next day, Marina brought home a pomegranate from the market. She cut it in two, and spooned out some juicy blood-red seeds.

"Have this. They're good for you." She handed me the spoon, and I tasted the fragrant, slightly sour taste of the pomegranate.

"And now . . ." She looked at me with knowing eyes, and gathered the remains of the pomegranate. She threw them into the wood stove and shut the steel door. I had no idea what she was doing.

After a couple of minutes, she opened the little door and poked in it with the fire tongs. She grasped something with the tongs, and carefully took it out. It was the pomegranate, perfect, intact, as if it had never been in the fire.

"You'll love again," she said, and put her olive-skinned, strong hand on mine.

I don't believe her, of course. But it felt good to hear words of hope, as if my life weren't over, as if there were still a future for me.

28
Shadows

The Earth turns
Stars are born
And a million hearts are broken

Walking up the stairs to John Burton's flat in Craigmillar on a cold autumn afternoon, you could have easily forgotten how beautiful Edinburgh is.

There was nothing beautiful about that rundown tower block and its dark, dirty stairs. From the window of each flight of stairs Sarah could see scores of grey buildings just like that one, with patches of sparse grass between each other. She wondered what kind of life she would have lived, had she been born there. Still better than the curse of the dreams, that's for sure – but such a tough existence.

She thought of her lovely sandstone house, and the oak trees of her garden. Life could be so unfair, and destiny such a lottery of fortune. She looked around at the walls full of angry graffiti, and longed to be home. Had she grown up in that estate she would have had an entirely different kind of demon to worry about.

Harry and Sarah climbed up three floors – Sarah was panting by the end of it, Harry had ran all the way and wasn't even out of breath – and knocked on a faded, scratched blue door. The steel number had been ripped off, and only a pale silhouette of it remained, a greyish little number nine.

A tired-looking woman opened the door. She had striking brown eyes, and a worn-out face. She looked older than her years, deep lines etched on her forehead and around her mouth.

"My name is Harry Midnight. I'm looking for John Burton."

"He's not here." The woman sounded like she smoked a few packets a day.

"We can wait."

"He won't be back. He moved."

Harry knew she was lying. Mike had checked the CCTV cameras dotted around the place. John was there earlier that morning. Right at that moment they heard the entrance door slam. They looked down the three flights of stairs. A man was coming up.

"Laura?" he had caught a glimpse of her standing in the dirty landing.

"John, go! They're here!" shouted the woman.

The man froze, and started running down the stairs again. Harry threw himself down after him, leaving Sarah standing in the landing beside the white-faced woman.

"We have nothing, OK? We can't pay!" the woman shouted at Sarah, her face contorted with distress.

"We're not . . . we don't want any money," Sarah said quickly. She felt desperately sorry for her, but she had no time to explain. She ran after Harry, down the three flights of stairs. As she got out of the building, she immediately saw John lying on the ground, with Harry sitting on his chest. A rivulet of blood was running out of John's nose. Sarah felt sick.

"Where is it? Where the hell is your demon?"

"I've worked on this for years. You won't talk me out of it."

Sarah noticed how thin he was, how sallow his skin looked in the light of day.

"Oh, I'm not going to *talk*, John. I'm going to move on to something else in a minute."

"Harry! Someone will call the police! Look around you!" Sarah gestured at the hundreds of windows in the high towers around them, looking down like hollow eyes. Harry grabbed John by the chest, grudgingly, and lifted him up.

"You don't understand. I needed a way out of this rut."

"Right. You've been learning black magic and evoking demons as a way out of here. Very sensible," Harry spat.

"I had no choice."

"No choice but to become part of the Valaya? Are you crazy?" Harry exclaimed. And then he stopped, abruptly.

He'd noticed his bloodshot eyes, his restless hands, the skin stretched on his cheekbones. The bruises on his arms, the face strangely elongated.

Heroin had shaped his face, and claimed John for her own.

That's what he's trying to pay for. Something as deadly as the Surari, but that takes a lot longer to kill you.

Sarah looked at John's troubled eyes. She could see it too, how he had chosen a slow, painful death for himself – and a life not worth living. *But there is a way out, for him. Unlike me, he has a choice.*

"I'm sorry," she said, unexpectedly. "You don't have to live like this." Sarah put a hand on his arm. Harry had to stop himself from seizing her arm and dragging her away from John. He hated her touching that pathetic, broken man. He thought that John didn't deserve her sympathy. He thought he'd brought all that on himself. He could not imagine how skilled, how sharp the people who had preyed on John were, who gave him the curse – they'd bite you once, turn you into one of them, and you were lost. Harry couldn't know how easy, how quick it had been for John to fall into the abyss – and how painful it had been trying to climb out, over and over again, and never succeeding. One day he was a young man with a job and a girlfriend – the next day he was one of the walking dead. He had managed to keep his job and his flat by turning his addiction into a routine – by conquering the pain he was in, constantly. But not for much longer. Heroin was taking over. He'd thought that Catherine Hollow had offered him salvation – he hadn't realized it meant becoming a murderer. And wrong choice after wrong choice, he realized he had sold his soul.

John Burton wasn't like the rest of the Valaya. Not in his heart.

He looked Sarah in the eye, for the first time. For a second he looked like a little boy. "It's too late. I can't control the demon. I can't call it back."

Sarah nodded slowly, her hope of not having to face another fight shattered.

"I'm sorry," it was his turn to say.

"If I survive I'll look for you, I promise. I'll help you," she whispered.

John shook his head. "You won't survive." Despair took him, and left nothing of him. He knew his soul was lost.

Sarah and Harry walked towards the car in silence. His demons would claim him soon enough.

"Poor man. And his girlfriend too."

"Yes, sure. And what about poor us?" Harry's voice was steely.

"At least we didn't do it to ourselves. We didn't destroy our own lives."

Harry stopped suddenly. He'd seen something out of the corner of his eye. Something that wasn't supposed to be there.

"Sarah."

"Yes?"

"I think the demon is here."

"Where?"

Harry took her by the hand and turned her around, gently, towards one of the grey buildings around them.

"Up there," he whispered. Sarah squeezed Harry's hand. She could feel his heart thumping, the blood flowing beneath the thin skin in his wrist. She followed his gaze up to a building beside them – first floor, a balcony with a broken chair; second floor, some washing left out in the drizzle; third floor, an empty balcony, but for a shadow against the whitewashed wall.

A shadow without a body.

Sarah swallowed and squeezed Harry's hand tighter. They both froze, not sure what to do. How do you kill a shadow?

Right at that moment a young man passed by, wearing a tracksuit and a baseball cap. He was walking fast, swaggering, trying to be cocky. He was thin and pale, like John.

The shadow leaped off the balcony, and landed right in front of him.

"What the hell . . . ?"

"Run!" Harry tried to call, but the guy was rooted to the spot, overwhelmed by horror and surprise. Harry and Sarah were only a few yards from him, but they couldn't reach him in time.

The shadow walked into him, and he was no more.

It was just like that. As quick and undramatic as that. No pleading, no blood, no dying screams. Not even a sigh.

The shadow had taken him, and there was nothing left.

Nearly nothing. A little black puddle was left on the pavement. A puddle that started to move, and take shape. The puddle quivered and then stood up. It wasn't liquid, Sarah realized. It was the shadow itself. The man in the baseball cap.

Like in a grotesque mime, the newly created shadow looked at its arms, then down at its legs, and seemed contorted with despair. It started running around, as if asking for help, and disappeared from view. Harry and Sarah looked on in horror.

"Well, that was something else." Harry murmured. Sarah clamped her hand on her mouth. She thought she'd never been so shocked in her whole life.

The demon-shadow walked towards them. It was as if it had decided to show them what it could do, and now it would be their turn. Sarah raised her hands, and felt them burning. Harry took out his *sgian-dubh*, and started whispering.

The shadow took a sprint towards them. Sarah flexed her hands, readying herself. Suddenly she felt something grab her shoulders and throw her on the ground. A wiry woman, punching her face and chest, holding her down. *John's girlfriend?*

Sarah had been taken by surprise, and she was trying to free herself, when Harry went for the woman with his *sgian-dubh*.

"Harry, no!" pleaded Sarah, trying in vain to get back on her feet. *We can't kill human beings.* But that wasn't what Harry had in mind. He raised the *sgian-dubh*, and started tracing signs in the air . . . Laura fell, unconscious, and buried Sarah under her weight.

The shadow had reached them by then, and Sarah could see its black shape right in front of her. She was still lying on the pavement, Laura's unconscious body heavy on her. Harry grabbed Laura and threw her roughly aside, and Sarah managed to slip from under her, taking Harry's hands to get up as quickly as she could.

It was nearly too late.

The shadow was right there before them, its arms out to touch them both. In a fraction of a second Sarah and Harry would become shadows themselves, condemned to a grey half-life forever . . . but just as the shadow was about to touch them something distracted it and made it turn around. Someone had called its attention. It was John. He was standing behind them, and was tracing signs in the air with both his hands. It was some kind of call, and they could see that the shadow had answered. But it wasn't an order to attack Sarah, like they'd thought – it was something else entirely.

John let his arms fall by his sides, and the shadow walked towards him. He stood there, eyes closed, wanting it, wanting it desperately. He sighed as the shadow swallowed him too, and it was a sigh of relief.

John asked it to do that, thought Sarah in horror.

The demon shadow turned around again, but Sarah was ready. Her hands were burning so hard they were sore – all she had to do was put them out, towards the immaterial being, and watch the black silhouette become liquid and fall on the ground with a swoosh. Beside it, another black puddle: John's shadow, slowly taking shape. Sarah's eyes filled with tears as she watched John's shadow stand up and look at itself.

What was left of John stood briefly in front of them, and then he went to crouch down beside his girlfriend. But she was slowly opening her eyes, and John didn't want to be seen. He ran away, before she could see what had become of him.

Sarah watched the shadow without a body disappear across the threadbare grass, over the motorway bridge, and on to the road, where car after car went through it without hurting it, without touching it.

He'll never die, thought Sarah, and shuddered.

"What happened? Where's John? Why are you still alive?" Laura struggled to get up.

Sarah couldn't reply. How could she tell her what had happened to John? Before Sarah could gather her thoughts, Harry was on Laura like a flash. He threw her down again with a brutality that shocked Sarah. He kneeled beside the woman, holding her down by the shoulders.

"Harry, let's go," pleaded Sarah.

"Not before I'm finished."

"Harry, what . . . ? No!"

She couldn't stop him. He'd taken the knife to Laura's face. The woman screamed and held her left cheek, blood trickling through her hands.

"Stay away from Sarah. Never, never touch her again," hissed Harry. He walked away from her, as if she were nothing – as if she weren't a desperate woman lying hurt on the ground. Drained by poverty, defeated by addiction, her heart and soul emptied bit by bit, since the day she last was happy, she last had pride. Sarah wanted to help her up – she took a step towards her – but the look in her eyes made Sarah stop and freeze. It was hatred, deep, absolute hatred, well beyond Sarah, well beyond John and his demons, reaching all the way back to a little girl who grew up too fast, who was made to grow up when she shouldn't have. Sarah felt a knot in her throat as their eyes met. *I suffered too*, she wanted to say, but she would not put herself in harm's way a second time.

Sarah was ready to walk away, when her mind registered something, something that wasn't right. The whole scene wasn't right. She surveyed the ground around them. No blackwater anywhere. The pavement was bone dry. Still, her hands were wet . . .

Goosebumps covered Sarah's arms, and the hair at the back of her neck stood up. *Something is very, very wrong*. But she couldn't figure out what.

After what he'd done to John's girlfriend, Sarah couldn't look Harry in the eye throughout the journey back. He'd cut her face. *What kind of a man is he? Who is he?*

Harry was looking resolutely at the road. To ease the silence, heavy on them like rain clouds, he switched on the radio. They sat in deep thought, listening idly to the flow of chatting and music. A few minutes later, an announcement caught their attention.

"The victim of yesterday's crash on the M11 has been named. Ms Sheila Douglas, a well known plastic surgeon from Aberdeen, with a thriving clinic in Edinburgh, died last night as a result of the collision of her car, a Mini, with a truck. The truck driver, Manuel Alvarado, from Madrid, was unharmed."

Sarah gasped. She couldn't believe what she'd just heard.

"You killed her." Both her hands were on her chest, as she was trying to take a breath that just wouldn't come.

"Looks like it," answered Harry, his voice even.

Sarah felt like she was swallowing nails.

"I'm going to practise for a bit," she said as soon as they got home, and ran upstairs. She didn't want to see Harry for a while.

Harry didn't reply. He went to the kitchen, and started making himself a double espresso. He knew he had shocked her. He knew that she thought what he'd done to Laura was wrong. But Laura had tried to kill Sarah. She would have gladly given Sarah to the demon-shadow. She deserved to be taught a lesson.

Really, Sarah was so naive! Where had she been all those years, while her parents went hunting? It's like they had sheltered her from the realities of life, *their* life, which was very, very different from most people's. She seemed to see her parents as these idealistic superheroes who always did what was right and never strayed. How wrong she was. The real Harry knew better than that. He had told him how ruthless his uncle and Anne could be. They'd *had* to be.

But Sarah was from different stock. Did she share their blood at all? Because he, Sean, seemed more of a Midnight than she did.

Sarah hated violence.

Sarah couldn't bear to touch a gun.

Sarah was in the habit of trying to *negotiate* with demons!

Her grandmother would have been shocked to have a granddaughter like Sarah. Morag Midnight was the toughest of the lot. The real Harry had told him so much about Morag. He would have loved to meet her. She was a warrior, an Amazon – ruthless, hard, even cruel at times.

Mairead Midnight had been different, though . . .

Sean sat at the table with his coffee, and tried to remember what the real Harry had said about Mairead. He'd said that she was a shy little girl, constantly frightened. That she had a lovely voice, and she enjoyed singing. Morag had taught her the hunting spells, but she didn't like doing them – she preferred the gentler spells, the protection charms, the potions, the invocations. Now that he thought about it, Mairead sounded spookily similar to Sarah. *It's such a shame that she'd died – maybe Sarah would have had someone to lean on now, someone to help her through all this madness . . .*

The real Harry hadn't gone into details about Mairead's death. He was just a baby when Mairead died; it was Stewart who'd told him all that he knew about her. He had just said that she was killed, and that it had something to do with water. She had drowned, maybe. Like Morag. From Stewart to Harry, from Harry to Sean, the stories about Mairead Midnight were losing details and becoming more and more threadbare.

"Hello! Anyone home?"

Harry jumped up and went into the hall. He could hear Sarah playing her cello upstairs, a haunting, beautiful sound. Before opening the door Harry checked he had his *sgian-dubh*.

"Yes? Oh, Bryony. Hello." *What is she doing here? Does she have a death wish?*

"Hi Harry. Is this a bad time?" Bryony had noticed the lack of enthusiasm in his voice.

"Yes. Sarah is practising – you know she has the audition in a month, and with all that's been happening . . . Maybe another time," he said ruthlessly. He liked Bryony, but he had no choice. He couldn't risk her life, he couldn't allow anyone else to share the danger they were in. He was about to close the door when a tall, lanky boy appeared from behind one of the columns. "Hello," he said awkwardly, as he realized Harry had noticed him.

"Jack." Harry's voice had just gone from cold to icy.

"Yes. I'm Sarah's friend. We were wondering if she wanted to come out for chips . . ."

"I know who you are. And she can't."

Let her say that, you freak! Who are you, her prison guard? Jack had disliked him instantly. If anything, because he looked like someone out of a film, and Jack didn't want anyone like that around Sarah.

"Bryony . . ."

Harry turned around. Sarah was coming down the stairs. Her hair hung loose over her shoulders, and she looked distraught, her eyes big and red-rimmed, her lashes moist.

"Sarah! Are you OK?" Bryony cried out when she saw her face.

"Yes, yes, of course. I was just playing." Sarah froze as she saw Jack.

Harry noticed that. *Good. Her face didn't light up as she saw him.*

"Oh, sweetheart, come here! What's wrong?" Bryony made her way into the house and hugged Sarah, leading her upstairs. "Jack, maybe another time, OK?" she added, barely looking over her shoulder.

"Right." Jack had got the message. *Between Bryony and Harry, Sarah is unreachable. I'll need to bloody phone them, get an appointment. Worse than trying to see the Queen,* he thought grumpily, and walked down the gravelly path.

Before he could stop them, Bryony and Sarah had gone up the stairs, arms linked. Harry heard Sarah's door closing.

Great. If something happens now, how do we explain it to Bryony?

He sighed, and went back into the kitchen. He didn't dare go down to the basement, in case something happened upstairs and he wasn't there to sort it, quickly.

"What's wrong?" Sarah looked into Bryony's soft brown eyes.

"Where do I start . . . ?" said Sarah desolately.

"Oh, Sarah." Bryony hugged her again, and Sarah held her tight, breathing in her bluebell perfume. Bryony was the closest thing to a sister she'd ever have.

"It's not Harry, is it? He seems strange. I don't know, he's so possessive of you . . ."

Sarah looked away. *He has his reasons, believe me.*

Bryony misunderstood Sarah's embarrassment. "Is it him? Has he been horrible to you?" Bryony was ready to go give him a piece of her mind.

"No, no. He's good to me. I don't know what I'd do without him. There's so much to sort out. You know the way my parents were . . ."

Bryony nodded. She thought that Anne was OK, but she had never warmed to Sarah's dad. She had always thought that there was something . . . hard about him. He had the same green eyes as Sarah, but their expression was completely different – James's eyes had something wild about them.

Anne was never there. She was dreamy, always doing something else – working in the garden, playing the piano, or down in the basement doing her art; she had told everyone that she was a painter, though nobody had ever seen a painting of hers. She lived in James's pocket – whenever he was around Anne wouldn't leave his side. She never seemed to have much time or energy for Sarah.

But James. He looked like someone you wouldn't mess with. Bryony remembered his tall, strong figure, his blond hair, fairer than Harry's – and those incredible green eyes, so piercing that she couldn't look straight into them. When they were wee girls Bryony used to be scared of him – he looked like the prince from a fairy tale, and then he looked at you like he was Bluebeard.

Bryony knew that she was being unfair. She knew that Sarah adored her parents. But she was a very intuitive girl and she felt there was more to them than met the eye.

"What do you mean? Is it about this house? Is it financial problems or something?"

"No, not financial. I suppose you can say problems . . . with the inheritance. Look, it doesn't matter. Really, I'll be fine."

"Are you sure you can make it for November?" asked Bryony, gesturing at Sarah's cello.

"I've got to." Sarah jumped at the chance to change subject. "And what about you? How's your portfolio? I'm so sorry, I haven't asked you in a long time . . ."

"My portfolio is nearly finished. Hopefully I'll get into the Glasgow School of Art. Otherwise there's always Dundee."

"You'll make it, I know. We can take the train to Glasgow together, next year . . ."

"Oh, and there's something else." Bryony looked all coy, all of a sudden.

I can see where this is going, thought Sarah. *Boyfriend number . . . what is it? Seven, eight, since we've started Secondary?*

"It's Michael, isn't it?"

"Yes. We're together!" Bryony beamed.

Sarah smiled. She liked Michael. She was happy for Bryony. *Thing is, it's going to last three months, maximum.*

"And what about you, Sarah? I suppose it'll never be Jack, will it?" she sighed.

Sarah shook her head, blood rising to her cheeks. "No. Not Jack."

"Wait a minute . . . There's someone! I can read it in your face!"

"Not really."

"Not really . . . But there *is*! You've got to tell me!"

"There's nothing to say. I met a guy, and I like him." *In my dreams, though.*

"At last! I can't believe it! This is the first time in the fourteen years I've known you that you tell me you like someone!"

"Well, I've always been busy."

"Yes, with that!" Bryony pointed at the cello. "That's your boyfriend!" Sarah laughed. "Now, who is he?"

Oh God. How am I going to explain? I met him in my dreams, he said he was sent to me, that he didn't expect me to be so beautiful . . . He saved my life, and gives me . . . leaves? I don't even know his real name.

"I'll tell you another time."

"What? This is torture! You can't do this to me!"

Sarah smiled. "Be patient."

"Sarah!" Harry was calling. There was an edge to his voice that Sarah didn't like.

"Wait here." She ran out, and down the stairs.

"You've got to send Bryony home," Harry whispered. Sarah sighed.

"Just a few more minutes . . ."

"Now."

"I'll go with her then," she retorted.

"Look." Harry took her by the arm, and led her to the living-room window.

Sarah couldn't believe her eyes.

Her oak trees.

They were bare. Completely bare. Not a leaf on them. The leaves were lying under them in a soft blanket, a few inches thick.

"Was this your friend, the one you call Leaf?" murmured Harry.

Sarah was horrified.

"I don't know . . ."

"You've got to send Bryony home now, do you understand me? I won't be responsible for her death. I won't tell her parents."

"Tell my parents what?" Bryony had appeared on the threshold of the living room.

Harry and Sarah rearranged their faces, quicker than the eye could see.

"To come and have dinner with us, soon. Bryony, I'm sorry, you need to go now. The solicitor is on her way. You know, those inheritance problems I was telling you about . . ."

"Of course, sorry. I'll text you later then."

Sarah walked her to the door.

"Oh my God, Sarah! What happened to the trees?" Bryony gasped, and brought her hand to her mouth.

Standing on the stony steps Sarah could take in the full extent of the devastation. The four oak trees at the entrance, two per side, were now bare skeletons, with their branches thrown up to the sky, like an invocation. The blanket of golden leaves at their feet was so thick that you could have slept on it.

"It's a parasite. A parasite of the oak trees," said Sarah in a small voice. "We need to get the gardener in."

"But they were fine when I arrived! Not even half an hour ago!" Bryony protested. Then she saw Sarah's face, and decided not to insist.

"Hopefully our garden won't get it," she muttered. She hugged Sarah quickly. "Call me if you need anything. Anything, OK?" she whispered in her ear.

Sarah nodded and followed her friend's flaming hair with her eyes, down the path and through the gate, as if she were watching the last beacon of normality leave her, before the night began.

29
Ley Lines

Wherever you go
I'll find you

Sarah looked up at the sky. It was darkening slowly, the afternoon turning into twilight. She shivered in the evening air, and went back inside.

"Harry . . . who – what did *that*?"

"I have no idea. Maybe it was your friend, the leaf man."

"That looks like a threat. Why would Leaf threaten me? He saved my life. Our lives. Twice!"

"I don't know. But I did say not to trust him, didn't I?"

"Yes, you did." Sarah lowered her head. Fear had taken hold of her mind, her very bones. She knew that what had been done to her trees was a warning of something horrible to come.

"It must be one of the two demons left. Simon Knowles's, or Catherine Hollow's. Or the Mistress's demon, if that's a different person altogether."

"Yes."

Could Leaf be Simon Knowles? No, that's impossible. It can't be.

"Maybe there's something about it in your mum's diary. Something about leaves, or trees . . ."

Sarah shook her head. "No. I mean, there's a lot about leaves and trees, but they're . . . ingredients, if you know what I mean. Nothing like this. The only thing I can think of is the sapphire's song, to tell us if there's any intruders."

"But if we do that . . ."

"We'd need to wash the sapphire in salt and water. And maybe it won't speak to us anymore."

"Exactly. I don't think we can do that one again until all this is finished."

"There's a scrying spell. It's to find demons, to locate them. It's one of the dangerous ones."

"What does it involve?"

"A map."

"That doesn't sound too dangerous . . ."

Sarah looked at him. "Wait 'til you see it."

The spell needed an object related to what they were looking for, something that would guide them. Sarah walked out into the garden in the purple-blue twilight, and grabbed one of the fallen leaves, one that was sitting on the last of the stony steps. *My poor trees*, she thought, looking at the devastation.

Harry was watching her, standing on the steps. *If Leaf is really a demon, well, all we need to do is destroy him. And that's a worry less for me. But if he's not . . . why on earth is he looking out for her, why is he leaving her those stupid leaves? What does he want from her?* He couldn't put the answer to that thought into words. He didn't want to think about it, because the jealousy he felt was too much to bear. He had never been jealous before, of anyone. Because he had never cared enough. It was a new feeling for him, and he didn't know what to do with it. All he knew was that he didn't like it.

"Come on." His tone was more brusque that he'd intended.

They went down into the basement, and Sarah placed the leaf gently on the table. Then she opened one of the boxes, took out a single white candle and laid it beside the leaf. In another box she found a little silver bowl. Next, she surveyed her mother's ceremonial knives, wondering which one to choose. There was a small silver one, beautifully carved with a Celtic pattern, and something engraved on the handle. It was a name.

Mairead Midnight

Sarah gasped. Morag Midnight must have given Mairead the knife and shown her how to use it for magic. Sarah sighed. Why did her mother not do that? Why did she always insist that she was too young?

Until it had been too late.

She touched Mairead's knife delicately, with the tip of her fingers.

I wish I'd known you.

"Harry, look," she whispered. She was choked. Harry took it, looked at the engraving, then gave it back.

"It's yours now," he said softly. "I'm sure Mairead would have been glad of it."

"Then why didn't my parents tell me about her?"

Harry didn't have an answer.

"I don't know." Once again, he wished he could have spoken to James and Anne, set them straight on a few things.

Sarah took a deep breath. "No time to think about that now. Can you go upstairs, get my duvet and my pillows, please?" The idea of upsetting her bed made her quite panicky, but it had to be done. The alternative would have been too painful.

"Right."

"I wish my parents had put carpets in here," she muttered under her breath. Harry looked at her. *No point in asking why*, he thought. *I'll find out in a minute anyway.*

"Oh, and the key to the map chest. The one around the doll's neck."

"Sure."

"Can you spread the duvet and pillows on the floor for me?" she asked when Harry returned. He obeyed.

It's a strange feeling, to follow instructions. To let someone else take the lead. I'm not used to it. It doesn't feel too bad.

Sarah opened the chest. "We need a map. But which one?"

"Maybe the Edinburgh one?"

"I'm thinking of what you said about the ley lines, remember? The way that map is used to locate things like freak bird migrations, crop circles, anything like that . . ."

"The falling of the leaves. Yes. It could be."

Sarah took out the Ley Lines map from the chest, and spread it carefully on the table.

"I just hope I don't break any bones."

Harry looked up, alarmed. "I have no idea of what you're talking about. I'll go with it, but be careful."

"I will be. Now, let's begin." She brought a finger to her lips. Harry nodded.

Sarah removed all her jewellery – her mother's diary said that metal could interfere with magic. She took the map, the leaf, the silver bowl and Mairead's knife, and placed them on the duvet, carefully. She kneeled in front of them. Finally, she lit the white candle. The spell had begun.

Sarah took Mairead's knife and cut her arm, only slightly, enough to get a few drops of blood. She let the blood trickle into the silver bowl. She took the bowl in her hands, her arm still dripping blood, and held it over the map. She closed her eyes, and the leaf started quivering. Harry stepped closer, making sure he could intervene if something went wrong.

The leaf began to float upwards, and over the bowl. It dipped itself into Sarah's blood, and then floated up again. There was a drop of blood suspended on one corner of it. Harry held his breath.

The leaf floated above the map, and then brushed it lightly with the bloodied corner, leaving a stain on the paper. It was a spot in the west of Scotland, just over a brown line.

"Sarah, this just tells us they're around here. We knew that, didn't we?"

Sarah didn't reply. The leaf kept hovering over the map.

"Sarah?"

Harry looked up. Sarah's eyes had rolled over, and they were now completely white. She was kneeling in the same position, her arms stretched out to hold the bowl over the map, as if she had been frozen. Harry took a step back and took out the *sgian-dubh*, just to be on the safe side.

Sarah opened her mouth to speak, but what came out wasn't her voice; it was a haunting, terrible sound, something between a wail and an echo.

"He will come out of the earth, and darkness will fall."

"Who? Who is *he*?"

"*The King of Shadows,*" answered Sarah, or whatever was talking through her.

The leaf dipped itself into the bowl again and marked another spot. Harry looked closer. It wasn't on the map, but somewhere right of it, on the duvet.

As if the map hadn't been big enough – or maybe it missed?

"Who is the King of Shadows? Where is he? When will he come?"

But Sarah was silent. Harry wanted to take her by the shoulders and shake her, make her come back, but he wasn't sure it was the right thing to do. He didn't want to put her in any danger.

Sarah started floating an inch above the floor. She was still kneeling, still holding the bowl. Suddenly an invisible force lifted her up, and threw her against the wall. She fell on the hard floor with a thud.

"Sarah!" Harry kneeled beside her.

"Ouch."

"Sarah, are you OK? Anything broken?"

"I don't think so. Just bruised. Oh, that hurts."

"That's why you asked for the duvet!"

"My mum wrote it could happen. What did I say? What did the map say?" She crawled over the duvet on her hands and knees, and looked at the map. "Where did the blood fall?"

"Where we are." Harry pointed at the stain just over the brown line. "And then . . . here." He pointed at the little blood stain on the duvet. "Out of the map."

"How . . . what does this mean?"

"Maybe it missed. Or maybe the map wasn't big enough. Had the map been bigger – well, that would be somewhere in Eastern Europe."

"Eastern Europe?"

Harry shrugged his shoulders. "Sarah, you said something strange, when you were in that sort of trance."

"What did I say?"

"You said that the King of Shadows will come out of the earth . . ."

"Right. I have no idea what that means."

The Enemy? The nameless, faceless threat that is destroying the Secret Families? Harry shivered. *Darkness will fall.*

"These spells always seem to work in weird ways." He got up quickly, taking Sarah's hands to help her up. He had to be alone. He had to speak to Niall and Mike. The King of Shadows – that must be the Enemy. It must be.

Sarah rubbed her back. "I'm just glad I didn't break any bones."

"That thing could have wrung your neck, Sarah."

"I told you it was dangerous."

"Next time, I'll do it."

Sarah laughed. "And what will I do? Knit? Watch telly?"

Harry smiled. "I'm sorry, I don't mean to . . . demean you. I know that this is what you have to do. It's just scary to see. I worry about you, Sarah."

"I worry about myself too, to be honest." She stretched, slowly. "Ouch! There, bruise of the day!" She turned around, and showed him a red, angry mark on her hip.

"That looks sore."

"It is. And the attack is still to come."

The King of Shadows. Harry felt cold. He knew what that lump in his throat was: it was terror. He was sure that they were closer to the heart of the threat, closer than ever before.

Sarah limped to the table and blew out the candle. They cleared up in silence. She folded the map away and locked the box, then she washed Mairead's knife and the silver bowl in water and salt.

They made their way upstairs. Harry went to his room, muttering something about an urgent call, and Sarah went to the living room to burn the leaf in the fireplace. Just as she was about to throw it in the flames, Sarah saw that there was something written on it, with the same old-fashioned hand-writing that was on the envelope she had received a few days before, the one with the red leaf inside. It was Leaf's handwriting.

I'll see you soon

Sarah swallowed. The room swirled around her.

She didn't know what to think. Leaf was involved with the destruction of the trees? It couldn't be. Why would he do that?

Then it dawned on her. When she'd gone to the garden, she had picked a leaf lying on the stone steps, not one under the oak trees. She had just assumed it must have fallen from the trees. But it must have been one that Leaf had left for her.

But then . . . had it been Leaf she was looking for, when she had cast the spell? Was the message about Leaf? Was he in danger? Was that creature – the King of Shadows – after him?

She threw the leaf into the fire and watched it turn to ashes. Better not to mention this to Harry. *Come to me, please. Come and tell me you are OK*, she prayed silently, hoping that Leaf would hear her.

Sarah decided that the best way to help her think and try to make sense of everything was to cook, as a way of meditation. She marched into the kitchen, tied the apron around her waist, and tied back her hair. She didn't stop or utter a word for two hours. At the end of her cooking session she had a lovely meal laid on the table: minted lamb and potatoes, and a dark chocolate mousse with a hint of chilli. She sighed and took the apron off, satisfied. The end of the world might come – the end of *her* world, anyway – but at least they would enjoy something *perfect*.

They ate, chatting about Harry's life in New Zealand and about Sarah's music. It was the calm before the storm, and they knew it.

Harry finished the last bit of his chocolate chilli mousse. "That was *amazing*. If I could choose my last meal . . ." He didn't finish the sentence, realizing what he had just said. But Sarah laughed, and he joined in, relieved.

"Hopefully your wish won't be granted tonight, Harry."

What else could they do? Their situation was so desperate, they would have had good reason to hide under the bed and wait for death. They might as well laugh. He looked at her fondly, her cheeks flushed, candlelight reflected in her deep, soulful eyes.

"So . . . Where did you learn to cook?"

"I taught myself. It relaxes me. Aunt Juliet likes cooking . . .

LEY LINES

my mum never had time. I won't either, probably, when all this is finished and I start hunting, like they did." She was polishing off the last of the chocolate mousse. Harry loved to see her eating heartily, for once.

"But you hate fighting."

"What choice do I have? Someone has to do it."

"You can't deal with it all by yourself. The dreams, the hunting . . ."

"I'm not by myself, though, am I?" she said. She got up and turned away quickly, busying herself at the sink, so that he wouldn't see her face.

"No. You're not by yourself."

Sarah smiled. Harry looked at her back as she was washing the dishes, her hair like a black waterfall. *She needs to know the truth. If I tell her the truth, she might see me with different eyes.*

She thinks I'm her cousin, for God's sake! It'd be . . . He couldn't even bear thinking the word. *But I'm not her cousin. I'm not.*

If I told her . . .

She'd hate me. She'd never forgive me for lying, for stealing Harry's life.

"I'll clear up, Sarah. Just leave it."

"It's OK, I'll help. I'm too sore to play, to be honest. Look." She lifted her top on her slim hip, and Harry saw that the bruise was beginning to turn blue. She slid down her jumper on her left shoulder, and there was another bruise, looking even worse than the other. "This one is agony. That's why I can't play."

"I've got something for it. Wait." Harry disappeared upstairs, and reappeared with a little tub of cream.

293

"It's Arnica. I used it a lot when I was hunting. As you can imagine." He handed her the tub.

"Can you do it?" she asked, handing the tub back.

Harry felt the blood rise to his face. *No? Yes?*

Yes.

He looked into Sarah's eyes, expecting to see an innuendo, a hidden message. Expecting to find out that she was flirting with him. But in her face he saw nothing but innocence.

How could that be? *She's seventeen years old; she should know how this works. She should know what it means, to ask me to touch her like this!*

Harry massaged the cream on her shoulder, then on her hip, breathing in her scent. She smelled of peaches, and her skin was soft as petals. Suddenly he felt terribly, terribly sad.

I can never have her, he thought desolately.

Sarah looked at him with those clear green eyes, and smiled. She leaned closer to him, nestling into him with a sigh.

Harry froze. *Does she know how I'm feeling? What other seventeen-year-old girl would not read the signs?* He thought of Sarah's girlfriends – that Alice, for example, or Siobhan – they would have read it in his eyes. Had it been them, this whole scene would have been completely different. It would have been about seduction.

But not with Sarah. With her, it was like trying to touch the moon.

Does she know?

"Cup of tea?" she asked softly, disentangling herself. "Oh, that's better already," she added, touching her hip.

She doesn't.

She's like a little girl. Like part of her has stopped growing. She stopped at thirteen, the day her dreams began. Shock and fear nailed her there. It's like that fairy tale, what was it? Briar Rose. *The girl who fell asleep for a hundred years.*

He wanted to be the one who put his lips on her lips, who broke the spell and woke her up. He wanted to be the one who made sure nobody would ever frighten her again, that she'd never be left alone again. The one who made sure no evil spell would ever be cast on her, that she would not prick her finger on some deadly spinning wheel.

Sarah handed him his cup of tea, looking him straight in the eye. She could have never imagined, not in a million years, what he was thinking right at that moment – she was still Briar Rose, asleep among the thorny bushes and the roses, still waiting.

30
King of Shadows

Lead me into the light
Let everyone know about our love

Grand Isle, Louisiana

The sound of the waves lapping on the shore was like oxygen to Niall, like the most familiar, oldest sound in his memory, second only to the beating of his mother's heart. He needed to be near the water, he needed time to just sit and think about all that was happening. To try and make sense of the events that had taken him there, to a beach on the other side of the world, beside a warm sea in a warm night, far away from the freezing waters and cold wind of the Atlantic, and all he that knew.

Mike had been incredible. To be a man who was there by choice and not by destiny, he was selfless and brave and endlessly resourceful. So loyal to Sean and to all they were fighting for. To think of what could happen soon to all of them – the Secret Families, the Gamekeepers, and then to all humanity, old and young, all over the world – if the Time of Demons came again.

Niall's grandfather used to tell him stories about the Time of Demons. He was the headmaster of the local school, a little white-washed cottage on the outskirts of Skerry, his home village. He was also a storyteller, a folklorist, and a musician, of course. He had the power of Song, a voice so potent that he could call storms, light a fire, change the colour of the leaves.

Patrick Flynn's stories were frightening. Members of the Flynn family had been telling them for generations, handing them from father to son and from mother to daughter – stories of a time when Donegal, and Ireland, and the world didn't belong to humans but to the Surari. Small tribes of human beings living a nomadic life full of danger and uncertainty, trying to survive the threat of the demons roaming the earth, owning the land. And then something happened. Special children were born to the human tribes – the ancestors of the Secret Families. They had powers that could tame the Surari, destroy them, or banish them to places that run parallel to this world, sealed away in space and time. Slowly the Surari grew weaker, and the humans grew stronger – until the earth belonged to humanity. The Time of Demons was over, and the Time of Humans began. The Secret Families watched the territory – they watched the openings between this world and theirs, destroying anything that managed to seep through.

When the destruction started, the Flynn family began falling ill. They grew weak, exhausted, unable to eat – Niall, his parents and his two little sisters, too young to even have Dreams yet. Some mysterious sickness was coming up from the land, slowly killing them. The people in Skerry and all around were suffering too – women were losing babies all around, children grew ill with blood diseases, and there was talk of the land being somehow poisoned, or the sea.

Something there was leaking death.

The Flynns sent their son away with Mike. They stayed, withering slowly, trying all they could to stop the sickness. Niall knew that his parents had chosen to die in the poisoned place – and he respected their choice. He would have gladly done the same. But he knew he had to go away, and survive and fight. And he'd do his duty.

He thought of Donegal, of how the land rolled sweetly, of how quickly the clouds would sweep the sky, of how perfectly silent and still the hills could be, so silent that you could hear the earth breathing.

This beautiful land he now found himself in, this place between the water and the sky, was full of soul – Louisiana, somewhere he never even thought he'd see. It was seeping into his blood, a watery, green, secret place where people were as proud of their traditions as his own people. And the music was amazing.

Still, it wasn't home.

"Niall!"

Mike interrupted his thoughts. He was calling him from the shack, waving broadly with his arms. Something had happened. Probably Sean-related.

Niall was dying to meet Sean Hannay, and the heron, the mysterious Sarah Midnight.

"Sean." Mike gestured at the phone sitting on the table, beside the computers.

Niall nodded. "How can I help?"

"Ever heard of the King of Shadows?"

The floor rose up to meet Niall, and the room danced around him as a buzzing sound filled his ears. He blinked over and over again.

Mike's voice came from afar.

"Are you OK?"

"Yes. Yes. I'm fine. Sean, I've heard of the King of Shadows before, yes. I've heard of him in . . . stories."

"Stories?"

"Stories that have been in my family for generations. As long as human memory goes."

"So who is this King of Shadows?"

"Try and avoid saying his name, Sean."

"Come on, Niall!" Mike laughed. Then he saw Niall's grey face, and he stopped laughing.

"What do you know about him?"

"He's a very, very powerful demon. The strongest of them all. He was driven back when the Time of Demons came to an end, but he was never truly defeated, just contained. Some say he rules the Underworld. Sometimes he's called Báis."

"What does it mean?"

"It's Irish. It means Death."

A pause.

"Where did you come across him?" asked Mike, grabbing the bottle of Bourbon. Niall saw that his hands were shaking.

"The heron had a vision."

"Sean. I need to come and see you and the heron. Now."

"It's too dangerous."

"If that's what's after you, you need all the help you can get."

"We need you alive, Niall. What else do you know?"

"Not much more. The stories say he brings death with a look of his eyes. That he hasn't seen the light for thousands of years. That's all I know."

"I see."

"This is really bad, Sean," Mike said.

"I know. Not good at all."

"The plan?"

"Keep going, I suppose."

"I'll try and get as much info as I can. I'll send it to you ASAP."

"Thank you, Mike."

"Not at all, my friend."

They heard a beep, and then silence.

"Not good at all," repeated Niall, and his words sounded like a song of mourning.

31
The Man Who Wasn't There

Hold me as if
I were about to disappear

"Them again?"

"Yes." Harry didn't look up from his iPhone.

"Who *are* they?" Sarah wasn't letting go.

"I told you, they don't want people to know."

"I'm not people. I'm family. And this makes me nervous."

"Don't be nervous. They're on our side."

Sarah sighed.

"I've got homework to do."

"Right, I'll leave you be." Harry got up from the sofa.

"No, no. Stay. I mean, stay if you want to," she amended. "I don't mind."

Harry stifled a smile.

"OK."

"I'll go get my books."

Sarah ran upstairs, grabbed her books, notebooks and pencil case and was down in a minute. She was about to step into the living room when something made her stop.

Harry was standing in front of the fireplace, still as the night, a strange expression on his face.

"Don't come in, Sarah." His voice was grey.

"Harry. What's wrong?" she whispered, her blood turning cold.

"Don't come in. Stay out. I think it's too late for me."

Sarah's head started spinning.

"What? What are you talking about?"

"Look at my feet."

Sarah looked down. The wooden floor was strewn with the lilac light of early evening, mixing with the light of the lamp on the coffee table and of the uplighter in the corner. All her radars started sending alarm signals to her brain, but she couldn't figure out why. There was something wrong with what she was seeing. Something was there that shouldn't have been there. Sarah swallowed. *What is it? What is it that doesn't look right?*

She looked again. The shadows.

The shadows were all wrong.

Harry had two shadows. And one of them was moving of its own accord.

All of a sudden, she knew. When they thought they had dissolved the demon-shadow, she had felt that something wasn't right. She'd thought the puddle of blackwater had disappeared too quickly, but she hadn't done anything about it. She hadn't even told Harry. She had buried her head in the sand, pushed the thought to the back of her mind. How wrong she'd been. What a stupid, stupid thing to do.

"Run," Harry begged her.

"I can't leave you."

302

"Whose life is more important, Sarah? Mine or yours? You need to save yourself. Please, Sarah, go."

Sarah shook her head.

"If you die there's nobody left. You're the one with the powers. Please go. Please go." Sarah had never seen him so frightened.

The demon-shadow looked around, as if to decide who to hit first. Then it turned towards Sarah. It had chosen. Harry understood at once.

"Sarah. Please, Sarah. Run." He pleaded again, taking out his *sgian-dubh*, slowly, an inch at a time.

"I can't leave you here. I can't." Sarah's hands were shaking so hard that all her books fell to the floor.

The shadow took a step towards her.

"Sarah!" shouted Harry. "Sarah, go!"

Sarah took a step back.

"Come here. Come here. Come with me," she whispered to the demon. It took another step forward, and Sarah took one backwards.

"Come with me."

"What are you doing?" Harry shouted in frustration.

"Getting it away from you." Sarah's voice was cold, even, but there was an edge of terror to it.

Run, please run. One touch is all it takes, and you'll be a shadow for all eternity . . .

Sarah took another step back. She didn't dare to turn away from the demon. Her hands were cold. She flexed them. She curled them into a fist, then unfolded them again. Cold. Still cold.

Harry followed them out of the living room and into the hall. The shadow took another step in her direction, a quicker one, and Sarah gasped. She jerked back, and tripped over one of her books, falling backwards and landing heavily on the first step of the stairs.

"Here! I'm here! Take me!" Harry shouted again.

But the shadow ignored him. Another step, and another, its hands out to get Sarah. She was desperately trying to get back on her feet, but kept slipping on the paper strewn on the landing.

Harry cried out once more, furious, desperate.

The demon reached out, its black hands as hollow, as empty as darkness itself.

Her hands were still cold – she lifted them in front of her face, in absolute, all-consuming terror.

The blackwater was failing her.

The demon crouched in front of Sarah. They mirrored each other, as if it had been Sarah's real shadow. Two beings, one with a body, one without, locked in an endless moment.

All of a sudden, the shadow turned around in a jerky, sudden movement, as if it had felt something. Sarah looked up, and there was Harry, sweat pouring down his face, his hands weaving the invisible runes in the air, the blade and Harry's fingers moving so quick it was impossible to follow. He was panting with the effort.

The shadow shuddered and arched its back. Harry yelled in anger and pain. Sarah saw that the hand holding the blade was bright red, dripping with blood.

The demon curled onto itself, and then shook its head back and forth. Harry fell on his knees, still tracing the runes, his shoulders shaking with the effort. The shadow started blurring, slowly. The mysterious force that held it together was faltering, and the particles that made up its body were beginning to drift away from their orbits, loose and lost. From black, it started turning into grey.

Harry moaned. There was a red stain on the carpet where his hand was dripping blood. *One last effort. One last effort*, he kept telling himself, as his strength faded, his hands trembled and the symbols became less and less defined.

But he was succeeding. The demon was now a grey, shapeless cloud. Just as Harry couldn't take any more, the shadow lingered for a long, painful moment, and then it was gone.

Harry let the *sgian-dubh* fall on the floor and leaned on his arms, on all fours, panting. His heart was beating so hard he thought Sarah could hear it.

He faltered towards Sarah, and he let himself fall beside her. He held her tight, too tight – as if the abyss were still there, and he had to stop her from falling.

"You're hurting me," she murmured.

He didn't let go.

32
The Heron

I can't speak to you
Not even in my dreams
Stay with me – I call
To nobody

Grand Isle, Louisiana

"Sean?"

"Niall." Sean's voice filled the little shack. The door was open, letting in the night and the sound of the waves.

"I had a dream."

"Oh, no."

"Unfortunately, yes. Now, it could be about something happening back home in Donegal. I mean, this is the way they're supposed to be. But I didn't recognize the place . . . it was on a football pitch. And the heron was in it."

"The heron?"

"Yes. And it was bad. She wasn't . . . herself. She *looked* like herself, but she wasn't. There was a demon inside her."

"A football pitch, you said?"

"Yes."

"Thank you, Niall."

"Sean. I'm tired of hiding. We've got to do something. We can't hide forever."

"I know. I know." His voice sounded exhausted.

"Sean?" Mike called.

"Yes."

"Ignore him. He's just fed up with eating shellfish every night. We'll stay here as long as it takes."

"No, he's right, Mike. We can't hide forever. They'll find us anyway, wherever we are."

"Sooner or later they'll make a mistake. We'll figure out who—"

"Stop. Don't say anything," Niall intervened.

"No. No, you're right."

"I'm going to go now. Take care. I mean it."

"And you, Sean."

They both looked at the computer, bright in the semi-darkness of the shack. On the screen, the website of Trinity Academy — a photo of the school orchestra, three rows of boys and girls in their uniform, smiling at the camera. They had zoomed in on a girl sitting at her cello, long black hair cascading over her shoulders, a shy, melancholic look in her eyes.

The heron.

33
The White Mountains

The day he went
Was the day I could not go back.
I thought it'd last forever

Castelmonte

Elodie

Still no powers. Like I'm not myself any more. No visions, no dreams, and nothing else. Water is just water, glass is just glass, and no visions come to me when I sleep. I don't get much sleep these days, anyway.

I mainly sit at the window and look at the mountains. At the beginning they felt like a cage, this huge barrier between me and the war I'm not allowed to fight. But I grew to love them, a constant, silent, protecting presence.

The other day we drove to Val d'Aosta. The Frisons were visiting some friends and they took me with them. We went to a little stony village that seemed to have grown out of the valley, between two enormous walls of rock at either side of it. A village that looks like a nativity scene, with a Roman bridge that crosses a white, ice-cold, glacier-born stream.

"At night you see some lights up there," Marina said, pointing up to the top of the mountain, somewhere impossibly high. "You might think they're stars, because you can't see the mountains, it all looks dark like the night sky. But they're houses. Can you imagine? Living up there?"

I pictured the lights hanging from the mountains like stars from the sky. I pictured living there, in a wooden house that gets cut off by the snow in the winter. Harry and me. And our children.

The thought cut me up like a blade right under my ribs, and I looked away. Marina read my mood. "Come on, let's go buy some treats."

The local bakery was a treasure trove, and we came out with our hands full of some flat, crumbly biscuits that they call *tegole*, 'slates', and some others shaped like little knots, sugary and buttery. *Torcetti*. The unfamiliar words rolled on my tongue and tasted as good as the biscuits, as I tried again and again to pronounce them. Marina smiled. She loves it when I try to speak her language.

We sat on the grass at the side of the stream to eat our goodies. The water ran so fast, from the glaciers to the valleys, on a bed of grey pebbles.

Marina was sitting beside me, her eyes closed against the autumn sun. A thin, chilly mountain breeze ruffled her hair. Aiko was throwing stones in the water, curling her chubby little fingers around the pebbles and giving little squirms of delight as they made an arc across the air, and a little splash in the water.

The scent of pines was sweet all around us, and the rock walls shone in the sun. They were warm to the touch, and they seemed to vibrate and hum very, very quietly – as if they were alive. It felt like they were giving out energy – like if I sat on them, I'd sort of plug myself in. Their strength seeped into me, thousands and thousands of years of being still under the sky, of watching the world changing, and never changing themselves.

These stones had seen the Time of Demons.

These stones might witness it coming again.

My heart grew cold at the sudden fear, and the pleasure of the moment was lost for me. I hugged my knees and rested my chin on them, deep in dark thoughts.

"Elodie?"

"Yes?"

"Don't worry." Marina put her hand across my shoulders, and her kindness filled my chest with unshed tears.

34
Losing You

What you call home
I call exile

"How are you doing, Sarah?" Mr McIntyre had stopped her in the corridor.

"Oh, hello. I'm OK, thank you."

"How are the audition pieces shaping up?" he asked, gesturing to her cello in its purple case.

"Very well, thank you. Mr Sands is helping a lot."

"We're very proud of you. You know that, don't you?"

Sarah smiled. "Thank you." Mr McIntyre walked away with one last encouraging smile. He was so kind. Always looking out for her.

The school had always made a fuss of her musical talent. It pleased her, and she was proud of it – but her shy nature stopped her from enjoying it fully. She felt a bit overwhelmed sometimes.

A shy performer. A contradiction in terms, really, but Sarah knew it was actually quite common among musicians. It's just that their love for music was stronger than the nerves that took them whenever they got up on stage.

"Coming for lunch?"

Alice was standing at the lockers, wearing the over-the-knee stockings she had bought in Accessorize a few days before, and attracting quite a few interested looks. And some envious ones.

How does she get away with wearing that? Only Alice could pull it off! thought Sarah, smoothing her uniform skirt over her opaque black tights.

"Yes. I've got food for you and the girls as well." Sarah cooked lunch for her friends sometimes. She took it to school in dainty little containers, and made their day.

"Oh, what a treat! Thank you!" exclaimed Alice, with genuine pleasure. For a girl who watched her figure she had a very healthy appetite.

Bryony and Leigh were waiting in front of the lunch hall. They sat at their usual table, the one in the back beside the window, and Sarah started taking out her treats.

"What is it?" asked Bryony.

"Ham and soft cheese crepes, and . . ." She smiled and produced a little floral box. "My famous homemade chocolates, Sarah's own." There was a flurry of *ooohs* and *aaahs*, and they started eating and chatting.

"I love your chocolates. Especially the white ones with the little sugar roses." Leigh licked her fingers. Sarah looked at her friend, with her cloudless blue eyes, the hint of freckles on her nose, her sunny smile. She wondered what it would be like, to have an easy life, to be a young woman without a curse. To be someone like Leigh.

A guitar sound came from under the table.

"Whose phone is that?"

"Oh, it's mine," said Sarah, digging in her bag. They were allowed to keep their phones in school, as long as they switched them off during lessons. Sarah always kept it on silent anyway. *I must have forgotten.* She looked at the screen. Harry. Something must have happened.

"Sorry, girls, just a minute."

She ran out of the lunch hall and looked for a corner where she could be alone.

"Yes?" she whispered in the phone.

"Sarah, they're in your school."

"What? Where?" Panic took hold of her.

"They just went in. You need to get out of there now. We can't fight them in front of everyone."

"What do they look like?"

"It's a man. I think it's Simon Knowles. He's wearing a tracksuit. There's a woman with him, I don't know who she is. She has brown hair, very short, and a blue coat."

So Leaf isn't Simon Knowles. Sarah drew a sigh of relief, in spite of the situation. "Going now. I'll meet you at the entrance."

She put the phone back in her bag, quickly. Simon was a football coach, it said on her parents' files. He was probably there under the pretence of training the school team. The most likely places to find him would be the gym hall, or the football pitches.

Sarah ran down the stairs into the entrance hall. Harry walked through the doors, looking cool and calm.

"Oh, Sarah. Hello. I was hoping to catch you," he said pleasantly. "I'm just going to report to the office. I'll be right back."

Sarah looked at him, wide eyed. His blood was as cold as ice. He would have made a great spy.

"Here I am." He was back after a few minutes, with a visitor's badge around his neck.

"What's your excuse?" she whispered.

"I'm here to see your Head Teacher. To ask how you've been doing."

"Right. No appointment?"

"Last-minute arrangement? Is that plausible?"

"Not really."

"Oh well, we'll just have to wing it."

Right at that moment, Sarah's heart stopped.

"Harry." She put a hand on his arm. "They're over there."

Sarah had seen them through the big glass doors at the back. They were walking towards the pitches.

"Stay here." Harry walked away quickly.

"No, I'm coming with you . . ."

"Sarah! Why did you not come back?" Leigh had just appeared beside her. "We ate everything, here's your containers. What happened?"

"Sorry, Harry said he was coming, and . . . Excuse me." Sarah ran after Harry down the corridor, and outside.

"Simon," Harry called calmly.

The man in a tracksuit and the woman in a blue coat turned around.

"There you are. I was just looking for you," said Simon, looking straight at Sarah. He was a young guy, tall and dark, with a big, friendly smile.

"I know." She was trying to be as cool as Harry, but her chest, rising and falling quickly, was giving her away.

"I wasn't expecting *you*, though," Simon said to Harry.

"I know." Harry echoed Sarah's words.

"Sarah?" Leigh had followed her outside, worried by Sarah's strange demeanour. "Is everything OK?"

"Leigh, just wait for me in class, I'll be there in a minute."

The red-haired woman smiled. "Are you *that* Leigh? Leigh Bain?"

Sarah felt like someone had stabbed her in the heart. *Leave her out of it. Please, leave her out of it . . .*

"Your dad told me so much about you. I'm Lucinda Hall. I work with him at Eastwood Park."

Sarah started breathing again. *She's not one of them.*

"Oh, Lucinda, yes. My dad's mentioned you."

"All good, I hope! We have a new football coach in the sports development team. Simon Knowles." Lucinda gestured towards him.

"Nice to meet you," said Leigh, smiling in her sunny way.

"And you. I hope I'll see you at the training sessions."

"Definitely. I love football."

"I can imagine, with that father of yours!" Lucinda laughed, a warm, friendly laugh.

"I won't be a minute, Leigh," pleaded Sarah.

Please, please go.

"OK. Nice to meet you at last, Lucinda. Bye, Simon."

"Nice meeting you." And then, "I can take it from here, Lucinda. I'll see you back at Eastwood Park . . . let me see . . . around three-ish, OK?"

"Are you sure? You all sorted, then?"

"All sorted. Will find my way around no problem."

"OK then, see you around three. Bye," she added, in Harry and Sarah's direction.

315

"Do you mind walking with me? I have a training session in half an hour." Simon started striding towards the pitches.

"Of course. We'll help you set up," answered Harry, like everything was normal, like nothing was happening. There were people walking by, and he didn't want to attract any attention.

They walked on to the football pitch, under the rain. It was deserted. The sky was grey and low, and it was dark, as dark as dusk. Every step they took squelched on the soaking grass. They stood beside the net.

"So how do you plan to kill me?" asked Sarah.

"Well, my demon—"

"Yes, I've heard it all before. 'My demon is the mightiest demon ever, you might have killed the others but not mine, this is the last day of your life . . .' I know, I know."

Simon laughed, and his chiselled face looked even more handsome. Sarah shivered. How appearances could deceive.

"No, what I was going to say is that my demon is *right here, right now.*"

Sarah and Harry froze. Harry took out his *sgian-dubh*, looking around. He hoped nobody would see them, or they would have a lot of explaining to do, but they had no choice.

"Harry, "whispered Sarah. Suddenly she understood what Simon meant, when he'd said *my demon is right here.*

Simon is the demon.

"Harry," she repeated, and looked at him. Harry wasn't looking around any more; his eyes had stopped on Simon's face. He understood too.

"You are a demon?" asked Sarah.

Here we go, thought Harry. *She's started making conversation again. Always trying to find a way out of killing.*

"Not exactly. I've got it inside me. And there's its slave around, too."

A slave? Is his demon a Sentient? Harry felt a chill down his spine.

"Right, I'm not interested. One more chance to call off your demon or I'll kill you," Harry intervened.

Simon laughed. *Why do they always laugh in our faces, like stupid pantomime villains?* thought Sarah, irritated. *What on earth is funny, in all this?*

"You won't do that."

"Watch me."

"Lucinda is with Leigh, right now."

Sarah gasped. The sky and the earth swapped place for a second.

"What?"

"Well, the *real* Lucinda is gone. *My slave* is with Leigh, chatting about her dad and about football."

"You're bluffing," whispered Harry.

"He's not," said Sarah, panicked. "He's telling the truth, I can feel it. Tell Lucinda to let her go. She hasn't done anything to you; she's nothing to you . . . Let her go."

"That is up to you. You let me kill you, and Leigh will be saved. Otherwise . . . well, my slave strangles very, very quickly. And quietly. It's a knack, I think."

"He's lying. He'll kill you, and Lucinda will kill Leigh," murmured Harry.

Sarah ignored him. "OK. It's a deal," she said, trying to sound firm, but sounding as if she was begging.

"It's no use. They'll kill Leigh anyway. Sarah, please," Harry pleaded.

"Tell her to find an excuse to come out on the steps. So I can see she's alive."

"I don't think you're in a position to bargain, Sarah." Simon's voice was pleasant, charming.

"I told you. They'll kill her, Sarah. There's no hope for her now," said Harry.

"It can't be. Come on, take me. Take me! I'm here! Look!" Sarah pleaded. She lifted her hands, and showed Simon her palms. "They're cold! I won't use the blackwater, I promise. Take me and let her go . . ."

Simon opened his mouth to reply.

There was the noise of a cork popping, and a small trickle of blood coming out of Simon's mouth.

There was the tiniest little hole in his neck, burnt around the edges. Simon collapsed on the wet grass with a thud.

Sarah turned to Harry in time to see, through a film of tears, that he was putting away his gun.

"What did you do?" she cried. "What did you do?"

"You weren't planning for me to be here," whispered Harry to the corpse. "But I was. And look what happened now." His eyes were shining in a way that made Sarah want to run away from him, as far as she could go.

Right at that moment a soft, white mist came out of Simon's mouth, and mixed silently with the mist rising from the ground, disappearing from view. Sarah was crying silently, in a haze of pain. Harry kneeled beside her, taking her face in his hands.

"Sarah. Listen to me. Listen. *Listen!* You need to dissolve Simon *now.*"

Leigh, Leigh, Sarah was calling silently.

"Sarah!" he shouted, making her flinch. She recoiled from him, but he held on to her face.

"You need to dissolve him before somebody sees us!"

"Harry . . . look," she whispered.

"What the hell . . . ?"

The white mist that had come out of Simon's mouth had started swirling around him in dusty circles, one inside the other, like a star in the making. After a few seconds it imploded, and collapsed into itself, a white, shiny little sphere, twirling, twirling.

"It's not dead. The demon is not dead," whispered Sarah.

Simon's corpse was lying with his mouth open. The sphere disappeared into it, and travelled down his throat. They could see it shining through his skin, taking place in his chest, where his heart would have beaten, had he still been alive.

Simon started twitching.

"Oh my God." They looked on, horrified.

Slowly, painfully, with jerky, unnatural movements that made Sarah feel ill, Simon's corpse got up, and looked around. Simon's face was still contorted in death, his eyes were still staring, his jaw slack – a death mask. All the blood had drained from him, and his lips were blue. He wailed, and took a step towards Sarah. Harry was on him like a flash, throwing him on the ground again.

"Now!" he called to Sarah.

Sarah shook herself, and sat astride Simon, putting her hands on his chest. Her face was just above his, as his skin began to weep. The white sphere emerged from Simon's mouth, suspended for a second, and it lingered around Sarah's mouth. Harry stood frozen. In an instant, he knew what was going to happen next.

It's looking for another host. Like in Niall's dream, where Sarah wasn't herself!

Harry threw himself on Sarah, just as the sphere moved, quick as a blink, ready to propel itself down Sarah's throat. It looked for her mouth, but found nothing.

Sarah was on the ground with Harry's arms around her chest, holding her so tight that she was nearly suffocating.

Without a host, the little white sphere dissolved into nothing, just as the last of Simon's body liquefied into black-water. The demon had been too late.

"It wanted to take you," whispered Harry. They lay together for a moment, Harry holding Sarah against him. She breathed in the scent of wet earth, the scent of death.

Leigh is dead.

After a few seconds, Harry let Sarah go, and he helped her up, his face cold and controlled again.

"You need to stay in school; we can't raise suspicions. You need to go back in and pretend nothing has happened. I can't help you with this. You have to do it by yourself. Do you understand me?"

"How could you . . . ? We could have saved her," Sarah whispered, but Harry had already grabbed Simon's sports bag, and he was gone, in his silent way.

Sarah sat there, trembling, for a while. Then she dried her tears, did up her hair again, and straightened her uniform. She composed her face, and she did it so well, so quickly, that nobody would have guessed there had been anything wrong except being caught up in a sudden shower.

She took a deep breath, and walked towards the main building.

Someone was screaming.

Leigh had been found.

35
Sorrow

Let me go

The sky had opened. The drizzle had turned into a downpour.

"They would have killed you too." Sarah was curled up on her bed. Harry was stroking her hair.

"I know."

"I'm sorry."

"I'll dream of her. I can feel it."

Harry thought of the sweet, quiet girl he remembered. *Leigh.*

"She'll blame me," whispered Sarah into her pillow.

"It wasn't your fault."

Sarah didn't reply.

She saw them both that night. Mairead and Leigh. They were on a windy shore, somewhere wild and bitter.

Sarah was sitting on the pebbles, waiting. She could taste salt in the air. The wind was so strong, it had tangled and matted her hair. She felt a hand on her shoulder, and there they were, sitting on either side of her. Mairead was wearing a short blue pinafore, her blond hair down on her shoulders. Leigh had on her school uniform, like the day she'd been killed.

"I'm sorry . . ." Sarah began, but Mairead put a cold finger on her lips.

Leigh leaned her head on Sarah's shoulder, and took her hand. They sat very close to each other, their hands entwined.

Sarah was too sad to even cry. After a short while of sitting in silence, Mairead and Leigh stood up. They had not spoken once.

Sarah watched them walk into the sea, until the waves swallowed them both. She saw brown hair and blond hair mixing, floating in the foam, then nothing.

The sky was grey and full of rain, ready to fall, like tears.

There was nothing left to say, nothing left to think. Sarah sat hugging her knees, waiting to wake up.

Maybe I'll soon join them.

The sea was cold, as grey as the sky, and so vast, so lonely.

When she woke up, Sarah didn't make a sound. She didn't want Harry to come. She didn't want anyone to come. She wanted to be alone; she wanted to be silent.

36
The Hand Holding Mine

Wilderness beneath my skin
Tooth and claw
The secret me

The aftermath was terrible. Sarah wanted to go to Leigh's funeral, but she knew that she couldn't; she knew she would have brought danger with her. She asked Harry to tell everyone that she was still too traumatized from her parents' death to attend.

Leigh was everywhere, everyone was talking about it. The girl killed in Trinity Academy. Not a trace, not a clue as to who'd done it.

Bryony and Alice called at the house, but Sarah asked Harry to turn them away. She couldn't bear to be near them. Had someone else died because of her . . .

The school was closed for three days, and it was the longest three days of her life. She refused to speak and she refused to eat, and Harry didn't force her. When he realized she wanted to be silent, he just went with it. All she did was lie on her bed, looking out of the window.

Harry hoped with all his heart they wouldn't attack now, or she would have been an easy target. Simon's slave was still around. What did it look like? Was it still possessing Lucinda's body?

Harry feared that Sarah couldn't have faced a fight in the state she was in.

He was wrong.

Sarah heard the growling first. "Harry," she said, and her voice was hoarse from the silence.

"Yes." Harry had heard it too. Simon's slave had arrived. The wait was over.

"Open the door and hide behind it," whispered Harry, for the second time since they'd known each other. Sarah looked at him, and didn't answer. Harry blinked. She looked strange. She looked different.

In an instant, Harry knew that she wasn't going to do what he'd said. Again.

Oh God, she wants to get herself killed! Harry thought in dismay.

But he was wrong again.

Sarah opened the door and stood there, unflinching. The woman that once had been Lucinda was growling, a low growl that came from the back of her throat. Lucinda had been dead for days now, and her body was beginning to come undone – her fingertips black already, her eyes empty, staring. The eyes of the dead.

Lucinda was poised to spring, her stiff body working to bend according to the demon's will. Her movements were painful, jerky. That split second allowed Sarah to look her straight in the eyes. Time stood still as the Midnight gaze worked on the demon.

Lucinda shuddered and tried to attack – but it was a faltering, lopsided jump that didn't take her anywhere. She wailed, a sound that was still horribly human.

Sarah grabbed Lucinda's short hair with both her hands and pulled her to the ground, holding her down without ever looking away.

Harry couldn't believe it. Was that Sarah? *How did she manage that?*

It dawned on him. He'd seen the real Harry do it. *Of course. The Midnight gaze. She had just looked at Lucinda, looked her in the eye, and it was enough. She had never been able to do that before.*

Lucinda whimpered. She couldn't move, her muscles twitching, drool coming out of her mouth.

"Harry, the dagger," called Sarah, keeping her eyes fixed on Lucinda.

Harry threw the *sgian-dubh* to her, and Sarah raised her hand to catch it, looking away for a split second. Harry caught a glimpse of her face. He gasped.

Morag Midnight.

The pictures that the real Harry had shown him. The same eyes, the same expression.

Finally. Sarah was becoming what she was meant to be. One of *them*.

And then a revelation: Harry *hated* to see Sarah like that. She was becoming a true Midnight now, like her grandmother. It was what was needed, what he had been trying to tell her since they'd met, but he hated it. It was like taking a rose and dipping it in steel. The realization made his head spin.

The moment that Sarah's gaze had left Lucinda had been enough for the demon to get on its feet, shaking its head stiffly, jerkily, to try and shake off Sarah's spell. They faced each other again, Lucinda's face contorted in an animal growl, Sarah's face as cold as the moon. The Midnight gaze was on the demon again, making it whimper and double over, legs giving way, until it fell. It wailed again, a cry full of pain.

This is where Sarah tries to spare her, thought Harry. *This is where she tries to get out of the killing.*

But it didn't happen. Not this time. Sarah grabbed the demon's hair, forcing it to raise its head and expose its neck. It was a deep, wide cut, from one ear to the other. Lucinda stood no chance.

A strange sound came out of Sarah, a growl of triumph and hatred. Dark blood sprouted from Lucinda's wound and from her mouth, trickling down her chin. She gasped and spluttered, struggling for breath, suffocating in her own blood.

There was no sign of mercy on Sarah's face. She waited until the demon stopped twitching. Then she stood up, without a word.

It was Leigh's death that did this to her. It was Leigh's death that changed her, Harry realized.

"Are you OK?"

Sarah looked at Harry to answer, but it was too soon, and the Midnight gaze cut him, a sharp pain, like a blade between his eyes.

Sarah blinked quickly. "Sorry." She took a deep breath. "I'm going to clean all this up."

Of course. What else is there to say?

Harry rubbed his forehead. It still hurt.

He watched Sarah kneeling beside Lucinda, ready to liquefy her; this new Sarah, this stranger that had taken her place. He locked the door, and chained it for good measure.

At least she's speaking again.

Sarah felt better after her hunt. She felt herself again, even if she was in so much pain for Leigh. She was ready to fight again. It was the first time, the first time in her whole life, that she had felt that sense of release. It was like she could understand them, now – her parents, Harry, her grandmother – how the hunt made them feel. Empty. Light. Spent. Like some terrible tension had gone from their minds, from their limbs.

Released.

Sarah knew the dreams would take her that night. When she felt sleep coming, she didn't fight it. She was scared, but she let it take her. She needed to see what the dream would tell her; she needed to bring all that to an end. Nobody else was going to get killed, she had sworn to herself. Nobody.

Sarah closed her eyes, and opened them in the dream. She was standing on the heather, in the familiar purple-skied place. The grass shone, wet with dew. Someone was walking towards her. Sarah recognized him at once – his way of walking quickly, as if he was always busy, leaning forward a bit, heading towards his next task, his next adventure.

It was Harry. Sarah started running towards him. They met halfway, on a little slope between two hills. She was so happy to see him. Him, instead of some horrible, horrible creature. She looked into his face, and he smiled, his eyes full of warmth. Sarah smiled back.

But the smile died on her lips.

There was something not right.

Harry wasn't Harry anymore. His face was changing, as if he was turning into someone else. One minute he was himself, with his startling blue eyes, and one minute he was a blond man with green eyes, the same shade as her own. The same *face* as her own. He looked like her father's twin. He looked like *her* twin.

Sarah was about to ask him who he was, when the man turned into Harry again, the clear eyes and the dimple in his left cheek. But he looked distraught.

"Sarah, I have to go," he said. His face was full of pain.

"You have to go? Where? I don't understand."

"I have to go. I have to leave you. I'm sorry."

Sarah felt like her heart was being ripped out.

"Why?"

"I'm sorry," he repeated. He turned away, and started walking. Sarah wanted to run after him, but she was rooted to the ground. She couldn't move.

"Harry!" she called.

He didn't turn around.

"Sarah! Wake up! Sarah!"

Harry knew that he shouldn't have woken her, that he should have waited until the vision was finished so that they could get the most information out of it. But he couldn't bear to see her like that.

Sarah opened her eyes, and saw Harry leaning on her bed. She threw her arms around him, and hid her face in his neck.

"Shhhh . . . it's finished . . . don't be afraid."

Harry felt furious, full of unspeakable anger. *Why does she have to be tormented like this? For goodness sake! Can they not help themselves?*

He had no reverence for the Midnight mission any more. No sacred respect. Being a Dreamer was just a curse, and he was quickly losing patience with it. They saved lives, yes. But not their own. And Sarah's life was all that mattered to him.

Sarah was shaking; she couldn't find peace. Harry started worrying. She should be a bit calmer by now. What did she see?

"Sarah, it's ok . . ." She clung to him even tighter. "What did you dream?"

Sarah shook her head. She didn't want to say. It was too painful.

"Sarah . . ."

"That you were leaving me," she whispered.

"I have no intention of going anywhere."

Sarah looked at him for a long time, as if searching for something in his eyes.

"I dreamt that you weren't . . . you. And that you were leaving me."

"Oh, Sarah." He took her face in his hands. "It was just a stupid dream. Not one of your visions. Everybody has dreams like that. I'll never go, I'll never leave you."

Sarah looked at him with desolate eyes, and took her place in his neck again. Harry stroked her hair and held her until she took a big sigh, and relaxed.

"That you weren't you," she said.

It couldn't be one of her visions. I'm never going to go. Unless she asks me to.

"You're all I have," he whispered into her soft hair.

"You're all I have," said Sarah in return.

What do you call this feeling? That you can't live without someone? I can't give it a name. I can't give a name to something I should not be feeling.

37

In Great Haste

All the dreams beneath the sea
Of all of them just one
Belongs to me

Grand Isle, Louisiana

"Niall, come here."

"What is it?"

"It's the Sabha. I think I've found some sort of channel they use to communicate.

Niall tore himself from his own computer and stood behind Mike's, leaning over his chair. The screen reflected their faces, Mike's as black as the night, Niall's Irish-white, both wide eyed, both horrified.

"My God. It's the traitors."

Niall felt dizzy. He looked out to sea, its opaque green waters under a yellowing sky. A fine drizzle covered the windows, its drops thickening by the minute. A storm was coming in, rolling in from the Gulf of Mexico. He could see the fog starting to rise, rolling towards the land like a marching army.

"We need to call Sean."

"I'm on it."

"Wait a minute. There's something else. Look." There was something in Mike's voice that sent a shiver down Niall's spine. Fear. Icy-white fear.

"Niall. It's a map – it's a satellite view of Louisiana. It's Grand Isle. Oh hell, it's our shack! They're on us!"

"Shut this down! Shut it down!" Mike grabbed the wires and tore them off the wall, while Niall was switching off any equipment he could get his hands on. The screens all over the room went dead, the computers buzzed softly and then they stopped. Without the glare of the screens the room looked suddenly dark, a surreal grey-yellow light, the light that announces a storm, seeping from the window.

Mike stood up and ran his hands through his hair. Niall looked into his friend's face, and a million unspoken words passed between them.

They both knew that it was too late. They both knew that they had been found, that it was just a matter of time before the traitors in the Sabha caught up with them.

38
Spell

On the threshold
Who am I?
I'm something soft, there is no fight

It was happening more and more often. Even when Sarah wasn't sleeping. Even when she just closed her eyes, she'd see Leaf.

Every time, her mind emptied, her heartbeat slowed, her thoughts blurred. She wanted to see him, and at the same time she dreaded it. Every time he was in her dreams it was as if she'd been bleeding for a long time, and she felt weak and hazy.

And still, she didn't want it to stop. She longed for him as much as he scared her. His power over her was addictive.

Once again, Sarah had barely closed her eyes when he came to her under the oak trees. The light was golden and the sky was a perfect blue, and she felt like she didn't know where she ended and the rest of the world began.

He was standing in front of her with his burning eyes, raven hair, his strange, earthy scent that made her head spin, like some sort of ether.

"Welcome back," he said. Sarah felt her legs give way, and he sustained her, his arms against her waist, his mouth against her ear.

"You've got to forgive me."

"Forgive you what?" she said dreamily, confused.

"You have to forgive me for this," he whispered, and without warning, he took a step closer to her. Sarah wanted to step back, but she couldn't – her limbs were unbearably heavy. She couldn't have lifted a finger.

He put a hand under her chin, to look her in the eye. When their gaze met, Sarah felt like she could never look away. He put a hand on the small of her back, and entwined the other in her hair. In spite of herself, she felt she was moving closer – her body did it for her, as if she had relinquished control, as if she were like seaweed carried by a strong current.

His face was against her, his lips were close to hers, so close . . .

It's happening. My first kiss . . .

"The Mistress is coming." A woman's voice had filled the moonlit room, and Sarah opened her eyes with a sharp intake of breath. The sapphire was shining on her bedside table, casting a blue light over the walls and ceiling.

Sarah drew herself upright. *It's not supposed to do that. That's not how the spell works!*

In her diary, her mother had warned her about spells working differently for each person who cast them, and being unpredictable – like a recipe coming out differently every time.

335

Was it always going to be that way? Casting a spell and not knowing what came of it?

She lay awake until dawn broke on the moors, wondering if the sapphire would speak again, thinking of her interrupted dream and fearing the day ahead.

39
Childhood Dreams

Wind and rain hiding my plight
Standing in the cold
Daughter of a place that is no more
Knowing you must go

The rain was tapping on the roof, trickling down the windows, soaking Anne's garden. It was dark, and the sky was so low, so swollen, that it looked as if it wanted to open up and swallow the earth. Sarah loved the rain, but she had a deep sense of foreboding that had followed her since the sapphire spoke, and the weather added to it.

When she'd told Harry about the sapphire singing again he had nodded quietly. It was as if they'd made the unspoken choice to wait calmly, to grab those last moments of peace. It had been a slow day, slow and dreamy, just the two of them in a world of their own. Sarah playing, Harry listening intently. Sarah writing her diary, Harry reading books he'd found among James's things. And then music, and tea, and chatting in a low voice about things that had nothing to do with death, and danger, and what was ahead of them.

Swirling in Sarah's head were thoughts of her almost-kiss.

Trust me to be weird in this as well. Can I not be normal, for once?

She drew a deep breath. *The Mistress. At last. At last. It's nearly over. There's only one name left on the list. It must be her. Catherine Hollow.*

"Not long to my audition," Sarah said dreamily, her fingers touching some music sheets piled neatly on the coffee table.

"Let's focus on staying alive, we'll think of your career later."

"Fair enough." Sarah sighed.

"If you don't get into the RCS then you can go somewhere else. There are plenty of places that teach music."

"My mum went there. And I don't want to leave this house."

"It'd only be for three years. I'd come with you."

"You'd come with me?"

"If you want me to," he added quickly. "Not if you'd rather share with friends."

"What would these friends think, when they see what I do at night?" she said sadly.

"I suppose. I'm used to that." He smiled.

"Exactly. And you keep the caffeine flowing." She smiled back.

"I'll cook for you and polish your cello."

Sarah laughed.

"Make you soup after the concerts."

"Iron my evening gowns."

"No, I'm terrible at ironing. You'd be one shabby musician."

They looked at each other. A few unspoken words.

And then Harry chose sarcasm. "Perfect timing, the Valaya. Just before your audition."

"Yes, perfect. Just in time to destroy my future!"

"As long as there is a future."

He has a point. She thought of Leigh, and a lump of tears formed in her throat. *How could I have laughed, just a minute ago? How can I ever laugh again, when she's dead?*

"I'm going to have a shower," she said, a catch in her voice.

Harry felt the change in her mood, and wished he could bring her back from the sadness. But he couldn't.

"I'll cook dinner," he said instead.

I'll look after you was what he meant.

Sarah undressed under Shadow's watchful eyes, and ran the shower. She sat on her bed, wrapped in a towel, waiting for the water to get hot.

A distant thunder resounded in the room, followed by another fanning of hard rain against the glass. The sky was yellow. A proper storm, coming in from the sea.

Sarah shivered. She couldn't get her heart to beat slowly; she couldn't get her blood to run the way it should. She felt anxious, as tight as the strings on her cello.

She closed the bathroom door and shut the world out. Steam had covered the mirrors, and the room was hot and damp. It was a world of her own, full of lovely scents and potions, the place where she could be alone and safe. Sarah folded the towel neatly, placed it beside the sink, and got into the shower. It was wonderful. She closed her eyes, letting the water run down her hair, her face, her body, like a hundred gentle hands caressing the fear away. She lathered herself in her peach-scented soap, breathing in the beautiful scent. A deep breath ran through her, releasing some of the tension.

Better.

Sarah couldn't let herself get away with more than fifteen minutes under the hot water. She forced herself to get out of the cabin, reaching quickly for the towel sitting beside the sink. She wrapped it around her, her hair dripping . . .

Standing in front of the steamed-up mirror, Sarah grabbed another towel and started drying the length of her hair. She caught a glimpse of herself, blurred by the steam – the ghost of a pale girl, white skin and night-black hair, troubled eyes, a long story to tell. She opened the body lotion and started massaging it into her legs, enjoying the sweet perfume and the feeling of softness against her skin. Her hands felt rough, made raw by the cleaning rituals. Sarah looked at them with a pang of shame.

A sudden cold current ran over the side of her body. The room changed in temperature, as if the steam had been let out. Sarah shivered.

She stopped dead.

The bathroom door had been opened, ever so slightly.

"Harry?"

He wouldn't walk in on me like that. He wouldn't come into the bathroom while I'm having a shower.

"Harry?" she called again.

She felt exposed, naked as she was and wrapped in a towel, her wet hair still trickling down her back.

It's nothing. It's a draught. It's nothing.

She stepped forward to close the door. Her hand was barely on the handle, when the door was grabbed from her and opened wide.

"Hello, Sarah."

A woman was standing in front of her, a short, blond woman with cold eyes and a black tattoo on the side of her neck. A ring. For a second, Sarah saw black and felt her legs giving way. Her heart was beating so hard, she thought she'd die of fright there and then.

The sgian-dubh is on my desk. My hands. I need the blackwater. Harry, she's here, Harry! Her thoughts were exploding in her mind like fireworks, the noise deafening, one of them stronger than the rest: *She's here to kill me.*

"Are you the Mistress?" she whispered, her voice coming from far away, as if someone else had spoken.

"I'm Cathy Duggan. Or Catherine Hollow, if you prefer. Come and sit down, sweetheart."

Sweetheart?

She touched Sarah's arm, softly, leading her towards the bed. Sarah jumped at the touch, and Cathy laughed.

"I'm not going to kill you yet, silly!" Cathy's fingers burrowed into Sarah's bare skin as she forced Sarah to sit down beside her.

Sarah flexed her hands, and felt the blackwater flow into them . . . but her instinct told her she had to listen to what Cathy had to say.

Cathy was smiling. She was beautiful, with those startling blue eyes, her high cheekbones and her fair, wavy hair around her face. Still, there was darkness in those eyes, infinite darkness. And something else.

Fury, Sarah realized. *Pure fury, and I'm the object of that rage. Why?*

"Why are you here if it's not to kill me?" Sarah was shaking so hard her teeth started chattering. She wanted to run away, she wanted to scream, but she couldn't move, she couldn't cry out. Her blood had turned to ice.

"I enjoy seeing you frightened out of your mind. That's why I'm here."

Oh God. She really is crazy.

"You have your father's eyes." Cathy stroked her face with cold, delicate fingers. "Shame about your mother's hair." She ran her hand through Sarah's wet hair, gently, then yanked it down suddenly, painfully, making Sarah cry out softly.

"It's nearly over," Cathy whispered, stroking Sarah's hair in long, soft movements. "You managed to kill them all, somehow. But not mine. It's the end of the Midnights."

"When?"

"Soon, my darling. I love to see you so scared, but it can't last forever, can it? Even the best things come to an end."

"Where?"

"I think you know. I've got a big surprise in store for you. Oh and by the way, keep practising your cello. I was told you're very good."

Who told you?

"Shame you'll die too young to do anything with it."

Crazy cow, Sarah thought, hate burning her up. Cathy touched her face again. Sarah recoiled.

"Soon it'll all be over, pet. Oh, and give a message to . . . *Harry* from me. Tell him I know." Cathy leaned over to kiss her, and the feeling of Cathy's cold lips on her cheek made Sarah heave.

Cathy's body seemed to blur, to lose its contours slowly. She rose from the bed and floated to the window, as if she'd been a ghost. She was now just a watermark etched against the glass, more and more see-through, until it disappeared completely.

All that was left was the noise of the rain tapping on the glass.

"She was here. The Mistress. She was in my room."

Harry looked up from his phone to see Sarah framed in the living-room doorway, white and shaking. She had thrown on a pair of jeans and a T-shirt, and her hair was falling in damp strands about her shoulders.

"Oh my God, Sarah, are you OK? Where is she?"

"She's gone. I'm OK." Sarah touched her left arm, leading Harry's gaze to it. The red imprint of cruel fingers, slowly turning purple. Harry took Sarah in his arms and felt her trembling.

"What did she say?"

"That they'll come for me. Soon. And that I know where it's going to happen. But I can't think where . . ." Sarah shook her head.

"Shhhh. Don't think about that now."

"She gave me a message for you."

Harry's heart stopped. *She knows. Oh God, she knows.*

"She said to tell you that she knows," Sarah echoed.

Yes. Of course.

Of course.

"What does she mean?"

"Nothing. She's just crazy."

Sarah studied his eyes. *He's keeping something from me.* But she couldn't think of that now, she had to hide her face in his chest; she had to breathe him in. *Harry.*

"She disappeared," Sarah said into his shoulder. "Sort of . . . dissolved. How did she do that?"

"I think . . . I think it wasn't her. She wasn't *really* there. It was her astral self – her astral *drop*, it's called. She can travel out of her body."

"She was real enough." Sarah showed him the darkening bruise on her arm.

"Astral drops can touch things, they can feel things."

"Can you do it? Can you travel out of your body?"

"No."

Sarah held him tighter. She wanted to hide her face in the crook of his neck and just stay there. Forever. They sat in each other's arms, in silence, each with their own fear, with their own burden. They both felt the ground was about to open under their feet – they both feared that the fall would kill them.

It was as easy as breathing, really, something Sarah's body did for her, something she had no control over. She had to be close to him, and that was it. She had to hide her face in his chest and hold him tight, she had to breathe him in, to touch the back of his head and braid her hands behind his back, to keep him there forever. She felt so alone she could have cried – he was the only one who could save her.

She wasn't expecting him to break the rules. She wasn't expecting him to push her down on the sofa like that, pinning her down by her shoulders. She couldn't have imagined that she'd *want* him to do that, as much as he wanted it, and more. She realized that until then she hadn't known what desire was; she'd never felt it before, and it felt as strong as terror, as sweet as love. And though she knew it was so, so wrong, the tingling feeling coursing through her body gave her no option but to give in.

A wave of tenderness swept her from head to toe, and left her warm and limp, ready to fall. She felt her loneliness melt away, and for the first time in her life, she felt safe.

Harry was drowning. He was afraid it'd all be over by tomorrow – he knew it would all be over soon, anyway – and he couldn't lose her without claiming her first. As she put her arms around him, tenderly, he couldn't take it any more.

I'm not your friend; I'm not your family.

I'm in love with you.

"You're all I have," he whispered in her neck. Their mantra, their secret code. The only *I love you* they were allowed to say.

He disentangled himself from her arms, took her by the shoulders, and pushed her down on the sofa – and stopped for an instant, horrified at what he was doing. She looked at him with wide eyes, surprised. But there was something else in her eyes, something that made him tremble. It was a yes. He took her face in his hands and kissed her slowly and deeply, while she wrapped her arms around him again and held him close, every drop of blood in her veins turning to honey.

My first kiss, she managed to think. *So this is what it feels like, this is what everybody talks about . . .*

Harry was afraid of his own desire, and tried to hold back. She was so small and vulnerable in his arms – he wanted to protect her, he'd never hurt her. And then the tenderness went, and was replaced by hunger, a hunger so deep it went beyond his will. *Just a little more, just a little more – I'll stop in a minute, before it's too late – I promise I'll stop . . .* She made a sound like a little animal, and held him tighter, harder. He knew then that he had to stop. *Not like this, not while you don't know who I am.*

He pulled his lips and his body away from hers, holding her softly again, like he used to.

Sarah sensed his change, and she was crushed, but she let him hold her in his arms, because to move away would have been like a little death. She felt liquid, shapeless; she needed him to stop her from dissolving into nothing. Harry felt her consternation, and took her face in his hands again. She looked bereft.

"Soon, when all this is over," he promised.

If he leaves me, I'll die, Sarah thought, and immediately pushed the thought away, as if it'd been a comet across the sky, beautiful and shining, but a sorrowful omen for everyone to see.

40
Eyes That Watch

Time to build, time to destroy
Not for you to keep

Cathy

I've been watching you for a long time, following you as you grew. I was there when you came out of the hospital in your mother's arms. I looked into your pram as you were sleeping in the garden. How easy it would have been to suffocate you, then.

I watched you from the window, playing on the rug and toddling around. I used to sit in front of your school, and wait for you to come out, in your little pinafore and your red coat. How easy it would have been to snatch you, and take you away forever.

I was there the first time you played, at the Concert for Schools, sitting where I couldn't be seen. It all made me sick. To see the daughter I was supposed to have, the life that should have been mine. Still, I couldn't stay away.

It didn't even occur to me, to have a life of my own. What life could be, without James, without his children? Without children at all?

I came so close to killing you, many, many times. Especially since Nocturne arrived. We watched you on the roundabout, in your little coat and your favourite shiny shoes, your hair blowing in the wind. How I hate your hair, your mother's hair! We watched you from the bushes along the river, silent and still.

You saw us, but I don't think it registered. I don't think you realized you were staring death in the face. You were only seven.

I nearly told Nocturne to go and wring your neck.

I nearly told him to bring you to me, so we could be mother and daughter. I could bring you up. But I knew it was impossible. You have *her* hair, an endless reminder that you're not mine. How could you be my daughter, when you have Anne's blood in your veins?

We waited, Nocturne and I, for the right time to destroy your parents. We're waiting for the right time to destroy you.

The last time I see your black hair down your back, it will have turned red.

My darling, darling Sarah.

41
Lies

I wish the world could change for us

They were in the living room, waiting. Sarah kept pacing up and down, straightening things as she went, sweeping away particles of dust, wiping invisible stains. She cooked lunch, something or other made with filo pastry, which they barely noticed, and barely nibbled at. They knew that they should have forced themselves to eat, but they just couldn't. They drank coffee, to keep them going. Cathy's words lingered between them: *I enjoy seeing you frightened out of your mind.* She was certainly succeeding in doing that.

Time went on, hour after hour, trickling like the rain on the windows. The house was shrouded in perfect silence. Night fell, and it wasn't much darker than the day had been. The rain was less intense, but there was still a drizzle that kept falling, falling.

"I wonder what Cathy's demon looks like?" Sarah was sorting her CDs into alphabetical order.

Harry didn't reply. He had a gun in his belt. He was ready to use it. He was ready to silence Cathy.

"Sarah, you need to sleep. They're trying to wear us out."

"So do you."

"I never sleep anyway. You go first. Come on."

Harry sat in Sarah's armchair, and Sarah lay in her bed, fully dressed. She tossed and turned for a long while, but finally fell asleep.

And she dreamt.

She was at the play park, on the roundabout. She could see her own legs, her own arms – but they were a little girl's legs and arms. She was wearing the red coat she had when she was seven, and her black patent ballerinas.

I'm a child again.

She kept going round and round. It was the middle of the day, but the light was muted and the sky clouded over. There was nobody around. Like so often in her dreams, she felt like she was the only human being left in the world.

As she turned, she caught a glimpse of something strange. Something was looking at her. Someone. It looked like a man, but he was very, very tall, and completely black. His eyes were shining red among the bushes, at the edge of the play park. He had huge arms that went down to his knees.

Sarah's little heart started beating in double time. She tried to stop and jump down, but the roundabout was going too fast. It went round once more, and she saw it again.

And again.

And no more. It was gone.

The roundabout stopped, and Sarah jumped off, terrified.

She looked around. She turned and turned, the grey sky turning with her, until she saw it once more.

He was right in front of her, lifting her up by the shoulders, to his face.

She screamed, and woke up in her room.

"Harry, the play park!" she gasped.

"What?"

"He's at the play park. I saw it. That's what she meant, when she said I knew where it was going to be." She jumped down from her bed. "Let's go."

They ran all the way, in the dark. Sarah wanted finally to end it, so badly. She wanted to be free, or she wanted to die. She couldn't live that besieged life any more.

She looked at her watch. One o'clock in the morning. The silence was uninterrupted, the darkness broken only by the streetlights and the neon signs of the takeaways on the other side of the river.

She stood beside the roundabout, and waited, Harry circling her slowly, the *sgian-dubh* in his hand, the gun in his belt.

And they came.

"Hi, Sarah. How are you, my dear?" Cathy strode up to them, smiling her showbiz smile, as if they were just meeting for a coffee. She sat on the roundabout and patted the place beside her. "Come and sit, let's have a chat," she said cosily. Sarah felt sick. "I can only stay a wee while. Then I'll leave you to Nocturne."

Harry gasped, and looked around frantically. He knew who Nocturne was. All Gamekeepers knew.

"Before you both die, there's something I need to tell you, Sarah. This man here —" Cathy pointed at Harry, as if she was telling some hilarious little story – "is not who he says he is."

Harry growled, and launched himself at her. Cathy fell, banging her head on the metal bar. She kneeled on the tarmac, holding her head.

"Harry!" whispered Sarah.

Something had come out of the darkness, something with red eyes and gleaming teeth. Something that had been watching them, hidden. Nocturne, the creature of Sarah's dream.

And then it clicked in Sarah's mind. *It wasn't a dream. It was a memory.*

She'd seen him at the same play park, many years before. Anne had gone to buy bread across the bridge, and she'd asked Sarah to wait for her. She'd sat on the roundabout, and she'd seen . . . him. In the bushes.

Had it been an omen of what was to come, ten years later? Is that how I'll meet my death?

Nocturne ran towards them and helped Cathy up, surprisingly gently.

"Sarah, don't listen to her." Harry's face was very white in the orange light of the streetlamps.

"This man is not your cousin," she hissed. "His name is Sean Hannay. He's been lying to you all this time."

"Don't listen to her . . ."

"He killed your cousin to take his place. He wanted to be a Midnight; there was nothing he wanted more. And he killed for it."

"What?" Sarah felt her head spinning. She looked into Harry's face.

Harry rearranged his features as quickly as he could, into a look of defiance.

"She's crazy! Don't listen to her!"

But it was too late. She'd seen it. She'd seen the truth in his eyes, just for a split second. She knew.

"Harry . . ."

"Sarah . . ." He felt the world crumble around him. Everything fell, and he stood in a desert of rubble and dust and nothing. Hope, love, pride – it was all gone, like sand between his fingers. He could not hold on. He could not stop it from happening.

"The dream I had last night – that's what it meant?" whispered Sarah.

She felt her heart breaking. It was so real a feeling that she brought a hand to her chest. *There it goes, it's breaking.* Fluttering like a dying butterfly.

"I didn't kill Harry. I would never harm him. Let me explain . . ."

"You lied to me. You lied all along."

A wave of rage overwhelmed her, drowning her. Like when she had destroyed her parents' room and burnt her dream diary. She was so angry that she was anger itself, an empty shell but for that all-consuming rage. She walked towards Harry, under Cathy's smiling gaze, and she lifted her hands. She felt her power flooding them, burning them . . .

Harry didn't move, didn't argue, didn't defend himself. He closed his eyes, and decided to let it happen.

But there was no blackwater. Instead Sarah went white, and stood frozen, looking at her shaking hands. They weren't burning any more; suddenly they were icy cold. Empty. Her power was gone.

The blackwater was gone.

The look of horror and despair on her face was such that it shook even Cathy, for a moment. Just for a moment.

There's nothing left. My power is gone. The blackwater is not mine any more.

She looked up at Nocturne. She knew he was going to do what he hadn't done all those years before, when she was a little girl.

Has he been waiting all along? Is this how I'm supposed to go?

She looked him straight in the eye. Nocturne tipped his head to one side.

Harry roared and put himself between Sarah and the demon, but Nocturne slapped him across the face, so hard that he fell unconscious on the tarmac. Sarah lowered her head and waited for the blow, waited for her neck to be broken.

"Leave her." A deep male voice.

She knew that voice.

She looked up. Leaf had materialized beside her.

"Who are you?" asked Cathy.

"I'm fire."

He crouched down, and touched a blade of grass with his index finger. The grass was soaking from the rain, and still it lit up. Tiny flames turned into towering ones, enveloping the trees all around.

I was right, he is fire, Harry managed to think confusedly. After the blow to his head he was between reality and a dream. He knew it somehow. He'd seen it in Leaf's eyes, when he'd saved Sarah from the mist.

Nocturne didn't let the fire distract him. He took two huge strides towards Sarah, and lifted her up by the shoulders, just like in her dream. Sarah thought her bones were going to break.

"No ..."

Sarah looked down at Leaf, and their eyes met. Cathy saw the expression on Sarah's face, and her eyes narrowed.

There's something between them.

"Get him!" Cathy shook Nocturne's arm, pointing at Leaf. "Never mind her! Get him!" She had found a novel way to torture Sarah, to inflict pain on her.

Nocturne obeyed and threw Sarah away. Literally. She landed on the cold, hard asphalt, and felt something crack. She lay there, bent in two, looking at the flames growing and growing around her.

Nocturne went for Leaf, who was looking at the demon with burning eyes. Leaf didn't move; he just stood there. Panicked, Sarah realized what he was doing. He *wanted* them to take him. So that she would be left alone.

"Leaf, no!"

Nocturne easily lifted Leaf and shook him until he was floppy in his hands. He disappeared into the night, with Leaf under his arm. Cathy walked to Sarah and kicked her in the ribs, trying to break another one, for good measure. Then she knelt down beside Sarah, her voice slow and menacing.

"There. Your boyfriend will suffer and it'll be all your fault. I'll take my time killing him. Make sure I enjoy it properly. Then I'll come for you. And there'll be nobody there to help you."

They walked away, into the darkness, and left Sarah broken among the growing flames.

"Sarah," Sean called. He never knew it'd be possible to feel so lost, so bereft.

Sarah looked at the black sky above her.

"Go away."

"Let me help you."

"I never want to see you again! You killed Harry! You killed the last one of my family!"

"Sarah, no, you've got it all wrong . . ."

With huge effort Sarah sat up, and then she stood, holding her side.

"Why? Why on earth did you kill Harry? Why did you pretend to be him? What do you want from me?"

"Let's go home, I'll explain . . ."

"That's not your home. I don't know who you are!" she sobbed, for the pain, the disappointment, the betrayal.

"Sarah . . ." He was crying too.

The sound of the fire brigade filled the night.

"I never want to see you again." Her words cut him like blades.

Sarah dragged herself home, every step an agony, and lay on the living-room floor until dawn, shaking with shock and fear.

42
Nowhere to Run

Pebbles on the shore
Every stone a thought of you

Grand Isle, Louisiana

Mike
They came from the sea, and slithered up to our cottage like snakes among the stones. We were expecting them. We knew they'd come.

We couldn't use our computers or our phones to tell Sean about what we'd discovered. But there was another way. Something I hadn't done before in my whole life, believe it or not. I wrote a *letter*, a proper letter, not an email. I wrote it in great haste, and I was about to drive away, to send the letter, not to escape – I knew there was no point in escaping, they'd find us anyway. Nowhere to hide at that stage. They'd find us. We'd stay and fight. Die, probably, but hey, we all have to die some day. The only thing that mattered was the letter.

I'd nearly made it to the car, when they came.

The letter burnt in my pocket as I ran towards the shack. I left it on the table, hoping and praying with every ounce of my strength that someone would find it and send it.

Then I walked out and waited. It didn't take long. They were on me in minutes, their tentacles long enough to wrap themselves around my waist and drag me down underwater.

How did I live to tell the tale? Nothing short of a miracle. I learned to swim in the icy Canadian lakes, and that helped. But the truth is, they were a lot more interested in Niall than they were in me. Which is why I'm alive and Niall is dead.

He distracted them as they were dragging me under, so that they left me alone, half drowned and concussed, but still alive. I saw them tying their tentacles around Niall's waist, and dragging him into the deep.

I thought they would be back to finish the job, but they must have assumed I was dead. I waited and waited, hoping that Niall would resurface; and he did, but he wasn't breathing.

I hid under the pier, among the rotting, salt-encrusted wood. I sat by my friend's body, drinking myself stupid to try to forget the pain. But how could I, when he lay so white, so cold, his lips blue, his hair matted with sand and seaweed? He was young, and he was brave, and he was dead.

Grief was like a boulder on my chest. I couldn't breathe; I couldn't raise my head, my very bones crushing under the weight of it. A little sliver of moon watched over me from above the water, and I sat and drank until I fell, until I felt the sand against my cheek and the water lapping at my toes.

43
Final Act

That moment I knew
It was all over –
I was the one outside the circle
I was gone.

By the time dawn had broken, Sarah realized she was definitely going to be killed. There was no way out. She knew it was going to happen; it was just a matter of time.

The blackwater was lost, and she was alone. She didn't want Harry – *Sean* – anywhere near her, and Leaf had been kidnapped. They were going to kill him, and yes, Cathy was right. It was her fault. She'd be responsible for Leaf's death, as she was for Leigh's.

And her own life was at an end.

What a shame. She was never going to fall in love, play her music . . . have a life, she thought, watching the sky getting lighter and lighter. She fell asleep again, a dreamless, black sleep where she knew no pain, a sleep that was a bit like death.

Maybe that's what it feels like, she thought as she was slipping away.

Two hours later, she woke up again. The pain in her ribs was horrendous, so bad that it made her sick.

Sarah dragged herself upstairs, followed by Shadow, and took two caplets of codeine to try to ease the pain. She realized she hadn't eaten since the day before. She went into the kitchen and toasted some bread. The smell made her feel faint with hunger. She made herself a cup of tea too, and polished the lot, quickly, greedily.

Harry.

Sarah felt her heart calling to him, calling, calling. She silenced it, resolutely.

Liar. Murderer. To think that he wasn't even that good a liar, to think that he had betrayed himself, in the end. She wouldn't have. She would have done it properly; she would have kept it going.

We're both rotten then.

Except she never chose to lie, she *had* to.

Why? Why did he kill Harry? Why did he pretend to be my cousin?

She looked at her watch. Nine o'clock. Nine o'clock on a Sunday morning, when families wake up to spend the day together.

She would spend the day waiting to die. Because they were going to come back, of course. And she had no way of stopping them. She had nothing, except a little dagger and a whole lot of weapons she didn't even have the strength to use.

Too late now. Too late for everything. She could only sit there and wait.

She wasn't scared. She was beyond that. She felt some sort of inevitability. Of course they were going to kill her. How could she ever think she'd survive the Midnight inheritance? She was the last of her family. Her parents were dead, so were her aunt and uncle, and now she knew that her cousin was dead too. There was nobody else to share their blood.

It's all over.

She went into the living room and tried to play, to lose herself in her music, but her ribs were too sore. No more playing her cello, ever again.

She desperately wanted to say goodbye to Bryony and to Aunt Juliet, but she couldn't put them in danger. She couldn't go anywhere; she couldn't see anyone.

I'm like a curse, a curse that's about to be lifted.

She sat at the window and waited. How lovely it all looked, now that she knew she wasn't going to see another autumn.

To think that only yesterday she and Harry had been chatting in that same living room, with the ease of two people who'd known each other forever. She could still see him sitting across from her, joking about making her soup after the concerts . . . She could see his face, she could feel his hands holding hers, she could hear his voice. Only yesterday.

Sarah didn't know that Sean was watching her from the garden, shaking with pain because of Nocturne's blow, but staying put. Just like when he'd followed her to school, or to the shops – invisible, but there.

Because he wasn't going to let her die.

He might have lost her, but he was going to protect her, until the very end. He was going to keep her alive.

"Sarah. Sarah, wake up."

Sarah opened her eyes in the darkness. She was in her room, and yet she was in a dream.

It was her mother, sitting on her bed again, her black hair shining.

Sarah gasped.

"Mum . . . They're going to kill me," she whispered.

Anne shook her head. "You need to be strong, you need to fight . . ."

"I'll be with you and Dad soon," Sarah said desolately.

"No, you won't. And Sarah, please forgive me. Forgive me for not having taught you more, for not having prepared you for all this. I'm so sorry. I was trying to protect you, and I put you in even more danger."

"It's OK, it's OK, Mum." Sarah felt the tears roll down her cheeks, and fall through her mum's immaterial hands.

"If I could do it all again . . ."

"No, please, don't blame yourself . . ."

"If I could do it all again I'd teach you all I know, like your grandmother did with Mairead. But I can't. I can't do it all again. It's your turn to live and be happy. Sarah, you must survive this, and live your life. Do you understand me? You must."

Sarah nodded over and over again. She was sobbing.

"I'll try. I'll try. Mum, are you with Dad? Where is he? Where are you?"

"I can't say. I'm sorry," Anne said, and she stood up, becoming more and more transparent, until she dissolved completely. "Forgive me," was the last thing Sarah heard her saying.

Sarah sat in her bed, stunned, until she felt some sense of reality come back to her. She grabbed her duvet and her pillows, and went downstairs. She got out of the house, and into the garden, followed by Shadow.

She walked to her mother's patch and lay there, wrapped in her duvet, like a chrysalis. She looked at the black, cloudy sky above her. Not one star was shining; the moon was nowhere to be seen. The silence was perfect. She closed her eyes and drifted off at once.

She opened them again as a grey dawn was breaking over the garden.

I didn't dream, was the first thing she thought.

She sat up, breathing in the lovely smell of her mum's herbs, and the scent of wet earth, and looked at the sky.

I must go and face them. It's up to me. Nobody will do it for me, nobody will help. I have to go and fight Cathy, if it's the last thing I do. And I know it will be.

44
Flames

Too late to care
Too late to tell the truth

Sarah took a hot shower, to warm her after the damp night in the garden. Shadow was pacing around her. She knew that something was terribly wrong, and she was scared in that electric, charged cat-like way.

Today is the last day of my life. But I'll fight. I'll fight. I won't go like a lamb to the slaughter; I'll fight as long as I have breath left in me.

The last day of this crazy, doomed life I was given.

To think that Anne had *chosen* that life. She must have loved her father very much, to let herself be dragged into all this.

I used to dream of experiencing that love. But I won't. I'll never know what love is now. Just like Leigh, I'll go before my life has even started. I'll see them all again soon. My mum, my dad, my grandmother. Mairead, Angela, Leigh. Leaf, if they have killed him already. Harry, the real Harry. My cousin.

She thought of Sean – she struggled to call him that; to her he was Harry – and it made her feel so alone.

I can't believe he's done this to me. She let herself imagine him calling her, or coming to the door, saying it had all been a mistake, that it was all a big misunderstanding. The thought of his face, of his voice, was like a stab through the heart.

But there was no mistake, no misunderstanding. He wasn't there.

What would happen, when she was gone? What would Aunt Juliet think when she saw her parents' things, their weapons, their magical equipment? Sarah couldn't imagine her reaction. She couldn't imagine anyone's reaction, in front of all that. Juliet would think that they were all crazy, that she'd been right all along, about her father, about the Midnights. That Anne should never have gone near them. What if Juliet tried to use anything? What if someone, something, got wind of it, and came looking for Juliet and her family? Sarah couldn't let it happen. She had to warn Juliet. She had to destroy her parents' things before she died.

Sarah hid her face in her hands. She couldn't bear the thought of setting fire to their things, burying them. She couldn't do it, not this way. She sat at the living-room window with her silver diary, and started writing.

She wrote everything, about the Midnights, about what her parents did, about her dreams. She wrote about the Valaya and how they'd killed James and Anne, and hunted her next. She also wrote what was going to happen to her at the hands of Cathy Duggan.

I know you'll find all this hard to believe. Just look at the things in the basement, and you'll be convinced. Don't use them though; don't do anything of what my mum's diary says. Burn and bury it all, quickly, the same day that you read this diary. I don't want them to know of you, I don't want them to come for you and Trevor and the girls. Forget about the Midnights. I'm so sorry . . .

She wrapped the diary in white tissue paper, and put it on the coffee table, with a note: *to Juliet, from Sarah.*

She sat and waited for the night to fall. As soon as she saw the shadows gathering on the moors she put her jacket on, and went out. The evening was bitterly cold, but it felt so sweet to her, the freezing air and the evening sky, as she was about to leave it all.

She started walking. She knew they were going to find her soon.

She wandered around for a while. Ghosts of herself appeared at every corner – Sarah as a child, walking down the street with her mum; on the swings in the playground of her old school; coming out of the sports centre after her swimming lessons, with wet hair and a little pink rucksack; in her school uniform, on an outing to the library with her class; with her cello in its purple case, waiting for the next train into town; chatting with her friends in front of the newsagents.

And finally, the ghost she was looking for: the little girl with the red coat, sitting on the roundabout, not knowing she was being watched, not knowing that death was so close to her that it could have brushed her face with its cold finger.

Everything was still and dark at the play park. Nobody around but drunks and police cars. A nightly world that was scary to most people – but not to her. The world she lived in was a lot more frightening.

She sat on the roundabout, beside the little girl. The seventeen-year-old Sarah and the seven-year-old Sarah looked at each other.

So this is who I'm going to be?

So this is who I was?

Sarah felt the irresistible urge to touch the girl's black hair, to hold her and protect her from what was to come. To save her from all that was going to happen, to save her from her dreams.

They looked into each other's eyes, and they were one again, the little girl taking her place inside the young woman, hidden, but there.

Sarah didn't have long to wait. Nocturne soon took shape, a mound of darkness against the river. He was holding someone by the arm – Leaf, battered and bruised, but still alive.

Sarah sprang to her feet.

He's alive. Leaf is alive.

Then Cathy emerged from the darkness, confident, smiling and cheerful, as if she'd been at one of her concerts, at some social event. Beautiful, slender, graceful.

"Ready, Sarah?"

"I want you to free Leaf."

"Oh, so that's his name. I don't think so. We'll kill you and keep your friend."

Sarah closed her eyes, then she opened them again, slowly. She looked into Cathy's eyes. Cathy moaned and folded unto herself, holding her head. She could see two green blades dancing in front of her eyes, cutting her over and over again.

Nocturne let Leaf fall on the ground, where he stayed, too weak, too hurt to get up, and ran to Cathy. He took her by the shoulders with incongruous gentleness, lifting her up and putting her down again, away from Sarah.

The Midnight gaze didn't seem to work on Nocturne. Sarah knew she didn't stand a chance, but she didn't want to just wait for Nocturne to wring her neck. The silence was deafening. Sarah wondered where the night noises had gone, the cars, the owls, the river flowing. She couldn't hear a thing, like everything was suspended, everything was waiting.

She looked into Nocturne's red eyes. He lifted his arms, those long, muscular arms hanging down to his knees. Sarah didn't look away, didn't whimper, didn't beg. She stood her ground, and looked at him. She felt that they were watching her – Anne, James, Morag, Mairead, Harry. She felt that the Midnight family was watching the last of their own being killed, and that she had to go with dignity.

"Nocturne!" someone shouted.

Harry's voice. *Sean's* voice.

He had materialized out of nowhere, the way he always did, silently. He had been watching her all along, Sarah realized, like he used to do when she was at school.

Sean raised the knife and started tracing signs through the air. Cathy started doing the same at once – it was like a strange duel, where they fought with their fingers, and without touching each other. Sarah could see the concentration on their faces. Under the orange light of the streetlamps, Sarah saw a drop of sweat trickling down Sean's forehead. Cathy lifted her other arm and gestured to Nocturne, still tracing the mysterious signs in the air. Sean growled, his movements growing quicker, sharper.

In the same instant Nocturne shuddered and shook himself, freeing himself from the invisible cage that Sean had built with his runes. He made a strange, deep sound, like a lament – then he grabbed Sean as if he'd been a doll, lifted him up, and threw him down on the tarmac. Sean didn't move again. Sarah saw his blood on the ground, trickling down from his side onto the grass behind him.

He's dead, she thought in despair, and she looked at Cathy with such hatred, such spite that Cathy felt herself burning up, burning with all the anger and jealousy she had accumulated through the years.

"You think you're better than anyone else, don't you? A *Midnight*! And your parents thought the same. They thought they ruled the world. You look at me like your mother looked at me. Like she despised me. Like I was nothing. And look at me now."

"Yes. Look at you now," said Sarah, with a calm, even voice.

Cathy couldn't bear it. She shrieked in anger, and for a moment she looked more like a demon than Nocturne.

"Just like your mother, aren't you? Looking at me like I'm nothing compared to you!"

Sarah shook inside at the mention of her mother.

"What do you mean, just like my mother? What did she ever do to you? What did I ever do to you?"

"Of course they wouldn't tell you, would they? I'm not even worth a mention. Like I never existed." Cathy's chest was rising and falling fast, her face contorted. Sarah felt struck by a wave of rage, and nearly took a step back as if it had been a physical blow – but she stood her ground, and waited. "It was all planned, all arranged. Morag had adopted me, she had taught me. James and I loved each other. Anne—" she spat out the word— "took everything away from me. Everything."

"My parents loved each other. You didn't come into it, Cathy. They loved each other more than anything else, more than they loved me." The realization of what she'd just said hit her hard, and her heart fluttered.

"James loved *me*, until Anne came. *I* was supposed to be your mother."

"But you aren't! You aren't my mother, are you? And you did all this . . . all this . . . because your boyfriend left you twenty years ago?"

A moment of silence.

"My *husband*. I was your father's wife."

What?

"Do you want to know why he cast me aside and married your mother? Because I couldn't have children. Our baby died. I was told that was it, for me, no more children. The same night, Sarah, the same night . . ." A sob interrupted her. "The same night Morag and your father told me I could take all the time in the world to recuperate. They told me they would pay for the best doctors. That they would look after me until I was better. And then, I was to pack my bags and leave their house."

Sarah gasped. "My dad wouldn't do something like that," she started. And then she stopped. He would. And so would Morag Midnight.

"I couldn't be your father's wife, because I'm barren," Cathy hissed, every word a drop of her blood being spilled. "They sent me away because I couldn't provide their precious heirs!" Her face was streaked with tears. For a moment, she looked like the heartbroken, abandoned girl she'd been twenty years before. Sarah shuddered.

Then she dried her eyes, and her faced changed – she was Catherine Hollow again, The Mistress. She was there to finish what she had started. She lifted her hand, and drew a rune in the air.

Nocturne heard her call, and he knew the moment had come, the moment to kill the last of the Midnights.

Sarah closed her eyes. The last thing she saw was Leaf, looking at her from the tarmac with those obsidian-like eyes, unable to get up. Then the blow came, and it was devastating. Sarah fell on the pavement, her head exploding with pain, and she saw black. *That's it, this is how it feels to die.*

But the grass and the asphalt came back into focus, and the feeling of the hard ground against her cheek.

I'm not dead. But with consciousness came pain, a sharp, terrible, sickening pain in her chest, every time she breathed. She started crying silently, because the pain was so strong, so unbearable, she couldn't take it. And it was just the beginning. She wondered how long it would take her to die, whether they were going to be merciful, and do it quickly – or let it linger.

She clutched her stomach and closed her eyes, waiting for another blow.

And then she heard a sound.
A suffocated scream.
It was Cathy.
Sarah opened her eyes, and what she saw was etched into her memory forever.

45
Nicholas

Time for me to burn,
Time for me to rise anew

Leaf was standing, one of his arms extended, the palm of the hand raised and exposed. Nocturne was immobile, frozen, his chin lowered to his chest, swaying gently from side to side.

Cathy was looking on in disbelief. This boy whom they had taken without him posing any resistance, whom they had tortured and played with – he had stopped Nocturne and was keeping him prisoner. How could it be?

"Who are you?" she shrieked.

"I am fire." His voice was soft, barely a whisper. All of a sudden, Sarah could smell dead leaves, moist earth, and smoke – all the scents that Leaf seemed to carry with him.

Cathy raised her hands frantically, trying to weave her runes. She suddenly looked very small, her beautiful face turned towards the night sky, as if in prayer. It was no use. The ravens were on her in a flurry of black wings, and this time they hit in perfect silence, without a single cawing. They covered her completely, so that all Sarah could see was the top of her blond head, now tainted with red, and her twitching feet.

When they had finished they raised in flight, dozens of little beaks lifting up what was left of Cathy. They dropped her in the river, her body disappearing in a gentle noise of waves and splashes.

Leaf lowered his hand – and for a second, a split second, Leaf and Nocturne looked at each other.

And then flames sprung up all around Nocturne, blue flames that rose up to the sky quicker than the eye could see. They licked Nocturne's body, then bit it, then devoured it, and still Nocturne wouldn't move, wouldn't cry out.

The blue flames burned and burned in front of Sarah's horrified eyes, until all that was left was a charred, shapeless mound, smouldering like coal.

Everything had happened in an eerie silence. Cathy hadn't even had time to scream, and all she could do under the ravens' beaks and claws was whimper; Nocturne hadn't made a sound, except the noise of his skin crackling, and a hollow thud as he'd fallen on the tarmac, half burnt already. The flurry of the ravens, the soft splash of the water as it swallowed Cathy's body, the hissing of the flames as they rose: the silence of the night had barely been broken.

And the whole of Sarah's world had changed.

Sarah had lifted herself up, kneeling on the tarmac, holding her side. She had blood on her hands, her own blood – but she wasn't sure where exactly it came from, where the cuts and bruises were, and she didn't bother to check.

It was over. Cathy and Nocturne were dead, at Leaf's hands. She saw that Sean was standing behind Leaf, stooped, shaking.

At least he's alive, she thought with relief. And then she remembered.

Murderer.

"Who are you?" Sean cried out at Leaf's silent figure. "And don't give me that *I am fire* shit. Who are you?"

Leaf turned around. Sarah had to blink as she saw his face – his eyes were so black, his skin so pale, his features were perfect, nearly angelic; it was as if she saw him for the first time.

"My name is Nicholas Donal. Of the Donal family."

"A Secret Family?"

A secret family? What does that mean? A family like ours, like the Midnights? Are there more like us?

"Yes."

"I've never heard of you."

"We're not in the Sabha. We keep ourselves to ourselves. Not that I owe you an explanation."

Sabha? Sarah's head was spinning.

"Go away, Sean." Sarah was trying to stand up, but her legs were failing her. Both men took a step towards her, but Sarah recoiled from Sean's hands and took Nicholas's instead. He wrapped his arms around her waist to sustain her. Sarah let herself go for a second. She was tired, so tired, and so sore. She clung to Nicholas, and her thoughts started to dissolve. The mist that Nicholas always brought with him started to rise, leaving her warm, dazed, unable to let go.

"Nicholas Donal," she whispered.

"I'll take you home. It's time for you to leave, Sean."

"Sarah . . ." he pleaded.

"I'm warning you . . ." Nicholas's eyes flashed, and there was the sound of wings flapping, somewhere among the trees.

"No, Leaf – Nicholas. No. Let him go!"

"He killed your cousin."

Sarah shook her head. To see Sean covered with those ravens, like Cathy had been . . .

"Please let him go."

Nicholas held her close. "All that matters now is you," he said, and his words sounded like a lullaby. She closed her eyes, resting her face on his chest.

Nicholas Donal. His name twirled in her head in a whirlpool of dead leaves and ravens.

"Take me home," she whispered.

46
On the Edge

And the words we said became
Echoes of nothing

Leaf
She had to be on the edge, looking down. She had to be sure
the end had come. I wanted her to feel total despair, complete
and utter lack of hope, before I intervened. The more pain
she'd felt, the sweeter my arms would seem to her. The more
afraid she was, the safer I would make her feel.

To see Cathy's reaction was hilarious. She thought I was a
helpless boy, a toy she could break to hurt Sarah. Her face
when I froze Nocturne! And the best thing – her expression
as my Elementals descended on her. I wish my father could
have seen that. I suppose pain was her redemption. And there
must have been a lot of pain.

It worked. Sarah believes in me now. And how beautiful she
looked, so pale, so frightened. Her blood is very red; her fear
smells like nightly flowers.

Nicholas Donal is now my name – how ironic, another man who can't tell her his real name, just like Sean. But that's all behind us now. Now we can start thinking of our life together.

47
Ash

Salty tears in salted water
The hand I couldn't see
To hold my restless thoughts
In his loving palm

Sarah couldn't remember how they made it home. It was as if she'd blinked, and they were there. He was opening her door, leading her in. They stood in the darkened hallway.

"Nicholas . . . The Secret Families . . . are there more like us? Like the Midnights?"

"Many more. And we're all in danger."

She moaned softly. Her ribs were hurting.

"Shhhh. You need to rest now. I'll keep watch, don't worry."

Will you stay? she nearly said. But she stopped herself. She needed to be alone. She needed to take it all in, Leaf's identity, Cathy's death. The Secret Families. Sean. The Sabha.

"When will I see you again?"

"Soon. I promise."

Sarah's face was raised towards him – and it would have been easy, so easy for their lips to meet – but Shadow came running down the stairs on silent paws and jumped straight on their entwined arms, so that Sarah had to catch her.

"Shadow!"

"Hello, lovely cat," whispered Nicholas. Shadow hissed. Nicholas ignored her. "Will you be OK? Do you want me to help you to bed?"

Sarah blushed. "No, no." She pulled away, holding on to Shadow like a barrier between them.

"I just meant . . ." He sounded embarrassed, confused.

"I know. I know."

"I'm going, then. Don't worry, I'll keep watch. You're safe." Sarah nodded.

"Thank you. Nicholas, I need to know. About the Secret Families, and the Sabha. I need to know everything."

"I'll tell you everything. They hid the truth from you. Sean, your parents . . . But I'll tell you everything." Sarah flinched at the mention of her parents. Cathy's revelations had been unbearable, so painful that she wished she hadn't known.

A soft kiss on her hair, one last breath of leaves and smoke rising from his chest, and he was gone.

Sarah took her clothes off carefully, trying not to rub against her cuts and bruises. She stepped into the shower. The scalding water washed away the blood, the dirt, the smudges of ash that had risen from Nocturne's pyre. She stayed under the shower for a long, long time, trying to untangle her thoughts.

Her parents' murderer had been a broken woman who had learnt the black arts. And that was all.

Or maybe not. If there were more Secret Families, more people like her, maybe there were other Valaya too. And a Council – Sabha, they called it – some sort of organization that united the families. But not her own. And not Nicholas's.

It was all a mystery. She couldn't wait for Nicholas to tell her everything.

Sean was gone. The thought flashed into her head, and she felt a stab of pain. Every time she'd woken up terrified after a vision, he had been there, watching over her. She thought of his arrogant smile, his fearlessness, the way he made her laugh even in the most frightening of situations. She thought of his eyes, so clear and bright. His voice, so soft – as familiar to her as her parents'. She could still hear it. She longed to speak to him so much – no, not Sean. Harry. She wanted her Harry back. She just wanted to close her eyes and listen to his voice.

But it had all been a lie. He was a murderer and a liar.

Sarah couldn't stand upright any more. The pain in her ribs was unbearable. She turned off the water, and wrapped a towel around herself, carefully. A deep tiredness overwhelmed her, and she could hardly move. She dried herself a bit, but had no energy to dry her hair. She slipped on her shorts and T-shirt, and lay on top of the blankets. A few minutes later she was asleep.

Shadow nestled herself against Sarah, and closed her amber eyes. She saw a black shape outside the window, and froze. It was the ravens. She jumped on the windowsill.

"It's OK, Shadow. They're friends," whispered Sarah, her head on the pillow.

But Shadow kept watching the ravens, her tail tapping the window seat in an anxious rhythm.

In closing her eyes, Sarah had hoped with all her might not to dream that night, to be allowed to rest. But what she wanted bore no influence on her visions.

She dreamt she was underground again, just like in the vision she'd had in the library. She was trapped in a little cave under a standing stone. Again she freed herself, squeezing out into the open. She found herself in the circle of stones in the middle of the night, under the whitest, purest of moons. The wind was cutting her face, and it smelled of winter.

There were lights dancing in the sky above her, changing colour as they moved – green, blue, yellow. The Northern Lights. It was beautiful beyond words.

Her heart missed a beat when she realized that Nicholas was there once more. His pale face, his black, burning eyes . . .

He raised a hand and showed her an opal resting in his palm. The quartz was shining with a light that came from its centre – a whirling light, turning and turning into the stone. Sarah took a step towards him – but Nicholas took a step back, as if wanting to stop her from coming near him.

Sarah felt that the opal was pulling her, as if she and the stone were somehow connected. She saw that what was swirling in the stone was a little white cloud, frantically folding and unfolding, trying to free itself.

Sarah looked at Nicholas, losing herself in his black eyes. His expression was unreadable at first. Bit by bit, Sarah saw his eyes changing. Something was taking shape, an emotion that she couldn't identify.

Guilt. Yes, that's what it was.

Nicholas's eyes were asking her to forgive him.

For what? He saved my life!

Sarah woke up. For a few seconds she waited for Sean to come in and ask her if she was all right. He'd sit on her bed and take her hand, leading her out of sleep and into reality. Out of fear, into a world she could control.

She forgot the vision; she forgot the swirling quartz and the circle of grey stones. She thought of Sean's hands holding hers, and burst into desolate tears.

48
Leaves

The world without you
The endless regret
The choice

"Harry . . . has gone to London for a few days. For work. To tie up loose ends or something. I don't know for sure." Sarah felt a bitter taste in her mouth. "No, there's no need, he'll be back soon . . . Thank you. Yes, I'll come up for dinner. See you tomorrow, then." She put the phone down.

I haven't lost it. I can still lie through my teeth, like I've always done. Not that she enjoyed it – actually, she hated it. To tell Juliet that Harry was in London had been a walk in the park, compared to the stories she'd had to invent to justify her chaotic, strange life.

"Don't lie about anything, ever, except for one thing: if it's to defend our secret. In that case, lie to your family, lie to your friends, lie to anyone who'll listen, and be convincing." That was what her father had said to her when she was five, and she had never forgotten it. She had never betrayed him, even when she would have wanted so desperately to reveal the truth, to lighten her burden a bit.

She had never allowed herself to do that.

She felt a wave of misery wash over her, and swept the immaculate coffee table with her hand, brushing away invisible particles of dust. Her eyes fell on the framed photograph of her parents' wedding. Anne was wearing a long white dress, and she had a bunch of heather in her hands, tied with a purple ribbon. She'd picked the heather herself, up on the moors, the day before the wedding. She'd said her bouquet smelled of Scotland.

You were so beautiful, Mum.

Sarah steeled herself. She had to keep Harry's disappearance hidden, at all costs, whatever it took. She couldn't leave the Midnight home. It would be like losing her parents all over again.

A week had gone by since the night Cathy had been killed, and with her, the Valaya. A week since she had lost Harry . . . *Sean.* Or whatever his name was. She missed him with an intensity that was almost physical, and it frightened her. She hated him for having killed her cousin, for having stolen his life – and still his absence was like a hole in her heart. The rip had been so sudden that she couldn't make sense of it; she thought he'd come into the room any minute, that he'd phone her any minute.

Why can I not stop thinking about him, why can I not tear him out of my head?

She had dreamt of Harry nearly every night. And they hadn't been visions, just dreams. Like normal people have. She had dreamt of a party in the Midnight house, on a warm summer night. The garden was dotted with paper lanterns, and there was a long table, full of lovely food and decorated with dozens of candles. Her parents were there, smiling, happy, and all their friends and family, the McKettricks, Bryony, Alice, Jack . . . And Leigh. They were laughing, eating, dancing. For once, their home was open to the world, not closed, hidden, isolated. Harry was standing beside her. He had turned around, suddenly, and kissed her bare shoulder. She'd laughed, surprised.

It had been a wonderful dream, so wonderful that when she'd woken up and she'd realized it wasn't true, she had felt breathless with grief.

Her parents were dead, Harry wasn't Harry after all, and Nicholas had disappeared. Again.

She sat at her window, contemplating the white light of the moon. She had wrapped herself in her woollen cardigan, and Shadow was asleep on her lap. She was holding the photo album with the silver cover, the one Aunt Juliet had given her. There were no photos in it, just dried leaves, some red, some brown, some yellow, carefully arranged, one in each transparent pocket.

I really am alone.

The garden was wrapped in shadows. She could barely make out his shape, as he came out of the trees and made his way among the bushes. But even before she could see him clearly against the white gravel of the path, she knew who it was that had come to see her.

Sarah ran down the stairs and opened the door with her heart in her throat.

"Nicholas!"

"Sarah. God, I missed you. I'm sorry it took so long. I had so much to sort out. I'll tell you everything."

"Come in," she whispered, not trusting herself to say any more.

There was a man leaning against Sarah's oak trees, invisible, still as the trees themselves. His hand was curled around a little red pouch he wore around his neck.

The man saw Nicholas walking up the path, and Sarah opening the door. He saw the black-haired boy walk in, into Sarah's home, into her heart, and then the door closed. To the hidden man, it felt as if the door had closed on all that he'd ever loved and wanted.

49
Masters of the Sea

Hair is seaweed
Skin is scales
Eyes are sea-shells
Breath the waves
Lips of coral
Heart the tide

Grand Isle, Louisiana

Mike opened his eyes in the grey light of daybreak. The first thing he saw was a white face, with red-rimmed eyes and blue lips, leaning over him. It was the face of a drowned man. His pale hands had him by the shoulders, shaking him.

"Jesus!" Mike jumped up, putting his hands out to keep the creature away from him. "You're dead. You're dead! Stay away!"

With shaking hands he tried to reach for the gun he always kept in his belt.

"For God's sake, Mike! Put that away!"

"Stay away from me."

"It's me. Niall. It's me!"

"You are dead!"

"Do I look dead to you?"

White-bluish skin, blue lips, blue nails. "Yes, actually! Look at your hands! And your face!"

"Oh, yes. It won't last. I'll be back to normal in a few hours. Mike?"

But Mike couldn't hear him, as he had passed out on the sand, unconscious, with his face in a tangled mass of seaweed.

Niall could smell the alcohol fumes coming out of his friend's body. He was coming to, blinking and rubbing his face. In spite of the fear and danger, Niall was finding the whole situation quite amusing.

"Jesus!" exclaimed Mike as he saw him.

"You said that before."

"You're dead!"

"You said that too. No, I'm not dead. Well, I was. But I came back."

"How . . . how . . . ?"

"Remember when you asked me what my power was? And I said the singing? I have another one. All Flynns do. We can't be killed by water."

"So you're alive?"

"As alive as you are."

"You're alive!" Mike threw his arms around Niall's neck, and immediately retreated. "Yes, well. I was worried." They both looked at the sand for a while.

"Have this." Mike took the hipflask out of his pocket.

"Oh yes. I need it." Niall took a greedy gulp.

"How was it?"

"The Bourbon? Oh, the best. You can't beat it. Except for Irish whiskey, of course, but you can't have everything." Mike noticed that Niall's voice sounded a bit gurgly, as if he still had water in his lungs.

"How did it feel to drown? To die?"

"Rotten. Still, it was my first time. My grandfather did it nine times, apparently."

They sat in silence for a while, looking at dawn breaking over the sea, while Niall was gathering his strength and warming up.

"So what now?" Niall untangled some seaweed from his hair.

"We need to get to Sean."

"They'll see us. They'll find us."

"They think we're dead."

"They'll soon realize we're not."

"We'll be in Scotland by then. Come on."

"To the airport?"

"To the port. I know someone who can get us into a freighter."

"Cool! A few weeks at sea!" Niall's face lit up.

"I could think of a few other words, to be honest."

"Ah, it'll be grand." He smiled, emptying his pockets of clams and barnacles that had gathered in them.

On their way to New Orleans, Mike dropped the letter for Sean in a mailbox. In case they didn't make it.

50
In Glass and Water

I'll never forget
The black-haired girl and her peaceful eyes
Too soon for her to go

Castelmonte

Elodie
I couldn't bear the wait any more. I was nearly relieved when they turned up at our door, all designer suits and sunglasses. The Turin Valaya had found us.

I let them in. I invited them to sit at my table.

Marina and Aiko had gone to a *fiera*, a fair, in a nearby village; Leandro was fishing. I was alone, thankfully. Better me than them. They had something left to live for.

Maybe this would be the time when I saw Harry again . . .

I shook myself. I couldn't let myself think like that. I had to fight. For Aiko, for the heirs.

"Where is the Ayanami heir?" they asked me in heavily-accented French.

"I don't know."

They laughed. Two men, both young, both handsome in that Italian, arrogant way. As if they owned the world.

"You're beautiful," said one of them. "That puts me in a good mood."

"Yes. Like we could take our time to get the truth out of you."

He put something on the table. It was a little vial. No mess then, no demons, no blood. A drop of that down our throats and we'd be the walking dead, like my husband had been for days, weeks even. All they had to do was convince us that dying would be better than living, and if I thought of what I'd heard the Valaya did to their victims, I had no doubt we would agree with them very, very quickly.

Still, I felt nothing. I wasn't afraid. I was getting ready.

Because seeing the future is not my only power; there's something else that we Brun carry in our blood. Something a lot more dangerous – something that, unlike the visions, had come back to me. I knew because I'd been checking. I'd tried it out on little animals, squirrels, birds, whatever I could get my hands on. Cruel, but necessary.

It had returned.

I brushed my hair away from my face. I could see the two men watching in appreciation. I was wearing a pair of jeans that clung to my body, and a strappy top. I thanked my lucky stars for having chosen that attire.

"I'm sure we can find an agreement," I said, getting up slowly, seductively, and walking over to where they sat.

The first man had jet-black hair and a million-dollar smile. He was looking at me like you'd look at something to devour.

I put my hand on his shoulder and sat on his lap, my face close to his. I brushed his cheeks with my hands.

"You can have them. Just let me go."

"You're one of the heirs, Elodie. We can't let you go," said the other man, with shining eyes.

"I'll make it worth your while," I whispered.

"I'll tell you what the deal is. You give them to us, and we take what we want anyway," said the man I was sitting on, with an ugly, angry voice, pawing at my waist, at my breasts.

"I see I have no choice," I purred in his ear.

"Exactly. You have no choice."

"No. I don't think you understand." I took his face in my hands again, and pulled it to mine. My lips met his lips, and he kissed me greedily for a few seconds, fumbling under my top.

Until he started gasping.

How ironic that my husband had to die of poison, that they wanted to kill me with poison, when I'm poisonous myself. The man gasped for breath as I set him free, falling on the floor, his mouth open like a fish out of water, desperately trying to inhale. His skin was turning white, a bluish-white like you would see on someone who'd drowned.

All I needed now was a split second, an instant where the other man would be too surprised, too shocked to move. And I nearly had it. But not quite. His gun was out already, and he was ready to shoot me. It would be nearly at point-blank range, straight into my stomach. I imagined myself on the ground, covered in blood, like the swan. The prophecy was about to come true.

But right at that moment the door opened, and an abyss of despair opened with it: Aiko and Marina were framed in the door, still smiling, not having registered what was happening inside.

The man turned around and fired. There were screams, and bodies falling. All I knew was that I had to put my lips on his, and I did.

The two men from the Valaya were lying on the floor, asphyxiated.

And so was Marina, holding her heart. Aiko was crying, her little hands covered in blood, tears running down her cheeks.

There was nothing I could do. By the time I'd kneeled beside her, she was already dead. It was her, Marina, the dead swan lying in a pool blood – not me. If that had been a sign of what was meant to happen to me one day, the chain of events that was going to lead to that must have shifted somehow, an imperceptible change that led to an entirely different outcome.

Or maybe that was just an accident. My prediction would still come true. The time would come for me to be the bloodied swan.

"We all have to choose a side," Leandro had said. Nobody is safe, nobody can hide. I left Aiko with him, in a tiny wooden hut in a secluded valley. That would work until winter closed in. Two months, and then the snowfalls and the cold would make the hut uninhabitable. Two months, and they would have to find another way.

But I knew that I couldn't be there any more. I had to follow the trail Harry had left, and destroy the Enemy.

But I couldn't do it on my own. And there was only one person I could trust with my life.

Sean Hannay.

51
Soul

Forgive me

Sean

Thoughts of her torture me every moment. I miss every second of every day. I can't lose her, I just can't.

She's not safe. That Nicholas Donal makes my skin crawl. I trust him as much as I'd trust those bloodthirsty ravens of his. I would ask Mike and Niall if they know anything about the Donal family, but I haven't heard from them in a while now. No signal. Their phone is down, they're impossible to contact. I fear the worst, that they've been found and killed – by the Surari by the Sabha, take your pick.

Nicholas has revealed to Sarah the existence of the other Secret Families, the existence of the Sabha. He has put her in the greatest danger. Does he not know that the Sabha have been infiltrated? Does he not know that we can't trust anyone? Or is he one of them?

I should have told Sarah everything. I made the same mistake as her parents – I kept her in the dark, thinking the time would come to tell her.

I watch her night and day. I look at her sitting at the window, brushing her hair. Oh, I remember the smell of her hair! I watch her going to school, and coming home. I'm so close to her at times that I could touch her – and she has no idea I'm there.

Tonight, I saw Nicholas walking up the path. I saw her face when she opened the door, her joy at seeing him. It was like being set on fire.

I have to find a way to get back into her life.

And I can only think of one way: telling her the truth.

Epilogue

I was beyond
I am Persephone

Elodie

I wasn't surprised when the vision formed in the aeroplane window. When I left Castelmonte I felt something in me unknotting, unfolding, flowing again – as if my power was a river, and a boulder had been blocking its flow. The rage over Marina's death, the sense of liberation that filled me when I got out of hiding and joined the battle again, had pulverized the boulder and left dust in its place.

I saw Sean, and a black-haired girl I recognized as Sarah Midnight. I saw her on her knees; someone was standing over her. I saw her soul leaving her, a little white light floating above her head in a crazy rhythm, upset and lost and confused, unsure of where to go. Sarah fell on the ground as her soul left her, like a puppet whose strings have been cut. The vision dissolved, and the reflection of my pale, haunted face replaced it.

My heart started racing, and bitter tears filled my eyes. My visions always come true. Everything I see in glass or water comes true.

And I've seen the death of Sarah Midnight.